. . . Then the wind gusted and cleared the smoke, and suddenly Tom had a good view of what was coming at him. To his dismay, the entire field was filled with the enemy, their weapons and bodies glittering and glistening in the sunshine. Instead of a few hundred, as he had thought, there were well over a thousand, against the remnants of the original rebel four hundred and fifty. Guns were volleying on every side, and rebels were steadily falling, whole families going down together—brothers with fathers and grandfathers, uncles and cousins, all wiped out in that fierce nightmare of slaughter and hellish noise.

Tom and his dogged companions withdrew toward the narrow gap fast closing behind them. They might have battled through, but then the enemy surged forward in a great mass, closing in on the survivors, overwhelming and cutting down the fugitives, and hammering against those few who, like Tom, stood to fight and die . . .

TRIUMPH

The Sixth Powerful Novel
in the Northwest Territory Series

A FAMILY FIGHTS TO STAY TOGETHER AS THE REVOLUTION BLAZES TO A CLIMAX IN THE OLD NORTHWEST

ELLA SUTHERLAND. Her happy refuge on the frontier is shattered by a war cry and a hatchet blow . . .

OWEN SUTHERLAND. His search for his kidnapped son pits him against an entire Indian nation and sets him off on one of the most amazing marches ever . . .

SIMON GIRTY. Slickest rebel scout in the Northwest, he can out-Indian any Indian and double-cross the devil himself . . .

DR. JEREMY BENTLY. He and his young wife hope to live and work in peace in the wilderness, but the war stalks them, waiting to strike . . .

GWEN BENTLY. A rebel in love with a British officer, she stands to lose all, even if her country wins...

BENJAMIN SUTHERLAND. Captured by marauding savages, Owen's son expects every day to be his last, until his fate takes a strange turn...

SUSANNAH SUTHERLAND. She is young, innocent, and in love, but the war will make her grow up fast...

JAMES MORELY. A genius at trading, he'll prove no man's his better, even if it means wagering his very soul...

BRADFORD CULLEN. The merchant Midas of the Northwest, everything and everyone he touches turns to corruption...

NORTHWEST TERRITORY · BOOK 6
TRIUMPH
OLIVER PAYNE

^{TM} **BCI**

Created by the producers of
Wagons West, The Australians, and
The Kent Family Chronicles.

Chairman of the Board: Lyle Kenyon Engel

B
®

BERKLEY BOOKS, NEW YORK

TRIUMPH

A Berkley Book/published by arrangement with
Book Creations, Inc.

PRINTING HISTORY
Berkley edition/April 1985

Produced by Book Creations, Inc.
Chairman of the Board: Lyle Kenyon Engel
For information address: The Berkley Publishing Group,
200 Madison Avenue, New York, New York 10016.

ISBN: 0-425-07644-X

To the memory of Clark's little army,
whose heroism played such a great part
in the winning of the Old Northwest.

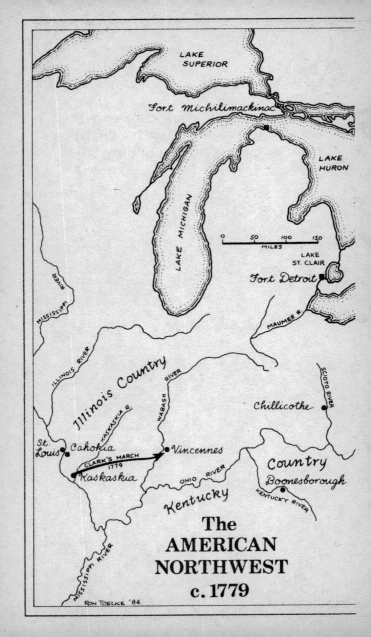

The
AMERICAN
NORTHWEST
c. 1779

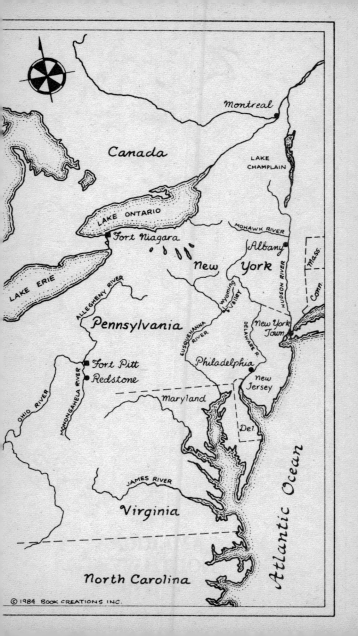

I told them … that none but men with arms in their hands were proper objects of the warrior's resentment, that to lose the name of Barbarians they must cease to act as Wolves.

—*Lieutenant Governor Henry Hamilton, addressing an Indian council. From his journal, December 24, 1778*

I told the [Indians] that I believed they were a set of Villains, that they had joined the English and they were welcome to continue in the Cause … [and] that I was a Man and a Warrior: that I did not care who was my Friends or Foes. . . .

—*Lieutenant Colonel George Rogers Clark, addressing Indians of the Illinois. From his journal, 1778*

TRIUMPH

PART ONE

The Frontier

chapter 1

ATTACK

The gray maples were naked against the snow, clattering their branches in a wind that swirled away down the ravine. Evening was coming on, and the smell of a storm hung in the air, mingling with woodsmoke from a few log cabins clustered at the bottom of the slope.

A blaze of orange flame blossomed in the center of the settlement, and seen from up on the wooded ridge, the bonfire was a hot, bright flare against the gloomy winter forest. Above the rush of wind in the trees lifted the keen lilt of a fiddle, light and carefree. Silhouettes could be seen dancing back and forth around the bonfire as it burned higher, sending billows of smoke into the darkening sky.

On the ridge, where bleak rocks crowded into shadows, a youthful figure knelt, unmoving. Wreathed in dimness, he seemed of stone himself, indistinguishable from his surroundings as he watched the settlement below. Only the wind gave him away, flicking the eagle feather that hung from his fur cap. In the hollow, where the settlers gaily surged about the bonfire, no one could tell they were being watched. No one would know until it was too late.

Soon other Shawnee warriors would join this scout, and before night fell, they would move in, silently, swiftly. By the time the snowstorm began, it would find the scout and his companions satisfied and warm in these cabins. When the storm ended, they would escape with their booty and trophies of war, fleeing on snowshoes through the northwestern wilderness, not stopping to rest until they were far away and safe from pursuit, in their own villages.

For generations, the warrior's path had led here to the Wyoming Valley of northeastern Pennsylvania. Time and

3

again settlers had been killed or driven out; time and again they had returned. Always they had been unable to defend themselves.

This little settlement would be no different. The scout expected it all to be over quickly, with the white fighting men being the first to die in a sudden volley of rifle fire from hidden warriors. The scout's father and grandfather had triumphed in this way, and tales of their victories had been sung through many long winter evenings. Still, the whites came back, no matter how many died. They came across the mountains to try where others had failed. They planted and built, cut down trees and drove off game, and infuriated the Indian.

Like the waxing of the moon, the return of the whites after a war was a natural process. Like the moon's waning, the massacre and the burning were inevitable, and the whites would depart. Now it would all happen again, just as it would in future wars, perhaps with the scout's own son one day striking the blow.

The fiddles played on. The bonfire was a beacon, fascinating and appealing to the scout. Its reflection glittered in his eyes, like the excitement that coursed through him. He was eager. He was confident. He was invincible. Soon another nest of whites would be wiped out, and all the warriors of the Shawnee nation would know of his brave deeds this day. Soon he would be warmer than ever before in his life.

How he liked that fiddle music. What a pity it, too, must be destroyed. He watched. He listened and he waited. Then, all around, he sensed the quiet arrival of the others. They were among the trees, the elder warriors drifting in the forefront of the advance. The young scout rose to a crouch and moved down toward the light and the fiddle music. It had begun.

At the edge of the noisy clearing where the cabins stood, a tall, slender young man in a bulky blanket coat and woolen hat took a last look at the people dancing on a puncheon floor near the bonfire. Bright reddish light glinted over his face, which was boyish and appealing. His dark eyes were large and soft, and a hint of humor glowed in them as he watched his friends celebrate New Year's Day. James Morely was about to take a turn on guard, having just replaced his older brother, Tom, who was already whooping and carousing with his pretty wife, Sally, in the throng of happy folk.

In the midst of the dancers were Ella and Owen Sutherland, both of them enjoying the lately popular dance called the German waltz. They were one of the few couples who knew it, and James admired them as they swirled around the floor. Ella's plain linsey and woolen clothes made her blond beauty even more striking, though she was past forty and had borne three children. Owen was in flannel and buckskin, his black curly hair tied in the back; at his side hung a Scottish claymore, a heavy, straight sword that he had carried since his days as an officer of the famous Black Watch Highland regiment. Sutherland was a bit older than Ella, but like her, he retained youthful good looks.

The Sutherlands were leaders here, looked upon as wise elders who knew about Indian warfare, about surviving in the northwest wilderness. Though Ella was of aristocratic English birth, and Owen was a native Scot, both had lived in the colonies most of their lives and were now ardent rebels, bent on winning American independence from Britain in the revolution that had been raging for nearly three years. James trusted their leadership, as did everyone else at the settlement.

The dance music ended, and some of the men called on Sutherland to share another toast to a prosperous and victorious new year. Ella parted with her husband and went to a large, three-sided lean-to where the youngest children were bundled under blankets, most of them sleepy from a full day of fun and feasting. The fiddles struck up a country tune, "Turkey in the Straw," and there immediately followed loud whooping as couples crowded onto the dance floor. Someone shoved a foaming mug of ale into James's hand, and he drained it in a long gulp and handed it back empty.

Hefting the rifle over his shoulder and shrugging his coat closer about his neck, James turned away and set off on guard duty. All trace of a smile vanished from his face.

The safety of the others was now his responsibility. He knew every last one of the forty or so people in the settlement, and he would not let them down by not being alert.

He glanced back over his shoulder, happy to see the others celebrating for all they were worth. It was no wonder that on this first day of January 1778 everyone in this isolated, unnamed community was joyous, for most of them were staunch rebels who had seen the tide of war turn sharply in their favor in the past few months.

James himself was not particularly for one side or the other in this bloody rebellion against England. He cared more for peace and prosperity than for political freedoms. He was a born fur trader whose life had always depended on a thriving Indian commerce, but unless there was peace here on the frontier, there could be no profitable trade with the redskins. James wanted terms to be reached soon by the rebels and the British, and he wanted the Indians to keep out of the fighting.

As he tramped through crunching snow up the trail toward the crest of the ridge, the happy sounds of the celebration faded. It did not matter now whether he was rebel or neutral or loyal. If Indians ever struck this settlement, they would not consider a man's politics. They would simply take as many scalps as they could and carry them back to the British fort at distant Detroit, to prove their prowess in battle. King George's officers were rewarding Indians for victories against rebel settlers on the frontier, and no one could say whether a scalp came from a rebel or a loyalist, or from the neutral James Morely.

A sensation crept up his spine—a feeling that was more than just cold, but less than fear. As he walked, the ashen woods gathered about him, and he kept a sharp lookout for any suspicious movement. It was still light enough to see some distance through the trees, and James was fairly experienced in the woods. Like his brother Tom, he had been brought up out at Fort Detroit in company with Indians and French who had taught him about the wild—in peace and in war. Though he had never been as tough or as apt as Tom, James knew enough to take care of himself.

Instinct prickled the hair on the back of his neck, but he

could make out nothing unusual in the drifting shadows, gray and cold, that filled the maple forest. The settlement's happy sounds were barely audible now. The party would end before long, for these days folks went inside at dark and stayed there until morning. Too often of late, stragglers had not come home at all, to be found in the morning, murdered by lurking Indians.

A twig cracked behind, and James whipped around, the rifle coming up as he dropped to one knee. His heart leaped as he saw his target. Shadows moved, and out of them stepped a slim and delicate figure, silhouetted against the distant blaze from the settlement. James released an annoyed sigh and lowered his rifle.

"Be you daft or simply touched in that girlie head of yours?" He stood up straight as Susannah Sutherland approached, trudging up the same path he had taken from the cabins. As she came near, James half smiled. She was a pretty one, even though she was only eleven years old. Her face shone from within the hood of the fine green frock coat she wore. They had known each other all their lives, and he knew she was soft for him—puppy love, his brother Tom rightly called it.

Susannah's voice was hushed as she drew her coat tightly about herself. "You talk too loud for a sentry, James. And you stand up too straight. Pa's right—you should stick to the fur-trading warehouse instead of being our watch."

James became unexpectedly serious at this remark, though Susannah had meant only to tease him in reply to his own barb. James turned and looked into the forest, which was steadily deepening in twilight.

Susannah came closer to him, clearing her throat. One slender hand played with a string of shell beads that hung at her breast; the other was behind her back, holding a sprig of mistletoe. As James glanced at her, she saw she had hurt him, and she was sorry. James was always too touchy about these things, as if he were not proud of being the most brilliant trader in the country—after her own father, Owen Sutherland, of course.

Trying to change the subject, Susannah again cleared her throat and smiled as coquettishly as she could. She wanted just the right moment to hold the mistletoe over the fellow's head and demand her rightful kiss. Though growing into an exquisitely lovely girl, with the delicate, fair looks of her mother, Susannah was not yet confident of her beauty. The past year had been spent in flight from her family home at loyalist Detroit, and then from Montreal, when the rebels had been driven out of that city by the British. She had been forced to journey hundreds of miles through wilderness, her girlish loveliness often masked by a riding bonnet, a tattered old cape, or by dirt and sweat. Few young men had been at hand to compliment her on how she was fast becoming a woman. Only James Morely had been there to notice her change, the way a man should.

Susannah knew he was too old for her, but he was such a fine man, brave and honest, with genuine good looks that many a female had commented upon within her hearing. And everyone liked and respected James—though Susannah's father had observed privately that he seemed more at home in a warehouse than on a scout for Indians. Indeed, Susannah was in love with James Morely—in love the way only an eleven-year-old girl could be in love with a sensitive, handsome bachelor of twenty-two.

For his part, as he let his eyes rove about the woods, James was aware of Susannah's feelings for him. He, too, was attracted to her, or perhaps to the woman she would become. In a few days he would be away in Albany, working to rebuild the trading firm known as the Frontier Company, in which he and his family were partners along with Susannah's people. He might not see her for years. Perhaps not until she was married and grown up, with her own children.

For just a moment he let himself look at her again, and her eyes held his. She smiled, and so did he.

"Your pa's right," he said softly, shouldering the rifle. "I'm meant most for business, not for the woods." He glanced about at the forest as the wind picked up. The trees seemed to hiss and creak more than before, but he noticed no danger.

"I feel safe," Susannah said, "knowing you're out here." She was sure the right moment had come, and was ready to reveal the sprig of mistletoe.

James gave a little laugh, and still staring at the trees, he said, "You'd be safer if I was alone, paying attention to the woods instead of listening to you prattle away." He looked kindly at her and said, "Best you go back down there. I'll keep an eye on you as you walk."

Susannah was disappointed and brought the mistletoe into both hands. "I came to talk to you . . . alone——"

Suddenly there was a crashing in the bushes, and James swung the rifle to bear and cocked the hammer in one fluid motion. Susannah cried in fright and sprang to his side.

"Don't shoot!" someone croaked. "It's just me! Hold your fire."

It was a familiar voice, and James saw young Benjamin Sutherland struggling to get free of a tangle of thornbushes, gasping and complaining all the while. Susannah stamped her foot in the snow, and the hood fell back, uncovering her long blond hair.

"Benjamin! You little sneak! You heathen! You skulking, sneaking . . ."

James laughed, uncocked the rifle, and reached to pull the lanky youth out of the bushes, where he had fallen after trying to climb on a rotten limb to eavesdrop.

Benjamin came clambering out of the thorns, half laughing, half in pain, jamming a three-cornered hat back onto his head. He said their father had seen Susannah leave the cabins and wanted her brought back immediately.

"I was coming to fetch you just as soon as I got up that tree there and spied out what you were——I mean where you were . . ." He winked at James, who nodded in mock agreement. Benjamin was thirteen, strong and wiry, quite tall for his age, and darkly handsome, like his father. He had a ready grin, which he could not contain as he glanced from the blushing Susannah to James and back again.

Susannah did not think it funny and looked in appeal to James, who became momentarily distracted as he turned to listen to the forest.

Susannah grumbled at her brother, "You just want to mind my personal business cause you think——" She glanced back at James, who was moving up the trail, paying no attention. Then she said in a whisper, "Benjamin, you're

wrong to think I'm trying to throw myself at his feet!"
Suddenly she remembered the mistletoe and whisked it behind her back. But Benjamin had seen it. He doffed his hat with a flourish, kissed it tenderly, then giggled in his infectious way. Susannah nearly smiled herself, but she was not sure just how to act, so she huffed and stuck out her tongue. Benjamin gave a soft whistle, then lifted his finger. A few seconds later a blue jay landed upon it, then hopped onto his shoulder.

"What d'ye think, Punch, my friend? Is Sis here old enough to throw herself at a grown man?"

The bird gave a squawk and fluttered its wings. Susannah frowned in exasperation, glad James had gone a bit up the trail and could not hear this embarrassing conversation. With her free hand she gave her brother a whack on the shoulder, but his thick duffel coat absorbed the blow, so she kicked him in the shins. Benjamin jumped back, chortling. The bird squawked and flew away.

Susannah tossed up her hood, then turned on her heel and followed James. She heard her brother hiss, "The snow's too cold to throw yourself at his feet, Sis. And you should wait until he's ready to catch you, first. About five years from now!"

Ignoring him, the girl turned the bend in the trail, out of sight from Benjamin, and found James leaning against a pine tree, head bowed. At first she thought he was listening to something, for his cheek was pressed against the bark, his rifle butt in the snow. She hesitated, shoving the mistletoe into a pocket of her coat. Then she was startled as James gave a groan and the rifle began to fall. She caught the weapon and clutched at his shoulder.

"James!" she gasped quietly. "Heavens! Are you ill? James?"

He let out another low groan, and as he tried to look at her she saw his eyes were out of focus.

"You're ill!" she declared, hoping Benjamin would come to help; but her brother was not to be seen.

In the distance she heard a burst of happy music and song. She wanted to get James back down there right away, but he would not go. He shook off her hand when she pulled at him.

"I'm all right..." he breathed, "all right..." Straightening up, he swayed momentarily and swallowed hard. Slowly, he shook his head and passed a gloved hand over his face. He muttered again that he would be all right.

"These ... these spells come on ... me, now and then." He let his head go back all the way, eyes closed.

Susannah was frightened for him, for she had never known James to be subject to fainting.

"Come down to the settlement!" she insisted, taking his arm. Once more he shook her off and reached with a trembling hand for his rifle.

"No!" He forced the word out, but appeared to be recovering. "No, I won't admit to anyone that there's ... there's something wrong with me! Especially not to your father. He already thinks I'm— I've got my duty, Susannah, and I'll not shirk it or be called ... weak!"

"Have you been ill, James?" She pressed close to him, her fingers touching his face. He yielded slightly and gazed into her lovely blue eyes. "You must have a care, dearest," she said.

James smiled and removed one glove; then he held her fingers close to his cheek. "When I'm in Albany, Susannah, I'll think fondly of you here."

Anxious and charmed at the same time, Susannah did not know whether to feel romantic, or concerned for his health. "But James, if there's something seriously wrong with—"

"No, no." He shook his head. "I've lived with this for years, and you're the first who's ever seen me take a fainting spell." Suddenly he became so grave that it dismayed her. "Listen, Susannah, do you care at all for me?"

"More than I can say!"

"Then promise me—"

"Anything!"

He squeezed her hand harder than he meant. "Promise you'll tell no one ... ever ... about this!"

"What? But—"

"Promise!" He brought her fingers against his lips, and she nearly melted with emotion. "If you truly care for me, Susannah, and if you truly want me to look for you when I come back."

"Oh, James!" She was thrilled beyond words. "Oh, James, I do . . . I promise! I'll not tell a soul."

"Never!" His black eyes flashed. "Tell no one, not even Owen, unless I give you leave. Swear it!"

"Never!" Her eyes closed with the intensity of it all, and she kept them tightly shut, whispering with a gush of passion, "Never, ever, ever!"

Then his hand went suddenly limp. She felt the weight of him sink down. "James!" she whimpered. He was fainting again. He was too heavy to hold up. The rifle struck the snow. She grappled for his waist, trying to ease him down. "James!" They fell together under the evergreen.

Then Susannah heard someone farther down the trail. She glanced back to see several shadows moving through the trees. At first she thought it was Benjamin with others, and knew she must say nothing to give herself away, lest they find James unconscious and his secret be discovered.

"James," she whispered ever so quietly, but he still did not move. She peered nervously at the shadowy men in the trees. James was breathing evenly, and she prayed he would wake up soon, before anyone found them. Fortunately, they were concealed by bushes all about and might not easily be discovered.

After a moment, when she thought they were alone, Susannah lightly slapped James's cheek. He began to come around, but his face was so pale that it seemed radiant in the gathering twilight. His eyes flickered, and Susannah was swept with relief. She murmured in thankfulness.

Abruptly there came shouting and the sounds of a struggle nearby. Something was wrong with Benjamin, for it was his voice, though partly muffled. James was not yet conscious, and Susannah dared not rouse him further, lest he cry out and give them away. She knew something was terribly amiss and grasped the rifle, cocking it. She listened, panting with fear, trying to make out where her brother was.

Then she knew, and terror rushed through her. She stood up slowly. Benjamin was cursing and growling in a stifled voice, being thrown about in the thickets. Susannah trembled. She could hesitate no longer and moved through the trees, whispering her brother's name, knowing the worst. He was being attacked by Indians.

"Please, God," Susannah whispered, over and over. "Please save him . . . please . . ."

Before Susannah reached him, Benjamin must have broken free, for he gave a bloodcurdling shriek, a ringing shout of warning for all down at the settlement to hear. The fiddle music stopped, and at almost the same moment Benjamin's fierce yell was cut short by a sickening thud. Susannah's mouth dropped open, but she managed not to scream. She was close enough now, and made out a warrior raising a club, about to strike again. She wailed and swung up the heavy rifle, and as it roared she was jarred backward by the recoil, smashing hard against a tree. Everything went black.

Ella Sutherland knew her son's cry, and in terror she screamed his name and broke away from the bonfire to dash for the opening of the forest path. The others stopped their dancing and music. For one brief moment they were frozen in surprise, firelight playing on them as they watched Ella fly toward the trail Benjamin had taken.

The instant passed, and as though they had rehearsed it many times, the settlers swarmed away from the firelight, women and children making for the stronger cabins, men grabbing rifles and pistols that were ready to hand. Ella heard voices cry for her to stop, but she forgot caution and scrambled into the trees. She had no idea how to save her son but could not prevent herself from making this headlong, mad rush to reach him before it was too late. When Susannah's gunshot sounded, Ella cried "No!" and ran even more wildly than before. She frantically called Benjamin's name as branches tore at her, catching the cotton mobcap and tugging at her apron. Her frock flew out as she ran, and her hair fell from where it had been pinned, dropping in straggling curls to her shoulders.

She was too distraught to hear the clamor of the people readying themselves back at the settlement, nor did she see the Shawnees in the trees, watching her pass—not until one rose up and shrieked insanely, painted like a devil, black and white and red, steel tomahawk gleaming. At that instant the rest of the Indians broke cover and opened fire at the settlement in a ragged volley.

Ella gasped and stumbled, trying to stop before she ran

into the warrior, a swarthy, overweight older man wearing greasy trade shirts and a bear-claw necklace. He whooped and swung his tomahawk. Ella ducked as the ax came down, and the blow just missed. She snatched at a stick as the Shawnee went for her again. She poked it at him, but he chopped it away and let out a grunt of anger as he lunged at her.

Ella was off-balance, on one knee when the man came in. Her hair obscured her sight, and she cried out in pain as his thick fingers clutched the nape of her neck, jerking her face back so that for a moment they stared into each other's eyes. Ella saw death there. Desperately she scratched and pummeled, only making the old warrior more furious. In one short stroke, he brought the tomahawk down at her head.

Ella saw it come, but there was nothing she could do to save herself. She crumpled heavily to the snow, her blood spilling out over the Shawnee's worn moccasins.

Racing up the path, Owen Sutherland saw the Indian tomahawk his wife. The horror of it gave him the strength to cover the last few yards in a leap, and he shouldered into the warrior with such force that the man smashed face-first against a tree trunk, collapsed, and lay still. Sutherland rolled and was on his feet immediately; springing around, eyes wide, he saw Ella lying there, saw the blood running away with her life. He cried her name, raising and shaking his claymore.

Groaning, he fell to her body, but suddenly he was attacked on all sides. From out of the dusk Shawnees came at him, howling and screaming like wild beasts, some firing rifles, others swinging tomahawks and war clubs. Sutherland slashed with the claymore, roared defiance, and leaped up, driving the first warriors back. More came in.

The claymore flashed and thudded. Tomahawks chopped down and were parried again and again, blows diverted, handles shattered by the sword. In the background rose the sound of fighting down at the settlement, but Sutherland heard none of it. Standing over his wife's body, he battled almost blindly, like a stag at bay fighting a pack of hungry wolves.

Twice rifle balls struck him, one passing through the flesh under his left arm and out the other side, the other cutting his thigh. Shrilling the battle cry of the Scottish Highlander—a war whoop as wild as any Indian's—Sutherland beat his opponents down, right and left, thrusting and blocking and hacking, and, when close in, punching wickedly with the claymore's heavy hilt.

How long the fight went on he could not tell. The shooting and yelling at the settlement began to die down, but Sutherland and his dogged enemies fought on over Ella's body, and over the bodies of at least seven Shawnee warriors. Darkness aided him, for the Indians could not see well enough to get clear advantage over so resolute an enemy, and even their strength in numbers was of little help in the close quarters of the trail.

But Sutherland began to give out. The Shawnees were simply too many. He swung and stabbed, fighting mightily, but his reactions were slowing. Then, unexpectedly, the shadows slipped aside and left him alone. The enemy were still out there, but they, too, seemed spent in the struggle against such brutal strokes of a sword that could hack arms in two or take heads off with one slash. Sutherland gasped for breath, body heaving, hardly feeling his wounds, but his heart was broken to think of Ella dying at his feet.

"Come on, blast you!" he shouted at the dark. His chest was bare, showing the green tattoo of a turtle, the mark of his long-ago adoption into the Ottawa nation. Sweat and blood covered his face and buckskin shirt. "Come, and I'll finish you all off! You can die like brave Shawnees want to die!"

This last he bellowed in their own tongue, for he knew the languages of many Indian tribes and could insult the best of them with their own galling sarcasm. He called them cowards, worse than dogs, and said they had not the stomach to face a man's death. He knew they were standing in the shadows, those who could stand. He heard shouts and cheering from the whites in the settlement and guessed the main body of attackers had been driven off. But it was still he against these others, who were determined to take his hair before the settlers came rushing up the slope to help him.

"Fight, you cowards!" he snarled. "Fight and die, or slink home in shame—"

Then Sutherland heard a ramrod sliding home and realized what they were doing. No sooner did he drop to the ground than five rifles exploded in the darkness from his left side. All missed. Without hesitation, he sprang up, screaming his war cry, and with claymore slashing went at the Indians where they stood in dismay. Two were so shocked that they were unable to defend themselves and died on the spot. There was a crash of underbrush as the remaining Shawnees took to their heels. In a twinkling, they were gone.

Sutherland reeled against a tree and, panting, collapsed to one knee. Then a chilling thought caused him to jerk around to look where Ella lay, a few yards off in the dimness. Through sweat and blood, he saw someone beside her, and the pale glint of a scalping knife. He shouted, but before he moved, there came a blur of white and a vicious snarling. His huge husky, Heera, bounded up the trail and struck the Indian, knocking him away from Ella. Sutherland followed, and soon another Shawnee lay dead.

Heera whined and lay down at Ella's side. Sutherland dropped to his knees, the claymore still gripped in his right hand. He whispered Ella's name, then picked her up. She was light, limp in his arms, and he felt the warmth of blood—hers, and his own.

Like a white phantom, Heera loped ahead as they hurried down the trail toward roaring fires. At the settlement Sutherland saw more blood and knew there were dead among his friends. Folks ran to him, crying out that the Indians had fled; they fell silent to see Ella in his arms.

He rushed with her straight toward their house. A nearby cabin was aflame, crackling and smoking. Children were crying, and women were kneeling over fallen husbands and sons. Sutherland stumbled over something and glanced down to see the body of a young warrior, no more than eighteen, lying as though asleep. A fiddle was clutched in one hand. Sutherland paid little heed.

"Susannah!" he roared through smoke that filled the clearing. "Someone get Susannah here! Tell her to come quick!"

Sally Morely, Tom's young, dark-haired wife, ran up to Sutherland. Her apron was torn, and gunpowder burns blackened her face and hands. She cried out in anguish to see Ella, who for years had been her foster mother. Sally hurried with Sutherland into the cabin, saying breathlessly that Susannah had not been seen since before the attack. Shaking all over, tears on her cheeks, Sally helped lay Ella on a rough-hewn bed in one corner of the main room, which was dimly lit by a fire in the fieldstone hearth.

Sally was overcome. "Oh, Ella . . . oh, dear heaven," she moaned. Ella's head was covered with blood, and Sally could hardly bring herself to look at the ghastly wound where the tomahawk had glanced off the side of the skull. Closing her eyes, she grasped Ella's limp hand and bowed her head to pray.

Sutherland hastily lit an oil lamp, then tore a sheet into bandages and snatched a jar of softened strips of chokeberry bark from a shelf in the far corner. He moved swiftly, and soon Sally recovered enough to help him. With trembling hands she stripped Ella's bloody clothes, fetched a basin of water, and carefully washed the wound. Owen pressed choke-berry bark into the gash to stanch the flow of blood and then rapidly stoked the fire to warm the room as Sally bound up the wound.

Outside, people of the settlement were shouting as they tried to put out the flaming house. The din became louder when the cabin door flew open to let in a portly, squat woman of nearly sixty, whose awful fear for Ella's life was masked by the resolution on her ruddy face. Lettie Morely Grey said nothing but knelt at Ella's side and examined the bandaging done by her daughter-in-law, Sally. She saw the bleeding had slowed, listened to Ella's heartbeat, then also began to pray. Her voice was soft, in an accent that recalled her native north of England.

". . . that Thy will be done, O Lord, is all we have the right to ask; but . . . if Thee can spare our darlin' Ella's life this day, we beseech Thee to let us have her a while longer. Lord, we need her so. . . ."

Heera lay by the hearth, pale eyes watching silently, head on his paws. Beside him stood Sutherland, gazing at his wife while roughly bandaging his own wounds. His clothes were torn nearly completely away, and the flannel shirt he had worn underneath his buckskin jacket was drenched with sweat and blood. Clean-shaven, taller than most, Sutherland was very broad at the shoulders and had long, powerful arms and legs. In the firelight, he cast a large shadow against the wall of the cabin.

He could hardly believe this had happened. He and Ella were in the prime of life, happy as any man and woman could be together. Though every husband on the frontier faced the same possible loss, Sutherland had never really thought it could strike him here, in such well-settled land. Not after Ella had spent most of the past fifteen years as his wife at remote Detroit, where Indian dangers were common, yet none had threatened her life like this.

How had it happened? How could the Shawnees have slipped past the guards? Sutherland was talking out loud and unexpectedly found Lettie gazing at him, her eyes running with tears. Her lower lip trembled, and she said with a dull, cold voice:

"My James was on sentry duty . . . I reckon they done for him first." She glanced at Sutherland again and wiped her cheeks with her sleeve. Sutherland's heart skipped as he thought of his own children, Susannah and Benjamin, who had followed James up the hill. Where were they?

He whipped around, sword again in hand, but before he could go out, the door opened once more and in rushed Susannah, who threw herself into his arms. Aching with relief, he gripped her close, grateful that at least she was safe.

Susannah broke away and ran to her unconscious mother, falling at the side of the bed, sobbing and wailing. Sally Morely drew her gently away and embraced her. Sutherland stood behind the kneeling women and stared blankly at Ella. Her lips were dry, parted slightly, and her breathing was no more than a frail rasp.

In a weary voice he asked, "Susannah, what of Benjamin and James?"

Susannah looked sharply up at him, a strange, anxious expression on her face. Sutherland thought she knew the lads were dead, and again remorse tormented him. But as he turned away, he saw James standing in the open door.

"James!" Sutherland put a hand on the young man's shoulders, drawing him into the lamplight. Lettie burst into sobs of relief and ran to her son. Sutherland had expected to find wounds or some sign of a fight with the Shawnees, but there was not a mark on him.

Sutherland stepped back. "How is it they got through, laddie? Where were you? And where's your gun?"

Before James could speak, Susannah leaped up from her mother's side and came between them, a frightened, haunted look in her moist eyes.

"Pa, I can explain—" But she was cut off as James eased her aside.

He faced Sutherland, whose expression was growing dark. James took a breath. "They . . . got past me without my knowing, Owen. I don't know how . . . but it was my fault. I'm deeply sorry—"

"Sorry?" Sutherland was now staring at his daughter, confusion and disbelief showing in his face. "Were you with him?"

James answered, "She was not responsible!"

Sutherland shot him a fierce look. "And my son? Where is he?"

James took another shaky breath and licked his lips before saying, "I'm not certain . . . it may be the Indians caught him." He closed his eyes. "I'm sorry, Owen, but—"

"You! You're sorry? You were the guard! You were chattering with this child! By the Lord, I should—" Sutherland raised his fist, forgetting that the claymore was in his hand. Susannah screamed, thinking her father was about to strike; but James did not move.

Clenching his jaw and quivering with anger, Sutherland let the sword down and turned to the fire. No one in the room said a word. Susannah and Lettie were crying, and James leaned dejectedly against the open door. Then Sutherland sheathed his sword, threw on a warm cape, and went to stand a moment over Ella's bed. Heera, his tail curled up in anticipation, was already by the door.

Sutherland knelt to kiss his wife's cold lips. "I'll find him, my darling," he whispered. "I'll find Ben . . . I promise you." He kissed her again and gripped her hand. To Sally and Lettie he said in a hoarse voice, "Keep her for me; keep her alive. I'll return quickly."

A tear ran down his weathered face, glinting in the firelight. He rose and, saying nothing to James or Susannah, took his rifle and ammunition down from above the hearth and left the cabin, followed by the husky.

The girl went again to kneel at her mother's side and began to weep uncontrollably. Sally put a comforting hand on Susannah's shoulder, and Lettie, sniffing softly, went to prepare food and tea. Downcast, James stepped outside, where the flames of the ruined building licked high into the night.

Owen Sutherland, with Heera at his side, was hurrying past a group of armed men, who listened to his rapid commands. At the edge of the trees, Sutherland paused as James shouted to him.

"Let me join you, Owen! I must go with you!"

James took a few hesitant steps forward. Without turning around, Sutherland glared back over his shoulder. Others in the settlement silently watched this exchange, all of them understanding that Sutherland blamed James for the disaster.

Sutherland made no reply. In a moment he was gone, vanished into the black forest. Standing alone at the door of the cabin, James watched him go. Then Susannah was at his side and touched his arm. He did not look at her as she spoke quietly.

"Pa will forgive you when he knows it wasn't your fault . . . that it was some—"

"Some other *weakness?*" James was icy. "What difference does it make? It all happened because of me, because of my . . . my weakness! Because of what I am, and what I can never be." His hands were fists. "No, Susannah, I can never be like the rest of them . . . and never be half the man your father is."

"James—" she began to protest, and found herself holding the sprig of mistletoe. James waited, as if to let her say what she wanted to, as if he needed some comfort in her words. But Susannah did not know what to say, and that told James all the more painfully that she, too, thought him a weakling. She, too, blamed him for a tragedy that might cost her mother's life, and perhaps had already cost the life of her brother.

chapter 2

DEATH'S DOOR

Snow fell that night, softly covering the battle scene, concealing the blood, and extinguishing the smoldering embers of the charred cabin and bonfire. The settlement was hushed, save for occasional sobbing heard from within one or another cabin. At dawn, when the wind dropped and the storm relented, the snow was a tranquil, beautiful blanket upon the settlement and in the forest.

The gray light had begun to brighten into day when a watchman on the ridge shouted Sutherland's arrival. Heera appeared first, then Sutherland followed, trudging out of the woods through six inches of new powder. His cape, fur hat, and leggins were white with snow, and his face was cold and red after a night of futile searching.

He had discovered nothing to tell him whether Benjamin was dead or alive. The Shawnees had fled swiftly, the snow covering their tracks. It would take hours, perhaps days, of hunting to the westward to find their trail again. The Indians might even have fled northward or eastward to throw off pursuit, intending to turn west only after they had gone many miles.

Sutherland knew that if Benjamin was a captive, a search for him meant a carefully planned journey of many weeks. He might even have to cross the Ohio into Shawnee country, traveling secretly and cautiously, until somehow he discovered where the boy was being held—if indeed Benjamin had survived.

Had Ella been unhurt, Sutherland would have gone off that very morning, not returning until the boy's fate was certain. Now he could not leave his wife, not like this, when she might be lost at any moment.

Heera bounded ahead to scratch and whine at the cabin door until Sally Morely opened it. As Sutherland approached on the run, he paid anxious attention to Sally's expression.

"She yet lives, Owen!"

He hurried past, throwing off his snowy cap and gloves and barging into the room, which was bright with daylight and warmly comfortable with its blazing fire and the fragrance of bread baking. He stopping short when he saw Ella lying in bed, as if asleep.

Something caught in Sutherland's chest; this moment seemed so familiar, like so many others of late, when he would tramp wearily in from the forest and Ella would come smiling to his arms. . . . He closed his eyes momentarily, trying not to lose the vision, but when he opened them again, the full impression of this simple, lovely room flooded his senses.

He had never noticed that the room was so bright, so filled with light. On all the windows were pale blue curtains, made of a printed cotton that Ella had somehow persuaded a packhorse trader to part with, though the material was supposed to go all the way to Fort Pitt, to the wife of an influential colonel of militia. But then Ella could charm a man into doing whatever she wanted, if she had a notion to. The room's walls were whitewashed and shone in the morning light, touched here and there with bright color: a painting, a small tapestry, some china, a fine silver vase on the mantelpiece. Ella had brought all these mementos safely from Detroit, when so much else had to be left behind. There were also Indian weavings on the walls and on the scrubbed plank floor, and she had laid one over the pine table Tom Morely had made for them.

The room was so much like Ella, so full of her life, that it took Sutherland a moment to regain his composure and look at her lying there. Her head was wrapped in clean bandages. The blankets were smoothly tucked in, and her arms were folded over a clean, turned-down sheet. Sally said the bleeding had mercifully stopped but that Ella was very weak, her heartbeat faint.

Sutherland moved toward her, unsure of what to do. She seemed so very fragile, as though he would hurt her if he dared touch her. It was evident she had been cared for with great love and diligence.

Sutherland stood over his wife, saying softly, "Aye, you've done well, Sal."

Sally sighed and answered, "Susannah's been here every minute; the child's exhausted, and just now lay down in her room."

They sensed another presence and looked around to see Sutherland's daughter standing in her white nightgown at the door of her bedroom. Father and daughter gazed at each other with unspoken feeling, and Sutherland felt an ache within. He held out a hand.

"Pa!" Susannah cried, and rushed to his embrace. "Pa, oh, Pa..."

"Hush, lassie." Sutherland spoke gently, stroking her blond hair, looking over her at his unconscious wife. "Hush, now, and let's hear no more of what happened. Done is done."

Susannah pushed back and stared, as though in appeal, at her father. "I want to...I want to make you understand, Pa, that it was not James's fault—"

He touched her lips with his finger, then kissed her forehead. "Let's not speak of it now." His tone was firm. "And don't you worry about your brother. I'll have him back with us soon."

As her father said this, Susannah searched his gray eyes; then she hugged him, sobbing and trembling.

He smiled wistfully. "There, I've got your best nightdress all wet with snow; you'll catch cold. Go now and sleep."

Susannah glanced at Sally, who assured her she would call her when needed; then the girl went to bed, half closing the door behind her. Sutherland and Sally sat on stools at Ella's bedside, and the Scotsman held his wife's hand. There was no feeling there, almost no life, it seemed. He felt so totally helpless.

"Come back to us, Ella," he heard himself whisper. "Come back, lass...back to us."

There was a soft knock at the door, and Sally let in her husband, Tom, a big, good-looking fellow with curly black hair and a lean, muscular physique. He wore linsey and flannel clothing, and he held a wide-brimmed felt hat in his hands as he approached the seated Sutherland. Like Sally, Tom was in his early twenties, and although he was an active trading partner in the Frontier Company, he was happiest as a cabinetmaker, a profession at which he excelled.

Tom cleared his throat, but before he could speak, Sally's baby, who had been sleeping in the back room, began to awaken noisily. Sally called Timothy Owen's name and went to him, cooing and urging him to go back to sleep, but he had to be picked up and brought into the main room. The child was more than a year old, dark like his parents, and the pride of his father. For this once, however, Tom did not pay heed to his son's crying. Something more important was on his mind.

Tom hemmed and cleared his throat, turning the hat over and over as he sought for words. Then he bluntly apologized for James's having failed them last night. Sutherland said no apologies were necessary.

"But they are," Tom said, his voice catching. "Four dead, and Ben missing . . . and poor Ella!"

"Tom," Sutherland began with a sigh, "what's done is done. Maybe it's our fault, expecting too much from James."

"Not so!" Tom said, his voice catching. "He knew enough to do his duty, but something happened, and he won't tell even me what it was!" Tom stamped about the room, slapping the hat on his leg, shaking his head. "Owen, I fear he plain froze in terror! I fear there ain't no excuse at all, and that's why I'm apologizing for my family name, because he sullied—"

"No!" Susannah was at the door, hands over her face, weeping. "No, that's not it at all, Tom, and you've got no right to blame him for what happened."

There was a weighty silence, broken only by the crackle of the fire and the baby's whimpering. After taking a slow, deep breath, Sutherland spoke to his daughter, who was staring at the floor, sobbing.

"You love the lad enough to believe anything he says?"

"That's not it, Pa! Not at all! But . . . but you're both wrong that he didn't do his duty! I know . . . I was with him!"

Tom was immediately furious. "Then what happened?"

He took a step toward her, crushing his hat in one big fist. "If he ain't at fault, then tell us what you know, girl! 'Cause I've a mind to whip him good, and unless you give me the answer, we'll throw him out—"

Sally put her hand on Tom's to steady him, and bounced their crying son in her arms. Tom turned away in anger as Susannah said, "I can't tell you. But you must trust me— and him! He did nothing wrong—"

"He's too old for you, girl!" Tom cried out, and Susannah gasped. "If you were the one who took his attention, then—" Tom gave a sound of disgust and yanked open the door, stopping when Sutherland spoke.

"Daughter, I do trust you, but if you won't tell us anything more, then we'll wait until James does. Let's not discuss it further." Sutherland called to Tom. "Don't be too hard on the lad. It's just that he's not made for this life. He belongs in Albany."

Tom gave another grunt of annoyance and agreed, turning to leave. Fighting back more tears, Susannah began to say something, when there was a shout outside. Everyone became tense, listening to the dreaded cry of warning.

"Indians!" Sutherland declared, leaping up to grab weapons and hat. He and Tom rushed outside.

There in the settlement's common ground they saw two warmly dressed Indians wearing snowshoes, surrounded by six cursing whites, whose rifles bore on them. Men were calling for their deaths, and others were saying they were either Shawnees or were allied with them.

When Sutherland and Tom approached, the whites parted to let them through. The Indians, swathed in furs and heavy blanket coats, were unarmed, having surrendered their rifles to their captors. The whites continued to snarl and threaten.

"Caught 'em comin' brazenly up the road, Owen," one grizzled man said, cocking his head, "just like they owned the settlement, or thought the Shawnees owned it by now!"

"Damned scouts, spies!" another growled and spat.

"Do for 'em, I say!"

Sutherland calmly called for silence, and the two Indians turned to face him. They were so bundled against the cold and snow that he could not see their faces. He knew they were not Shawnees; judging by the design of their snow-shoes, or *racquets,* as they were called, these two had come from the distant northwest.

Before the Scotsman could speak, the taller of the two Indians muttered through the opening in his fur hood, "There was a time when a Chippewa was welcome in the house of Donoway, and a man out of the storm could find shelter and food."

The other Indian spoke up before the startled Sutherland could respond, saying, "Mebbe tobacco for empty pipe, little rum for empty belly!"

The other settlers were angered at this impudence; they did not recognize the name Donoway, which was Sutherland's Ottawa title. But Sutherland, despite his sorrow, was moved to cry out for joy. He went to the Indians, helped remove their hoods, and embraced them gravely and with great affection. The whites were astonished and stepped back to grumble at one another.

To the elder Indian, a heavyset man with a florid face and small, beady eyes, Sutherland showed the utmost respect, holding this man's forearms. "Uncle," he said in Ottawa, using a younger man's term of reverence for a warrior of considerable age. "Your visit to my new home honors me. Welcome, Mawak, and have no concern for your safety among these good folk, who last night were attacked by Shawnee raiders.

"And it is good to see my brother Tamano," he said in Chippewa to the taller and younger of the pair, whose wide shoulders he gripped. "You have come to me in the deepest distress of my life, and as ever, my brother, you are welcome in my heart and in my house."

While the puzzled, dubious whites muttered in anger, Sutherland ceremoniously greeted the two men. Both dwelt at Detroit, nearly five hundred miles of wilderness to the northwest, and had long been Sutherland's closest friends among the Indians. Though Sutherland guessed they had come to find him on some extremely urgent matter, he first paid them every formal courtesy. Indians considered it uncouth and disrespectful to blurt out a message without first taking the time to contemplate how it should be said, and

as one who had been adopted by the Ottawa twenty years
ago and who had once been married to an Ottawa squaw,
Owen Sutherland observed decorum.

When Tom Morely enthusiastically embraced the Indians, and even Sally and Lettie came dashing out to welcome
them, the other whites were amazed. Children clutched their
mothers' aprons or were shooed indoors, and the older settlers gaped in fascination, though many were revolted at
such a show of affection for Indians. Then Lettie's husband,
the huge, aging Jeb Grey, came lumbering toward Tamano
and Mawak to shake their hands warmly and ask of news
from Detroit. At this, the dumbstruck settlers drifted off,
heads wagging.

Sutherland was not surprised by the reluctance of the
others to show courtesy to Tamano and Mawak, for he knew
that frontiersmen in this part of America were far different
from those who had lived out at Detroit, in the heart of
Indian lands. Traders there were friends of the Indian for
the most part, needing their furs as much as the Indians
needed the white men's manufactured wares in return. But
on the frontier of more settled country, along the borderlands
from Pennsylvania to Georgia, whites and Indians fought
continually for possession of the land. Hatred was the only
emotion the two races shared, and what mattered most when
they met in the forest was who struck the first blow.

Sutherland called out to the others in the settlement.
"These are my trusted friends, and they have come here to
find me. If you will open your hearts and your minds, they
will be your friends, too."

The remaining onlookers eyed one another, and a few
nodded curtly at Sutherland, saying they would abide by
his will in this matter. But they would not offer these Indians
hospitality, and certainly not their trust.

Sutherland accompanied Tamano and Mawak to his cabin,
and as they walked he spoke of what had taken place last
night. Both Indians were moved deeply when they saw Ella
lying in bed, so close to death. With Sutherland, they sat
cross-legged on the floor beside her, not speaking for some
time, until long after the others had left the cabin. When
Tamano and Mawak were ready, they would be fed and

refreshed from their hard journey; but first they had to pay their respects to Ella, whom they had known for many years.

At last Mawak spoke to Sutherland. "This old medicine man still knows a thing or two, Donoway. Will you have me tend your squaw?"

Sutherland gladly accepted Mawak's offer, for the ancient Ottawa was respected as a healer, though he was far past his prime when it came to rigorous ritual dancing and week-long meditation without sleep. After a few words with Sutherland, Mawak left the cabin to find Sally and procure various herbs for a concoction to help heal the wound. Sutherland knew Mawak would chant over the spilled contents of his medicine bag—a crooked bird's leg, a shell or two, and the powdered gall of a bear—but it was the Indian's herb lore that could help Ella most.

Sutherland and Tamano rose from the floor and went to sit before the fire and share some tobacco. After passing the pipe, the Chippewa said, "I have come with tidings, and to tell you I no longer like what the great white father across the sea is doing to my people." Speaking slowly and deliberately, Tamano said that for the first time ever the northwest Indians were unified in their preparations for an all-out war.

"British soldiers are giving our young men gifts of muskets and ammunition, scalping knives and sharp steel tomahawks, in numbers never before seen in my country. Every minor chief wears a medal from King George on his breast, and every lodge is rich with gifts of blankets, clothing, beads, vermilion, mirrors."

Tamano went on to explain that the British were calling for a full-scale rising of the northwestern tribes next spring. Sutherland listened, but his sorrow for Ella made the Chippewa's words seem remote. He and Tamano had been the closest of friends for years, until the Scotsman had become a rebel against the king in 1775. At that time, Tamano had believed the best choice for the Indians was to support the British government and remain loyally neutral; and although the powerful Iroquois to the north of the Wyoming Valley had taken up arms with the British, most other Indians of the northwest had been slow to accept the red-painted hatchet sent by the British from nation to nation. Of late, however, the British had been more persuasive and more generous with gifts and arms.

Tamano stared at Sutherland. "I know, Donoway, the Indian cannot win anything in this war. We can only die well. I have seen your great cities, and I have seen the power of the armies. I know the great white father in England will not win this war, and those Indians who join him will suffer and will lose all they have."

"You see these things clearly, brother," Sutherland said. "I only wish my stepson had your wisdom."

Sutherland referred to Ella's son by her first husband. Now in his middle twenties, Jeremy Bently had been raised at Detroit and educated in Edinburgh; he was a respected physician and lived at the Sutherland family home near loyalist-held Fort Detroit.

Sutherland stared over at Ella, recalling how deeply she had been hurt when her son had joined the enemy. Often she had voiced the hope that when peace was made they would all be reunited. At first Sutherland had shared that hope, but now he was not so optimistic. Last spring Jeremy had accepted a commission as a British officer, a surgeon major in the Eighth Regiment of Foot under Lieutenant Governor Henry Hamilton, commander of British troops in the northwest. Sutherland had last seen his stepson several months ago, after a terrible battle to the north, at Oriskany, in New York's Mohawk Valley. Jeremy had been captured by the rebels, though later he had been exchanged and allowed to return to the northwest. Sutherland presumed Tamano had since seen him at Detroit, and was surprised when the Chippewa said he had not.

"I have come here, Donoway, because I thought that Jeremy was in a rebel prison." Tamano said he had been in Montreal that autumn, to learn what he could about the British army's plans for its Indian allies. While there, he had also discovered startling information concerning Jeremy's closest friend, a British officer who had been killed under mysterious circumstances two years previous.

Reaching into his deerskin pouch, Tamano handed over a small leather-bound journal, which was stained with blood.

Sutherland took it, reading the familiar name written neatly on the first page: Lieutenant Richard Weston, Seventh Welsh Fusiliers. Sutherland had never met Weston, but Ella had, and she had often spoken highly of him.

As Sutherland thumbed through the book, Tamano explained the roundabout route whereby it had come to him. It had been found by Hurons who had camped at the scene of Weston's scalping. Expecting to receive a reward for the journal, the Hurons had brought it to a British officer at Montreal, a man known to Tamano. The officer had asked Tamano to carry the journal back to the commander of Fort Detroit, where Weston had been stationed. It was believed that Weston had been scalped by rebel scouts, who had left him for dead. This cruel act had helped drive Jeremy into joining the British army to fight the rebellion. Tamano had also known Weston, and being curious, he had asked a white friend to read the entries telling of the officer's final campaign.

Tamano said, "If your stepson reads this, Donoway, he will see that it might not have been rebels who killed his friend, but a king's officer."

Startled, Sutherland paged through to the final entries. If what Tamano said was true, Jeremy might come to realize he had misjudged the rebellion. He might even be persuaded to abandon the loyalist cause.

Sutherland looked over at Ella's pale face, wishing she could hear him. Then, forcing himself to concentrate, he began to read the clear, fine writing, beginning at the entry dated April 18, 1776. "Somewhere on the Saint Lawrence River."

Weather good, windy. Our march has been most trying ever since we left Fort Detroit. It is not so much the rigors of the journey that have caused hardship, but the savage tyranny of our commander, Captain Mark Davies.

Sutherland's eyes stopped at that familiar name, and he glanced up at Tamano. Mark Davies was a scoundrel, and had long been Sutherland's enemy. And Weston, Sutherland

knew, had once fought a duel with Davies, even though
Davies was his superior officer. Sutherland had been away
from Detroit at the time, and Davies, taking advantage of
his absence, had publicly threatened Ella. Weston had come
to her defense and had faced down Davies with pistols.
Davies had fired hastily and missed, whereupon Weston had
deliberately discharged his weapon into the ground, satisfied
to have made his point. But Davies had been even more
furious than before.

Sutherland frowned, already suspecting what the following
pages would reveal. He quickly read on:

> How profoundly Davies loathes me! He tries in
> every way to break my spirit. He sends me on night
> patrols without rest and orders me to carry out petty,
> dirty chores. These I suffer to do, but I'll not submit
> to his browbeating. This morning, when I demanded
> he stop his Senecas from torturing a prisoner, a sus-
> pected rebel, he flew into a rage and nearly drew his
> sword on me.

It was clear to Sutherland that Weston felt very alone on
this expedition, which apparently had been composed mainly
of Indians, with a few British soldiers along to direct them.
The diary entries were concerned less with the march than
with Davies and the Senecas, one of whom was named
Manoth, a war chief who had died last year in a battle with
Sutherland's folk. It was Benjamin who had shot down this
feared Seneca, and when Sutherland read the Indian's name,
he again thought gloomily of his missing son.

He skimmed on to the last pages:

> It is late, and I write in my bedding by candlelight.
> Once again I have earned Davies's and Manoth's hos-
> tility for preventing the torture of a rebel prisoner.
> God forgive Davies for allowing his Indians to roast
> four poor souls. . . .

This entry went on to tell of how Davies and Weston
had again nearly come to blows over the mistreatment of
prisoners. Sutherland read on:

... I'm not given to imagination, but even at this very moment I feel as though there is an enemy lurking in the bushes near my dying fire. The Indians and even the other officers give me wide berth because of my opposition to Davies. Still I am firm in my resolve to stand against him, as any honorable officer must do.

The very woods seem hostile tonight, and

The pen had suddenly scrawled off, as though Weston's hand had moved abruptly, and on this page were drops of blood. Sutherland turned the page. There were no other entries. Apparently the journal had been lost to sight in the struggle.

Sutherland was almost certain it was Mark Davies, or Manoth acting on the captain's direct command, who had murdered Jeremy's friend.

He closed the book. Again he looked over at Ella and saw that she was breathing hard, more unconscious than in a restful sleep. Then the door opened, and in tumbled Mawak with an armful of dried herbs. He began bustling about at the hearth with water and iron kettles.

Sutherland said to Tamano, "Jeremy might feel differently about the British cause when he reads this."

Tamano nodded once. "I will take this book back to Detroit and give it to him."

"No," Sutherland said, rising and going to stand near Ella, gazing longingly at her. "No, it's for me to talk to him, though he be in a British fort. It's for me to show him the truth and persuade him to come back to us while he can ... before the loyalists are driven out forever."

Tamano and Mawak watched in silence as Sutherland knelt at his wife's side, holding her hand. He whispered, "Ella, if I can bring your sons back to you, I will; won't you live for that?" Bowing his head, he closed his eyes and murmured, "Live for that!"

Some time later, as snow again began to fall outside the cabin, old Mawak prepared to treat Ella. Sally and Lettie had returned for an hour and carefully unbound and cleaned the wound, but they did not know how to bring Ella around.

Now Mawak would try. He, Tamano, and Sutherland were alone in the cabin with her.

While the sky darkened as the blizzard brought an early nightfall, the cabin's main room glowed with whale-oil lamps and firelight. Sitting cross-legged near Ella's bed, Mawak worked without speaking. Slowly and carefully he spread a blanket on the floor and laid out objects from his hide pouch, their arrangement as important to him as the actual attempt at healing that was to come.

Sitting in a chair by the fire, Sutherland watched in silence. Every hour of unconsciousness brought Ella closer to death—and took Benjamin farther away from them. By now Sutherland believed the boy was alive, for the pet blue jay, Punch, had not been seen in the settlement that day. The birdhouse hanging against the cabin's clay-and-stick chimney was empty, and Sutherland was sure Punch had stayed with his owner, probably flying overhead as the Shawnees fled homeward. Sutherland longed to go after his son, but he would not leave Ella like this.

Mawak began to chant softly in a throaty, deep voice. He had finished laying out the contents of his medicine bundle: three ball-shaped objects wrapped in leather; three slim, hollow bones; a black charm-stone, such as was carried by every Indian sorcerer; three dried fruits; a small stone pipe; a thong with one bear claw; the deformed leg of a bird. Sutherland knew that this last object was considered extremely potent, giving special powers of communication with the manitous, or nature spirits.

To another white man, Mawak's deliberate preparations and the superstitious charms might have seemed pure nonsense, but Owen Sutherland had witnessed much of Indian medicine since the day he had been captured by Ottawas. He regarded his left hand, which was missing the last three fingernails. He had lost them during a brutal session of torture; but he had not cried out. That had won him the admiration of the chieftain Pontiac, who had ordered his release and adoption.

They had made him one of them, tattooed the green turtle on his chest, and renamed him Donoway, "fearless in the flames." He had lived as an Ottawa, hunted, celebrated,

suffered, and eventually married an Ottawa squaw. He had
often seen the work of medicine men such as Mawak, members of the revered medicine society, the Midewiwin, and
knew their healing powers. He could not explain how they
succeeded, but they often did, and he trusted them. As
Mawak sat with bowed head, turtle-shell rattle slowly shaking in his right hand, Sutherland leaned forward, watching,
waiting. Mawak had already applied a compress of yarrow
to the wound and had forced some unknown solution into
Ella's mouth. Now he chanted to Menabozho, the mighty
manitou who had given the secrets of healing to the *mide*,
as the sorcerer was called. The chant was languid, hypnotic.

Sutherland gazed at his wife, who, so close to death,
seemed more beautiful than ever. Mawak's voice rose and
fell, as outside the blizzard howled around the cabin, blowing snow under the door. Now and again the old Indian
paused a few moments, then resumed with the same nasal
sound. Tamano occasionally plied the fire with dry logs,
but otherwise remained silent and unmoving, seated against
one wall.

Then Mawak stopped chanting and picked up one of the
three hollow bones, leaning over and touching the end of
it to Ella's temple. He put his lips to the other end and drew
slowly, deeply. Sutherland knew he was attempting to suck
the bad spirits from the victim and into his own body.
Suddenly Mawak jerked back and seemed to convulse, taking air in a quick gulp; he appeared to swallow the bone
whole. Sutherland knew this was a sleight-of-hand typical
of medicine men, symbolic of ingesting the bad spirit.

Mawak repeated this same process with the other two
bones, each time convulsing wildly as the bone disappeared
somewhere—seemingly into his throat, but likely into his
shirt.

After a while Mawak sat with head bowed low, the rattle
again in his hand, but not moving. Then the rattle sounded,
and he was chanting once more. This was the approach to
the climax of the ceremony.

Tamano came to Sutherland's side, knowing Mawak's
medicine had to work now. The two men watched Ella for
the slightest indication that she was awakening. The rattle

and Mawak's voice rose and fell, rose and fell, and at last became still.

Sutherland wanted to speak his wife's name, but to interfere with Mawak's medicine would be a grave transgression. He stood there. Every minute dragged past like an eternity. Ella was so fair, seemingly alight with some inner radiance; yet she did not awaken.

More than a half hour passed. Sutherland felt a tremendous weight about his shoulders and neck. Whatever magic the old Indian medicine man could conjure up had not been powerful enough to restore Ella.

As the three men sat in silence, the wind sounded mournful, battering the shutters, stinging snow against the cabin. Sutherland slumped near the fire, feeling the heat on his face. His mind began to whirl. What should he do next? Should he leave Ella like this and rush away to find Benjamin? He looked a moment at his wife, who was hardly breathing. What would she want him to do?

She would want him to go for Benjamin.

"Yes," he murmured, finally. "That's what you would want."

Her expression, pure and pale, did not change; yet he thought he could hear her saying, *Owen, find our son. Bring him home. Bring home both sons, Benjamin and Jeremy.*

Sweat began to bead on his forehead; breathing was difficult, and he swayed briefly before springing to his feet to cry out Ella's name. He gazed at her, his fists clenched, never before feeling so useless.

Mawak spoke. "She hears you, nephew, but she cannot answer. Not yet."

Breathing fast, Sutherland looked down at the wizened old man, such a wrinkled, brown contrast to the fair Ella with her long lashes and beautiful lips. Sutherland wanted to call out again, but what was the use?

He took a step toward the bed. "Ah, Mawak, uncle, can't you bring her back to me?"

The Ottawa answered, "Maybe there is a way . . . a way taught to me by your son Jeremy."

Sutherland looked in question at the Indian, who drew from the medicine pouch a steel lancet, evidently a gift from

Jeremy. Mawak contemplated the sharp, glittering blade, saying Jeremy and he had exchanged lessons in medicine many times, and that the art of bleeding a patient was one he had learned not long ago.

It was dangerous. Sutherland knew enough of modern theory to suggest that the blade be heated over a flame, then washed before being used. Mawak nodded his head and handed the lancet to Sutherland, saying with much gravity, "This washing and burning ceremony is a sacred one, I know."

Sutherland held the blade in the fire—a procedure that, contrary to what Mawak had observed, not all physicians believed in. Sutherland had read, however, that sterilization was worthwhile, and his stepson was of the same opinion. Though Sutherland had never attempted a bleeding, he knew that it was sometimes used to revive an unconscious patient. He had seen Jeremy do it to Tom Morely, who had been wounded in the head, similarly to Ella, three years ago.

Tamano and Sutherland both knelt at Mawak's side, with towels, bandages, and hot water. The medicine man leaned over Ella, touching the sharp blade to the skin behind the ear. Carefully and delicately—obviously well trained by Jeremy—Mawak made several shallow incisions. Blood trickled down to a towel that Sutherland held beneath the cuts. Ella was already so pale that he feared for her, worried that Mawak would take too much blood.

Mawak made an incision in a small vein. This released a copious flow, causing Sutherland to gasp audibly. The Indian's thick, callused hands were amazingly light as he continued to make more small cuts, swabbing them with a warm, wet towel to encourage the flow. Sutherland thought this would never end; one towel after another was soaked red as Tamano stood by with a lantern.

Then Sutherland thought Ella moved. Or was it his imagination—emotion drawn taut by strain and weariness? He must have been wrong, for she still lay unconscious. Mawak laid aside the lancet, dabbing the wounds steadily, controlling the flow by pressing a cloth against the bony skull. Eventually, he and Sutherland had four towels at their feet, all soaked with Ella's blood.

"It is enough," Mawak said, and called for the softened chokeberry bark, which Tamano brought. As Sutherland reswathed Ella's head, Mawak sat back on his blanket and again took up the rattle. The old Indian's clothes were stained with Ella's blood, and the strain had begun to tell even on his dark and inscrutable face.

Sutherland finished his bandaging, ran a hand gently down Ella's cheek, and sighed. He sat there, bloody towels in hand, and watched her. He knew that when bloodletting was successful, the patient usually became conscious immediately. He stood up nervously, his mind agitated. She was not recovering.

chapter 3

FAREWELLS

In a cabin just forty feet from where her mother lay near death, Susannah Sutherland prayed. She sat out of the firelight, near a small window with frost creeping up its corners. She could see little outside, and scarcely noticed the snow swirling past the small, thick panes. Her attention was focused on the faint blush of red light at her family's cabin window, which grew brighter as the night deepened.

Her father had insisted on the utmost privacy for Mawak, so she was with Mel and Hickory Webster, a childless couple who had fled Detroit with the Sutherlands. Though politically neutral, the Websters had stood by Ella and Owen in time of trouble, and now hoped to live here peacefully until the war ended.

A lanky, blond fellow in his thirties, Mel had a thin, friendly face and an easygoing nature. He was stooped over a workbench at the far side of the room, binding a book with leather. Susannah turned from the window to watch idly, hardly thinking about Mel, whose tongue stuck out as he pressed the rolling fillet tool around the border of the leather covering.

Bookbinding was Mel's latest passion in a seemingly unrelated chain of hobbies, inventions, and harebrained notions—as most people termed his attempts to build flying machines or to design something called a submarine, which, according to Mel, a rebel inventor had already devised and used unsuccessfully against British ships in New York harbor. Bookbinding, fortunately, was a safer pastime than breathing underwater or leaping with wood-and-feather wings from tall trees, and Mel's friends were relieved that he was finally putting his talents to safe and constructive use.

Along one wall of the rough cabin were dozens of bound volumes, some in cloth, some in soft, imported morocco, others in calfskin or sheepskin. Many were only of pasteboard or thin scaleboard, but otherwise extremely well done, with gilt lettering stamped on a patch of leather glued to the spine. Some of these volumes contained only a few editions of the *Pennsylvania Gazette* or someone's collection of random letters that Mel had agreed to bind for a small price. Mel had taught himself this craft, and now the cabin was half given over to it: a workbench with a tabletop sewing frame, neatly arranged clamps, trimming press, hammer, needles, awls, threads, fillet stamps, and piles of papers, board, and leather.

The other half of the cabin, where Susannah sat awaiting word from her father, had a couple of repaired chairs, a rough rag rug, and a seaman's chest, which held Hickory Webster's few clothes. Hickory, who sat at the fire reading a Mohawk-language prayer book, was a sturdy, dark, thirty-year-old woman, almost as tall as Mel and built somewhat more powerfully. Her full name was "Hickory splitter who is stronger than white lumberjack," and she was an Oneida, a member of the only tribe of the Six Nations of Iroquois that supported the rebels against the British government. The other five nations had remained loyal to the king.

Mel had met Hickory in his years of travel among the Indians as a teacher and instructor in white language and civilized crafts. A ready hand at everything from metalworking to fruit-tree growing, Mel had generously shared his knowledge with the Indians, as well as his love of music. He was such an adept fiddler that his Indian friends called him Singing Bow; now his battered old violin hung on the wall, above a pile of yellowed journals on science and invention.

When he finished with the filleting stamp, Mel held up the book to examine it in the firelight. It was a small volume, about five inches long and four wide, and had required meticulous skill to bind. With a satisfied nod, he rose from his seat, crossed the room to Susannah, and handed her the book. "See this, my girl, and tell me if you think it's a fitting gift for your father."

Susannah ran her fingers over the beautifully wrought leather, then opened the cover. The title page was written in Mel's own flowing hand, and she read it aloud:

"Discourses, essays, and occasional poems by the noted American author, philosopher, and frontier gentleman, Owen Sutherland. 1778, Wyoming Valley, the Independent Commonwealth of Pennsylvania."

It was a collection of her father's writings that had appeared in various American and British publications over the past ten years, and Susannah was impressed. She forced herself to smile.

"He'll be most grateful, Mel, I'm sure," she said, then added with a sniff, "I'm afraid he would have been better able to appreciate it had not my ... mother ... my—"

Mel patted her shoulder. "There, there," he said softly, wiping away a tear that appeared at his own eye; Hickory was staring at them, sadness in her kindly face. "Why don't you just peruse this book and distract yourself by reflecting on how remarkable a man Owen is, and how he's voiced so perfectly what so many of us Americans are thinking these days."

Susannah blinked away tears, her mouth working involuntarily. She closed the book and gazed at it.

"Oh, I know ... I know only too well what a great man he is ... as everyone says—"

"You proud?" Hickory said, smiling. "We proud to know him, proud to know him." She often repeated herself.

Susannah nodded hastily and looked back out into the darkness, at her family's cabin window. "Very proud. I love him so, but sometimes ... sometimes I think he expects too much of folk ... too much of ordinary folk like me, and ... and ..." She began to sob and fumbled with a handkerchief.

"James Morely?" Mel's voice was hushed, but pierced Susannah as if the name were something sharp; her head jerked around so that the long blond hair flew in her face.

Biting her lip, she nodded once and stared at the floor. "He blames James, hates him for what happened ... for Ma lying in there, and for those poor folk who died."

Mel said quickly, gently, "He admires James as a trader, a merchant. There's nobody except your father slicker at a trade than James. We all know that."

Hickory joined them, the prayer book held at her waist. She said, "Your pa upset, you know; he come to again, when your ma all right. He no hate James. No hate."

"Maybe not hate!" Susannah blurted out. "But he has no respect for him." She lost control and cried loudly, "My pa doesn't respect James as a man!"

Mel and Hickory began to protest, but a sudden chill rushed against their backs, and they turned to see the door wide open, cold air pouring in. Standing there, struck by what Susannah had said, was James Morely.

With a shock, Susannah rushed to take his hands, stopping short of embracing him, and hurriedly asked that he come in and sit. Though the young man's eyes glowed with fire and injured pride, he was able to master himself and closed the door, removing his cap and nodding to the Websters. He was dressed in his best brown duffel coat and with new fur leggins that Hickory had made especially for his trip to Albany.

James was close friends with Mel, particularly because they shared a common interest in booklearning, although James had little formal education. Mel had made a point of overcoming that lack, and along with Susannah, James was a star pupil in Mel's occasional school, held in this cabin.

Self-conscious as he came into the center of the room, James said he had been out for a walk and thought he might visit awhile. He asked if there was word of Ella, and being told there was not, he said blankly, almost hoarsely, "I'm departing in the morning."

Susannah's hand went to her open mouth. James cleared his throat and looked away as Hickory helped him take off his coat. Seeing the book in Susannah's hand, he deliberately changed the subject. "Is that Mel's most recent creation?"

Susannah came to herself and handed over the book. When James read that it was a collection of Owen Sutherland's work, his face fell. Still he was polite enough to ask casually how Mel had gone about cutting up all those periodicals and assembling them so neatly. Offering him a chair, Mel began to explain at length, and Susannah went back to her solitary place by the window.

Hard as they all tried, they were far too uneasy about Ella to conduct the usual cheerful conversation. After a while James went to Susannah, and she turned to stare at him as he held out the book. She knew he must have noticed the tears streaking her face, but he seemed not to want any more unhappiness. He looked past her, at the red glow of the nearby cabin window.

"Your father is a wonderful essayist, Susannah, an important voice for America. Maybe one day this book will be set in type and printed up somewhere . . . likely by your pa's friend, that old publisher Ben Franklin."

He smiled, and Susannah nodded, doing her best to support his effort at congenial conversation. She asked him if he had heard any news lately from Frontier Company partners in Albany, and James eagerly launched into an explanation of the current state of the fur trade. Obviously he was relieved to talk about business matters, even though they all knew that the company was by no means prospering these days.

In fact, since the war had begun in 1775, the once-flourishing Frontier Company had faded fast. Most of its principal partners, like her father and James, were rebels, but the fur grounds of the northwest were in British hands, as well as all the major trading posts and the shipping routes to the ocean. A new wave of loyalist traders had taken over where the Frontier Company had once been active. Even the few company partners who had continued to do business as loyalists had lost much ground to the new associations of traders from Montreal. James said this was largely because company sources of credit in Britain had been lost in the upheaval. The names Frontier Company and Owen Sutherland were too closely associated in most British minds, he said.

Once again there was an uneasy silence; then Mel spoke. "I'm sure the company will come out of the war in fine shape, particularly since you'll soon be helping out in Albany, James."

Susannah thought James felt a great burden just then, for he briefly closed his eyes. It might be that the entire future of the Frontier Company rested on his shoulders. In the flight from Montreal, company members had saved all their cash, amounting to nearly five thousand pounds sterling in paper money—a vast sum when sterling was such a precious commodity in a sea of almost worthless congressional notes. It was up to James to find a way to make that last sum of company money reestablish the firm's vigor.

Albany, Susannah knew, was the ideal place to do just that; some company members lived there, overseeing warehouses and dockyards that still belonged to the company, although they were mostly empty and unused these days.

James seemed conscious that Susannah was watching him. Her hazel eyes were soft and beautiful, and he blushed noticeably as he returned her gaze. Her voice was slow, halting: "How long will you be gone?"

He pursed his lips, unconsciously turning Sutherland's book over in his hands. "Perhaps two years . . ."

She gave an audible gasp, evoking sympathetic looks from Mel and Hickory, who had taken seats together by the fire to give the young folk more privacy.

"Or perhaps I'll be back sooner, if matters turn our way." His eyes took on a strange light, and his voice grew determined. "However long it takes to put the Frontier Company on its feet again."

"Oh!" Susannah declared, "Pa would be so proud of you if you did that!"

James reddened at the mention of her father. He avoided looking at her, then nodded almost imperceptibly. "If he would, I would be glad."

Susannah saw resentment in his eyes; his handsome face was almost contorted. She reached out to touch his hand, to calm him. At first he did not respond; then his other hand covered hers, and his face softened, the boyish beauty returning.

"Come back to us soon," she said quietly.

"Soon will still be too early for you, Susannah." He spoke plainly, and she thrilled to grasp the meaning of his words. "Become a woman in your own way, and for a time put me from your mind . . . if not your heart." He smiled warmly, and she felt his goodness. "Think of happier things, as you ought to at your age. Susannah, I'm going out of your life for now, and that's best for both of us."

Susannah thought she would cry. She knew he was right, that their ages were far too different; yet she loved him all the more for his cool wisdom, and, more important, his words had proved that he loved her, too.

Then, unexpectedly, she felt a tremendous rush of emotion, and it was as if her mother was calling her. Cold fear surged through her body, and she stared out the window, feeling more than seeing.

Owen Sutherland leaned against the mantelpiece, staring into the roaring red blaze. Behind him, Mawak and Tamano sat in silence.

For the first time in years, Sutherland sensed words come from his heart and into his mind, unwilled words that collected in a flow and rhythm, in structure, like a poem. He had no wish to put them on paper, yet they came and stayed with him, like an echo, a call, as though they rose from the fire and not from his own tormented soul.

> My love and passion, life and longing,
> Heart of hearts, forevermore.
>
> Love and passion, dream and waking,
> I shall love you, evermore.

Again and again those simple words came and went, and he shut his eyes, as if to see them. He saw Ella instead, so full of joy and life. Their children were running happily behind—Jeremy, Benjamin, Susannah—and Ella was laughing and calling his name. The fire was hot on his body. He absorbed the power of it, feeling it surge through him, whispering, "I shall love you, evermore!" And Ella was calling his name, coming closer, her beautiful eyes all for him—

"Owen . . ."

He whispered, "Evermore."

"Owen."

He became conscious of where he was. The wind outside

was blowing harder than ever, and the fire grew hotter every moment he stood there.

"Owen."

His eyes opened, heart pounding. She was with him! He whirled. She was conscious, gazing at him, almost smiling, one hand weakly out to him. Mawak was grinning and nodding his head. Tamano stood and yelped for joy.

Sutherland breathed Ella's name and moved toward her with halting steps, as if afraid she would go away again. He said her name, and Ella held out her other hand. With a cry, he rushed into her arms, and they embraced, both trembling with emotion, unable to speak.

In a moment, Mawak and Tamano had left the room, the door opening with a blast of cold, fresh air, then closing again. Sutherland kissed his wife gently, lips and cheeks and bandaged forehead.

Overjoyed, he grinned at her. "So you mean to stay with us, then?"

She ran her fingertips behind his head, then drew him very close. "I do..." Then a look of fear came over her, and she gasped, "The children? Owen, our children!"

Though she tried to sit up, it took no effort to hold her down. She asked a delirious rush of questions about the attack, about Benjamin and Susannah, but before Owen could answer, she began to moan, dizzy and exhausted, her head moving from side to side.

The door opened just then, and Susannah rushed in, caped and hooded against the storm. Doffing her cloak with a gasp of joy, she fell to her mother's bedside, head on Ella's breast. Sutherland stroked his daughter's hair, guessing that Tamano and Mawak had told her of her mother's recovery. Or perhaps the strong, unspoken bond between mother and daughter had brought Susannah here at just this moment.

He observed them both a little while, then rose to fetch some broth. He was awhirl with relief, yet tried to clear his head to think of what must be done next. Susannah, he was glad to see, had managed to comfort her mother, and by the time he brought the steaming cup to the bed, Ella appeared calm and ready to hear him out.

Slowly, choosing his words with care, he told her everything he knew about the attack, reassuring her there was good reason to believe Benjamin was alive and saying he would start out after the boy now that she was recovering.

After Susannah had fed Ella the broth and Sutherland had given her a dose of laudanum, he again took her hand. "Ella, before you sleep, there is one more thing you should know—it's about Jeremy."

Her eyes widened in alarm, and he patted her hand reassuringly, telling her about Tamano and Mawak's arrival and Richard Weston's journal. He said he intended to meet Jeremy secretly, as soon as possible.

"I'll do my best to bring him out, too, my darling."

"Oh, Owen, if only you could!"

He smiled, and his eyes lit with the bold confidence Ella so loved to see. "This will be a journey to remember," he said, "when we're old and gray and in our rocking chairs!"

She smiled, too, tears in her eyes. "I'll be waiting for you . . . for all of you! Have no fear for my sake, Owen. I mean to live awhile yet, until my family is united again, and peace is . . ." She faltered, trying to catch her breath.

Owen and Susannah were staring intently. Ella went on slowly, every phrase a strain. "I know this war will soon be over. I know you'll come home to me, and we'll be together . . . in peace . . . as we have dreamed . . . back at the straits. At our Valenya . . ." She became distant as she recalled their grand house at Detroit, where Jeremy was now living with his young wife. She and Owen had built Valenya to fulfill a dream, but two years ago the war had forced them to flee. That was why they were here on the frontier, poised to return to Detroit with the first rebel army that could be organized to strike westward.

"Valenya," Sutherland said quietly, echoing Ella's faint murmurings as she fell into a tranquil, restful sleep. "Yes, my Ella, one day we'll go home to Valenya. One day, when peace comes."

James Morely was ready before dawn. His packhorse was loaded, and his mount, waiting in a three-sided shelter, was frisky and eager to move out. James left his mother's cabin after a breakfast that he ate more out of duty to her than because of hunger, for he was tense and anxious to be on his way.

The morning was dark and very cold, but James was dressed warmly in his mink cap, duffel coat, and new fur leggins. It was a journey of four weeks to Albany, and he would be in company with six trusted men leading several packhorses laden with pelts. In a money belt around his waist James had five thousand pounds sterling. He knew it was risky to carry so much cash, but the woods between the Wyoming Valley and Albany were well patrolled by colonial militia. Also, James had a written pass from the militia commander at nearby Forty Fort, so he could travel undisturbed by Congress troops.

The money was a secret, unknown even to the men going with James. The fact that Owen Sutherland and other members of the Frontier Company had trusted him with all their cash should have told James how highly he was regarded as an honest merchant; but his shame at having let them down when the Indians attacked was a painful burden he could not forget. He was sure Owen Sutherland thoroughly reviled him and was allowing him to take the sterling only out of respect for his mother, Lettie, and for the memory of his dead father, who had been Sutherland's friend. But James was sworn to prove Sutherland wrong to think him incompetent.

As James helped ready the horses, his mother stood watching, her chubby face glistening with tears, visible beneath her hood. His stepfather, the former regular soldier Jeb Grey, stood hatless beside her, hands in pockets, head bowed. They were both relieved that Ella was recovering, and James knew their greatest concern now was for him.

A small crowd had gathered on the common to say farewell to their men. Everyone was quiet, chilled by the pre-dawn cold. Torches were lit, and swigs of rum were downed as fortification against the long winter trail. James embraced his mother and stepfather, then went to Sally and his brother Tom, both of whom wished him a warm farewell. Any disappointment Tom felt at his younger brother's recent failure was not evident as the two of them shook hands.

James smiled. "I'll write you, Tom, whenever I can."

He turned to his horse. The absence of the Sutherlands was unpleasantly conspicuous, but no one spoke about it as he prepared to mount. Then there came a cry from the Sutherland cabin, and he turned to see Susannah dash out the open door and scamper across the snow, her frock coat over a nightgown.

James hugged her, and she panted, "I was asleep, but Pa woke me up and told me it was time to . . . to say—" She broke down and pressed her face against his chest. He kissed her on the head, and after a moment gently pushed her back to Sally Morely. Susannah cried, obviously not caring what anyone thought.

James touched her under the chin. "Take care of your ma, girl. How is she now?"

Susannah sobbed, "She's fast asleep and much better already!"

James had been invited into the cabin last night, and though Ella had been kind, it all still pained him.

"I'm glad to hear it," he said. He was about to turn away when Susannah handed him something wrapped in a silk handkerchief. As he began to untie it, Owen Sutherland stepped into the torchlight nearby.

Sutherland offered James his hand, and the young man tucked the handkerchief away to accept the greeting. The Scotsman gripped his shoulders in a gesture of affection. "Make the most of Albany, laddie; your father, Garth, was a trader of traders, and he'd be proud to know his son had such an opportunity."

Sutherland had meant this as encouragement, but James took it as a challenge, and stood straighter, chin thrust out a little.

"You can depend on me, sir." He and Owen looked each other in the eye, and James said, "Nothing will keep me from success; wait and see." He glanced at Susannah. "Nothing."

As James mounted up, Susannah pressed against her father, who put an arm over her shoulders. Sutherland, too, was dressed for traveling, in buckskins, linsey, and furs. Nearby were Mawak and Tamano, both carrying snowshoes. James knew they would soon be on the westward trail to find Benjamin.

As the party formed into a file and moved off toward the dawn, the shouts of farewell rose, then faded. James waved back to everyone, and last of all to Susannah.

chapter **4**

WABETE

In two weeks, the fleeing Shawnees had not paused to rest more than a few hours in any one place. The gray, snowy hills and dense forests of western Pennsylvania were as dangerous to them as to any of the bands of white hunters or scouts roving the woods. A trail belonged to the strongest party, and these Shawnees were few, dispirited, and hungry. They had much to fear until they crossed the Ohio River, many miles westward.

They were sure white scouts were on their trail by now. Whites always came after a retreating war party. The blizzard had given a precious day or two of cover, but since then the weather had turned milder, perfect for following the tracks of fifteen bone-weary fighting men, three of them wounded, one borne on a sapling-and-rawhide litter. There had been no time to hunt, little enough to rest; even water was taken only occasionally, at brief stops near unfrozen springs.

If they discovered a lonely cabin— always abandoned, because the settlers were bunching together these days or fleeing back over the mountains—the Indians took shelter there. They dared not light a fire, lest their smoke be sighted; but a house was better than a cold bed of balsam pine, with a man's back huddled against a hard boulder or ledge.

How disappointed they had been by their bitter defeat. Before the fight, not one of them had doubted they would destroy the settlement and return home with scalps at their belts and bags full of food, drink, tobacco, and booty. There should have been thirty of them, exulting in triumph, confident that an equal number of frontiersmen on their trail would be cautious of a trap and therefore keep their distance, glad simply to see the Shawnees depart. But so many good men had fallen in that disaster—grimly confirming what other warriors had been saying of late about the new breed of white settlers on the edge of Indian country.

In days long ago, when the British warred against the French, it had been the settler and the soldier who had guarded against ambush, and the Indian had been the master of cunning; but this generation of whites was tougher, better armed, and knew how to fight like the Indian. It seemed white scouts—Indian spies, as they called themselves— were everywhere, as elusive as the fox, and as vicious as a trapped wolverine.

Even speed, formerly the Indian's exclusive defense, was no longer reliable for escape. The white scouts—the toughest were from Virginia and were called Longknives—kept on pursuing, sometimes striking deep into Indian country before calling off the chase. And so often the whites had known precisely when to turn back, as if smelling danger, pulling their men off the trail on the brink of a devastating ambush.

Such thoughts haunted these beaten warriors as they fled westward, day and night, until snowshoes snapped, leggins were worn away, and clothing was in shreds. More than once a lookout had given the warning that an enemy was near, and several times white scouts had been spotted, examining the trail the Shawnees had used, or a clearing where they had paused ever so briefly.

Early on this cold, clear morning, the weary fugitives rested at a spring not far southeast of the large white settlement at Fort Pitt. They carried their *racquets* slung over their backs now, for the snow was not deep, and it was imperative they move fast. This was extremely dangerous country, and the Shawnees would be grateful to get out of it after a few days of hard marching. Around the slushy watering place they slouched in exhaustion or sat with bowed heads, backs bent. Feathers were limp, war paint was smeared with sweat and sometimes blood. The wounded were silent, their pain so unbearable that it consumed their minds and left them dazed. No one had eaten anything yet today, save for some pinecones, chewed and chewed until soft enough to swallow.

Soon they would reach their canoes, which had been hidden near the Ohio River, the Spay-lay-wi-theepi. There was a cache of food there, too, enough to keep them going for another week if managed sparingly. Until then they would suffer silently.

The leader of the war party was an aging, strongly built chieftain named Wabete, or Elk. He was clad in a dirty blue blanket with holes cut for head and arms, and a red beaded belt was wrapped about his large stomach. His hair, like that of the others, had been plucked or burned off clean on either side of his head; the remainder had been stiffened into a high ridge, fitted with two eagle feathers, and braided down the back, in brazen defiance to anyone who might lust after his scalp. The bear fat that had been generously rubbed into the hair had lost its shine, however, and most of the shells and ornamental stones had been torn off in the hand-to-hand fighting.

Wabete sat on a fallen tree trunk, idly tossing a pair of lead dice over and over again, thinking, resting, planning. His blanket sagged to reveal two greasy red trade shirts with patched and tattered sleeves, and his faded, blue flannel leggins only partly covered his white-man's boots, a gift from the British at Detroit. Most of his war paint had rubbed off by now, and beneath it could be seen black tattoos covering his leathery face and hands. Another warrior, slouched on a nearby log, was garbed much the same but was skinny, with the look of a weasel about his pinched face. His name was Amaghwah, the Beaver, and he was a few years younger than Wabete.

A dense growth of evergreens surrounded the spring, and there was little sound save the rush of wind through the branches and the low voices of the two older Indians.

"These people of the Wyoming are not Longknives," said Wabete, "but they know how to fight...aiee, how they know!" He gingerly touched a bloodstained strip of cloth wrapped about his left shoulder, where he had taken a flesh wound.

Amaghwah gazed around the clearing at the sullen war party. "It is not like the days of our youth, Wabete, when we could scare whites like pigeons and shoot them down like deer." His gravelly voice was slurred from exhaustion, and his long, hooked nose made him look very sour.

Wabete stared at the dice in his hand, nodded thought-fully, and rubbed his belly, which rumbled constantly now. Indeed, these days it seemed cabins were all forts, and settlers were quick and accurate with their long rifles. Few Indians had such fearful weapons or could shoot as well, and they were dependent on white gunsmiths to repair even the smallest malfunction.

Wabete threw the dice again, thinking. To an Indian, dying in battle was no glory. To live, to win honor, and to boast about it afterward was the Indian's greatest triumph. If only one man was lost in a victorious engagement, a whole nation would mourn for him before permitting itself to revel in triumph.

Fifteen men had been lost in the attack against the Wy-oming settlement, and there would be no victory celebration. Wabete picked up the dice and sighed heavily, feeling the pangs of hunger that plagued his stomach. Fifteen men. His pride and reputation had been shaken. The village would hold him responsible, and all he had to show for the attack was a boy captive, whose burning at the stake would do little to soothe the sorrow of his people.

Wabete glared through hard, slitted eyes at the boy, who sat upright, long legs crossed, his arms tied tightly behind his back. An ugly bluish lump stood out on his forehead, the result of fighting Amaghwah just before the attack on the settlement. The boy had other bruises and cuts, most of them from the frequent cuffs and kicks he had received to hurry him along the trail. Some of the warriors had ex-changed their clothing for his, leaving him only his blue silk shirt, which had been torn to shreds in the first struggle. Over this the boy wore two old buckskin jackets that did little to keep off the chill, and a tattered and dirty fur cap that stank. The leggins replacing his own fine fur ones were sorry even by the standards of the poorest Shawnees, worn thin and full of holes.

The aging chieftain spoke again to Amaghwah. "Even this whelp fought well, though you tried hard to keep his mouth shut!"

Amaghwah grumbled that he should have killed the boy

for giving the settlement warning. He spat toward Benjamin, fingering the scalping knife at his belt. "A whelp he is," he hissed through large front teeth that protruded over his lower lip. "Just a pup . . . but there are uses for pups." Something came into his eyes, and he hissed again. "I hunger, Wabete, and I will not wait for food until we reach our canoes." He drew the knife from his belt.

Wabete's thoughts were far away, and he did not pay attention as Amaghwah moved into a squat, his gleaming eyes on Benjamin. "Have you had man-flesh of late, brother? Do you hunger as I hunger?"

Wabete scarcely heard, his mind still on the defeat, and he mumbled that even half-grown whites fought well these days. "If they all fight like this one, this wildcat, it will take all our power combined with the power of the Redcoats to drive them—"

Wabete stopped short, for his companion was on his feet, scalping knife out, hatred and craving in his eyes. Amaghwah's limp was noticeable; somehow he had been shot in the thigh when fighting the boy. Wabete had come on the scene soon after and ordered that the half-conscious Benjamin be carried off for later sacrifice.

The other warriors noticed Amaghwah advancing. The boy had become tense, but showed no sign of fear.

To Amaghwah's surprise, Benjamin suddenly stood up, squarely confronting him. Amaghwah snarled, turning the knife over in his hand, eyes locked on Benjamin's. As an elder warrior, Amaghwah could be stopped only by Wabete from doing what he was about to do. Though few liked or respected him, and some even thought him cowardly, Amaghwah was of an age that gave him privilege among these warriors, most of whom were quite young.

Benjamin stood his ground. Amaghwah was several steps away, his pinched face drawn into a ferocious scowl. His black and red war paint had streaked and run, making him look all the more vicious. As Benjamin planted his feet, readying himself to fight, Amaghwah laughed and brought the knife-point up, just a few feet from his victim. Wabete rose to watch, impressed with the boy's courage, almost sorry he was to die now, before being brought back to the village to run the gauntlet and be roasted at the stake. But perhaps Amaghwah was right to kill the boy, for this would excite and instill courage in the exhausted warriors and give them the strength to go on.

Some of the other Indians were getting up, joking and calling encouragement. Amaghwah was in a low crouch and had the look of a snake about to strike. He flicked the blade and said in Shawnee, "I thirst for your blood, for your flesh to get me home, dog." He limped forward, and the severe pain of his wound showed in his eyes. In English he hissed, "Afraid, boy? Goddam! Want knife? Son of a bitch! Cut your rope?"

Benjamin spat defiantly at the ground. In Shawnee he shouted, "Speak plainly to a man! Do not attempt to fool me! When you make your move, I'll fight you."

The other Indians muttered in surprise, for this was the first time their captive had spoken during the journey. They moved closer to see what would happen next.

Amaghwah, too, was startled, and squinted out of one eye, trying not to yield to the agony of his leg wound. Enraged at this insult but momentarily confused by a white lad speaking like a Shawnee, he glanced at Wabete, who said nothing. Amaghwah cackled and turned back to Benjamin.

"So the young dog knows the true language, does he? But it is the language of men"—his voice rose to a half-screech, as though he was trying to summon enough wrath to finish this work—"and you defile it with your white dog's mouth!"

Amaghwah still was surprisingly cautious about stabbing, and Benjamin spat out, "I speak as a man, whatever language comes from my white mouth! Show me if you are a man, or—"

Amaghwah screamed and lunged the knife at Benjamin's throat. The boy ducked under the thrust and kicked viciously, hitting the warrior full in the stomach and sending him with a groan to his knees. The other Indians grumbled and moved closer, hands on weapons, not liking to see this after their earlier humiliation. Yet clearly they were fascinated by the courage of their young prisoner, and it was

funny to see a man like Amaghwah so angry. Wabete motioned for them to be still, and they hesitated as the gasping
Amaghwah steadied himself and got to his feet, cursing and
threatening. He advanced again, feinting, determined to get
the boy this time.

He grunted and slashed with the knife, but once again
he missed and Benjamin caught him with a swift kick, this
time under the chin, sending him reeling a few feet, his bad
leg sliding painfully on the slick ground. Wabete grunted
in approval, perhaps even in admiration, and the rest of the
party chattered in surprise, one calling to Amaghwah that
he should use his rifle if the bound boy was too formidable.
Another offered to tie Benjamin's feet, at which the rest
laughed heartily.

Amaghwah became crazed. He got up and charged, though
slyly enough to keep his prey from guessing how he would
make his final, killing move. Benjamin feinted in turn, but
lost his footing and went down on one knee. Amaghwah
gave a shriek of joy and slashed at the lad's face, missing
by a hair. The second thrust came quickly, cutting Benjamin's shirt at the shoulder, and then Amaghwah was in
close, his sinewy hand catching Benjamin's throat, throt-
tling him. Benjamin struggled to stand, but the ground was
too slippery. Amaghwah brought the knife back and gave
a terrible cry that the young Indians caught and sent up to
the sky.

Suddenly, something like an arrow struck Amaghwah
squarely in the face. He staggered, and Benjamin took the
chance to scramble to his feet and deal the Indian another
wicked kick, right between the legs. Bleating in breathless
pain, Amaghwah hunched over, and something came at his
head once more, accompanied by an ear-splitting squawk
of fury. Benjamin kicked again, nearly cracking Amaghwah's jaw and knocking him down, unmoving in the slush.

As the others stood there, the blue jay, Punch, whipped
down for one last peck at the enemy's head, striking with
such force that the sound of it was distinct in the hushed
clearing. The Shawnees watched with amazement, none
more astonished than Wabete.

Benjamin whipped around to confront them all, trying

to catch his breath, clearly expecting to die. Tomahawks and blades appeared, but the Indians were still taken aback by all they had seen. Finally, several young braves began advancing. Up in the trees Punch gave a shriek of defiance, fluttering his wings, ready to strike once more. The Indians involuntarily glanced up at the bird, aware that it had been following them ever since the Wyoming Valley battle. Twice they had tried to snare it, but both times it had been scared off by the white boy, who had made what they then had thought was an unintentional noise. Now they were understandably leery of the warlike blue jay.

Benjamin backed up against a tree, bent forward at the waist and ready for whatever might come. The advancing Indians turned their full attention to him.

Just then, Punch shot down again and landed a nasty peck on one man's head. The brave shouted in pain, swinging his ax at the air, hitting nothing. Benjamin laughed, hooting and calling, "Let 'em have it, Punch! They'll sing songs about you afore this is done!"

He repeated this in Shawnee, and a couple of the Indians tried to cover a smirk as their unlucky companion shook his head, which was bleeding. Once more the Indians came in, four of them in a semicircle, all aware of the bird flitting and darting close above. When the Indian who had been struck gave an unexpected sound of annoyance and swiped again at the bird, Wabete began to chuckle. The other warriors glanced back at their leader, then at the pouting man who had been injured. He did look ridiculously peevish and wary of the bird. Then Punch zipped down at the biggest Shawnee of all, who ducked and slipped on the ice as he swatted clumsily—and his friends truly had trouble staying in a killing mood. The harder they tried not to laugh, and the more the big man tried not to show his embarrassment, the more the Shawnees lost their composure.

Wabete cried out that the bird protected the wildcat, and no sooner had he spoken than Punch pecked at yet another warrior, who yelped in pain. The elderly chieftain, hands on hips and eyes closed, leaned back and gave himself up to laughter. At that moment, with everyone else watching Punch's flight, the blue jay chose Wabete as target. No one gave a warning, and the bird's beak hit Wabete right on the point of the nose, knocking him backward, head over heels, into the slushy spring. Suddenly the clearing became a wild clamor of howling, screeching Indians, nearly hysterical, bent over and holding their sides. They pointed at Wabete's feet high in the air and slapped one another on the back, occasionally giving a cry of delight as Punch came whizzing down at them.

Benjamin was nearly forgotten, and only the recovering Amaghwah, with a glowering look on his thin face, was not part of the fun. Then, as the Indians saw him sitting up, looking so upset, the hilarity redoubled. Even Wabete, holding his bruised nose, his cockscomb headdress wet and disheveled, could not restrain his laughter, which sent him falling backward again.

Punch landed on Benjamin's shoulder and gave a squawk, and as the laughing died down, the Indians watched in admiration while Benjamin spoke to the bird and nuzzled it affectionately. It was apparent that this little devil on wings belonged to the white boy and had been trained by him in the arts of war.

Wabete did his best to regain a measure of sobriety. Like most Indians, he had a well-developed sense of humor, especially when it came to practical jokes that made someone look silly. But empty stomachs and losses in battle were hard to forget or laugh away.

Slowly, Amaghwah struggled to his feet, knife again in hand, blood running from a burst lip. Benjamin once more braced for trouble, and Punch flared his feathers.

The Indians quieted down, resigning themselves to what was about to happen, for they now had some feeling for this bird-tamer. Amaghwah, still dizzy, staggered toward Benjamin, the knife held before him.

It was Wabete who stopped things from going any further. He stepped between Amaghwah and Benjamin, and, at peril of imminent attack from Punch, spoke quietly to the warrior, saying:

"It is my right to decide if the prisoner lives or dies, for it is I who ordered him taken, brother."

Amaghwah was furious. He protested, "You would have

allowed me to slay him a moment ago! Now he has insulted me, and his life is forfeit—"

"His life is mine!" Wabete declared.

Amaghwah knew better than to defy so powerful a chieftain, for that surely would mean a duel, for which he had no stomach. He was shaking, almost frantic, clearly out of control.

"Kill him, then! Kill him, and show that no white whelp may insult a warrior of the Shawnee!"

Wabete was grim, slow to answer, though Amaghwah held up the blade, wet with snow, before his face. "In time," Wabete said in a deep, steady voice, "he will meet his fate; but it is not my pleasure as yet. Come, we must be off. We have a long way to go—"

"And are in need of flesh!" Amaghwah screamed, shaking, spittle flecking his thin lips. He grabbed Wabete by the shirtsleeve.

Wabete glared at Amaghwah's scrawny hand, and it was immediately removed, a frightened apology in the man's eyes as he turned away from the chieftain.

"We go on," Wabete said.

The others seemed relieved; they were in no mood to slay this young prisoner, who had entertained them with his bravery and with his bird's remarkable feats.

To mollify Amaghwah, Wabete gave him a valuable shark's-tooth necklace that he had worn beneath his blanket coat, surprising the others with such a generous gift. Then Wabete took personal charge of Benjamin; he motioned the boy to shoo away the bird, then shoved him onto the path, telling him to keep up or be killed on the spot.

They began to run, with Wabete in the lead, Amaghwah limping painfully a few paces behind Benjamin, as though waiting for the boy's strength to give out so he could slay him. As they settled into a steady trot, Wabete made a sound of approval deep in his chest and muttered over his shoulder, "A real wildcat you are! A wildcat!" He chuckled and called back to the others, "A cat, with a jay for a friend!" And the Indians laughed again, despite their hunger and weariness.

Mile after mile they journeyed along the tortuous winter trail, following the ridgelines, high above forests, open meadows, and winding rivers. Wildcat. *Peshawa,* in Shawnee. It was an appropriate name, Wabete thought.

chapter 5

GEORGE ROGERS CLARK

The weather held clear and cold as Owen Sutherland pursued Wabete's raiders through the winter forest, following tracks, losing them, sometimes scouting an area for hours until finding the trail once more. Traveling narrow forest paths on horseback with Mawak and Tamano, he had kept within a few days' journey of his prey but could not catch up, for the Shawnees were pressing to the limit.

By now Sutherland knew Benjamin was alive. Time and again he had prowled through the hasty campsites, scrounging for evidence that the boy was with the Shawnees. Eventually he had found what he was looking for: a scrap of blue silk cloth, torn from the shirt Benjamin had been wearing the evening of the attack. Although Benjamin would have had to take care in leaving traces of his presence, lest he be caught and killed on the spot, he had also managed to pluck and scrape the rough bark from an old maple tree, in the form of a *B*. Sutherland guessed that the lad had been tied and had managed this at night, with hands behind his back.

It was Mawak who noticed the same bird tracks at each place the Shawnees had paused; he said they were the marks of a blue jay—undoubtedly Punch.

Sutherland and his friends pressed on faster, with renewed hope. Yet every sign that his son was still alive made Sutherland that much more anxious to catch the Indians before Benjamin was killed. When they came to the watering place where Benjamin had fought Amaghwah, Sutherland felt terrible, cold fear at the sight of blood. There was no body to be found, however, and a day later Mawak once more picked up the blue jay's tracks in the snow near where

Benjamin must have sat. By now they had an inkling as to
which tracks at campsites were the boy's; on the trail, however, every print was mingled with many others. In time,
the snow had become so deep, the trail so twisty and hilly,
that horses were useless and had to be left with a settler in
a hamlet near the Youghiogheny River.

Once on foot, the three of them gained time by leaving
the main trail, cutting through trackless forest, anticipating
the movements of the Shawnees. They were always right
in guessing the path the war party would take. The Shawnees, they knew, would expect white pursuers to hold their
noses to the tracks and stubbornly dog the trail. But with
Sutherland and the two Indians taking shortcuts to river
crossings or to the kind of high ground Indians always
favored, the Shawnees were gradually losing their lead.

An hour's sleep was a luxury, as was a handful of dried
corn, or occasionally a hot meal of pemmican boiled with
hickory nuts raided from a squirrel's den—and once the
squirrel itself. They seldom risked a fire, lest their smoke
be seen, and in any case it took time to kindle a flame, time
to get themselves warm—and they had no time. They had
to catch the war party before it got over the Ohio to the
Shawnee side, where whites were prey at every step.

They were nearing a settlement called Redstone, on the
Monongahela River. This was hilly, forested country where
a man could walk straight between enormously tall, ancient
trees and never see a bush, nor hear a bird twitter. It was
like a great, endless cavern, even though the sun was bright
and the trees were without leaves. Everything was shadowed
gray by dense branches overhead and straggling vines that
clutched the tops of trees like massive, strangling veils.

On a wooded bluff near Redstone, Sutherland stopped
and listened. He could hear the gurgle of water under ice,
and before them was the wide Monongahela, the sunlight
making it a swath of glaring brightness through the naked
trees. But it was not the river or shifting ice he was listening
to, and in a moment they all knew a group of whites was
at hand. As the wind changed direction, they could clearly
make out distant shouting and the whack of axes biting into
trees.

They went on, leaving the Shawnees' trail—which curved away from the noise and seemed to be heading upstream, obviously to find a crossing place out of sight of enemies. Sutherland and the two Indians came to a cliff over the river, and looking down across snow-covered rocky outcrops, they saw a huddle of rude cabins and makeshift lean-tos, all with the wood still bright where it had been recently cut. Acres of fresh stumps surrounded the encampment on three sides, with the river on the fourth. A little downstream was an older stockaded settlement, the one Sutherland knew as Redstone.

They watched the whites for a while. There were women and children, and the encampment was alive with wagons, handcarts, mules, horses, cattle, pigs, and goats. Honking geese and clucking chickens fluttered and squawked among the children playing on the snow. The newness and bustle everywhere told that these people had arrived not long ago.

Tamano said, "Longknives," and Sutherland nodded, noting the white woolen hats that many of the men wore, as was the style in the western Virginia mountains.

"Going somewhere else, I'd guess," Sutherland replied. He estimated about three hundred people, crammed into two dozen cabins and lean-tos and a few canvas tents—and some apparently living under flatboats overturned on racks near the river. "Probably waiting for the spring thaw, then heading down the Ohio for Kentucky."

Mawak rubbed his belly. "Smell pig meat roasting!" He closed his eyes, savoring the aroma.

Suddenly there came a crackling sound, much closer. Men were approaching up a steep trail to the left, and had been out of sight till now. Sutherland's group quickly took shelter away from the cliff face, not wishing to be seen and perhaps challenged and brought in for questioning. Sutherland stood motionless behind a massive maple as a score of well-armed Virginians came tramping past, only fifteen feet away. They looked like strong, healthy fellows, with fine clothes and good gear. In the lead was a tall, strapping, red-haired man in buckskins and linsey, with a broad felt hat. He looked familiar to Sutherland, who had met many Virginians in the war against the Shawnees a few years back, in 1774. Some Longknives had little love for Sutherland, for he had helped arrange peace terms with the Shawnees before the two thousand victorious Virginians could finish their bloody work, meaning to wipe out the entire nation if they could.

The irony of it flashed through Sutherland's mind. Had he kept out of that affair, the Shawnees may well have been exterminated, and Benjamin would not now be their prisoner. Back then the mightiest Shawnee leader of all, Cornstalk, had been persuaded to make terms just in time. Now Cornstalk was dead, murdered last October by some fool of a Pennsylvania militia officer, after the chieftain had come to council for peace. That crime had sent the Shawnees on the warpath this winter, long before most other northwestern tribes had been ready to strike.

Sutherland realized one of the whites had fallen out of the column and was pretending to tie the thong of his moccasin. All the while, this short, scraggly fellow, with braided black hair under a flat black hat, and wearing remarkably filthy buckskins, was casually eyeing the trees where Sutherland and the others were hidden. The man knew they were there. If he suddenly gave warning, the startled Virginians might begin firing.

But Sutherland had belatedly recognized the red-headed man in the lead, as well as this dark, smallish fellow. Stepping from behind the tree, hand raised, he shouted, "How, Girty! Hello, Mr. Clark!"

Like a snake slithering away from surprise, the Virginian column recoiled; but before they could unshoulder their rifles, Sutherland cried out, "Hold your water, lads—we're friends."

Simon Girty was laughing with a shrill cackle, delighted to have been so neatly ambushed by a white man. He took obvious pleasure in the shock of the Virginians, more than one of whom cursed and told him to shut his mouth. Girty was more Indian than white, having been taken prisoner by the Senecas as a boy and favoring their way of life ever since. He was a well-known army scout and interpreter and had met Sutherland during the Shawnee campaign in '74.

The Virginians glared at the newcomers—especially the

Indians—but their leader, George Rogers Clark, trotted jauntily back along the line, obviously happy to see Sutherland. These two had also met in '74, and Sutherland's stepson, Jeremy, had fought at Clark's side during the hottest part of the battle. As Sutherland shook hands with Clark, then with Girty, there came muttering insults and rude noises from the slouching, confident Virginians.

Tamano and Mawak ignored the comments about "red weasels," "red stinks," and "skulking devils," knowing they were outnumbered by whites here and had better let Owen do the talking. Sutherland turned to the Virginians with a black look, but even after Clark loudly introduced him, the Virginians were not impressed. They cared nothing for anyone's warning looks, and they crowded closer, as if to start trouble.

Clark spoke calmly to his men, his voice deep and clipped: "Hold your tongues, gentlemen, or you'll find that you've signed on for Virginia-army discipline as well as free land!"

Evidently his words carried authority, for the sneers and insolence quickly abated.

"These are friends and will be treated as such as long as they are here." He turned to Sutherland, his hazel eyes bright under their bushy red brows. "Will you be my guest tonight, Mr. Sutherland? Perhaps we'll have something of interest to discuss."

"I'd be greatly honored, Mr. Clark, and the Lord knows my friends and I could use a rest. But my son is the prisoner of a party of Shawnees that went through here a day or two past . . . have you seen them?"

Clark sobered at this, and the Virginians took the occasion to curse the Shawnees, calling down hell's fury on every man, woman, and child of them. This time Clark did not silence them. Finally he answered, "Sorry to say, Mr. Sutherland, two days ago our party came close to tangling with those devils, but they must've seen us coming and got away somehow. All we found was a dead one who'd gone under from his wounds. They didn't even have time to rack him in a tree."

Simon Girty, chewing on a large wad of tobacco, spat, then turned away, seeming somewhat self-conscious. Clark was giving him a look that was clearly an accusation.

Sutherland heard a Virginian mutter, "My grandma coulda follered that Injun sign better'n Girty!"

Another agreed, saying aloud, "Mebbe Girty didn't want nobody snarin' his Shawnee friends!"

"Leastways," one of them chuckled, "I got me a trophy from that dead buck!" He held up a fresh scalp, and another man shouted that he had skinned the Shawnee's thigh to make a fine, soft tobacco pouch.

"We shoulda all got hair 'n pouches," someone declared. "But your Injun scout's mebbe too much an Injun when it comes to runnin' Shawnees to ground, Colonel Clark. Too many cousins among 'em, to his mind!"

Girty craned his neck at them like a wounded badger and showed his teeth. Sutherland thought there surely would be a fight, and he spoke up:

"It sounds to me like every one of your brave lads is an expert scout and tracker, Mr. Clark"—this raised some mutters, but he went on—"though few of them would've grown up to be here now had Mr. Girty not scouted for the army at Bushy Run in '63, or been Colonel Bouquet's interpreter at the peace council. Of course some of you boys may not remember that far back."

At the mention of this famous battle and the brave officer who had defeated a superior force of Shawnees, Mingoes, Delawares, and Senecas, the Virginians became grudgingly silent, although one of them mumbled, "Times've changed! Past is done."

Girty remained silent, but Sutherland sensed the man's gratitude for what had been said in his favor. It was not easy to still a band of cocky Virginians.

Clark broke the tension. "We're grateful to you, Mr. Sutherland, for being Colonel Bouquet's adviser at Bushy Run." The men shifted uneasily. "At any rate, we are glad to have these mangy Shawnees out of our hair." Then he said that if Sutherland could not stay long, he could at least come down to the camp for dinner and to replenish his supplies.

Sutherland was still reluctant and began to say he must press on, when Clark looked directly into his eyes and interrupted in a slow voice, "I have something very important to tell you, sir; something to which you must swear secrecy and never repeat. It'll be a grand adventure you'll learn about!"

Sutherland shook his head; all he could think of was Benjamin.

Clark glanced at Girty, who was off to the side, talking with Tamano and Mawak, and could not hear the conversation. "It may mean your son's liberty, Mr. Sutherland."

Sutherland's expression immediately changed. "Very well, sir. I'll come—on the condition that my two friends are welcome in your cabin."

The Virginian heartily agreed, and with Girty shambling along, they set off down to the crowded settlement, the dismissed troops hurrying ahead, hooting and cheering for all to hear them come in.

The place smelled of too many people, Sutherland thought, of smoky fires and overused latrines. Clearly the buildings here were not meant to be permanent, unlike the well-constructed, stockaded settlement of Redstone a few hundred yards downstream.

On the common ground, forty thickly-clad men were drilling in two companies, a few officers stamping back and forth, calling out marching commands and showing justifiable frustration and anger when these backwoods troops fumbled about and lapsed into comical confusion. This attempt to instill military order puzzled Sutherland, for these men were best at fighting as individuals in the woods; even their hometown musters and drills back in Virginia would seldom be taken seriously, usually turning into turkey shoots and occasions for community picnics. Sutherland had at first thought the people here were simply pioneers with newly bought deeds to distant lands—lands that would have to be fought for before they could be called home. Now, and in light of what Clark had hinted, he was not so sure. This looked more like the makings of a small army.

The drilling Virginians gawked as Sutherland and his two friends walked past, Mawak and Tamano making some comments in Ottawa about soldiering that caused Sutherland and Girty to laugh.

Sutherland again heard Clark greeted as "Colonel," and upon asking him, learned the man had been so commissioned by Governor Patrick Henry of Virginia and was now military commander of Kentucky. Virginia's leaders, Sutherland knew, wanted to populate the Kentucky country before North Carolina further pressed its own claims. The Carolinians had already founded a major settlement at Boonesborough, named after their leader, Daniel Boone. Sutherland wondered what these Virginians were up to.

Girty wandered off, and Sutherland's group went into a small cabin, where Clark and a few officers lived. It was cramped but neat and clean, furnished with an iron stove, a plank table, and benches of green wood, with cots and straw bedding.

Laying aside his weapons and outer clothing, Sutherland stood in the heat of the stove, rubbing ice from the curly beard he had let grow. The Indians also removed hats, mittens, and coats and stood by the stove, as Clark ordered hot food brought in. Then they all sat around the table, the Virginian generously sharing a jug of sour-mash whiskey.

Uneasy and edgy to get going, Sutherland began the conversation by learning all he could about the Shawnees who had Benjamin. Clark told him they were moving fast and would be across the Ohio and in Shawnee country in a week if not cut off.

They all fell silent, knowing what danger that meant for Sutherland's son. Clark rocked back on the bench, leaning against the cabin wall as he puffed on a corncob pipe. Changing the subject, he asked about Jeremy Bently.

"The lad's loyal," Sutherland said softly, and his gaze fell to the tabletop before him. "He's in the Eighth Foot as a surgeon, up at Detroit."

Clark was impassive, and after some time Sutherland spoke again.

"I have my hopes of persuading him to join us yet, Colonel."

Clark nodded and puffed his pipe before saying, "Good man, he is. Tough as they come, and slick as my Virginians in the woods."

Jeremy had been seriously wounded in the '74 campaign

when he and Clark had gone to fetch water for their thirsty company. Since Jeremy had been with Clark's unit purely by chance that day, his willingness to risk death to find water for men he did not know had meant much to the Virginian.

Sutherland said, "But first I mean to find Benjamin."

"Simon Girty'll maybe go a piece with you, Mr. Sutherland, seeing as how his work is done here."

Sutherland was surprised by the offer. There was no better tracker, Indian or white, than Girty. "Isn't he going with you, Colonel?"

Clark in turn seemed surprised at Sutherland's question and hardly looked up as two orderlies brought in a pot of thick stew, fresh corn bread, a jug of cider, and bowls of sweetened corn mush. Tamano and Mawak fell to the food ravenously.

"Good as Girty is," Clark said, "he's not liked here, and that's bad for morale. Too many folks think he's a British spy . . . and maybe he . . ." Abruptly changing his train of thought, he asked what it was that made Sutherland think these Virginians were going somewhere else.

Sutherland was collecting food on a wooden plate, and when he finished, he said, "What you have here, Colonel, looks very much like an army, except for the women and children." He began to eat, adding, "But then you need an army in Kentucky if you want to stay there, and women to keep the army happy. As for the children, I guess your army means to sink roots and hold on even after the Indians give up." The stew went down well, the first hot solid food in almost a week. "And I suppose if you meant to stay here you would've come sooner, built better, and wouldn't have the look of a field expedition, drilling and parading and marching like new-recruited Redcoats."

Clark grinned and got some food for himself. He said they indeed were on their way to Kentucky, to make a fort or two south of the Ohio. Sutherland sensed that Clark was reluctant to say more in company with the Indians; nevertheless, the Virginian politely waited for Tamano and Mawak to finish their meal before he suggested they go to a nearby shed to renew their provisions and find the leather and tools needed to repair their battered snowshoes. He quickly wrote a note to requisition the necessary items and called for the orderly to escort them.

As soon as the Indians had left, Clark lit candles, offering the taper to Sutherland for his pipe. Clark got to the point immediately, asking first for Sutherland's oath of secrecy, which he received.

"We all know Detroit is the center for the Injuns' raids, from the Wyoming Valley to Kentucky and even into Virginia; and the British at Detroit think they're safe up there, fat and cozy, protected by hundreds of miles and by half the Injuns on the continent. But they're not so safe from me!" He thought a moment, candlelight illuminating his craggy face and red hair: he looked young, not yet thirty, but had the presence and demeanor of a much older man. "There's a way to get to Detroit . . . a way that's not well protected, not once a fort or two's taken—forts that don't have more'n a dozen British regulars protecting all of 'em!"

Eyes gleaming, Clark was looking at Sutherland, who found his own heart quickening. A campaign against Detroit was what he had long dreamed of. He wanted to hear more.

"You mean to go up the Mississippi and attack Detroit by the back door? Hah!" He slapped the table and poured himself and Clark mugs of cider. "You'll need more than a couple of hundred Virginia buckos to get that far, laddie! Unless . . ." As he drank, he eyed the grinning Clark over the mug. Clark was watching him closely, and Sutherland was thinking fast. Already he had a glimmering of Clark's full plan.

Clark said, "As a fur trader out there, you know the Illinois region better than any Britisher or American, Mr. Sutherland." He leaned forward, almost whispering. "You know what's possible for a determined force that strikes boldly and swiftly." Sitting back, he said, "You also know what's in store for us if the British at Detroit raise the tribes of the northwest in a coordinated assault on the borders. Even Pitt will fall. And that's exactly what will happen before the year is out, I'm thinking, unless someone proves to the redskins that Henry Hamilton at Detroit is not the invincible great white chief they've been told he is."

Clark made it plain he intended to take his little army down the Ohio, build a fort at the Falls, and join that summer with another force from Virginia. Then he would march overland against the weakly fortified settlements of Kaskaskia and Cahokia on the Mississippi and Vincennes on the Wabash. He would take them and hold them through the winter, intimidating the French and Indian inhabitants of the region, and next spring would advance on Detroit.

Sutherland was smiling, imagining what it would be like conquering his former home in the name of the independent American states. He was well aware of how weak the British were in the northwest, and that their French and Indian allies were fickle at best, anxious to back the winning side. They might just keep their heads down while the others fought it out.

"Aye," he murmured, "it can be done."

Clark said enthusiastically, "My Virginia militia will number five hundred men soon after I reach the Falls. After we take Vincennes and Kaskaskia, Virginia will send another thousand fresh militiamen downriver. Tell me, Mr. Sutherland, can the British muster even five hundred white fighting men like ours?"

Sutherland knew they could not. Hamilton had a hundred Redcoats at Detroit and perhaps another hundred between Fort Michilimackinac far to the north and the Ohio River to the south. The French population in this vast wilderness numbered several thousand, but they had little love for the British or the Americans. The Indians, Sutherland knew, were the real danger. If Hamilton learned in advance of Clark's plan, he might quickly muster three or four thousand warriors to oppose the Virginians. And if Clark were defeated, every tribe in the northwest would be tempted to rise against the frontier settlements; the rebellious states would be hard put to protect their backcountry, having to draw off thousands of troops from the desperate struggle in the East.

Sutherland brooded at the prospect. "I assume that if you succeed, Colonel, the government of Virginia will repay your men with land."

Clark nodded. He got up, lithe and strong and decisive,

and began pacing the room as he said, "But success will go to the best men—and I must have the best scouts!" He stopped pacing and looked straight at Sutherland. "I don't trust Girty, so he knows nothing. I don't trust anyone I don't have to trust. Mr. Sutherland, I know you well enough to have told you what most of my men out there won't know until we reach the Falls of the Ohio. They think we're only going to defend Kentucky, and in a way we are."

He drew out an envelope from a leather satchel lying on his cot. "These are sealed orders from the Commonwealth of Virginia, authorizing me to take whatever action I deem necessary after we reach the Falls. You understand, sir, how much it means to have Virginia as my authority and support."

Sutherland was well aware that no other former British colony in America had the wealth or power of Virginia.

"What exactly do you want of me?"

"Join us! I propose that you be my leading scout, my interpreter, and my liaison with the French and Indians." Clark planted his hands on the table, a fierce light in his eyes. "One day, Mr. Sutherland, we'll march into Detroit itself, and the entire northwest will be ours! You'll have greater honor and prestige than ever before!"

"It's my son I want."

Clark slammed the table. "And we'll find your son! I mean to make every Indian from Pitt to Michilimackinac grovel at my feet, Mr. Sutherland! They'll bring in their white prisoners, and I'll give a special order for release of your son, or else those who are guilty will suffer the ultimate penalty!"

Sutherland was silent, and Clark backed off, going to a window to let him think.

Night was falling fast, and Sutherland knew he must get on with the search. He thought of Simon Girty, aware that the man's uncanny ability in the woods might make all the difference; yet apparently Girty had failed to lead Clark's men to the Shawnee party a couple of days earlier. Perhaps it was because Girty had no love for Longknives. If Girty wanted to catch Indians, he could do it, and he might just do it for Sutherland.

Clark turned toward him and said quietly, "We'll be at the Falls until midsummer; you can join us there. Other than the rescue of your son, your reward would include a land grant from Virginia after the war. I know that to a wealthy man such as yourself that might not be much, but I also suspect you'd like to see Detroit in our hands."

Sutherland rose, his muscles and bones stiff from the unaccustomed luxury of sitting. Giving Clark his hand, he thanked him for the hospitality and for the offer. "If you do not see me at the Falls by July, then you'll know I'll be of no help to you for some time to come." His eyes were dark and weary as he said, "Aye, I want to take Detroit and get this war over with, Colonel Clark, but I'm not at liberty to promise you anything until I've done all I can to see my boy home safe." Sutherland was tempted to say something about his stepson Jeremy at Detroit, but refrained. As a British officer, Jeremy would be squarely in the path of the tough Virginians.

Gathering his weapons and clothing, he added, "Be assured your secret is safe with me, Colonel . . . and whatever I can do to aid your campaign, I will do." He went to the door. "I know where you're going, and I'll come to you if I can."

Clark seemed satisfied, and there was nothing more to be said on the matter. Before they went outside, he asked, "Will you take Girty along on your hunt . . . at least as far as he'll go with you?"

"Yes, I will, Colonel. I understand now why you want to let him go from here."

Clark said, "I can't trust him to keep his mouth shut, even if he's not a British spy, as some would think. Anyhow, he's too much like an Injun for my taste—partial to squaws, bad liquor, and eating bugs and rotten meat. You won't have to pay him much, Mr. Sutherland; he'll be happy to leave us."

In the darkness, Sutherland, Tamano, Mawak, and Simon Girty moved carefully across the ice of the Monongahela River, again on the trail of the Shawnees. Sutherland had offered Girty generous pay, in sterling, and the little man had grinned and said they would run the Shawnees to ground in three days.

"You hosses know something about the woods!" Girty muttered as he confidently guided them on the floes, which were like huge stepping-stones in the black, rushing water. He had cat's eyes, seeming to have no need of the bright moon rising on the eastern horizon; soon there would be enough light to lead them along the trail that night. "You're not like 'em Longknife varmints . . . all piss 'n' wind, nothing more!"

Girty sprang across a dark opening between floes, cackling in that high, keen way he had: "But these Longknives gonna talk polite to this child come spring, when Congress makes old Girty a sure enough cap'n in the Continental rangers!" He cackled again, glancing back at Sutherland, who was surprised to hear such expectations after having seen the man so mistrusted and rudely treated by Virginian rebels. "That's right, hoss! Cap'n, pension, land grant and all! Come spring, I was promised!"

As he darted nimbly across the shifting ice, Girty boasted that he had helped raise a company of woodsmen in western Pennsylvania and that this feat alone qualified him for a captaincy, which a ranking officer at Pitt had promised him.

"But you know Longknives and Pennsylvanians like to fight one another as much as they like to fight Injuns and Redcoats!" He shook his head, pausing in the middle of the broad river, as the others came alongside. He said with bitterness, "Like as not, 'em Longknives mislikes me 'cause I raised a Pennsylvania militia company for Pitt, and that means more Pennsylvanians to challenge the Virginia claim to this country! Pah! Let the bastards howl!"

He gave that keening laugh and sprang away once more, cursing all Virginians and calling back to Sutherland that he would prove he could track any Shawnee born of a squaw.

"I know where they cache their canoes and some food . . . same place these war bands allus cache their grub!" They were nearly across the ice, water roaring, wind strong and cold in their faces. "They'll take a roundabout way there, jest to throw off company, but we don't need to sniff at their tails! Let's hump some now, and I'll show you Injun trails even Injuns don't know about."

Off they went into the forest, under tall, broad trees that were like great pillars holding up the sky. Sutherland trotted behind Girty, who was a flitting shadow in front, hunched down Indian-style on the trail. Behind Sutherland came Mawak, strong despite his years, then Tamano, alert for every sound.

Sutherland had refused a last-minute offer from Clark to send along some men to fight the Shawnees, for that would mean extreme danger to Benjamin. Even woods-wise Virginians could not move as quietly as this small party, and they would be too eager to start shooting. The Indians had to be surprised, tricked somehow. If he could, Sutherland would rescue the boy without fighting. By now he did not burn to take revenge for the terrible injury done Ella. He did not hate these Shawnees, but he sorely wanted his son back, safe and sound.

chapter 6

SIMON GIRTY

Past noon on the second day out of Clark's camp, after forty hours of almost constant moving, Sutherland's group descended into the steep Valley of the Ohio. Fresh snow had fallen, and everything was frozen and white, clear across to the high, forested bluffs on the other side of the river.

Girty chose a campsite overlooking a hillside trail that he said was used often. Sutherland noted that the trail was hard-packed under the new snow, though he could detect no sign that whites had been here. Girty was sharing an important secret, if this indeed was where the Shawnees regularly cached their food and hid their canoes. Fort Pitt was only a few miles eastward, and Sutherland was amazed that any war party would pass this close to a major outpost. Yet perhaps such daring gave them an advantage, for rebel scouts would not expect them to slip through here on their way back from raids to the east.

As Girty scouted down by the river, the others made a fire to keep warm, using dry wood to keep the smoke down. The Indian crossing place Girty had indicated was upwind, so the Shawnees would not smell the smoke, nor would they see the fire, as long as it was daylight.

Huddled in his cloak, the exhausted Sutherland sat on a boulder near the fire, his rifle across his knees. He was able to see the trail winding below but was confident of being unseen. Nearby, Tamano and Mawak were fast asleep in their blankets, using snowshoes for pillows. Sutherland could not help but wonder at the array of hazel branches Mawak had stuck in the snow around his bedding. Hazelwood was unfailing protection against rattlers attracted by the warmth of the fire, the old medicine man claimed. If anyone knew such lore, Mawak would.

Sutherland turned his attention toward the river and strained his eyes to spot Girty, but could not. He would have been surprised if he did. These past two days, Sutherland had stuck close behind the scout, who had moved like a wraith, nimbler than any white Sutherland had ever known. It had not been easy to keep up with him as he slipped effortlessly down stony, crumbling trails or hopped with the surefootedness of a goat up icy ground. He seemed to glide along watercourses, never getting his feet wet, stepping quickly on stones and logs, never losing his balance.

Sutherland had stayed with him, though. The Scotsman was as good as the best on the trail, and Tamano the same. Mawak was too old, however, and he had labored at the pace, though he had never complained. Whenever Sutherland had called for Girty to slow or rest, the scout had reluctantly obeyed, for he was always respectful to old Mawak; but in minutes he would be urging them to move on, saying he would show them how to snare a Shawnee. And as the other three sat on logs or under pine trees, Girty would only crouch on his haunches, gnawing a piece of jerked meat, always rinsing it down with rye whiskey from a flask he carried.

Girty had offered them his firewater, but after the first sample, Sutherland and Tamano had refused, finding it bitter and foul. Mawak, however, was never one to decline a drink, and it seemed to give him strength to get up and go on at the same steady, grueling pace. When Girty spoke during these rests, he became steadily more excited about outwitting the Shawnees. Sutherland could tell by the light in his eye that he loved the idea of out-Indianing an Indian.

Girty's heavy drinking did not alarm Sutherland, though he had heard Girty had a reputation as a mean drunk, often getting into fights. It was not Girty's heavy drinking, Sutherland knew, that put off men such as Clark's Virginians, for they had enough reason to distrust a half-Indian scout who once had made his living working for the British army.

These thoughts troubled Sutherland, yet he sensed that

Girty was sincerely trying to head off the Shawnees, if only to prove what a man he was. In any case, there were few woodsmen Sutherland would rather have on his side just then.

Again he thought of Benjamin, who soon would be within reach. As he scanned the trail below, Sutherland recalled what Girty had told him about the boy's captors. The dead warrior left behind when Clark's men had chased the others off was from the large town called Chillicothe, on the Scioto River. Girty knew the man, and said he was undoubtedly traveling in company with others from that village. If something went wrong and the Shawnees got across the Ohio, it would be best, Girty said, to make for the Chillicothe trail by careful traveling. If they could head off the Shawnees, perhaps the boy could be spirited out.

Sutherland gazed beyond the trail to the half-frozen river, which was lined and slashed where the ice was broken up, and black where the river ran free. Girty had said the Indians would use their hidden canoes to get over, picking their way through open channels. For a moment Sutherland wondered why Girty had not told the militia commander at Pitt about this spot; but that was Girty's business. For now, all Sutherland cared about was getting his son back. It would not be easy.

Sutherland took note of a likely crossing place upstream, to his right, where immense blockades of driftwood had backed up the river and slowed the pace of the ice floes. Good paddlers could slip a birch boat safely through the dam's quiet, nearer side. The driftwood, piled high with masses of snow and great cakes of twisted ice, would be an ideal place to hide and await an opportunity to try for Benjamin.

It was then that Sutherland saw Girty, darting over the ice at the very spot he was watching. The scout was hunched low, bounding like a creature that was half deer, half panther, leaping across the floating ice until he reached the bank directly below. Surely Girty, too, knew that was the place to make their move for Benjamin, who would be in a canoe with only a few Indians instead of guarded by a dozen or more.

Girty came straight up the slope at Sutherland, who had thought himself concealed to sight. Girty lightly sprang over the boulders and slouched down nearby, hardly breathless after such strenuous exertion.

Lighting a pipe quickly, the scout said, "I reckon 'em Shawnees'll be scurryin' along by dark, and this child'll bet they'll try to cross after the moon rises."

He yanked out the dented flask, offered Sutherland some, then guzzled quite a deal of it. "Got a awful dry!" he hissed with a burp, and drank some more. "Rotgut poison! But it's all the sutler at Clark's would sell me, that bastard Longknife!"

He gave Sutherland a sly, sidelong glance, as if to see what the Scotsman thought of Virginians and of men who reviled them. Sutherland changed the subject to the Shawnees and began to plan their move. Girty agreed it should be made from the driftwood barrier, against the canoe that held Benjamin. After they were satisfied with their tactics, Girty finished the flask to the final drop, cursed, and shoved it into his deerskin pouch. Sutherland saw he had another in there.

"This hoss could use a good feed!" Girty looked upriver, where shadows of twilight were beginning to creep over the water and hills. "When we're done with this business we should make Pitt by dark . . . but we gotta keep a sharp lookout when we go in there!" He spat. "Longknife sons of bitches patrol everywhere, and if they know it's me, they'll act big and important and grub us for passes and such, as if they don't know I'm the child what scouts for 'em hereabouts and keeps 'em from getting their hair lifted!"

Girty went on like this, venting spite for rebel militiamen, especially Virginians. More than once he had fought them, he said, and their officers had locked him up, even beaten him with no good reason. Sutherland suspected that he must have been drunk to be jailed.

Girty bit off a chew of tobacco, looked down at the trail, paused as if listening, then slowly chewed.

Sutherland remarked, "The army must be paying you well to put up with it."

Girty glanced around, snorted, then turned his attention

back to the trail. "Not enough . . . though I take some pleasure in proving 'em all dandies and no-account greenhorns
whose scalps'd be hanging in the wind if I didn't keep 'em
outa trouble!" He spat again and cursed.

Sutherland said, "At least they're getting the upper hand
around here, now that Burgoyne's army's been taken and
the loyalists are staying at Niagara and Montreal."

Girty gave him an unexpectedly savage look. "Getting
the upper hand? Hah! You'd sing a different tune, Mr.
Sutherland, if you heard what I hear the redskins say . . .
how the Tories're massin' for a strike this spring, and how
they're going on the warpath with Injuns from twenty nations, thousands of 'em!"

Suddenly Girty became tense. He was peering across the
river at the dim far bank, however, not at the Indian trail
below.

He whispered, "Here's a few of those lumbering udder-
suckers from Pitt right now!"

He nodded with only the slightest movement, and Sutherland saw the men, three hundred yards across the ice, in
the trees close to shore. Sure enough, it was a militia patrol,
and they seemed to be hunting for a place to cross over.
There were about a dozen of them, clumsy and uncertain,
some slipping on the icy bank, others testing the ice and
accidentally getting wet. It was obvious they were not experienced woodsmen; Sutherland guessed they were farmers
from the Virginia hills stationed out here on a three-month
tour of duty. No doubt they were anxious to get away from
the Indian side of the Ohio and back to Fort Pitt before
dark.

Girty was cursing, saying they would spoil everything
by blundering through here. "Shawnee'll be by any time,
and these bug-tits'll raise hell tryin' to cross, hollerin' and
bawlin', maybe shootin' at squirrels. . . ." His voice trailed
off in a mixture of curses and Indian talk.

As they watched, it became clear these men were indeed
intent on crossing the ice here. At the rate they were going,
however, it would take them at least an hour, if they did
not drown.

Girty shook his head and snorted. "Dumber 'n Redcoats,

they are sometimes." In a wink he was gone, calling back to Sutherland that he would get rid of these green soldiers.

Sutherland, Tamano, and Mawak readied themselves above the Indian trail, in case the Shawnees suddenly appeared. Darkness was closing in fast, and already the men on the far bank were barely visible; but even from here Sutherland could hear their loud chatter. He grew worried when the noise continued long after Girty must have gone as far as he dared across the ice and signaled them to turn back.

Sutherland had no doubts that it would be better to intercept Benjamin with just the four of them rather than ask the help of these inexperienced troops. He could not see the militiamen at all now, but still they were making noise. He grew increasingly uneasy. Why had they not shut up when Girty met them?

Eventually they did quiet down, and Sutherland supposed that they had finally turned back. He looked at the sky, which was clear, dark blue, the stars twinkling on, cold and sharp.

It was another half hour before Girty appeared out of the darkness, but not from the direction of the river. Instead, he trotted down the trail the Shawnees were expected to use. At first Sutherland was surprised at such carelessness, but then Girty was uncannily knowledgeable in these things, and Sutherland was still confident the Shawnees and Benjamin would be here when Girty said they would. The moon would rise in two hours, and the Indians would want to cross just as it came up. That still left plenty of time for the four of them to move down to the river and take up their positions.

When Girty joined them, out of breath and stinking of whiskey and sweat, he said that the militiamen had gone back upriver.

"I told them there was big army doings here, and they was wanted to watch the fords upstream." He chuckled and munched some beef. "They didn't like being officered about by the likes of me, but I told 'em a full colonel was over here, and he'd beller like a bull if they dare come over and spoil things! They gone for good."

Sutherland asked why Girty had been on the Indian trail, and the scout pulled out the flask, threw some down, and answered in a slow, almost apologetic voice.

"Seems I missed my guess, Mr. Sutherland. Ain't this here crossing at all they'll use." He did not look at the startled Sutherland or the two Indians, and Sutherland felt a strange uneasiness, almost mistrust, though he could not tell just why.

Girty drank once again and said, "We got to hump some for a mile or so downstream; I scouted around and saw the food cache'd been already rifled by another war party, and the canoes ain't where I thought they'd be." He cleared his throat and wiped the back of his hand across his mouth. "This Shawnee bunch'll make for the next crossing down-river—you can count on it."

Girty insisted they had to move at once, taking the shore trail, which he knew well. Then they would make their plans for the ambush at another and even better spot down-stream. Sutherland had no choice but to follow, though he noticed Tamano also seemed unsure of Girty's new plan.

An hour later they were at a second crossing place. In the dimness, however, Sutherland could not make out any good spots to ambush the Shawnees and get Benjamin safely away. Girty said they could see the ground better and plan a course of attack when the moon came up.

As if something were eating at him, Girty hastily downed the rest of his flask. Then he proceeded to cut himself a few balsam branches and bed down on them some distance away. Pulling his blanket over his shoulders, he told the others to wake him once the moon came up, when they would decide on the next step.

Sutherland did not like it and said so. In reply, Girty snarled that this was how it had to be done and he was too tired to stay awake if he did not have to.

Sutherland and the Indians were as weary, so while the others slept, Sutherland stood guard. There was no real plan, and they would have to improvise one if the Shawnees appeared suddenly. As Sutherland sat on a log, he could hear nothing save the rushing of the mighty Ohio. In a few weeks the spring flood would make it impassable, but soon

afterward Clark's flatboats and his small expedition would
make their dash downstream for the west. Clark's plan just
might work, Sutherland thought, as long as the British and
Indians did not get wind of it. He wished he had as good
a plan right now.

He stared into the night, searching for the slightest movement that would tell of the enemy's approach. At least
darkness would be on his side. If he snatched Benjamin
quickly and managed to get a lead, the Indians probably
would not pursue and risk wasting the chance to cross the
river in moonlight. Or perhaps he could grab the boy and
spring out onto the drifting ice while Tamano, Mawak, and
Girty distracted the Shawnees with hot firing.

By the time the moon rose and spilled a milky blue sheen
across the river and snowy hills, Sutherland felt better, more
sure of what he would do when the Shawnees arrived with
Benjamin. He knocked the powder from his rifle's pan and
reprimed to ensure against a misfire. Then he turned and
called softly to Girty. There was no answer.

Tamano and Mawak awoke as Sutherland again called
the scout's name. No reply. Girty was gone. Persuading
Sutherland to share a cold meal of beef jerky and ground
corn, the Indians allowed that Girty was a strange one, but
no doubt would have an explanation when he returned.
Sutherland wanted to agree, but all the same he felt a creeping uneasiness in the pit of his stomach.

Girty did not come back. Nor did the Shawnees appear. By
morning, when the sun rose to overpower the pale moon
and cast reddish fire on the distant hills of Indian country,
Sutherland was seething, furious to have been left waiting
like some green militiaman. Then again, maybe Girty had
been caught and killed by the Shawnees; maybe the Indians
had smelled a trap and escaped to another crossing place.
Whatever had gone wrong, Sutherland was determined to
find out quickly.

While Tamano and Mawak scouted the nearby trail, Sutherland followed Girty's tracks, which headed back upstream
toward the original crossing place. Girty was moving fast,
taking long, sure strides. The farther Sutherland went, the

more an unreasoning anger gripped him, causing him to run, though he knew he could be ambushed. Had Girty gone off to Pitt, forsaking the chase in favor of drink and warmth? Had he gone out to do more scouting and been waylaid? Why had he abandoned Sutherland without a word?

The sun was high and golden in the eastern sky when Sutherland reached the first crossing place and found part of his answer: the Shawnees had come through here after all, and were already across! And Girty's tracks were mixed in with theirs, even crossing the river, as if he were one of them!

Sutherland was quivering with fury. He peered over the wide Ohio for some sign of the enemy or Girty, but there was nothing. Surely they had crossed no more than a few hours ago—and Sutherland would, too, as soon as he found his companions.

Suddenly he heard a distant burst of riflery from upstream, across the river. They were Indian weapons; he could tell by the rifle charges, which were always lighter than white charges, in order to conserve gunpowder. Sutherland waited and listened, soon hearing what he feared: a few white-men's rifles going off, scattered and irregular, in a feeble reply that could not have had much effect.

Sutherland stared helplessly upriver. He knew that the militia patrol must have camped on the opposite bank for the night, and now it was being hit by the Shawnees. He could never get there in time to help.

The firing went on for another minute or so, then stopped abruptly. Sutherland took a deep breath and rushed off to find Tamano and Mawak; together they would go upriver to see what had happened—as if he did not already know. His heart sank as he again prepared himself to view the aftermath of an Indian massacre.

A few hours later, Sutherland and his companions silently gazed from the bushes at the sunny clearing. There lay the bodies of the militia patrol—thirteen of them, apparently surprised while at breakfast. Their naked bodies were scattered around the campsite, every one of them scalped and gruesomely mutilated. Still, the Shawnees had apparently been in a hurry, for they had not been as hideously thorough as was their custom.

Sutherland and his friends had seen death often, but a massacre was never a scene that one became used to. They approached reluctantly, going from body to body, finding most had been shot from a distance. Few had found the chance to put up a fight.

As Tamano and Mawak looked around in the bushes for other bodies, Sutherland inspected the tracks of the departing Shawnees. As he expected, they had dashed away westward, well aware that white troops would come racing after them as soon as word of the ambush got back to Fort Pitt. The Shawnees would be doubly on their guard for the next few days; it would be even more difficult to surprise them and get Benjamin free, if he was still alive.

There came a soft whistle from Tamano, and Sutherland turned to see the Indians carrying a wounded militiaman from the woods. They laid him down carefully, for he had been shot in the stomach and was still bleeding. He was a slight man of middle age, fair-haired and wiry, with good clothes that spoke of some wealth. His hair and beard were crusted with snow and pine needles; apparently he had crawled away to lie concealed by bushes. He was lucky the Shawnees had overlooked him.

Gasping, he took water from Mawak. He was pale with shock, but no blood came out of his mouth; he might live if they got him back to the fort. After a moment, he began to speak.

"Was . . . damned Girty!"

Mawak had been tearing the shirt from the man to make bandages, but like Tamano and Sutherland, the old Indian stopped short to hear this.

The man coughed, wincing with pain. Every effort seemed to cause him excruciating agony. "Girty joined up with 'em . . . just like everybody said he . . . said he would! Dirty Tory bastard!" He moaned and rolled on his side, legs curling up as the hurt overwhelmed him.

Sutherland could not figure why Girty had done this, when for years he had made a good living answering to whatever officer commanded at Fort Pitt—British, Virginian, Pennsylvanian.

The wounded militiaman answered the unspoken question, struggling to remain conscious in order to tell of Simon Girty's treachery.

"Our officer told Girty last night . . . shouted over the ice . . . Girty best get his arse back to Pitt and report!" He gasped for breath. "Girty's been cashiered, fired as scout by Congress after . . . after so many officers wrote complaints agin him . . . about his Injun ways and how he weren't to be trusted!"

Grimacing in pain as Mawak bandaged him, the man went on to describe how Girty had bridled at the news of his firing, how he had roundly cursed the militiamen, who wanted to arrest him, and would have done so if Girty had not scrambled nimbly back across the ice-laden river.

"We weren't no redskins," the man muttered, hardly aware of Mawak and Tamano tending his wounds. "We couldn't git across the ice like him . . . damned wolf . . . dirty varmint . . . murdering white savage!"

Sutherland anxiously asked if there had been a white boy with the Shawnees, and felt a great relief when the man confirmed this, nodding. He was barely able to speak.

"Yeah . . . tied up . . . they . . . made him watch. . . ."

Sutherland felt sick at heart to think of what his son must be enduring. Yet the boy was alive, and for that he was thankful.

Mawak got the militiaman well bound, but by now the man was delirious. He rambled on about Girty's reviling the dying militiamen, brutalizing them, and cursing Congress and all rebels.

Soon the man's strength gave out. Sutherland mixed up some laudanum paste, administering it with water that still stood in a pot on the campfire ashes. Then the three of them quickly fashioned a sling of cloth and thongs and bore the militiaman along the shore trail toward Fort Pitt.

There was no doubt now Girty had told the Shawnees that Sutherland was on their heels. Sutherland knew that if he pursued swiftly, they would be ready for him, and he would be cut down from ambush. He must think of something else. Besides, this man's life was in danger; and if Tamano and Mawak brought him into Pitt alone, they might be abused by angry whites.

The Shawnees had kept Benjamin alive this long, so they apparently intended to bring him all the way to their village—Chillicothe, Girty had said. Tonight, Sutherland thought, he would set off for Chillicothe, avoiding the warriors' trail to stay clear of ambush. That would mean moving even faster than before, mostly at night, and old Mawak would not be up to it.

Mawak and Tamano should both go home to Fort Detroit, Sutherland decided. One man could get through to Chillicothe where three or even two would surely be seen. One man could travel faster, hide more easily, and eat next to nothing yet still go on.

Also, Tamano could bring word to Jeremy Bently that his stepfather wanted a secret rendezvous. If the time to free Benjamin was not right, or if something worse happened, then Sutherland would make for Detroit and try to change Jeremy's loyalty by showing him Weston's journal. As a last resort, it was even possible that Jeremy, as a British officer, could enter the Shawnee village and purchase his half-brother's freedom.

At least Sutherland was fairly certain that Simon Girty would not remain in the way for long. Once Girty realized Sutherland was not on his trail, he probably would head for Detroit to sell his services to Henry Hamilton in time for the spring fighting.

As Sutherland had thought all along, Simon Girty was a strange character, definitely the wrong man to have as an enemy. Yet Girty could have led the Shawnees to him last night and killed him then and there, earning great honor in their eyes. But he had not, and Sutherland could not puzzle that through.

chapter 7

WYOMING VALLEY

Instead of replacing the cabin that had burned down in the Shawnee raid, the people of Ella Sutherland's settlement began to raise a stout blockhouse. The Jenkins family, whose home had been lost, were willing to move into the blockhouse, which would remain available as shelter to all in case of another attack. Also, because the head of the family was a god-fearing Connecticut Congregationalist and something of a preacher, the blockhouse would be used every Sunday as a place of worship.

Joshua Jenkins was a tall, dark-bearded man, a barrel-maker by trade. Back east, as a devout elder of his village congregation, he had stoutly resisted the radical "New-Lighters" who had begun to dominate the community and change its form of worship. Like many Connecticut Congregationalists over the past thirty years, he had pulled up his family, sold their holdings, and come to the Wyoming Valley.

The Jenkinses were hardy, courageous folk, and these qualities had served them well in this difficult time, for they had lost nearly everything in the fire. Friends and their five children had helped Joshua and Ruth save some of their furniture and household goods before the cabin was totally consumed, but so much had been destroyed that the family was destitute.

Not only was the community constructing a new dwelling, but its womenfolk were sewing, weaving, mending, and making gifts for the housewarming. Ella Sutherland, though still weak, spent much of her time with Susannah, working on a new quilt for the Jenkinses.

As the sound of hammers, mauls, adzes, and saws went

on outside her sunlit cabin, Ella sat across the pine-plank
table from Susannah, the bright quilt taking shape between
them. Although most settlers in the Wyoming were well-
to-do New England folk, none of the families here was as
well-off as the Sutherlands, whose quilt would be fashioned
of the very finest fabric. It had done Ella's heart good when
Susannah had generously offered to cut up a pretty yellow
Philadelphia-bought gown to use in the pattern.

Ella was thinking of Owen when she looked up from her
stitches to steal a glance at her daughter, who was sewing
nimbly. Susannah's fair hair was tied back like Ella's, and
like her mother she wore a drab linen apron over a com-
fortably soft, dark-brown cotton frock. Ella thought of her
own youth, as the daughter of English aristocracy, and remembered dreaming of going to America to find adventure
and see a land of unsurpassed beauty.

Now she was here, having married a Massachusetts man
who fell in Braddock's defeat near Fort Pitt, back in 1755.
John Bently had eventually died of his wounds, and afterward Ella had gone to Detroit with her son, Jeremy, to be
with her brother, the Redcoat major in command of the fort.
There, during Pontiac's outbreak, Ella had met and fallen
in love with Owen Sutherland. He had just lost his wife,
and what had begun as kindness from Ella had eventually
turned to passionate love. Their life together since had gone
far beyond passion, and they had raised a family and built
a great trading company. The revolution, however, had
broken up both family and company, as Jeremy Bently had
chosen the side of the loyalists, and the Frontier Company
members had gone their separate ways. Now Benjamin was
gone, too.

She stopped to think of her son by Owen, closing her
eyes, believing intensely that he must still be alive. If he
lived, Owen would get him home safely. As for Jeremy,
Ella found it painful to imagine him in a scarlet uniform,
although in years past she had been proud that her brother
was a respected British officer. She had not seen Jeremy
for more than two years.

How her life had changed, and so quickly! With a sigh,
she resumed her sewing, hearing the singing of men at work.

She wished it all would change once more, for the better, and for peace in America.

Susannah tied off what she was sewing and began to cut some more of the yellow fabric.

Ella smiled, and without glancing up from her work said, "I would have thought it pained you to sacrifice that dress, dear; you loved it so much."

Susannah pouted and pretended to look bored. "Yes, I did like it, but it's quite out of style these days. Anyway, fashion doesn't seem very important out here, and this dress will see better use as a quilt for Ruth Jenkins."

Ella smiled to hear this. "When your father and Benjamin come back . . ." She almost added Jeremy's name, but that would have been too much to hope for. She held up patches of fabric, trying to match them. "When they return, and after the Redcoats leave Philadelphia, we'll make a trip there, and you can choose another dress, perhaps even two or three."

Susannah jumped for glee and began to talk about Philadelphia, a week's journey to the southeast, the second greatest city in the British empire after London. It was occupied by the king's troops, but rumor had it they would go back to New York Town this summer to consolidate their forces. Suddenly Susannah's expression changed to a look of concern, and she said, "Mother, do you think we might go to Albany instead?" She sat down and went abruptly back to her work, not looking up, but obviously she was hanging on the reply.

Ella knew Susannah would require some time to get over James Morely. She laughed, saying, "I don't think Albany will have the dressmakers who can fashion a Marie Antoinette, dear."

Susannah glanced up, then back at her work; she gave a long sigh of tedium. "Well, perhaps it's not all that important, but I would like to visit the Defrieses and see Jeanette again."

It was true that Susannah had not seen her friend in years; Jeanette was the daughter of Frontier Company partners Peter and Mary Defries, who oversaw the company's affairs in Albany.

Susannah said, "I'm sure Jeanette will know all the latest fashions, and surely she has a wonderful dressmaker who'd do right by me...." Her words faded off, and she stopped working. "Mother, do you think Jeanette would be—I mean, do you think James and Jeanette could ever be..."

There was a moment of uneasy quiet as Ella thought how to reply without hurting her daughter's feelings. The white husky, Heera, lying near the door, gazed at Ella, as though he too sympathized with Susannah's youthful heartache. Indeed, Ella thought, James Morely and Jeanette Defries would be a fine match, Jeanette being of more eligible age for marriage than Susannah. Before she could reply, however, a shout came from outside. It was the excited voice of Tom Morely, saying Mel was "gonna have a go at it!"

Ella and Susannah were both expecting this. After a morning's furious work, Mel had finally managed to get his levitation machine ready to fly, and they wanted to watch. Ella grew slightly dizzy as she rose to her feet, and Susannah excitedly came to take her arm and help her to the cabin door. They stood there viewing the sun-filled common ground, Heera at their side. The world was white with snow, but the sunshine felt warm.

The settlement was all confusion and noise, with workmen leaping from their scaffolding around the second floor of the unfinished blockhouse. Men threw down tools, women lifted infants from their cradles and hurried outside. Children abandoned their hoops, balls, and snowmen and dashed through the settlement toward the open field where people were gathering.

Ella and Susannah put on warm capes, and Sally Morely joined them outside, coming to Ella's other side as they walked to the field. Any prolonged standing made Ella feel dizzy, but she needed this diversion, and would not give in to her weakness. In any case, the wound had healed well, her hair concealing the scar above her left ear, and she was determined to be as good as new by the time Owen returned.

Ella smiled when she saw Mel Webster, who was shouting orders and running frantically about. Just yesterday he had finished sewing a large bag of patchwork cloth ten feet across, with a paper lining stitched inside. She had marveled

at the work that had gone into it, and now, as they neared
the open, snow-covered field, she could see that the entire
contraption had been propped up on poles and stretched
with ropes above a roaring hot, smoky fire. The bag seemed
to be rising in the middle, as if some great force was pushing
it from beneath.

"Heavens to Betsy!" cried Sally Morely. "There're four
people holding down the corners, and it still wants to rise
up! Mel must be right . . . there's something—a gas or
something—in the smoke that makes the bag rise! It's amazing!"

The women hurried on, as fast as Ella could go, all of
them eager to watch the fabric fill. It was beginning to lift
high enough so that the poles were not needed and the people
holding it down had to move closer together. Tom Morely
was at one rope, boys from the settlement at two others,
and Hickory Webster, strong as a man, at the fourth. They
were leaning back, putting all their weight into the effort.
The four ropes, Ella could now see, were attached to a
wooden-framed opening in the bottom of the bag, into which
the smoke billowed. With every passing moment the bag
rose higher and grew more distended, beginning to resemble
a large, upside-down spittoon. The laughing people on the
ropes were finding it increasingly difficult to keep from
being pulled too close to the fire.

Portly Lettie Grey, standing nearby, was unaccustomedly
nervous, calling loudly for her son Tom to stop this sorcery
and release his rope before it was too late. Mel himself,
deaf to her pleas, was leaping and cavorting for glee around
the contraption, shouting, "I knew it would rise! I knew it
would!"

Big Jeb Grey, his beefy face intent, joined the three
women. He rubbed his chin and stared, perplexed, as the
aerostatic machine, as Mel called it, grew ever more full.

Lettie murmured, "I pray dear Mel ain't going against
God's law! It don't seem right, no." She screamed, "Tom!
Thee take care, now, hear?"

Jeb shrugged and grumbled, "Ain't nothing wrong with
foolery that don't hurt nobody, girl." He nodded to himself,
saying, "Interesting, that's sure; but what good is it?"

"Don't seem Christian," Lettie said.

"Mebbe; but what good is it?"

Ella smiled, enjoying every moment, standing in the bright sun of this crisp February day. She had become attached to the settlement and to these people, and for a moment she stopped thinking about Owen and her sons, content to be here with Susannah and friends—especially friends as delightfully eccentric as Mel Webster. He had just grabbed the line held by a boy whose hands had been rope-burned from resisting the balloon's sudden shift in a gust. For extra security, Mel wrapped the rope around his chest, tied a quick hitch to keep it there, then shouted for joy:

"This proves my theory, and the theory—" The wind shifted suddenly, and he struggled to keep his feet. "The theory of Gusmao, who said air will rise if it's heated—"

Abruptly he and the others were yanked off-balance by a strong gust, but they held on to their ropes. Lettie was shouting that they should let go before they were all dragged into the bonfire, which crackled furiously, still sending billows of smoke and heat upward into the framed opening.

"Now!" Mel declared loudly, being jolted and tugged, "you're all witnesses to history, and this experiment... will be recorded... like Franklin's key and kite flying! It's a landmark—"

The balloon started rising irresistibly, dragging them all toward the fire—but the rope ends had been secured to pegs, and one by one the lines grew taut and held—all save for Mel's. When another gust jerked the balloon, his line tore free of its peg, and Mel was pulled sideways and up. With a yell of surprise and delight, he was whipped twenty feet high.

The crowd screamed and gasped as the balloon lurched and jerked at its moorings. All that kept Mel from being lashed across the field like a slingshot stone was the rope hitched around his chest. He could not let go, and could not get down for long. Whenever he did, the rope yanked him back upward, then plunked him down again, so that he hit the earth on the run, repeating this jarring process again and again. He squealed in delight and terror at the power of his discovery, and might have been knocked to pieces in his joy had not half a dozen men leaped on him. Several were pulled off their feet before they mobbed him and held him down long enough to undo his harness and secure the rope to its peg once more.

Finally Mel was safe, and the others had let go of their ropes, allowing the pegs to keep the balloon steady. Awed, the onlookers stood back to gape at the massive cloth bag floating above the fire. It was majestic, incredible, a sight never imagined possible by any of them.

"Isn't it beautiful?" Mel cried to Ella. "Make it big enough, and find a way to carry fire, and it'll fly a man to the clouds, to Philadelphia, to Paris, to Moscow, to China, to—"

Suddenly, as if it were tinder in a bonfire, the balloon erupted loudly into flame, sheets of fire and smoke bursting high into the sky. Everyone was driven back by the heat, and Ella, Sally, and Susannah had to tug on the dumbstruck Mel's arm to drag him to safety. The flames rose, then fell back onto the fire below with a mighty roar. Mel was open-mouthed, and the others were frightened, not knowing what to make of it.

Lettie shrilly declared, "It ain't Christian! It ain't for men to dabble in levitation machines and such devilish sorcery! No!"

Ella was standing near Mel, whose joy had turned brutally, suddenly, to utter disappointment. He was rubbing his rope-burned hands and sore chest as Hickory came sadly to his side. Other friends approached to console him, and the rest of the settlers shook their heads and muttered about all they had seen.

Jeb Grey put a consoling arm on Mel's shoulder. "It was amazing while it lasted, Mel . . . truly amazing." He nodded slowly. "But tell me, son—what good is it?"

Owen Sutherland moved alone down the frozen Ohio River, keeping to the Kentucky side, watching for sign of Indians and making sure he was not easy to see from a distance. He had decided on this route after talking to a few Kentuckians back at Pitt. To cross the Ohio near the fort, they had said, would make him easy prey for Shawnee scouts who watched the borderland trails. Sutherland knew that they were right, and he also knew that Girty might be there, waiting for him.

The land south of the Ohio would be safer. Although it was legally Indian territory, white settlers had trickled in during the past few years, and for some time any redskin caught at a disadvantage here had been as good as dead. Entire Indian villages had been moved north of the river, which had served as a boundary line, and a lone man crossing into enemy country—on either side—was either foolhardy or desperate.

But even on this side of the river caution was still necessary. Since the outbreak of hostilities, the Kentucky shore had been gradually abandoned by white settlers—including the ones Sutherland had spoken to—though a few still held on at Boonesborough and Harrod's Station. Those settlements, however, were too far to the southwest to be of any help to Sutherland. He meant to swing north across the half-frozen Ohio well before then, up the valley of the Scioto River for Chillicothe.

February had turned bitter cold, which made for hard traveling, though the river remained choked with ice floes, thus allowing Sutherland to go far downstream and still be able to cross. The closer he got to the mouth of the Scioto before crossing, the better were his chances of remaining unobserved. No Indian would expect a lone white man to come over the ice and enter the Scioto Valley. That was Sutherland's only advantage.

He had thought over every possibility, time and time again. Back at Pitt he had visited an old *voyageur* trader and fitted himself out as best he could; now, besides rifle, claymore, and pack, he carried a *voyageur*'s deerskin pouch, stuffed with items he might need if he made it to Chillicothe.

He moved by day and sometimes by night, resting when possible in abandoned cabins. He lit no fires after dark; instead, in the afternoon he would find a safe place to build a blaze and stay there just long enough to get warm, thaw his clothes, and eat a hot meal. Afterward he would move some distance away to a cold camp for the night, in case the smoke had been seen and Indians came to investigate.

Food was scarce, and he carefully rationed his cornmeal and pemmican. If he found a beaver lodge, he would go at it methodically, driving the beavers from one tunnel to another. Eventually he would corner them in their escape hatch, marking their location by the bubbles rising from under the ice. He would kill one or two, eating what he needed and saving the rest of the meat, which he bundled in the skins. At other times he made do with raiding squirrel dens for hickory nuts and acorns.

Day after day he traveled, seeing many ruined, blackened cabins with bloodstained floors and broken doors. Night after night he lay bundled in the warmest place he could find, though it seemed he was never really warm. After a while, even the brightest campfire could not drive out the chill that seemed to have settled in his very bones. He also sank deep into the condition that oppressed every white man on a long wilderness journey: loneliness.

Since parting with Mawak and Tamano near Fort Pitt three weeks earlier, he had not spoken to another human being. He passed much of his time thinking, or singing softly as he plodded along the trail, watching the snowshoes incessantly rise and fall, flopping down, scattering powdery snow, moving in time to his tune. At night he was too hungry to sing, too exhausted to lie awake and think for very long.

Still, there were times in those hidden camps when he would have liked to have pen and paper, to compose an essay in the voice of the fictional Indian sage Quill, the pen-name Sutherland had often used to write on American politics and colonial government. Quill had gained quite a reputation both at home and abroad and had been translated into French and German. His opinions, many of them humorous and bitingly revealing of British incompetence, had even found an audience in England.

Since the war, however, Sutherland had been too caught up in the fighting or in protecting his family to write much. Even the poetry that years ago had captured the fancy of Philadelphia's elite had stopped coming to him. But now, in this desolate, awesomely beautiful country, Sutherland felt he could have composed verse after verse. He laughed at the irony of it, for a winter trail was not a place for a working poet or essayist, no matter how inspired. Yet he often wished he could have written down his thoughts, calling for Americans to reunite, to see how magnificent and huge their country was and put aside differences that had erupted in civil war and revolution far beyond anything the average man had expected back in '75.

He thought about Jeremy Bently at Detroit; certainly Jeremy would understand the need for reconciliation. Neither of them wanted to prolong a war that had divided families and friends. If only Congress and Parliament could compromise and get to the peace table, there was hope that the killing would stop. But what would it take to make the king's ministers admit they could not stand in the way of American liberty?

Sutherland did not know. Even Quill could not deal with that question. Often Sutherland fell asleep wondering how and when the war would end. Nearly always his dreams were of Benjamin, the captive, and of Jeremy, the enemy soldier. For all his bodily need, Sutherland did not sleep well.

By the end of February, he was so weary of the trail that he considered hardly anything except aching muscles, stiff bones, wet feet, a growling, empty belly, and the cold, bitter air that gnawed at him, burned his windpipe, and stung his face. Nothing seemed important, save for taking another stride in the snow, going on and on with his obsession to save his son. Eating, hunting, sleeping, hiding, walking, and walking . . . all done as if he were moving through a dream, drifting and unreal. The only moments that seemed real were when danger was present. Often, as he moved farther west, Shawnee hunting parties would pass by, unaware he was concealed just a few feet away, his rifle trained on them.

But all other times the trail seemed the same: narrow and winding; black and gray naked branches; white and gray bare snow; blue and gray cold sky. Day after day, one step and then another; a meal where it could be found; a fire where it might be safe, or where he could not go on without it; and Ella foremost in his mind. Now, when he had the

will to think at all, Sutherland's strongest thoughts were of
her; but after a while these, too, ran into one another, with
no beginning, no end, no sense of time or place. He simply
saw her, felt her as if she were present in his very soul,
keeping him going with her love for him and with her need
to have Benjamin back home. Ella and Benjamin; snowshoes and snow; thinking and living like a hunted beast,
and like a hunter.

By March, the blockhouse at Ella's settlement had been
completed. It stood solid and squat in the center of a cleared
area and could be held for many days by a handful of brave
men against a hundred Indians. Within a few feet of one
wall a spring had been tapped to provide water for a deep
pool, so that a bucket could be lowered at night if the place
were under siege.

On the evening the work was finished, after the Jenkins
family had labored all day with friends to move in what
possessions they had made, saved, borrowed, or been given,
the settlement lay in silence under the starry winter sky.
Tallow lamps glowed inside the blockhouse, throwing slants
of yellow light through the half-closed shutters and glinting
on precious panes of glass donated by some generous soul.
Then, out of the shadows of the other cabins, dark forms
appeared, approaching swiftly but not very silently, heralded by clatters and bumps, stumbling and shushing as they
crept closer to the new blockhouse.

In an hour or so the Jenkinses would be asleep, the door
barred, but now they were still vulnerable, with even the
shuttered windows unsecured. Shortly the settlement became hushed once more, and there was no sign of movement
anywhere. Then two figures, hunching low, ran at top speed
toward the blockhouse door and with a shout threw it wide
open. A mighty yelling and racket erupted, as torches flared
alight, dogs barked, and a deep grating, droning noise echoed
off cabin walls.

A startled Joshua Jenkins came to the door. Standing in
the glare of a dozen torches, he laughed to see friends and
neighbors crowding toward his house, encircling it, whack-
ing spoons and sticks against tin plates, shaking tambourines

and old Indian rattles, and shouting, "Char'vree! Char'vree, Jenkins!"

Though their French pronunciation left something to be desired, Jenkins knew this was a *charivari,* or mock serenade, as prelude to a housewarming.

Mrs. Jenkins and the children came laughing to the door, waving and acknowledging the celebration, the little ones holding their ears against the deep grating noise of the horse fiddle—a well-rosined empty barrel energetically bowed with a split rail. Tom Morely and Mel Webster winced at the bone-vibrating drone as they dragged the rail across the barrel's side, sending out a hollow, moaning din that set Heera and the other dogs to yowling.

The party quickly moved inside the blockhouse. Real fiddles played by Mel and Sally started the music, tables and chairs were pushed aside, toasts of cider and whiskey were drunk all around, and the dancing took hold like a magic spell. Food was brought in by the other women, and the feasting began with a passion not seen here since the New Year's Day party that had ended with the murderous Indian attack.

Ella Sutherland enjoyed herself thoroughly. After presenting the finished quilt to Mrs. Jenkins, she and Susannah joined the festivities, though Ella was still weak and soon retired to a nearby cabin with the community's youngest children. There she rocked babies to sleep and sang lullabies in quick time to the rollicking, jigging music going on inside the blockhouse. Sally Morely and Lettie joined her from time to time, and Susannah came in even more often, claiming she took little interest in the young men—boys, she called them—who asked her to dance. After some encouragement from her mother, however, Susannah rejoined the party and eventually seemed to forget her longing for James Morely as she was swept up in the laughter and music.

It was quite late when a warning shout went up from a sentry, who said horsemen were approaching along the eastern trail. In a few moments most of the settlers had barred themselves in the blockhouse and other cabins, as a small party of armed men went to investigate the alarm. Heera ran in front, and the men were ready for a fight, but the horsemen turned out to be a packtrain of horses and mules, managed by six stalwart traders. They had come all the way from Albany, they said, to sell their wares and supply the militia forts in the region, and were pushing to reach this settlement before bedding down for the night.

The packers were warmly welcomed, and after they had cared for their animals, they joined the dancing and feasting. The celebration took them so much by surprise that at first the master of the train neglected to deliver a package of letters from James Morely. His offhand announcement of the package touched off a flurry of excitement among James's friends and family. Susannah immediately forsook the lads trying to charm her and almost dragged Ella back to their cabin to read the letter addressed to the Sutherlands in care of Ella.

With the party sounds faint in the distance, mother and daughter sat before the fire while Ella read aloud. This letter had come even sooner than Susannah had hoped; it and several others for the Morelys and the Websters had been posted less than a week after James had arrived in Albany. He had spent a goodly sum to have the master of the packtrain carry the package right to Susannah's settlement, and although this letter was properly addressed to Ella, Susannah was certain it was meant for herself.

James had written most of the letter during his journey, while staying overnight in private homes or at inns or taverns. He asked first about Ella, Benjamin, and Owen, anxious for any news, then spoke of a hard but uneventful trip across the mountains, and of meeting many rebel patrols. There had been no sign of Indian raiders or loyalist militia, and he had safely deposited the five thousand pounds sterling with Frontier Company partners Peter and Mary Defries.

As Ella read on, Susannah gazed into the flames of the fireplace. Heera was at her feet, and she fondled the husky's ear as she listened to James's words.

> . . . Albany is as grand as I thought it would be—a fine, prosperous city built all of bricks, with dockyards enough to support a thriving commerce, although they are not nearly as busy as they would be in time of

peace. And you were right, Susannah, when you told
me about the Dutch folk, jabbering in a tongue that
sounds stranger than any Indian talk.

This was the first time James had been to Albany—the
first time in the past fifteen years, in fact, that he had been
anywhere out of the northwest, save for Montreal. Susannah
had seen much more of the world than he had, and she
smiled slightly to hear him describe Albany as grand, when
she knew it was nothing compared to Philadelphia or New
York.

The city is full of rebel generals, soldiers, and
sympathizers who have gathered here following the
defeat of Burgoyne at Saratoga. Everyone's proud and
a staunch rebel, it seems—although there's a good
deal of profit being made by professed rebel merchants
who charge Congress's troops an arm and a leg for
barrel-scrapings, goods that the thievingest northwest
trader wouldn't palm off on a drunken Indian.

James said that rebel forces in the north were always on
guard in case the British massed another large army in
Canada to strike southward against Albany and the Hudson
Valley. The rebels, however, were having trouble collecting
war supplies, since they had little money to pay for what
they needed.

Our company's old nemesis, Bradford Cullen, is
making handsome profits by gouging the army all he
can. Save for our sterling, he seems to have all the
hard cash in town, and has cornered the market on
everything from old muskets to old hats, molasses to
dried peas. . . .

Bradford Cullen, Susannah knew, was an elderly mer-
chant who for many years had ruthlessly battled the Frontier
Company in an effort to monopolize northwest commerce.
Her father believed Cullen was only pretending to be a rebel

and would eagerly turn his coat if the British appeared to be winning the war. Cullen would stoop to any tactic, it was said, when it came to gaining wealth and influence, including hiring assassins. Despite his reputation, he held great sway over important rebels in Congress, many of whom were in debt to him.

James wrote that Cullen obviously was making money hand over fist, yet Congress's representatives remained grateful for his capacity to supply its army.

Of course he never quite finds enough munitions or equipment to outfit an expedition fully, for that might mean a strike at Canada, thus angering his British friends (as rumor has it). Although it cannot yet be proved, I'm sure he is buying up and shipping war essentials abroad from Boston, keeping them out of circulation.

At any rate, I'm not interested in the war at the moment and mean to concentrate on turning our own resources to a profit. I must admit it troubles me that Peter and Mary spend all their personal cash to supply the rebel army, when all they get in payment are worthless Continental dollars.

Susannah was surprised to hear James sound so disapproving of Peter and Mary. She knew that James was no ardent rebel, but did not think he should criticize the Defrieses for having forgone profit for the sake of the war effort.

Ella, too, seemed troubled as she read on:

Peter and Mary, I'm sorry to say, have allowed Frontier Company business to languish, while Bradford Cullen, realist that he is, continues to profit. Cullen does not throw *his* money down the vast hole that we call the Continental army!

Ella laid the letter in her lap. "James almost sounds as if he admires Cullen—"

Susannah nearly jumped from her seat, and Heera quickly

raised his head as the girl cried out, "Oh, no, Mother! You mustn't think that! It's not true! I'm sure he's just trying to succeed for the sake of us all, and it must make him . . . frustrated! Yes, frustrated to see Cullen taking advantage of everyone, using the war for his own advancement, while an honest man like James meets so many difficulties. . . ."

She sat down, fingers knitted in her lap, her heart thudding, and stared at the fire. Her mother sounded so sharp about James, and that was not fair. When James one day succeeded against the odds, then her mother and father would feel differently. They would be grateful for his efforts and for his genius in business.

Ella read on as James changed the subject to how much he missed everyone in the Wyoming Valley. Susannah's eyes filled with tears, but she tried to keep her mother from noticing.

> . . . It seems I've been gone for years, and that this strange and foreign city is a place gone mad compared to our peaceful homes at Detroit and, yes, even our little cabins in the Wyoming.
>
> Maybe I'm not the city lad some folk like to think; maybe my heart really does belong in the northwest wilderness. Certainly it is not in Albany, for all its bustle and excitement. My heart, my thoughts, are often elsewhere, often with you. Soon I shall write again, for it gives me comfort to speak to you this way. It would give me more comfort if you would honor me with a letter in return, those of you who care that I am gone.

Susannah was breathing hard, sure that those last words were meant for her in particular. Already she had written a long letter, although it was not nearly long enough to tell James all that was in her heart. She wanted to send it, but hoped her mother would not ask to read it, for it contained some passages that perhaps were not reserved enough for an unmarried woman.

Ella seemed to have read Susannah's mind. "Why don't you write something to send to James? The packtrain master surely would agree to carry it back to Albany."

Susannah lifted her skirts and dashed to her bedroom, returning with her letter—all twenty-five pages of it, wrinkled and dog-eared, more than one sheet stained with tears. Susannah was too discomposed to notice the amused surprise on her mother's face.

"James surely will be less lonely when he receives this." She took the rumpled pages and organized them neatly, Susannah all the while dreading that she might begin to read them. Ella did not even scan what had been written, however, and asked Susannah to fetch sealing wax, the stamp, and a ribbon with which to tie the letter.

"A lot of ribbon, dear—and I hope our packtrain master won't have to buy an extra mule to carry this one."

A wolf was howling louder than the wind, and Owen Sutherland could not imagine what the beast was doing abroad in this blinding snowstorm. Sutherland was huddled under a rock ledge, with an enormous fire crackling before him. All about, snow was piling up, whirled into powder by the northern wind, drifting ever closer to Sutherland's campsite. Several times he rose and stamped around with snowshoes to keep the snow down. Beyond his work, drifts mounted steadily.

The wolf howled, lonely and mournful, probably lurking not far away, watching the glow of the fire. The desolate wail went unanswered, as the pack did not respond or gather to observe Sutherland.

Gusts twisted and changed direction, making the shelter of the rock sometimes useless. Sutherland was gloomy, gaunt, hunched down, listening to wolf and storm, the fire hot on his body. He was bundled in a blanket and beaver pelts, and beside him was his rifle, wrapped in a fur case against the cold and damp. His food was gone, and he had wanted to hunt this afternoon before crossing the Ohio, somewhere out there in the black night and swirling snow. But the storm had swept in suddenly from the western horizon, driving game to shelter. Perhaps the wolf was hungry, too.

It was March, the Moon of the Big Winds, the time of

blizzards. April was the Green Moon, but April was far away from this lonely camp in the middle of nowhere. April, Chillicothe, Benjamin, Ella . . . all so very far away. Jeremy, Susannah, Detroit, Valenya. Loved ones and home, food, warmth, and Ella. The wolf howled.

It would have been good to have Tamano sharing this hunger and danger. That audacious Chippewa would have had stories to tell to pass the time, and he would enjoy Sutherland's old tales, though he had heard them over and over again.

The wolf howled. Sutherland thought he could see his eyes, even through the snow, reflecting the firelight.

"Could I share this fire with you, lad, I would; but you've no manners . . . no sense of gratitude, you wild one."

The wolf's howl rose, quavered, and fell away on the wind. It was almost company to hear the sound, for the wolf, too, was enduring the snow and the cold and the solitude.

When the call went unanswered, Sutherland put back his head and howled. His cry was long and lonely and, in its way, comforting to a man who had no one else to talk to.

chapter **8**

CAPTAIN DAVIES

Simon Girty did not stay long with the Shawnees. Benjamin guessed that he was heading northward, perhaps to the Senecas who had raised him, or maybe up to Niagara.

Benjamin had been surprised when the scraggly white scout had shown up, and even more surprised when the Indians had spoken his name familiarly. He had heard of Simon Girty, of course—everyone had. But he had not expected him to be in league with the Shawnees. Girty had glanced at him once or twice, but otherwise had displayed no interest. Benjamin had watched Girty closely, however, and had overheard him warn Wabete that scouts were on their trail. But the man had said nothing about who those scouts were, and now he was gone.

Benjamin hoped one of them was his father. The Indians certainly would be astonished to learn they had caught the son of Owen Sutherland. Benjamin suspected they would find out sooner or later, but for now he would not give them the pleasure of knowing it. The Shawnees were already too cocky—they'd been that way ever since ambushing the unsuspecting militiamen camped near the river. That grisly triumph had lifted their spirits tremendously, and most of them now sported fresh, stinking scalps on their belts.

Benjamin still shook to recall that day. At first he had been gagged and kept a ways off; then, when the shooting was over, they had dragged him into the camp and forced him to watch the brutal torture of those who yet lived. It was as if Wabete had been testing him. He had tried not to give in to revulsion, not to show weakness. Only later, when no one was watching, had he vomited and wept.

But he had not wept since. He knew this was the Indian

way of war, and the way of many white frontiersmen as
well. The hideous experience near the river had hardened
him, made his blood run cold, and even now, weeks later,
the memory of it gave him the strength to remain stubborn
and defiant at every turn.

At least he was no longer alone. This morning the Shawnees had met a large raiding party of their own nation, more
than a hundred and fifty strong, bearing trophies of war that
made Wabete's sorry little group flush with envy. The leader
of this other party was the famous Blackfish, and his warriors had captured thirty white men from the Kentucky country, without firing a shot. Thirty whites! All roped together
like packhorses and forced to carry captured provisions and
gear for the jubilant Indians.

Since early evening they had all rested at a watering
hole, where Blackfish had invited Wabete to feast and hear
the tales of triumph. Wabete apparently was greatly respected, for Blackfish had given him a place of honor at
the fire. Off in shadows, Benjamin sat tied up with the
doleful Kentucky whites, many of whom were sleeping.
They, too, had endured a long, hard march, though their
journey was far from over. Benjamin had learned they were
being taken all the way to Detroit, where they would be
sold to the British.

The cold night air was strong with the aroma of woodsmoke and roasting meat, mingled with the smell of tobacco
and greasy, sweating Indians. Beyond the main council fire,
Blackfish's men were dancing and chanting around a spitted,
roasting ox, some warriors beating on tom-toms, others
twanging jew's harps. They were happy, proud, and boastful, making Wabete's band seem gloomy by comparison,
for they had far less to brag about.

Benjamin leaned back against a tree, again thinking of
the massacre. The unlooked-for victory over the militia had
encouraged Wabete's men, and the food, weapons, and
clothing of the dead whites had been welcome. As the war
band had traveled deeper into Indian country, they had
marched proudly through village after village, boasting of
victory, showing off their scalps and prisoner. Inevitably,
Benjamin was attacked by the squaws and children, who

would curse and kick and beat him with switches and small clubs until Wabete hurried him to shelter. He had almost grown accustomed to such treatment.

Benjamin smiled to himself. Punch, too, had attracted much attention, not only for his response to Benjamin's whistles, but also for his mischievous behavior. He was becoming a notorious thief, whisking away with jewelry or beads or small pieces of glass, which he would drop by Benjamin's bedding. More than once an angry squaw had come charging into his lodging to retrieve some precious token swiped by the jay.

"Psst." One of the Kentuckians kicked his foot to get his attention. "They kept you alive for long, boy?"

Benjamin said ten weeks.

"Lucky those red devils got no liquor tonight, or we'd all be goners."

"They'd make mincemeat outa us," said another grizzled man, lean and sallow-faced, with ragged flannel and buckskin clothing that did little to keep off the cold. Like Benjamin, the other whites had been robbed of their clothes and given louse-ridden, decrepit gear in exchange.

Glaring at the raucous Indians around the fire, the second man grumbled, "Nothin' meaner'n a drunk Injun—especially a drunk Injun with a score to settle, like this bunch who brought you in from the Wyoming, boy."

Benjamin slowly nodded in reply. As he turned his gaze to Punch, who was perched on a branch overhead, he felt the eyes of the Kentuckians on him. Most were from the Carolinas, a few from Pennsylvania and Virginia. He looked back at them and saw the bitterness there, and the humiliation, but none seemed in any way resigned to death. One, a sturdy, fair-haired fellow in his middle forties, stared at Benjamin with alert blue eyes that seemed to penetrate the lad's mind. Benjamin stared back almost insolently, until the man nodded, introduced himself with a name Benjamin did not catch, and said he had also come from Pennsylvania, a long time ago.

"Near Reading I was born, when it was frontier and the Wyoming was Injun country; but things've changed, and the borderlands've been pushed westward some." He became thoughtful a moment and said, "But I reckon border-lands're wherever the warpath leads Injuns, and these days Philadelphee best be on its guard."

He was a friendly man, Benjamin thought, and seemed to be regarded highly by the others, who listened to him talk on about Pontiac's war and the French and Indian fight-ing, which was before Benjamin's time. The man said he had been a teamster with Braddock and had seen the Indians at their very best. A few of these Shawnees, including Wabete and Blackfish, had fought in the Braddock disaster, he said, in which nearly a thousand Redcoats and provincial militia had been massacred in one of the worst defeats in British military history.

As the Kentuckian spoke, one of the warriors drifted closer to listen. He was tall for an Indian, wrapped in a white, hooded blanket-coat and wearing a fine beaverskin hat pulled down close to his eyes. It was hard to make out his face in the play of firelight and shadows. Benjamin thought the man was listening to the whites converse as though he understood their tongue. He must have been a sentry, for he carried a rifle and paced slowly past, to lean casually against a tree.

Benjamin noticed he did not walk in the half-stooping manner of most Shawnee warriors, and his garb gave no hint of his tribe. Benjamin found his attention going alter-nately from the Kentucky man's conversation to this silent warrior.

Then Benjamin realized the Kentuckian was addressing him, and he turned to hear, ". . . been long in the Wyoming Valley, young fella?"

"What? Oh, no, sir, just a few months." The Kentuckian eyed him curiously, obviously expecting more, and Ben-jamin went on. "We're not from Pennsylvania at all, sir. We've just been there since Montreal fell to the British, but we're not from Montreal, either. . . ."

Benjamin was distracted by the feeling that the tall Indian in the white coat was listening. He had no desire to say anything that might be of interest to the fellow, but the frontiersman went on talking, showing no anxiety. He said that out here everyone was from someplace else; even the

Indians had shifted their villages and council fires many times because of white encroachments.

"Taking us's the first big win the Shawnee've been able to claim in plenty of years," said the Kentuckian.

The man with the gaunt face spat and declared, "'Specially nabbin' you, Dan. That there Blackfish's prouder'n hell to take you to hair-buyer Hamilton!"

As though the Indians crowding around the council fires had heard, one of them got up and approached the seated white prisoners, kicking and pushing his way through until he found the man called Dan, who had been doing most of the talking to Benjamin.

"Up, son 'a bitch!" the warrior grunted, motioning for the man to rise and follow him. "Blackfish want Boone now!"

The other frontiersman muttered, "Gonna show you off to old Wabete, Dan'l! Better shine yer shoes and powder yer wig!"

Not until then did Benjamin realize, with a start, that this was the well-known Daniel Boone, a leader of the few whites tenaciously holding on to new settlements in Kentucky. Benjamin was awed to think he was in company with such a hero, and forgetting himself, he called out to Boone:

"My pa said he met you years back in the French war, sir—his name's Owen Sutherland!"

At that, not only did Boone turn in surprise, but the tall Indian nearby in the blanket coat stood up straight and took a step forward. Daniel Boone laughed and nodded once.

"Sutherland's son, eh? Wisht I coulda had your pappy along when these here Shawnee snuck up. They might not've got close enough to surprise us, if'n I remember his knack at scouting! Hah! Proud to meet you, son."

The Indian who had come for Boone snorted and yanked ineffectually at the prisoner's thick arms, which were tied behind his back; no doubt Blackfish wanted Boone present while he gave his speech on how the great long hunter had been captured without a fight. Even Benjamin was curious now; so far he had been told only that the whites had been surrounded at a place called Blue Licks. Outnumbered five to one, they had immediately surrendered, counting on being brought to Detroit and sold to Hamilton.

As Benjamin watched Boone being led toward the fire, he again became uncomfortably conscious of the Indian in the white blanket-coat. The man's left eye glinted in the shadow, and Benjamin tried to look away, yet was strangely attracted to this ominous figure. It certainly was not Amagh-wah, who could never afford a long rifle or such fine cloth-ing.

Blackfish was on his feet, wildly gesticulating and grunt-ing in his guttural language. He pointed at Boone, who was standing ramrod straight, his arms now unbound and folded across his chest. Blackfish was acting out the capture, and the Indians, including Wabete, shouted approval.

Benjamin became absorbed in the story. After some time, when the speech appeared to be drawing near an end, he was relieved to note that the man in the white coat had left and was nowhere in sight.

His attention returned to the circle around the fire, and he was amazed at what he now heard: Blackfish was actually lauding Boone, as if the frontiersman were a Shawnee and not a longtime adversary. It sounded very much like Black-fish intended to adopt Boone, to replace a young, renowned warrior killed last year. Boone showed no emotion at this, though it meant he might not be sold to the British at Detroit, as surely he had hoped. Benjamin knew that any man who tried to escape after having been adopted was condemned to instant death. If Boone succeeded in getting away and were ever recaptured, he would be killed on the spot.

The captives seated near Benjamin began muttering as those who understood the Shawnee tongue explained what Blackfish was saying. They looked at their leader with pity, realizing he was being condemned to remain on the knife's edge of death. At least those bought by Hamilton would soon know their fate.

When the speech ended, Boone was tied once more and roughly pushed back to the group of captives. The other Kentuckians glanced at him furtively to gauge his reaction; but if Boone felt troubled by the news, it did not show. He simply yawned, and after a while said that the Shawnee would be happy to get back to their lodges to celebrate capturing so many Kentuckians.

"They'll be crushed to the marrow, though, when I show 'em my heels and scurry off home at the very first chance." Home, Benjamin figured, was Boonesborough.

He told the men not to worry, because they would be safe once they arrived at Detroit. Hamilton, he said, was not the cruel hair-buyer that rebel pamphleteers said he was; he would ransom them all and pay the Indians generously— more than they would get for bringing in scalps.

Benjamin felt his empty belly turn and rumble. Thinking of Amaghwah, he said, "There's Indians among these who'd like to make some mischief, though, especially after the whipping we gave them . . . I mean the whipping my folk gave them." He reddened somewhat and said, "I guess I wasn't much help getting snared like I did."

Boone leaned over and said with a wink, "Sometimes even the best of us get caught off-guard, lad. If we live to tell of it, we're that much better woodsmen next time."

Suddenly a ripple of movement went through the Indian throng, as all their attention turned to one figure. Boone was distracted by it. Benjamin, to his surprise, saw it was the warrior in the white coat. He was standing in the fire's red glare, about to speak. His hood was back, but the fine fur hat was close about his head. He must have been a person of some importance, for even the leading Indians paid close attention as he began a speech in Shawnee, offering ropes of tobacco and a bag of new scalping knives as a preliminary gesture of respect.

The man's accent was queer, his voice high-pitched, somehow familiar, Benjamin thought, as he heard him saying that the fortunes of war belonged to the Indians tonight, and that King George was justly proud of his red children.

"The mighty Blackfish has triumphed, and he shall carry his prisoners back to the great and potent Henry Hamilton, right hand of the king, scourge of his enemies, and unmatched commander of British troops. The fearless Blackfish will be marked as a leader among leaders of the red children, who are the pride of the king in America. . . ."

Benjamin listened closely as the speaker presented Blackfish gifts of a medal, a hat, and even an officer's scarlet coat. He flattered Blackfish and all the Shawnees at length, and spoke of Lieutenant Governor Hamilton as a prince who

ruled half the continent, a warlike potentate who would call
down the wrath of empire upon rebels who threatened Indian
country. At every turn of flowery phrase the Indians called
out, "Ho! Ho!" in approval and became ever more excited.
Eventually, Benjamin noticed, the man's praise shifted from
Blackfish to Wabete. He said that one misfortune in war
would never diminish the chieftain's reputation. Wabete
puffed up at these words, and his men joined loudly in the
chorus of approval.

". . . and to prove the high regard in which Wabete is
held, it does me great honor to offer him, in the name of
the king, this symbol of the love that his father across the
great water holds for him—"

To the cheering of the Shawnee, the man held out a
second scarlet tunic, replete with gold buttons and braid.
Wabete's eyes lit, and his followers stamped their feet,
shouting with glee.

At that instant the speaker theatrically tossed aside his
white blanket-coat and stood in the glare of firelight.

He was a Redcoat, a captain in the British army—and
he was staring right at Benjamin.

Evidently the Indians had known all along who was addressing them, but the Kentuckians were surprised, as they
grumbled and cursed under their breath.

Even the easygoing Boone became cold with hatred.
"This scum's a prime hand at leadin' war parties against
the settlements," he murmured to Benjamin, who was gaping at the officer. "He's more Injun than an Injun when it
comes to torture and liftin' hair. Damn, but I'd like to put
that lobsterback under!"

"I know him," Benjamin said dully, to Boone's surprise.
"Mark Davies. He once sent Senecas to kill my mother."
Benjamin explained that when his family had still lived at
Detroit, near the beginning of the war, they had continually
had trouble with Davies, ever since Owen Sutherland had
humiliated him in front of his men.

Boone frowned and glanced from Benjamin to Davies;
the officer's arms were wide as he lavished praise on Wabete, who had put on his new red coat. Boone remarked

that it was unusual for an officer to praise an Indian who had just been defeated.

"...and further to honor Wabete," Davies went on, "I propose that he need not make the tedious journey to Detroit to turn in his lone, young captive for a reward!" As if on cue, half a dozen Indians in Davies's service pushed through the crowd, each one laden with gifts. First came three beautiful rifles, then bags of lead ball, two small kegs of black powder, jars of vermilion paint, several sacks of beads, hand mirrors, hats, and several thick blankets, all laid at the astonished chief's feet.

Davies went on: "The band of Wabete may now accept the king's thanks and return to their lodges accompanying their chief in his scarlet coat, so that their people might rejoice in how the king, their father, has seen fit to honor them...."

Boone leaned over to Benjamin and said softly, "Davies means to buy you, lad."

Davies was peering across the campfire straight at Benjamin, with a thin, wicked smile that clearly revealed his intentions. Wabete, nodding, looked almost giddy as he inspected the goods at his feet, while his warriors called out that this indeed was a fine reward. Though they had lost a battle, this British officer had confirmed their worth; now they would be able to go home with fine presents, which would soothe the weeping eyes of the squaws and children and make the deaths of so many good warriors easier to accept.

But Wabete's swelling pride and the laughter of the Indians ended abruptly as a voice rang out in Shawnee, high-pitched but clear and loud.

"Beware, Wabete—this red-haired dog would cheat you!"

To everyone's disbelief, Benjamin Sutherland was on his feet, striding defiantly toward the fire. Several angry warriors rose to block his path, and one cuffed him sharply for his insolence. Wabete appeared startled, as did they all, but he smiled when Benjamin recovered from the blow and began to speak again.

This time, however, the Indians immediately shouted him

down; he was a mere pup, with no right to address a council of warriors. They shoved him roughly backward into the gloom, though he struggled to speak over the tumult of voices. Again he was struck hard, and he fell back, half-stunned, beside Boone.

Davies had recovered from his astonishment and was again smiling. As soon as old Wabete signaled to his followers to pick up the presents, Benjamin would belong to him, to do with as he chose.

Then the clamor of furious Indian voices was cut through by another shout, this time deep and powerful, addressed to Blackfish himself. The noise abruptly died down, and everyone stared at Daniel Boone. Many of these Indians knew Boone personally, and all respected him as they did few other whites; if he dared risk his life to speak out of turn at council, then it must be to say something extremely important.

Blackfish was grave behind his painted mask of white and scarlet, like a fiendish judge with black, glittering eyes.

"Boone," he rasped, "you have no right to speak here; therefore sit down with your people, or Blackfish will allow my brother Wabete to decide your punishment for defiling a ceremony in his honor!"

Boone did not back down. "It is for the great Wabete's sake that I rise to speak, Blackfish, full knowing the peril if my words fall on deaf ears." After a properly formal pause, in which Blackfish's silence meant Boone could go on, the Kentuckian said, "Let not these gifts cloud your eyes, O noble Wabete, and the false words of this British snake stop up your ears!"

Davies's hand went to a pistol at his belt, Benjamin noticed, but stopped there. Boone had been given the floor, and there was nothing the officer could do about it.

Boone loudly declared, "This British snake means to cheat Wabete and his men, steal their glory, and cheapen their success by exchanging a few paltry tokens for . . ." He paused, motioning with his head toward Benjamin, who was kneeling, blood trickling from his mouth where he had been struck. The Indians leaned forward, anxiously awaiting

Boone's words. Not a sound could be heard. In an orator's voice, Boone cried out, "For the son of the mighty Donoway!"

The Indians began to murmur among themselves, obviously moved to hear that Wabete had battled none other than Donoway, a man as famous as Boone among the northwestern Indians. Davies glared at Boone; he looked as if he would explode at any second.

Boone declared, "This British snake meant to slip away to Detroit with Wabete's prisoner and claim the glory for himself! But it is the rightful honor of Wabete and his men to take the son of Donoway to Detroit and present him to Henry Hamilton, for a reward that will make them all very rich Shawnees."

Boone glanced at Davies and added in a sarcastic, sneering voice, "Even this officer, a man said to be honorable, knows what great gifts will be offered to Wabete in exchange for the son of Donoway—far more than—"

"Enough!" Davies shrieked hysterically, barely composing himself enough to ask Blackfish leave to reply. He said hurriedly, "I shall offer whatever Wabete desires in exchange for the captive! But this Boone lies to say the identity of the prisoner was known to me!"

Davies immediately called for the last two kegs of powder, another rifle, a crate of steel-headed tomahawks, six British military pistols, and more blankets—apparently all the goods he had left with him to reward Indian victories. This was an amazing trove of wealth to offer for one prisoner.

Boone's face fell as the additional valuables were laid at Wabete's feet. The old chieftain's men crowded closer to gawk, nearly slavering with anticipation. As Benjamin struggled back to his feet, he noticed that even Amaghwah seemed to have lost his lust for blood; no doubt he would prefer a new rifle to a boy's scalp. Already he and the others were pointing to what would be theirs after the deal was closed.

Boone glanced almost apologetically at Benjamin, who did not have to be told what the frontiersman feared—that no Indian could refuse such bounty. Davies was smirking again, his pale eyes bright as he watched the excitement rise among the Shawnees.

Wabete, his own expression indecipherable, turned his gaze back to Benjamin. He spoke slowly, almost kindly. "What do you say about this, Peshawa? Do you think it will go worse for you with this soldier than it would if I keep you to run the gauntlet, or to meet whatever fate awaits you in my village?"

There was silence. Blackfish's men seemed spellbound by the drama; Wabete's men looked annoyed, impatient.

Davies stood haughtily, arms folded, head high, like a stuffed figure on a stage, reminding Benjamin of a farce he had seen performed by rebel soldiers at Montreal. The caricatured Redcoat officer in that play had looked remarkably like Davies. A smile crept over Benjamin's face, and he looked away from the posturing Davies and directly at Wabete.

"It is not my decision, Wabete. But if I had to choose the manner of dying, I would prefer it to be at the hands of the Shawnee warriors rather than at the hands of a British capon like this one!"

After a few seconds of stunned silence, Davies moved forward threateningly, shaking a fist and shouting in English that Benjamin would suffer for this. However, when Wabete languidly held up a hand for quiet, Davies halted in his tracks and held his tongue, though he glared at Benjamin.

Benjamin was no longer so full of confidence, for the comic image of Davies had been quickly replaced by this dangerous, vengeful creature who wanted his head. Still he forced himself to show no fear, knowing how Indians respected bravado and enjoyed a brassy insult from a prisoner facing death.

Wabete spoke slowly. "Few warriors have the chance to choose their moment to die, Wildcat. My own son, my pride, died of the lung fever before he set foot on the warpath." For an instant, Wabete's eyes lost their clarity, but only for an instant. Head raised, he turned to address his own men.

"We know now, brothers, who it was we fought, and

who was following us so closely. And though we have been honored tonight, I believe there is an even greater prize, an even greater honor to be won in the moons to come."

The Shawnees from Wabete's village seemed unsure what he meant, until he added, "One day, the famous Donoway himself will seek out his son—will seek him in our lodges— and then we will take him, and we will avenge our defeat. . . ." His voice rose as he cried, "We will have our vengeance! We will glory in our triumph, and honor will cover the graves of our fallen warriors!"

His Indians were beginning to understand, and so was Davies, who was obviously dismayed.

Wabete looked at each of his men individually, then asked, "Will you trust me to lead you to victory and to wealth, as ever I have in the past? Will you refuse the gifts that lie before us, in the belief that we can win much more if we keep the captive and bait our trap for the great Donoway himself?"

Though more than one of the warriors cast longing glances at Davies's gifts, most of them heartily agreed, shaking tomahawks and crying out that they would abide by his decision. Amaghwah, however, had already moved off into the shadows, away from the others. He was staring at Captain Mark Davies.

Wabete, too, looked at Davies, whose pale face was mottled from frustration.

"Thank you, Captain, for your generous offer," Wabete said, and then, though still speaking to Davies, he turned toward Benjamin. "I will keep the prisoner and take him to meet our uncle, Henry Hamilton. Then we will see what he is really worth, and what he is worth along with Donoway. Wabete is finished."

Wabete sat down beside Blackfish, and all the Indians were quiet, thinking about what they had seen and the fortune that had been turned down. Benjamin took a slow breath and sat shakily beside Boone and the other prisoners, all of whom were gazing at him.

Then, with a snarl like a wild animal, Mark Davies spun on his heel and left the firelight, darkness swallowing him. Behind him followed the slinking shadow of Amaghwah.

chapter 9

AN OLD ENEMY

James Morely was a happy, exhausted, proud young man, and with good reason. Though he had been in Albany less than two months, he had found his way through the ins and outs of the network of regional merchants, shippers, and brokers, then had gone right past all of them, directly to the source of the one commodity the Continental army needed most: gunpowder.

Before the revolution had broken out in 1775, Parliament, foreseeing trouble, had strictly controlled the importation of gunpowder into the colonies and forbidden the manufacture of black powder here, except that sold directly to the army or navy. Most colonial powder works had quickly gone out of business, though a few had gone underground, producing small, secret stockpiles for men who were preparing to rise when the rebellion's time came.

When war did break out, smuggled arms and captured gunpowder had gone a long way to keep the army of Congress in the field, and individuals had donated their personal powder to the cause. Still there was not enough. After Lexington and Concord, many small powder works had sprung up, especially in the north, and the precious supplies they produced were purchased by rebel headquarters.

As the war dragged on, however, the growing worthlessness of Congress's currency had all but shut down most of these mills. The Continental dollars with which mill owners were paid could not buy adequate equipment and raw materials or pay wages. Even the most ardent rebels had become reluctant to accept continentals in lieu of hard cash, unless a coat of tar or a spell in jail were the alternatives. The new states for the most part were even too poor to offer raw goods as payment to powder manufacturers.

This was the case, James had found, in upper New York, where small powder mills had been established wherever saltpeter could be dug and sulfur and charcoal were readily available. Most of these mills had not been adequately repaid for supplying last year's campaign against Burgoyne; yet with General Washington now besieging New York Town, and with the southern and middle colonies expected to come under British attack this year, more of their powder was desperately needed. It was said that promissory notes from wealthy rebels were on their way, but James had seen his opportunity.

While the weather was still cold and snowy, he had ridden out alone to the mills, contracting for powder, paying in advance, and paying well, in sterling. Moving swiftly from mill to mill, he had worn out several horses but had not neglected a detail, even arranging cartage well ahead of time to fetch the powder when it was ready.

Now it was early spring, and while most of the wharves on the Hudson River were idle, the Frontier Company docks and warehouses were bustling, swarming with laborers loading the gunpowder recently delivered from twenty small mills. James stood on the wharf near the company's vessel, a two-masted sloop, which was already low in the water with the cargo destined for General Washington.

A large portion of the five thousand pounds sterling entrusted to James had gone into buying this cargo, but seldom had Frontier Company money been better spent. James knew that those promissory notes from rich rebels, when signed over to him by Washington, would be as good as gold to the Frontier Company, although they would have been useless to the mill owners, who needed cash on the barrelhead. Contentedly, he watched the kegs being loaded, each marked "Grease." It was best to keep the nature of this precious shipment a secret, although it had been necessary to warn the workmen to handle the kegs carefully and not to smoke.

James leaned over a large crate, writing with a quill in a ledger spread before him, noting precisely how many kegs, and of what weight, were being delivered. Behind him Albany's red brick houses spread up a long hill and along the waterfront on either side. Rebel soldiers were drilling in the street nearby, children watching or else standing near the wharves, observing the Frontier Company ship being loaded. It was a bright, sunny day, the world pleasantly mirroring James's own high spirits. He could not help thinking that Owen Sutherland would be proud of what he had done—particularly since it was Bradford Cullen's agents who usually bought up whatever gunpowder could be manufactured at these small mills. James had beaten Cullen at his own game, accumulating several tons of gunpowder, although it had cost him more than Cullen would have paid. And he was ready to ship it south before Cullen had even sent out his buyers to place orders!

James was mentally toting up the profits, which would be considerable, when a burly, blond-haired man of middle age and ruddy complexion came up behind and thumped him soundly on the shoulders. James was sent staggering, almost spilling his ink, and he knew right away he had been greeted by Peter Defries.

"James my man, you've outdone us all with this neat bit of horse-trading!" Defries was much bigger than James, with a thick neck, and arms and chest like a bear. James turned and smiled; Defries, it seemed, was always in good spirits, except when he was hungry or annoyed at whichever government was in charge of his life at the time. The burly Albany Dutchman was rubbing his thick hands together and chuckling as he looked the ship over.

Suddenly a workman pushing a handcart became careless and lost control; the cart swerved, and a keg fell on its side and began to roll off to the ground. With a loud "Ho!" Defries lunged and nimbly caught the keg with one hand—though it weighed nearly eighty pounds—and gently righted it on the cart again.

He shook his head at the carter. "Won't do to bust a barrel and spill grease all over, now, will it, friend?"

The fellow was bored and tired, and he had a slow-witted look about him—a look that changed to wide-eyed alarm as Defries clamped a huge arm around his shoulder and squeezed. "Spill even an ooze, friend, and it'll like to make you slip, right over that there dock, into that there water ...I guarantees it!"

Defries winked at James as the carter trundled his load away and ever so cautiously pushed it up the gangway onto the sloop. Defries was well known in Albany as a trader as well as a brawler, but to men such as this dock-worker, it was the brawler who earned respect.

James smiled, glad for Defries's company and his amazing ability to acquire and organize the men, supplies, and ship needed to get the gunpowder down to Washington's army. James had not even objected greatly when Defries had insisted on shaving the sale price to make it easier for Washington to afford the powder. Defries would no doubt spend his own last farthing on the rebel war effort, even if it meant the Frontier Company's demise. James did not hold to that philosophy, but getting anything done in Albany required the cooperation of Defries and his wife, Mary, who was also involved in company matters here, her late father having been a trader.

James watched as the last kegs were taken up the gangplank, and he made a note and closed his ledger. "Enough powder to take New York, and some left over to hold the city when the British come to take it back."

Defries snorted. "They won't try to take it back! They ain't got the stomach left for this war. Only reason they're keeping on looking like our enemy is they're prouder than they're smart. They're beat, and it's only time now afore they got to admit it."

James was not so sure. "At any rate, we've got what Washington needs, and there's no harm in making a little something for ourselves at the same time we help him out."

Defries frowned, his heavy brows knitting. "Wisht you'd sound a bit more like you're on our side, James. If'n you ain't a rebel, at least don't make it sound like we're buzzards picking the bones after a battle."

James blushed slightly. "I suppose I do sound a bit like Bradford Cullen."

Under his breath, Defries grumbled, somewhat sulkily, "That you do, son . . . and it ain't how a Frontier Company man should sound—not by a long shot!"

Then Defries recovered, shrugged his shoulders, and said, "Well, here comes the woman and the girl!" He waved enthusiastically as Mary and his daughter, Jeanette Marie, stepped down from a carriage driven by a black man in fine livery.

James turned to watch them approach as Emmy, the Defrieses' elderly black servant, hurried to keep up. Peter's wife was in her late thirties, blond like him, and stunningly beautiful in a fashionable blue riding cloak and matching frock and petticoats. Jeanette, however, was the one who caught James's eye. She was almost fifteen, dark and petite, and radiantly dressed in the finest silks and satins. Her blue eyes flashed as she threw herself into her father's arms and then welcomed James with a demure curtsy. Jeanette had been away for much of the winter, visiting relations and receiving a ladylike schooling in Bennington, and James had not seen her for several years.

"Jeanette—you've grown up!" he declared, smiling, and temporarily at a loss. "Why, you're old enough that I best take care how I compliment your beauty."

Jeanette smiled, and without the slightest bashfulness said, "Compliment me all you want, James, for everyone else thinks I'm still a child. Do I look like a child to you?"

Before James could reply, Mary took her husband's arm, saying, "Have a care, James, for she's a flirt, and those who've tried to catch her have grasped only air!"

Peter rumbled, "Hot air, at that." Jeanette playfully hit him with her fan, and Peter chuckled. "When you're really grown up you won't have to tell us you're grown up! And you'll stop flapping those saucy eyes of yours like that, or you'll be sorry!" He turned to the servant. "Emmy, can't you teach this brat the difference between flirting and downright enticement?"

The chubby Emmy frowned, saying, "She well knows which is which, sir, and chooses the one that suits her best!"

Jeanette flushed, absently toying with a tulip pinned at her breast. James, who was still staring at her, grinned as he said, "Most of the time I can't tell the difference myself. I probably wouldn't notice."

Emmy went on about how Jeanette had been spoiled at school, and for a few more minutes they all enjoyed the banter, everyone in good cheer at the approach of a new era of prosperity for the Frontier Company. James was invited to dinner the next evening, and when he accepted, Jeanette seemed to light up with excitement. She was indeed lovely and very much a young woman; by comparison, James thought, Susannah was but a child.

Just then a man came up and, touching his hat and presenting himself as a "messenger from a gentleman," handed James a sealed letter. Peter, respecting James's privacy, led his family toward the loaded ship, whose hatches were being closed. The workmen were filing down the gangway, sweat and grime on their faces and clothes. Defries yelled congratulations to them for loading the ship in remarkable time.

While the messenger waited, James broke the seal and read the letter. Immediately his face darkened and he glanced toward Defries, who was still chatting with some of the laborers. James curtly told the messenger he would send an answer later that day, then went to the Defrieses and excused himself, saying he had an appointment.

Hurrying off along the docks, James clutched at the letter, all other concerns gone from his mind. He was startled and shocked by what he had read, and he needed to think.

After a few minutes he stopped at the end of a deserted wharf and opened the letter again.

I would be greatly obliged if you would come alone to my house this evening at eight to discuss a matter of urgency. Certainly the unexpectedness of this invitation will cause you to hesitate, but be assured that my intentions are forthright and that the business at hand is of profound concern to the interests of both your company and mine. I trust you will be farsighted enough to disregard whatever unfortunate misunderstandings may have gone before.

> Until we meet, I remain,
> your humble servant,
> Bradford Cullen.

That evening, with the distinct sense of entering the lair of a dangerous beast, James went briskly up the steps of an elegant Dutch-style town house. It was an imposingly large imitation of earlier, more modest dwelling, with a steep tile roof and the gable end of the house facing the street. The mansion overlooked the Hudson River, which lay quiet and dark, save for glowing lanterns on anchored ships. With some effort James fought the uneasiness that kept warning him to turn back. He repeatedly told himself that Owen Sutherland had confronted and beaten Cullen when it was necessary, and if he, too, were to make himself a formidable leader of commerce, he must do the same. This was as good a time as any, he decided, but still he was nervous.

The door was opened by a tall, reedy Frenchman with a hooked nose and an exaggerated air of haughtiness. In contrast to the servant's fine gray satin coat, matching breeches, and shimmering silk stockings, James wore but a plain dark-blue coat and smallclothes, and he immediately felt out of place. The servant nodded him into a high, chandelier-lit vestibule with a shining balustrade, winding stairs, and costly rugs and side tables. James thought that for a Boston-born Puritan, Bradford Cullen had developed rather worldly tastes—indeed, the taste of a prince who enjoyed displaying his wealth.

The butler showed him into a plush sitting room, where a fire crackled brightly, then left to announce him. An instant later James's attention was caught by the swish of a woman's gown. He turned to bow to a short, dark-haired woman, probably almost forty, who stood framed in the double doors as if posing for a painting. James knew this was Linda Cullen, Bradford's daughter. The dozen years since she had last been in Detroit had not improved her thick, homely features.

Linda smiled and wobbled a red fan before her face, which had too much makeup; James was unsure whether she was winking at him or had something in her eye.

"Mistress Cullen," he said, smiling cordially. "I've come at your father's request. Please present my compliments to your mother."

Linda advanced a few paces, then curtsied so low that

her ample bosom was clearly displayed. For a bulky woman, she seemed agile enough to curtsy right to the floor. James thought she could not have done greater homage to King George himself.

She offered him her hand, and he helped her rise, at the last moment realizing she wanted him to kiss it. Though startled by such an indulgence on her part, James gamely brought her hand to his lips, tried to smile politely, then gestured for her to sit on the settee. She beckoned for him to join her, but still did not say a word.

James cleared his throat and sat down, close enough to feel the breeze from her fluttering fan.

"How are your mother and father?" he asked. Helen Cullen was an ancient prune of a shrew, one of the few people who could bend Bradford to her will.

Linda replied in a breathy voice, "Mother is ill; Father, as ever, is strong in his heart, but suffers from gout and from the years. He's well into his eighties, you know."

They spoke of Albany and the weather for a few moments, then Linda gave a coy smile and, hiding behind her fan, said, "I'm so glad Father finally invited you, Mr. Morely. It's been so long since we've seen you, and you certainly have grown into a handsome man."

James smiled, fingering his collar.

Linda sighed dramatically and pouted. "There are so few real gentlemen left in Albany. Most of them have fled to Montreal or New York because of the rebellion." Abruptly she glanced at James. "Of course there are fine gentlemen amongst the Congress party as well, but . . . you must realize that all of us have lost the companionship of many dear friends and acquaintances to the loyalist side."

James nodded. He did not have to be reminded that most of the wealthiest families had remained loyal to the king and had either fled to loyalist territory or been forced out and dispossessed by the rebels. Owen Sutherland had said that Cullen himself was ready to turn his own coat and join the loyalists, but that the wily old merchant would bide his time until it was clear who was winning the war. Cullen, James knew, had long been obsessed with gaining control of the northwest fur trade and making the wilderness his

personal empire. If he chose the losing side, that burning
ambition was as good as dead.

Again James smiled weakly at Linda. She and her husband—if she ever married—would inherit the Cullen
empire, and that thought, for some reason, made him
uncomfortable. He knew that Linda, hard as she and her
mother had tried, had so far failed to land a proper husband,
Tory or rebel. No doubt Cullen wanted someone of his own
character, someone who could manage a financial empire
as brilliantly and harshly as the old man himself. That someone must be found before much longer, James guessed, for
even the indomitable Cullen would not live forever.

James realized that Linda was talking away, asking question after question with hardly a pause. Did he prefer Montreal to New York? What was his taste in wine, women's
fashions, men's wigs? Did he prefer English furniture or
French? Was he planning to marry anyone in particular very
soon?

James suppressed a cough. "Actually, Mistress Cullen,
I'm far too busy with company affairs to consider marriage."
Even as he spoke, however, he thought of Susannah Sutherland and wished he could be with her now. True, she was
far too young, and he was not certain he loved her; but it
felt good to think about her. A letter from her had come
that very evening, just before he had set out for Cullen's
house. Now he wished he had read it first.

Linda snapped her fan closed and gave a throaty sound
of approval. "Oh, Mr. Morely, I admire you for that, and
so will Father! He respects a man who puts work before
home life. After all, an understanding woman will respect
her husband's needs, putting herself second in all such
things...." She flipped the fan open and covered her
mouth, her eyes glittering. "Save for affairs of the heart, of
course."

James did not know what to say.

"Don't you agree, Mr. Morely?"

James tapped his fingers on one knee and again cleared
his throat. He was vastly relieved when the French servant
appeared at the door and announced that Mr. Cullen was
waiting. James rose, excused himself, paused—came back

to kiss Linda's offered hand—then followed the Frenchman down a long hallway to the back of the house. There he was ushered into a small, dimly lit office, with its own fireplace at one side and two whale-oil lamps glowing on a massive, polished table.

James's eyes were unused to the dark, and at first he could not see Cullen, whose gravelly voice came from the gloom somewhere behind the table: "Ah, there you are, young man! Come in, sit down. Forgive me for not rising, but I'm not young like you." Cullen sounded far older than James remembered, and he wheezed more than ever, with a rasping weakness that spoke of extreme old age.

James advanced, and the door was closed behind him. Then he saw Cullen, who leaned forward, his face suddenly illuminated by the shaded table-lamps. His first impression was of an overlarge, bewigged head, with rolls of white curls falling straight to the chest, as if Cullen had no shoulders at all. The little eyes, set in a fleshy, pallid face, glinted in the yellow light. Below them was a genial, disarming smile.

James bowed and took a seat in front of the table.

Cullen chuckled, "So this is James Morely, son of my old compatriot Garth, eh? My, my, but you have grown, just as my dear child Linda and my wife said you had! Yes, indeed!"

James listened, surprised, as Cullen said Linda had spoken much about him, having seen him several times at various functions in the city. Cullen said Linda had expressed amazement that James so closely resembled his late father.

James was taken aback. "I never realized you knew my father."

"Knew your father? Why, young man, your father and I did business long before the last French war! Hah! Yes, Garth and I made a few pennies in military procurement, and he was always one as could teach me a few things about how to keep the troops buying what they needed from us, and only us!"

Cullen released slow, rolling laughter, and launched into a long tale of happier, innocent days, before civil war, when the enemy was a French foreigner and not former friends or neighbors. James was pleased to hear his father so well spoken of. Garth Morely had, with Owen Sutherland, been a founder of the Frontier Company, but a couple of years later, in 1765, had been killed by white renegades while leading a freight convoy into the Illinois. Owen Sutherland had found the body.

Cullen rumbled, "Garth was a master trader, mark my words, he was. And from what I've heard about you out at Detroit, up in Montreal, and now here in Albany, you're a fellow as will walk his footsteps and take commercial matters even further!"

Cullen said it was a pity that Garth had never become the effective leader of the company instead of Owen Sutherland, who was a stubborn, hard man to deal with and had unnecessarily caused much of the conflict with Cullen and Company. James was self-conscious at these compliments, for he knew well that Cullen was ruthless and greedy and had caused the trouble himself. Nevertheless, James inwardly agreed that Garth Morely was every bit as good a trader as Owen Sutherland and would probably have been a more hard-headed businessman in these perilous times.

James heard Cullen out, then replied. "Sir, leaving aside the blame for our differences, it's obvious that as a Frontier Company representative, I am quite out of order to be here in private. Our meeting, I must tell you, will be reported to my partners, so you are forewarned. I have honored your request that I come alone, however, so would you please proceed to the matter at hand."

"Honored, indeed." Cullen nodded slowly, his glittering eyes half closing as a frown crossed his face. "Fair enough, Mr. Morely." Cullen leaned closer, and James thought he felt a chill draft, although no doors had been opened and the lamps continued to burn steadily. "You are, as I had hoped, Mr. Morely, truly a man of your father's stamp. Yes, even to your ability to supply an army with——" He gave a snort of mirth. "——with what it needs most. Grease!"

Cullen smiled in such a warm and engaging way, totally unexpectedly, that James could not help joining in. Chuck-

ling, Cullen offered a glass of sherry, and James accepted.
The old man languidly poured, and James saw that his fat,
wrinkled hand was perfectly steady.

"As you can imagine, Mr. Morely, your arrival and
movements in the city have not gone unobserved—and I
mean by more than my dear wife and daughter! To put it
frankly, your every move has been followed, and the five
thousand sterling you brought with you has thus far been
used wisely—may I say, brilliantly."

He handed over a glass and chuckled again. James was
shaken that Cullen actually knew to the pound how much
he had carried. The rumors about Cullen's vast spy network
must indeed be true.

Cullen went on, "You've given poor, plodding Peter
Defries a lesson or two, by Jove, although the best teacher
in the empire might be wasted on such a droll fellow...."

The conversation—or rather lecture—that followed
moved alternately from criticism of Owen Sutherland to
praise of James and Garth Morely, mingled with gentler
remarks about the good, harmless qualities of the likes of
Peter Defries and other company members. Cullen knew
them all, but apparently not that several of the families were
now living in the Wyoming Valley.

After a few more sherries, James was not sure whether
Cullen hated or merely tolerated his competitors. It was
certain, James thought, that Cullen firmly held the upper
hand in Albany, which was the hub of the region's trade,
dealing directly with most of the northeast and much of the
rebel-held interior.

Finally James interrupted. "Please, Mr. Cullen, come to
the point. Why have you asked me here?"

There followed a brief silence, marked only by Cullen's
slow, wheezing breaths.

At last, Cullen said, "To look you over; to see what sort
of fellow could have outdone me with that gunpowder deal."

James stiffened.

Cullen spoke in a tone of resignation that seemed touched
with admiration: "Yes, young man, you outfoxed the sly
old fox. I just wanted to see you for myself...." He leaned

back in his chair. "And as you may know, I dote upon my daughter, and it was something of a favor to her to bring you here. She wanted to meet you in person. Will you forgive an old man his indulgence with an unmarried daughter who is fast growing past her prime?"

James did not know whether to be angry or to laugh at Cullen's ploys. He absolutely did not trust the man, and no amount of flattery would change that. At the same time, he sensed that Cullen was telling the truth insofar as wanting to give Linda a chance at some small pleasure. More than that, though; perhaps he really did admire what James had done with the gunpowder.

Rising, James said, "Whatever your motives, sir, I'll now excuse myself, and hope that in future our rivalry will be dignified with honor and mutual esteem."

Cullen lowered his head slightly, eyes closing. "As long as Owen Sutherland is not stirring up my blood, and you, Garth . . . I mean James, are the gentleman who competes with me, I'm certain there will be no acrimony."

He rang a small bell, and the French servant opened the door. As James bowed, Cullen said there was another reason for inviting him, one having to do with the "similar interests" mentioned in the letter that afternoon.

"It might be," Cullen said, staring intently at James, "that your presence in this city will be a blessing, a way for both of us to begin anew, a chance to mend our differences once and for all."

James did not know what to make of this. Cullen went on smoothly: "An opportunity to cooperate in commercial affairs that might very well enrich us both. Why sap each other's energy and finances for the sake of old, forgotten quarrels, eh?" He sighed most convincingly. "Ah, well, perhaps that could better be discussed at some other time. Until then, good evening, young man. I envy your brains and vigor. You remind me of myself, when I was young."

A few days later, James and Jeanette were strolling arm in arm beside the Hudson, enjoying a warm and lovely spring morning. Peter and Mary were seated on a blanket a little upstream, and in the bluish distance Albany made a colorful backdrop, with its trees in bud and ships' white sails visible in the harbor.

James was content with the way things had developed, including how he had impressed even old Bradford Cullen. Defries, when James had told him about the meeting, had warned against overconfidence, but James was not concerned. Already he was thinking that he might do equally well by arranging to drive herds of cattle into the no-man's-land near New York, straight through to Washington's lines.

He mentioned this idea to Jeanette, but she sighed and waved such thoughts away with her pretty, slim hand. As usual, she wore a fresh flower at her bosom, and it looked charming there.

"Politics, business, war, commerce!" she complained, brushing back her long raven hair and closing her eyes to face the sun and wind. "It's spring, in case you hadn't noticed!"

Having left her bonnet with her parents, she looked like springtime itself as the breeze pressed against her soft white clothing, outlining her shapely figure. James thought she was beautiful, intelligent, and witty. Thanks to Mary's persistence, Jeanette had received the best education possible for a woman, even in a city that had a goodly share of wealthy families. Jeanette was an only child, and James wondered briefly whether there was any truth in the rumor that she actually was the daughter of the Delaware war chief who had abducted Mary during Pontiac's uprising. Of course, James thought with annoyance, such rumors were cruel and probably nonsense. Even to think of such lies about Jeanette in her presence made him feel ashamed.

Just then, Jeanette turned abruptly and said, "May I ask you a personal question, James? Tell me, why do you always carry that silken handkerchief just inside your blouse?" Jeanette gestured at the tip of one corner, which protruded between two buttons of his waistcoat.

James glanced at the handkerchief, which was the one Susannah had given him. He smiled as he drew it out. "It reminds me of home."

Jeanette looked perplexed and stared at him strangely. "That's funny—it reminds me of Susie Sutherland."

As James blushed in surprise, Jeanette broke into laughter, her bright eyes teasing. She said, "I gave it to Susie as a gift the last time I saw her. I thought it was precious to her, not something she would give away to just anyone."

James smiled. "She does regard it as precious, Jeanette. You see, Susannah believes she's in love with me." He carefully unfolded the handkerchief. "She gave me this sprig of mistletoe as a keepsake—though she's a bit too young for me to use it."

"Susannah, you say? Not Susie?" Jeanette turned away and leaned against a willow tree that hung over the placid river. "Little Susie's very pretty, and she'll be even prettier when she's old enough for you to kiss. You ought to keep that mistletoe safe; perhaps one day you'll be first in a long line to give Susie a kiss."

"She's not so little, Jeanette, and she's old enough to call herself Susannah." He grinned, raising the sprig, threatening to hold it over her head. "Lucky for you it's not Yuletide, or I might—"

Suddenly there came a shout from Peter, who was standing beside a man James knew was an employee at the company office. Peter beckoned with his hat and began running down the shore. Startled, James hurried to meet him, Jeanette following.

"Damn them damnable Britishers!" Peter was shouting, and James saw that Mary was still seated, face in her hands, apparently weeping. "Damn them all!"

Defries was red in the face, big fists clenched. Jeanette and James called out to ask what was wrong.

"Gunpowder's lost!" James stopped in his tracks. Peter raised his fists and kicked a tree, shouting, "Ship got caught by loyalists! Spies done for us! Everything's lost!"

James closed his eyes, trying to catch his breath. Was this a dream? A nightmare? Jeanette gasped and turned away.

Defries approached and declared, "Ship was boarded at night . . . the boys fought back and woulda held it, but it got blew up, near everybody killed! Near everybody!"

James staggered; he felt physically sick, as though he would vomit. He broke into a sweat, and he was trembling, feeling the horror of a fainting spell coming on. He must not pass out! Not now! Jeanette was against him, shaking, and he struggled against his body's distress. Letting his head back for air, he whispered to himself, "Oh, no, no, no . . . I lost it all! I've failed! It's my fault, all of it!" He felt dizzy, but forced himself to breathe deeply. Gradually his head began to clear.

Jeanette gripped his arm. Her father had turned back, head down, and was striding angrily toward the messenger and Mary. Jeanette whispered:

"It's not your fault, James! It's not! You did all you could! We all did!"

James was sure now he would not faint, but that deep, sick feeling persisted, and he wanted to be alone. He wiped away sweat, and felt the mistletoe in the handkerchief scrape against his forehead. He looked at the handkerchief and wondered what Susannah would think of his failure. What would Owen Sutherland think of him now? James was crushed. He had squandered well over three thousand pounds sterling on a disastrous enterprise. What did he do wrong? How could he ever recover from such a staggering loss?

James walked back slowly with Jeanette to Peter and Mary, his mind awhirl. His head was throbbing as if it would burst. Jeanette was saying soothing, kind words, but he did not hear. In his mind was Owen Sutherland, and also Susannah. He wanted to push them both from his thoughts, but could not. He wanted to think of nothing but the future, but it seemed there was no future. Instead there were only Owen and Susannah Sutherland—one accusing, one blindly forgiving. He had never felt so thoroughly defeated.

James soon learned there was no point trying to collect more gunpowder. Bradford Cullen had already done so, his own powder vessel having left Albany the night of the Frontier Company ship's sinking.

There seemed little doubt that Cullen was behind the loss

of the shipment. James was sure the rogue had invited him to his house simply to gloat, to enjoy his own private joke. He promised himself to make Cullen regret having played him for a fool.

Already he had another scheme to earn the Frontier Company large profits, and he threw himself into it with feverish intensity. One way or the other, he vowed, he would redeem himself, and the next time he gambled, he would win.

PART TWO

Indian Country

chapter 10

CHILLICOTHE

Full spring came suddenly upon Indian country north of the Ohio, with a sun warm and glorious and a soft breeze coaxing the world back to life, giving it strength again.

Willows sent out slender green shoots, and other trees followed with bud and leaf, darkening the woods in shadow and sheltering forest trails from sight. In cold streams trout jumped at darting flies, and in swamps the beaver broke through fragile shore ice to waddle up on land and feast on new growth. Birds came back, flocking and whirling by the thousands, ducks and geese settling on ponds, pigeons blackening the sky before taking their rest in treetops, seeming more numerous than the leaves.

As he traveled, Owen Sutherland saw game enough at hand, though he ate little. Deer slowly fattened up, and sluggish bears wallowed out of hibernation, chunky and slow and possible to kill with the tomahawk if a man were bold and quick. The warm weather made Sutherland's long journey easier, but that much more dangerous, too, because Shawnee hunters were everywhere, glad to be roving the forest after a long winter lazing about their smoky lodges.

Sutherland had avoided them since crossing the Ohio, following little-used tracks that once had served now-abandoned villages. Often he had been forced to take the long way around Shawnee towns and hunting camps. Whenever he could, however, he traveled in a straight line, though always proceeding cautiously, covering no more than eight miles in a day. And there were so many days when Shawnee camps or villages seemed to spring out of the ground as he came around a hillside or found himself near a forest clearing. Then he had hidden, had stayed quiet and unmoving, sometimes for days on end, until the moment was right to push on past and head once more for Chillicothe, a name that meant "Home of the People."

Now it was April, and time seemed to have passed like water in a stream, hardly noticed until it was gone and the weather had changed from bitter cold to thaw to balmy. He had made his way far up the valley of the Scioto, starting almost at the river mouth, near the great promontory called Raven Rock, where always there was an Indian lookout watching for movement of whites down the Ohio. He had passed cautiously, unseen, and followed close beside the Scioto Trail, or Warrior's Path, as it was known, being the direct route to the Kentucky settlements, as well as the way south to the Creeks and Chickasaws, traditional enemies of the Shawnees.

The trail followed flats much of the way, past villages and lone lodges with their cornfield stubble and barking dogs, scalp poles tufted with hair blowing in the spring breeze, and elm-bark boats overturned on racks near the water. Here Sutherland became even more vigilant, usually moving at night or in the early hours and resting through full day. Often he was close enough to see women coming and going with their noisy children, toting water, skins, or firewood; and always there were those mangy Indian dogs, nasty and bristle-haired, all spine, ribs, and fang. More than once he had been sniffed out and had barely escaped a snarling, snapping pack close on his heels.

It had been a long journey, lonely and wearying, always fraught with the chance of discovery and death. As far as Sutherland knew, no other white man had come up the Scioto alone and lived to tell about it. This was the very heart of Shawnee country, with high, wooded hills, steep ravines thick with hemlock, and huge gray boulders and cliffs that seemed to frown down on him, watching. The Shawnees held this land sacred and jealously protected it from white eyes. Even such well-known woodsmen as Kenton and Boone had not ventured up this valley—though Girty might well have been through.

Four years ago, however, a white army had come near here for the first time. As Sutherland traversed meadows

and bottomland within a day of Chillicothe itself, he marked
distant hills and solitary knobs that he remembered looked
down on the flats called Pickaway Plains. Back in 1774 he
had been there on an Indian campaign with two or three
thousand Virginians, and the Shawnees had sued for peace.
That was when he had first met George Clark, who had
commanded a company of tough Virginia woodsmen, all
of them hungering to obliterate Chillicothe and keep on
marching from town to town until every Shawnee was driven
out or killed.

Sutherland had helped negotiate that peace, and the dis-
gruntled Virginians had gone home disappointed, though
more triumphant than any militia army had ever been against
the tribes. Looking at the blue-gray northern hills and the
configuration of ridges, Sutherland presumed the Indians
who had caught Benjamin had reached home already. Although the Shawnees had named several of their towns
Chillicothe, the one ahead was by far the largest, and doubt-
less the one Girty had meant.

He pushed on, through dense bracken and along dark
ravines, now avoiding any open country where he might be
spotted. Brambles tore at his clothes, but he paid them no
mind. Anyway, by now he was in rags, his deerskin outer
clothing mended and patched and mended again until parts
had fallen away. Using the frontiersman's common sewing
kit, he had repaired what he could, and once had been
desperate enough to slip up on sleeping Indians to steal
gear. The booty he had taken, however, had been as miserable and worn-out as his own. Now, save for his long
rifle and claymore, and the *voyageur*'s deerskin pouch that
had been carefully protected since Pitt, he looked like the
poorest poordevil—as whites named impoverished Indians—who ever walked the Scioto Trail.

Yet there was the unmistakable lean quality, the whip-
cord strength and quick grace that marked him as a fighting
man of the first rank. Sutherland had always been anyone's
match in hand-to-hand battle, and after the ordeal of the
last three months, he was as fit and hardened as ever.

And he was driven. The constant vision of his son's face
had forced him onward; the memory of his wife lying weak

but courageous in her bed urged him to move whenever he ached to rest. These things had kept him going at times when his secret journey seemed impossible, when he wanted to step from cover and parley with the first Indian who happened along.

But now he was almost to his goal.

That evening, Sutherland swam across the Scioto, floating his gear on a makeshift raft, and after cautiously advancing to within half a mile of town, he took shelter on high ground for the night.

The next morning, he crouched on a promontory over-looking the valley from the west. Below, the Scioto ran placidly through rolling bottomland, its water reflecting bright sky and a few knobby hills dotting the eastern plain. In the still morning air, hanging wisps of smoke marked the ninety or so dome-shaped bark lodges clustered among elms near the river; each lodge, Sutherland knew, housed several males of warrior age and their families. In the meadows along the river, herds of horses and cattle grazed peacefully in grass that was already ankle-high and a rich green. This was magnificent, lush country, Sutherland thought. It was no wonder the Shawnee were bent on holding it against white settlers.

From the deerskin pouch he had protected for so long he now removed a spyglass, and, remaining well concealed, settled down to watch the village, trying to get a glimpse of Benjamin. For hours his glass followed pony races involving forty or so young men and boys, for he thought that Benjamin might have been long enough with the Shawnees to be challenged to ride against them. But he did not see his son; nor did he see him later when he watched dozens of lads throwing tomahawks in a competition not a hundred yards from his hiding place. Perhaps Benjamin was too rebellious and had been tied up or forced to stay close to a lodge. But rebellious captives quickly made Indians sour, and often they were killed. Sutherland hoped Benjamin knew better than to annoy his captors too much. He must be alive! Sutherland forced away any other consideration.

Chillicothe was a busy, crowded place, but by midday

Sutherland felt as though he had seen everyone. In the afternoon he observed knots of youths dancing around a pole, as they did before going on the warpath. Squaws and girls were everywhere, many laboring with wooden hoes at the fertile, black earth. Others carried papooses, or sat outside lodges working skins into leather; the older women were forever bent over cooking fires. Mobs of children romped together with dogs on the outskirts of the town, played with balls or wrestled, exercised horses or went off to fish in the river.

Hour after hour Sutherland watched, seeing canoes come and go, hunters arriving with deer slung on poles between them, and riders approaching from the north. Several times he saw small parties marching single-file down the Warrior's Path toward the Ohio. It was frustrating to see so many folk perfectly well through the glass, yet not see Benjamin. Still, Sutherland was sure his son must be here—and there was one way to make certain.

As the sky darkened to twilight, he left the lookout and went to a secluded brook. Again he opened the deerskin pouch, laying out the rest of its contents on the ground.

At dawn the next morning, dogs at the northern edge of the Shawnee town went wild with barking, and people came out of their lodges to see what was the matter.

To their astonishment, out of the morning mist strode a tall, dark man in a yellow blouse, blue woolen breeches, and scarlet waist sash and stocking cap. His clothes were of the best quality but soiled, and the trousers were torn, telling of misfortune in his journey from the north country. There was a small gold crucifix around his neck, and for a weapon he carried only a walking stick, though there was a dirk tucked in his stocking.

He raised a hand in greeting to knots of Indians who had gathered to watch. This man was obviously a French *voyageur*. If he had been followed by assistants bearing trade goods, as was usually the case, the village would have burst into life, excited squaws jabbering at their men to fetch hides and beaerskins to buy something for themselves or the children. This *voyageur*, however, carried only a deerskin pouch that could not have held much in the way of trade goods. So why was he here?

Owen Sutherland kicked at snarling dogs, loudly cursing them in French. He joked with several little boys who sprang out and pretended to shoot toy bows at him. Then he politely greeted an elderly man seated outside a lodge. He addressed the man in a broken form of Algonquian, supplemented with French and pidgin English, which usually served for the purposes of trade.

After a few questions, he left a small gift of tobacco and followed the direction of the man's gnarled hand, which was pointing to the council house, a long, oval-roofed building in the center of town.

The men of the village were not sure what to make of this stranger as he strode confidently through a cluttered alley between rows of lodges. He seemed at home as he passed dugout canoes lying on blocks, racks and piles of skins stretched to dry, little garden plots of black soil that had been recently turned. Already he had an escort of several dozen males, nearly all of them armed and looking stern. Normally, the approach of a French trader would be heralded well ahead of time, and the Indians would be waiting, cheerful and eager to begin trading, especially after a long winter without white goods.

Sutherland stopped to speak to a sturdy warrior whose high scalp-lock and many feathers and beads spoke of authority; he said he wished to meet with the chief to explain this unceremonious arrival. The warrior ordered word sent ahead, and Sutherland moved on slowly, to allow the chief time to ready himself. As he walked, he looked around for Benjamin, glancing sidelong into lodge entrances and scanning the crowd. If his ruse failed, neither of them would likely get out alive.

The throng of Indians, by now well in the hundreds, drifted ever more thickly behind and alongside Sutherland, and he did his best to walk jauntily and behave like a Frenchman. He was sure he looked the part well enough. He gambled that in his disguise and with his beard, he would not be remembered from the days when he counseled these Shawnees to make peace with the Longknives. Many elder warriors had died in fighting since that time, and so far he did not recognize any of the leading men gathering alongside him.

When Sutherland reached the council ground—a broad, grassless area in front of the council house—he was informed that he was in the presence of none other than Catahecassa, second chief after Blackfish in all the Shawnee nation. Along with ten other headmen, old Catahecassa, thin and gray-haired, sat before the council house, robed in a buffalo skin, with a silver medallion of King George around his neck—a token from the British to chieftains of importance who had allied against the rebels.

Sutherland approached the council circle, which had assembled swiftly upon news of his approach. He knew Shawnees did not like to parley without being allowed time to adorn themselves formally, but the arrival of a trader from the northwest was an occasion of interest to all. Or perhaps they had gathered so promptly because they hoped he would bring news of gifts from the British at Detroit.

As was proper, Sutherland walked to the right, outside the seated circle of dignitaries, for it was rude for a visitor to pass between anyone and the fire. When he came to the right rear of Catahecassa, he stood until the chief's bony hand motioned him to sit. Sutherland could consider himself a guest in this town, for the moment.

On another motion from the chief, Sutherland rose and stepped into the center of the circle, this time near the fire, which had been kindled so recently that it had hardly taken hold of the wood. Catahecassa's eyes were cold and sharp and never left him.

"It is the honor of Jean Longshanks of Detroit to address the council of Chillicothe," Sutherland said with gravity, after a formal greeting to the chiefs. Now he spoke in a tongue that was closer to Kickapoo and clearly understandable to the Shawnees; the casual language of the trader was inappropriate in council. Catahecassa looked impressed.

"I have come to the land of the Shawnee for two reasons—one, the reason that took me from my home, the other a reason that found me after I reached this country." He deliberately left his words mysterious, knowing Indians loved obscure talk that led to an unexpected conclusion.

He reached into his pouch and laid several twists of tobacco on the ground at Catahecassa's feet, and alongside he placed the spyglass. An immediate rush of whispering rose from the Indians; they well knew what a rare and valuable present this spyglass was. They had captured similar glasses in attacks on surveying parties, but none had ever been traded outright to the Indians.

Showing no emotion, the chieftain took up the tobacco, broke off some for his own pipe, then passed the rest to the warriors, who numbered more than three hundred by now, all seated in successive circles. Many pipes were lit, and Sutherland returned to his place behind Catahecassa until it became his turn to smoke. A prolonged period of contemplation followed, the quiet broken only by the barking of dogs and the crackle of the fire. Sutherland saw that Catahecassa had lost his right ear; hanging over what was left of it was an eagle feather, symbol of valor.

Near Sutherland sat several medicine men; they were painted in garish designs and dressed in bearskins and feathers, with buffalo-horn headdresses. Sutherland noticed they were wearing amulets of bird heads, snakeskins, eagle claws, and what appeared to be human teeth. They were grim, surly-looking men, unlike the rotund and jolly Mawak of the Ottawas. Sutherland marked them well, to see whether they would be taken in by his plan. They had better, or he was finished.

When Sutherland was again called to the fore to speak, he said he had traveled all the way from the British post at distant Michilimackinac to trade and to visit the famous Shawnee, and to learn if it was true that they were the scourge of the Longknives and had captured many whites in the latest fighting.

"I came far, and my canoe was laden with the finest gifts for the mighty Shawnees," he said with all the feeling he could summon, accompanying his words with sweeping gestures. "But three days of hard marching from here my boat was swept under the rapids, and all I had was lost; thus it is my deepest regret to appear before you with so humble an offering, as my only expression of homage to the Shawnees."

He sensed suspicion, uncertainty. Catahecassa's eyes narrowed, and a gleam of dislike came into them. A stranger who had penetrated this country without scouts or hunters detecting him was indeed remarkable. Sutherland ignored dark looks and piercing glares, putting on a show of utmost innocence. He indicated the medals he had pinned on his chest, saying they were gifts of honor from the British, who had found him a useful friend in the past. The Indians close at hand leaned forward to inspect them; truly, they were different from the cheap medallions handed out so liberally to Indians. Anyone with such fine medals must be a friend to the king.

"The river spirit has been enriched by my misfortune, but I have come at last to my destination, to look upon the Shawnees and learn of their triumph in warfare, and to see the whites who have been taken captive. Then I shall offer enough British paper money to buy many canoeloads of presents, and shall purchase whites in the name of our great father, King George."

There was an ominous silence. Sutherland let his eyes fall to the ground, as if he were thinking very deeply. It was not unusual for British officers and agents to go among Indian villages to purchase rebel captives and take them back to Detroit; but Jean Longshanks had come alone, unannounced, without troops and without trade goods.

Sutherland had to play his second card.

"Before I ask leave to see the captives, it is my earnest desire that something puzzling be explained to me." He looked in appeal toward the gloomy medicine men. "It is a dream that came upon me the night before my canoe went under with so many friends. . . ."

Sutherland related in detail how a rattlesnake had spoken to him in this dream, warning him of the rapids and telling him it was his destiny to end his journey under the protection of the spirits.

This immediately caught everyone's attention; even the somber Catahecassa looked eager to hear more. Indians held that dreams were of divine origin and that a proper understanding of them not only was critical to the future conduct of one's life, but told whether a person stood in favor with the gods. And the rattlesnake, Sutherland knew, was venerated by the Shawnees, who believed it an incarnation of the great spirit.

"Perhaps the medicine men of this town will enlighten an ignorant Frenchman by interpreting the snake's last words, which were: 'You are like unto the manitou, and what you wish to purchase must be sold to you.'"

The Shawnee audience was shocked. The medicine men were wide-eyed, sitting up straighter. Sutherland was well aware that a meaning of the word "manitou" was "he who walks with the serpent." Sutherland had just declared that a mighty spirit had spoken to him and promised to protect him in time of danger. Not only that, but he was to be sold whatever he chose to buy.

Sutherland knew he might be pushing the Indians' credulity too far, yet he desperately needed time in the village to locate Benjamin. This ploy, he hoped, would give him that time.

Sutherland sat back down, knowing the medicine men were intensely thinking of a way to challenge this grand title he had so brashly taken upon himself. Manitou was a name none of them would dare assume. Catahecassa rose to formally welcome Jean Longshanks, as was appropriate at this time. The old chief was not smiling.

"For a white stranger to appear from the mist and ask to buy our white prisoners is unusual," he said in a harsh, throaty voice. "But for a white stranger to ask our medicine men to interpret such a momentous dream is indeed beyond this old chief's experience. But then, I am not fully knowledgeable about the ways of . . . manitous!"

He looked long at Sutherland, then briefly at the medicine men, who appeared extremely dour.

"We must allow the wise ones to consult with their own manitous and ask what should be done with a Frenchman who claims to walk with serpents." Unexpectedly, Catahecassa became cheerful, a smile transforming his gaunt face, the feather shaking as he laughed hoarsely. "It might give us entertainment to test you, Longshanks-with-the-snake-dream—but it will give us far more entertainment to punish you, should you be found false."

Sutherland bowed forward, in the manner of saying yes.

He was also smiling, but the medicine men could not have looked more moody and spiteful.

Catahecassa motioned for Sutherland to be led away to a lodge, while the medicine men ruminated over all they had heard. The rest of the Shawnees dispersed; they would be called back when the council was resumed—perhaps that evening, or if the medicine men needed more time to cast bones and meditate, not until the next day.

Sutherland was left alone in a dark, warm lodge with a small fire. He sat cross-legged on a bearskin rug, eating corn mush, broiled bear meat, and turkey, served on birch-bark bowls with wooden spoons. It was delicious, besides being the first hot food he had had in weeks. As he ate, he heard the distant chanting of the medicine men, their rattles shaking and drums thudding as they pondered how to challenge this Frenchman's assertion that the serpent had spoken to him in a dream, promising to protect him.

There was one sure test. No one could deny the fact of his having the dream, but the Shawnees had a quick, simple, and deadly method of verifying its truth. As the day wore on, Sutherland lay down to rest. Though exhausted, he dared not sleep, for he knew what was to come. Now and again he caught himself nodding off, but each time forced himself awake. He wished the medicine men would get on with their business. Their drums kept beating, rattles sounding.

It was a considerable risk he was taking, but he knew no other quick way to win the confidence of the Shawnees and have the freedom of the village. He could not hide for weeks at the edge of the woods hoping to spot the boy, then wait for a chance to find him lightly guarded; surely he would be discovered before then.

Finally, near sundown, the drumming and chanting stopped. The entire village was quiet, as though awaiting something. Above his head, the smokehole had changed from blue to gray, and the small fire had burned down to coals, no squaw being permitted to enter the lodge of a man whose fate was in the hands of the medicine men.

Sutherland lay quietly, listening, soon becoming aware of movement outside the lodge. They had come at last, as he knew they would. This was the moment. The flap of the door opened slightly, and something was thrown inside to land nearby with a soft thud. Sutherland could see it in the half-light, slithering and coiling, then becoming motionless. He sat very still, but his heart leaped before he calmed himself.

The rattlesnake was huge. Its eyes glinted, the head steady until it saw him. Then the rattle flared, loud inside the lodge, and the snake writhed suddenly into a tight coil, its head rearing back.

Sutherland lay on his side, eyes on the snake, sure that he was being watched by medicine men at peepholes around the lodge. The snake rose high on its coil, white fangs gleaming, tongue flicking. Sutherland drew himself slowly up, keeping his feet between him and the rattler. The snake's head wove back and forth, just inches away. Cautiously, Sutherland reached for the journal of Richard Weston, which was close at hand. He opened it, almost casually. As the rattlesnake bobbed its head, Sutherland pretended to read, nonchalantly taking the stick he had carried into the village and poking the fire with it. Then he absently laid the stick between himself and the snake, which backed away slightly. Sutherland turned a page. Slowly the snake let its head drop. Sutherland yawned. The snake rose again, as if it would come at him, but instead uncoiled backward, the rattle falling silent. Sutherland turned another page. The snake withdrew into the shadows of the lodge.

Sutherland wondered if the medicine men could see the sweat beading on his brow. There were murmurs outside. He watched the snake slither against the wall of the lodge, and then it was gone.

Soon the voices were no longer there, and it was dark enough in the lodge for Sutherland to remove the anklets of thin hazel branches from beneath his trousers and quickly unwrap the strips of hazel bark he had wound about his waist. If a wise enough medicine man saw the hazel, he might know just why the rattlesnake had been so reluctant to come near Sutherland.

He tossed the hazel onto the coals, and as the fire flared up brightly, illuminating his face, he smiled to think how remarkably often Mawak's lore was true.

* * *

An hour later, Sutherland was escorted from the lodge, with respectful medicine men on every side. A great bonfire had been lit, and drums, rattles, bells, jew's harps, cymbals, and tambourines sounded in a rising storm of excitement. The council ground was filled with Shawnee warriors, and Catahecassa had resumed his place at the head of the circle.

"Manitou, manitou," people were murmuring as they stared with awe at the strange Frenchman.

Relief swept through Sutherland, and with it a taste of success. He stood facing the old chief, who rose to lay a fine white trade blanket over his shoulders, saying the village would provide Jean Longshanks with new clothing, a canoe, and weapons for his journey home.

"In the morning, Longshanks, you may look upon our white prisoners, and those you desire will be yours."

This was all Sutherland could want. Solemnly he thanked the chief. The rest of his mission, he knew, would be difficult enough: flight through the woods with Benjamin and other white captives might yet end in death—but at least the riskiest part was over. Tomorrow he would claim Benjamin and any others, then make for Clark's rendezvous at the Falls of the Ohio.

Sutherland turned to thank the Indians around the council circle. He smiled at the medicine men. Their eyes glittered as they smiled back; they continued beating drums and shaking tortoise-shell rattles. To them he had the power of a protected one, and they would do anything to appease the will of the spirits.

Sutherland felt so good that he nearly smirked.

"Jean Longshanks," someone chuckled from not too far off.

Sutherland's heart skipped.

Across the bonfire from him, grinning, sat a short, swarthy figure in filthy buckskins, with a feathered, broad-brimmed hat.

It was Simon Girty.

chapter 11

THE CLIFF

Sutherland was sure it was all up for him, but he showed no emotion and avoided looking at Girty. Instead he gave his attention to the throbbing drums and chanting of the medicine men. Catahecassa was completing a lengthy speech, but Sutherland heard hardly a word of it. When the chief gestured for him to be seated, Sutherland went back to sit at the chieftain's right hand. His mind working furiously, he glanced over to where Girty had been, but the man was gone.

It was a long, noisy feast, and Sutherland had no appetite. The Shawnees, though, were doubly excited, for to them he was good luck, and they were preparing to go on the warpath. The young men leaped up to chant war songs, boasting of past deeds and deeds to come, while driving tomahawks into a tall post set up in the center of the council circle. Meanwhile, Sutherland continued to look around for Benjamin, but there was no sign of him or any other white prisoners, and probably would not be until morning . . . if Sutherland lived that long.

Girty could give him away at any moment, and then the post that the warriors were dancing around and sticking with hatchets would become a stake where he would be slowly roasted to death. Every friendly word from the chief or from other Shawnees who came over to greet him could be transformed instantly into a scalping cry, a shriek of hatred. Yet he dared not try to escape, lest Girty be waiting for the attempt. And even if he did get away, what would happen to Benjamin?

Knowing his slim chances, and hoping against the worst,

Sutherland forced himself to join the feasting, though he could not help thinking that this was his last meal.

The revelry went on long after dark. Still Girty had not made a move, and he was not to be seen even after Sutherland had been allowed to return to his lodge. Politely declining the company of a squaw for the night, he ducked through the door flap, his mind full with plans, none of them very useful. Inside, a freshened fire was burning, filling the top of the lodge with smoke, and a thick bed of buffalo skins and rabbit fur had been laid out.

Immediately he sensed another presence. As his eyes became accustomed to the thick atmosphere, he saw Girty seated cross-legged beyond the fire, that same fierce grin on his face. Sutherland had the urge to spring across the fire and throttle him, then slip away and search out Benjamin. Or perhaps Girty knew where the boy was kept, and could be forced to lead Sutherland to him after the village went to sleep.

Girty and Sutherland stared at each other for some time, as outside the clamor of dancing and singing continued. Sutherland thought of the dirk in his stocking; he noticed that a pistol and tomahawk lay ready at Girty's side.

"How, Sutherland."

"How, Girty."

Sutherland sat down on the bedding. Girty said nothing more, but filled a pipe with tobacco, lit it, blew smoke to the heavens, earth, and winds, then handed it over the fire to Sutherland. Girty was more Indian than white.

When they had smoked the pipe down, Girty laid it near the fire. Then he spoke:

"They wanted to bed you with a purty squaw, Sutherland—nothing but the best for a manitou!" He grinned again, his beard black against the flashing teeth. "Neat trick—slick it was, indeedy." He nodded, clucking his tongue, and pulled out his flask, offering some. Sutherland declined, and Girty guzzled a powerful swig that made his eyes close and his breath catch.

"Got a awful dry!" He put the flask away and eyed Sutherland before turning to the fire, poking at it with a hazel rod, freshly cut. He muttered something about hazel being a useful wood at times, then complained, "'Em damn Shawnee medicine men ain't like northern shamans—don't know more'n a gnat about hazelwood 'n' rattlers!" He spat into a corner of the lodge. "Too busy fighting Longknives, I reckon. Ain't got time to listen to their grandpappies."

Sutherland leaned back on his hands. "You mean to give them instruction in the old ways, Girty?" They locked gazes, searching, sizing each other up.

Girty poked the fire again and replied casually, "If I was, I wouldn't tell you . . . just yet."

When Girty looked over at Sutherland, the dirk had materialized, held loosely but ready in the Scotsman's hand. It could strike before Girty was halfway to the pistol.

Girty smiled and kept on poking at the fire with the hazel rod, letting the sharp tip flare, then removed it from the fire and blew it out. It would make an effective weapon.

Sutherland's anger was rising. He was in no mood for games. If it was blood Girty wanted, then it would begin now, before the Indians came.

"Why are you here, Girty?"

Girty sat back, frowning, then took a long, deep breath. Staring at the fire, he said, "I ain't on the warpath agin you, Sutherland." He turned to face Sutherland. "Your boy ain't here."

Sutherland's blood was up now. This was the last thing he expected.

Girty said quietly, "He's gone to Detroit with Wabete, the chief what took him and aims to sell him to Hamilton, I reckon."

With an oath, Sutherland threw the dirk into the earth. His elaborate ruse had got him into the midst of the largest Shawnee town, but it had all been in vain. Now he had to get out and rush northward—if Girty was not lying. He eyed the scout.

"What do you care about me or my son?" Sutherland wanted to believe Girty, but one mistake, one lost opportunity, might spoil everything he had done to get this far. "I didn't come in here to be led off on a goose chase—especially by a traitor who sent a patrol to their deaths!"

Girty leaped to his feet, clenching his fists. "They got what was coming, 'em Longknife bastards! Got what they deserved, and there'll be more of 'em pays afore I'm done!"

He backed off a step as if to govern himself; his face was contorted with rage. Trembling, eyes bulging, he growled, "You stood by me on that trail when 'em Longknife dogs cursed me, but . . ." He shook his head. "I ain't sayin' I owes you anything, but you take what I'm giving, Sutherland, or your boy and your hair'll both be raised by Shawnees—"

Abruptly his face lit in a strange expression of glee, and he laughed that high-pitched way that told he was not completely master of himself. "Good joke, eh? Hair and kid raised by Injuns! Hah!"

He paced back and forth, mumbling something that could not be heard over the raucous sounds of Indians celebrating outside.

Sutherland began to believe Girty, but did not take his eyes off him. There was no reason the man needed to be here, in this lodge, in danger of being killed. Girty was actually humming a tune as he paced, his hands behind his back, gaze on the ground. He was half mad, but no doubt meant what he was saying. Sutherland decided to accept it.

"You'd be a big man here if you turned me in, Girty," he said, putting the dirk back in his stocking.

Girty stopped pacing. "I'm already a big man here," he cackled. "I'm loyal, and an adopted Injun; and I got Henry Hamilton for a friend!" He cackled once more and gave Sutherland the corner of his eye, as if to see how Sutherland took his implicit confession that he had been a loyalist spy all along. Sutherland did not respond. He had seen every sort of man in his days, even spies.

Girty resumed pacing, saying, "Sutherland, you're a rebel, but I ain't set agin you—not yet, leastways. But I got a notion that these here medicine men ain't so keen on a white man, even a Frenchy, claiming the title manitou, and they'll likely test you other ways—meaner ways—a few more times, if'n you stay much longer."

The noise outside was at last dying down, the light of the bonfire fading where it came through the lodge flap.

Sutherland had to escape soon, while the town was asleep, but he did not know for how long Girty would help him. Woodsmen like him were strange characters, in many ways as unpredictable as Indians; but when it came to personal loyalty or hatred, they were always unswerving. One day Girty might become a mortal enemy, and when that happened, there would be no mercy given or asked. For the moment, however, he was offering Sutherland his life.

"I'm going for my boy," Sutherland said.

Girty sat down. "These Injuns like having a manitou around. They'll be sorry you up and left without a good-bye party. Might even guess you made fools of 'em . . . might come after you." He thought a moment, then went on. "Keep close to the Scioto Trail; it'll lead you past Mingo Town and to Upper Sandusky. . . ."

Girty swiftly explained the route to Sutherland, who listened closely as landmarks and villages were described. It would be another two hundred miles of hard, dangerous country. Before dawn, Sutherland would be on his way, and soon afterward the Shawnees would give chase. The more he ran, the harder they would try to catch him, and the angrier they would become. Girty was offering a chance at death in another place, but all Owen Sutherland asked was a few hours' head start.

Not long after Sutherland reached the place where his gear was concealed, he saw the Shawnees coming for him.

He was climbing a rocky cliff above the flats, and could make out the village a few miles in the hazy distance, with the soft light of early morning just touching bark roofs and dew-wet grasslands. After pulling himself over a ledge, he had turned to rest briefly and look back at the town—and saw horsemen riding out in every direction, galloping across the meadows and searching for his tracks, which would be well marked in the morning dew.

His absence had been discovered sooner than he had expected; he had gained no more than an hour's start, some of which had been wasted retrieving clothes and equipment and swiftly changing into his worn buckskins.

He had thought his best chance lay in getting over the

rocks, where he would leave no tracks. If after that a few warriors found his trail, they would likely pursue him without returning for help, which would better the odds. Now, however, he probably would be sighted before he cleared the top of the cliff. Already a dozen horsemen were heading in his direction.

No doubt each man wanted the honor of capturing him. Surely they did not know he was Donoway; but as Girty had said, they would be angry at him for slipping away in the night, proving he was afraid for having tricked them. At the very least they would force him to run the gauntlet, and perhaps imprison him until they found out who he was.

He continued ascending the cliff face, straight upward, now knowing for sure they would soon spot him. The riders were closing in, but by the time he was high enough to be easily sighted, he should be near the top. The Indians would lose the advantage of their horses when they set out to climb after him.

Up he went, scrambling along narrow ledges, pulling himself over sharp rock-shelves that broke and crumbled under him. It was slow, dangerous going, with a drop of already more than a hundred feet should he slip.

Soon the mounted warriors were directly below, looking up, pointing, and shouting at one another. They did not fire their guns, probably not wanting to attract other competitors for their prey; instead, several leaped from their mounts and began to scale the cliff. Four others, Sutherland noticed, rode off into the trees, as if they knew a way to cut him off.

He struggled on up the rock face, sometimes moving rapidly, at other times finding himself at a dead end, without handholds on the stone. More than once he was forced to work backward or to leap across to another shelf—his rifle, pack, and claymore flapping like deadly weights, trying to throw him off-balance. At other times he had to inch along, scant toeholds and fingerholds all that kept him clinging to the rock.

Up here it was windy, and the breeze buffeted his clothing, whipping at his hat and coat, trying to snatch him from the cliff. He looked down, and it was dizzying. Already the

Indians had made good progress. Probably they knew this place well, having climbed it often as youngsters; and they were not encumbered like him. He inched on, pressed hard against the gray rock, moving sideways more often than upward, but now less than sixty feet from the top. How he was to get up there he did not know, for there was no obvious route of ledges to follow. Twice more he came to an impasse and had to work back hurriedly and start up another ledge; each time the Shawnees below came that much closer. Had they wanted to kill him, he would have been shot down by now. Instead, they whooped and shouted as if it were a game, and continued nimbly up the treacherous rock, steadily gaining.

"Listen, Frenchman!" called the leader of the party, a short, muscular fellow of middle age. "You are taking the wrong way, and will have to grow wings to escape us!"

"Do not fall, French squirrel!" a rather fat warrior, a little beneath the leader, shouted with a breathless, puffing laugh. "We are coming up a long way to snare you, and it will anger us if you fly all the way down!"

"Fly if you must!" a third Shawnee shouted loudly. "But wait until we come higher and can watch you from a good place!"

The Shawnees went on like that, enjoying themselves and climbing ever closer. After a little while Sutherland saw they were right: he had taken a route that led to a wide abyss. He was on a ledge less than a foot across, his face and chest against the rock, his heavy rifle and pack pulling him backward.

Quickly he considered his alternatives. The climb must have been too difficult for most of the Indians, he noticed, for only the three who had mocked him were still in sight. The others had descended, to wait far below. He took a quick glance at the abyss. It was far too wide; it would be better to get back along the ledge and find another way to the top.

But now the Shawnee leader was boosting himself onto the same ledge, not far off. The man stood up, laughed, and yanked out a tomahawk, apparently more interested in taking a scalp than in returning a wayward Frenchman to the village.

Sutherland felt for the hilt of his claymore and waited for the Shawnee. He knew that as soon as he killed this man, the watchers below would open fire.

"Go back!" he called to the first man, who was just a few yards away. "Go back before this French squirrel makes you wish you had wings!"

At that, the warrior gave an exultant, toothless grin and shouted, "Squirrels chatter loudly when they are afraid!"

Careful to keep his balance, the warrior edged closer and taunted with the tomahawk, poking and jabbing, uttering little grunts, trying to terrify Sutherland. He seemed brave enough, but unsure of how to strike without losing his balance and falling two hundred feet to his death.

Sutherland did not want to kill if he could avoid it, nor did he want to become the target of musket fire. The Shawnees below were shouting and whistling, clapping their hands and calling for their friend to knock the Frenchman down to them. They promised to save the scalp for him, but each claimed part of the white man's gear.

"His rifle is mine!" bellowed the fat one from nearby. He was panting as he, too, edged onto the ledge. His presence seemed to make the first warrior all the more anxious to kill.

Pressing his chest against the rock face, Sutherland surprised the first Shawnee by quickly drawing his claymore and presenting the point of the weapon just inches from the man's face.

"Go back, Shawnee, before I make wolf meat of you and your fat companion!"

The first Indian edged back a few inches, startled at seeing death so unexpectedly near; but the second howled in anger at being insulted and tried to force past his friend. It was awkward and dangerous, and Sutherland laughed at them.

"Push him off, fat one!" he shouted, and that angered the first Indian as well. "Come on, fat one, and I'll let you be first to taste this steel! Hear me now! I'm no Frenchman, but Owen Sutherland—Donoway to you—and I thirst for Shawnee blood! Go back, or I'll have yours!"

He poked the claymore at the front Indian, who struggled back in earnest now that he knew who it was he faced. The fat Shawnee also hesitated, but the encouraging cries from his friends below and the gruff shouts of the third man, now coming up, compelled him to be brave.

"Donoway?" the third man bellowed in astonishment, and was heard down below. The Indians at the foot of the cliff shouted and whooped in excitement, and Sutherland saw them loading their muskets. He had expected this. Each was eager to be the one who killed Donoway, and the loud protests of the three who were brave enough to climb up after him were of no avail. A musket cracked, and a ball smashed off the rock near Sutherland's face, spraying shards of stone at him and at the Indians, who again called out for their friends to stop shooting. But a second and a third musket went off, both near-misses as Sutherland ducked to one knee.

At that instant the first warrior gave a screech and threw his tomahawk. Sutherland deflected it with his claymore hilt, but the steel axhead glanced sidelong against his head. He reeled in pain, and the Shawnees shouted. He was losing his balance. The first Indian now was coming on with a knife. Sutherland, still on his knee, struggled to grip the rock face and blindly stabbed with the claymore. The Indian gasped and dived back, upsetting his friends, who almost toppled over.

They began screaming for Sutherland to surrender. Another musket went off, the bullet ricocheting loudly and close. Though dazed, Sutherland maintained his balance, one hand clutching the rock. He was a step away from the end of the ledge, with a breathtaking gap between the brink and another narrow ledge farther down, where some juniper and scrub pine clung to the rocks. After that, it was a long way to the bottom.

The fat man was reluctant to press the attack, but shouted, "You are our prisoner, Donoway! Come peacefully, and you may die at the stake like a man! Fight, and you will be shot like a pigeon." To stay here was certain doom; even if he overcame the three men trying to get at him, he would be shot by the others. There was only one way out. He shook off his dizziness, slowly stood up, and shouted at the three Shawnees.

"Follow me, if you're as brave as the squirrel!"

Then, with a Highland war cry, he spun, crouched, and flew into the air. Across the wide abyss he floated, dropping down and down, at last striking the cliff face and clutching at scrub pine. The first bush gave way. He fell, his feet and hands scraping at the rock. He was sliding backward, losing the ledge. The Shawnees shrieked with delight. At the last moment he caught at a juniper, slowing his fall, swung in, and landed with his arms on the lower ledge. Now the three Indians screeched in anger. From below, the view of the other Shawnees was blocked by an outcropping, and Sutherland was safe from their gunfire for a minute or two, until they were able to change positions.

First he had to fight his way up onto the ledge. Struggling to keep a hold, he kicked one leg up. The fat Shawnee bellowed, and Sutherland instinctively moved—and just in time, for the tomahawk smacked rock nearby and bounded off, falling into the valley far below.

With a grunt of determination Sutherland clambered all the way up and, breathless and bruised, turned to face the Shawnees who were clinging uneasily to the rock face about thirty feet above him. They were without firearms, and for them that distance might as well have been a mile. They were in a fury, and the third one clumsily managed to heave his tomahawk. Sutherland did not flinch as the weapon flew wide. He laughed even louder.

"Jump, if you're men! Come on—I'll catch you!" He held out his hands, as though they were children. Now the Indians only glared, their fury quenched by insult and cold fear.

Sutherland nodded his head. "Have a care going back down!"

Then he bounded around the corner and was gone from their sight. Still chuckling to himself, he loped ahead on the trail, which was widening, although the wall of rock to the right was too sheer to climb, and the drop on the left was precipitous. The track was steadily rising, and he figured he soon would reach the top, where he could break away for woodland shelter and lose all pursuit by nightfall.

The track wound around the face of the cliff, and Suth-

erland ran steadily, putting good distance between himself
and the abyss he had just leaped. He was thinking of both
Benjamin and Jeremy, for they might be together at Detroit
by the time he got there. Perhaps they could have a secret
meeting at the house at Valenya, and some of their friends
could be invited for old times' sake. . . .

As he rounded the corner, he confronted a horse that
screamed and reared in fright at his sudden appearance. The
four Shawnee riders! He waved his arms to drive the horse
up again as its shouting rider fought to bring it down. The
other three horsemen were close behind on the narrow trail,
and they whipped out tomahawks as Sutherland ducked back
around the bend, the way he had come. The Indian horses
thudded close behind, and at the instant the first one rounded
the bend, Sutherland darted into a deep, narrow fissure in
the cliff face. Feeling his way quickly into the darkness, he
hoped the Indians had not seen him take cover. After they
galloped past he would escape and run back up the trail.

Panting, Sutherland unslung his rifle and crouched in the
blackness just inside a larger chamber at the end of a narrow
passage of a dozen feet. It stank in here, and he guessed
some animal had made it a den. He heard the horses stamping and saw the Shawnees stop, springing down from their
mounts, guns in hand. He listened to their muted voices;
obviously they were discussing how to get at their quarry.
Sutherland thought he might handle the first couple easily
enough, but this was too tight a spot to be trapped in. If
they could not flush him out, they might keep him here
until he gave up—or they might decide to burn him out.

He looked for another way to escape, glancing around
at the rock walls, which were more visible now that his
eyes were used to the dark. He was sure he smelled the
distinct reek of bear—

Suddenly he realized that the faint light in the chamber
was coming from somewhere above. He stepped quickly to
the opposite rock-face and looked straight up. The glare of
day was sharp and bright. The cleft seemed fifteen or twenty
feet high and only a foot or two wide at its narrowest part,
but he was sure he could climb it.

Preparing to leap up for a handhold, he slung his rifle

back onto his shoulders, at the same time seeing the Indians edging into the entrance, guns at the ready. He crouched to jump up, when something small and furry—two things small and furry—rubbed against his legs, so startling him that he almost fell over. They were newborn bear cubs, and Sutherland's spine tingled before the ear-splitting roar of the mother bear confirmed the worst.

There was no time to jump. Instantly the bear was upon him, long claws swiping from the darkness. He dived sideways, jarring against the rock wall. All he could make out were flashing fangs, claws, and points of light for eyes that kept lunging at him. He scrambled back to where he had been, trying to get into position to leap up into that shaft of daylight.

The snarling bear clawed at his left foot, hooking him to a stop. He braced himself and kicked powerfully back with the other heel, catching the animal's snout and freeing himself. But the she-bear came right back, and there was not even enough room for him to draw his claymore. From the corner of his eye he saw the startled Indians silhouetted in the tunnel, the sudden commotion transfixing them. He whirled and gave the bear another staggering kick on the snout, grabbed one bundle of bear cub, then the other, and tossed them squealing into the midst of the Indians.

Suddenly it became very crowded and noisy in that narrow passage as the cubs howled, the mother roared, and the first Shawnee fired his musket with a shattering boom, while trying desperately to push backward through the others. The Indians were all shouting, for the mother bear was upon them, going for its cubs. Sutherland leaped up into the shaft, wedging there with legs and arms.

Without pausing for breath, he scrambled upward as fast as he could. When he was halfway to the top, he heard another musket go off and the bear roar and Shawnees scream. Then the noises suddenly grew fainter, telling that the others were outside the cave. He could hear more shouting and horses neighing, and another shot was fired, though it, too, must have been ineffective, for the bear was snarling as wildly as ever.

Sutherland forced himself higher up the cleft, despite the

pain in his left foot, which had been clawed right through the leggin and moccasin. Hands and feet, then knees and elbows pressed against the wet, cold sides of the rock opening, which narrowed steadily. Only a few feet from the top, he became jammed, the cleft too narrow for his body and the knapsack.

Wedging his feet against the opposite wall, his muscles trembling with exertion and his injured foot throbbing, he laboriously undid his gear. Somehow he slung it all onto his left arm and shoved it through the gap, climbing with only one hand and his feet. It was brutal going, but after what seemed like ten minutes—during which the noise below quieted and the she-bear growled up at him—he thrust his head into sweet air. Clambering out through bushes, he lay gasping on level ground once more.

His injured left foot was bleeding, but there was no time to waste. Even though the Shawnees might think he had been killed by the bear, they would come back to hunt the beast and find his remains. He found a stream, washed his lacerations, and bandaged them with strips from his yellow shirt. Then he shouldered his pack and rifle and set off once again, limping painfully, but glad enough to have run into the she-bear, who had saved his life. Still, it had been a close call, and the next time he might choose instead to climb over the cliff edge. Indian marksmen were less dangerous than she-bears with cubs.

chapter **12**

JEREMY BENTLY

Morning came to the straits at Detroit in a soft mantle of April light, slowly putting out the stars. As the sun rose over the horizon, its rays touched the roof of a large house on the eastern shore, then glowed pink on whitewashed clapboard walls, casting shadows that stretched down to the water's edge. The house faced the broad straits, which were still dark and obscure, though the high ground on the far shore was beginning to turn red under a pale blue sky.

Few houses anywhere in the northwest compared with this one, which was called Valenya. It was of two stories, classically proportioned, with a grand front door crafted of oak. To each side of this door were large sash windows such as were seldom found west of Fort Pitt, and above them, just under the eaves, were two horizontal windows, lighting the second floor. The roof was cedar-shingled and steep, in the French-Canadian style.

Downriver a little distance, silhouetted against the sunrise, were seven looming stones of monumental size, clustered together as if some giant hand or God's whim had stood them there on end. These monoliths were sacred to the Indians, who had named them the Singing Stones because of the keening wail the north wind made when it blew between them. It was a testimony of the Indians' respect for Owen Sutherland that they had regarded him as the guardian of these seven stones.

Valenya had been built by Sutherland and Ella as the fulfillment of a dream, but the war had forced them to abandon their home, and now it was occupied by Ella's son, Jeremy Bently, and his new bride, Gwen Hardy Bently. Though Jeremy had helped to erect Valenya, he always

165

considered it his parents' home, a place to which they would one day return, when there was peace.

On this fine April morning, with the wind blowing hard and fresh from the west, Jeremy moved about near the back of the large common room, where a fire crackled in the hearth against the early spring chill. The room was bright and airy, furnished with a large trestle table, comfortable chairs close to the fire, Persian rugs, and a spinet standing near one wall. Jeremy was preparing tea over the stone sink against the back wall, and the tea's fragrance and the smell of bread warming in the brick oven filled the room.

When he had finished, Jeremy retrieved his scarlet tunic from the chair-back where he had carefully hung it. As he put it on, fastening the brass buttons, he thought, as he often did, of how pleasing this room was, and how tastefully his mother had decorated it with paintings, weavings, and furniture from Philadelphia and Montreal. Since he had moved back here two years ago, he had done little to change anything. Of course now that Gwen was with him, things would have to be arranged more to her taste, but eventually he would have another home built somewhere upriver, where the straits flowed down from Lake Saint Clair. The war would not last forever.

The light of dawn, low in the eastern windows, glinted on Jeremy's brass, red tunic, and polished black leather. He wore the uniform of surgeon major in the King's Eighth Foot, the regiment garrisoned at Detroit. Because of his staff position, however, and the lack of suitable housing at the fort, Jeremy was permitted to live at Valenya, a few miles upstream and across the straits from Detroit.

He spent several days a week in the fort, at a hospital he had established two years ago with Gwen's help. It served soldiers as well as civilians and Indians and, more often of late, rebel captives brought in by raiding parties. This morning he would have to paddle across to Detroit, although it should have been his day off.

"Come back to bed, darling." It was Gwen's sleepy voice, calling from the bedroom.

Jeremy frowned. He was in no mood to go to Detroit, and when Gwen repeated her sleepy summons, he had the strong impulse to stay at home.

"In a moment, Gwen." Jeremy moved to the front window, to gaze at the straits. He was a handsome man, in his middle twenties, with very broad shoulders, powerful arms and legs. He was taller than most, and his scarlet uniform made him look imposing and older than his years. His long blond hair was tied in a queue at the nape of his neck, so that it almost resembled a regular officer's powdered wig.

Jeremy heard his dog come padding into the room, and he spoke quietly to her as she lay down near the door, ready to go out. Cape was her name, after the Cape of Good Hope, where she had been born. She was big, sleek, and bony, with ears that flopped over at the tips. A ridge of short hair ran in the wrong direction along her spine, marking her as a southern African lion dog, or boerhound, as they were called.

"You know this is your day to play in the forest, don't you, girl?" As Jeremy struggled to button the tight stock at his neck, which was always so uncomfortable, Cape watched, her large head cocked, brown eyes soft and friendly.

"Well..." Jeremy managed at last to fasten the button, and he shrugged his shoulders to make the tunic sit right. "Well, Cape, I'm afraid you're out of luck today."

The dog snuffled and laid her head on her massive paws, baleful eyes on him.

"I'm sorry. It bothers me, too." He retied his queue to make it look more military. He hated the officer's powdered wig with its two curls on either side, and thus far no one had expressly ordered him to wear one—probably because he was a doctor, he assumed, and not expected to be so very military.

Unlike most of the Redcoats at Detroit, Jeremy was native born, from Massachusetts. These days there were not many like him. It used to be that half the Redcoats in America were enlisted from the colonies, but the king no longer depended on loyalists to wage his wars. Jeremy well knew that many Redcoat generals despised American fighting qualities, and the British army had declined, time and again, to fill their regular regiments with loyalists. He objected to this British snobbery, because loyalists made brave, desperate enemies of the rebels.

But as a physician trained in Philadelphia and Edinburgh,

and as a fighting man who had learned the ways of frontier war from Owen Sutherland and Tamano, Jeremy had been a welcomed addition to the small British army holding the vast northwest. Indeed, Lieutenant Governor Henry Hamilton had known his worth well enough to personally offer him a commission last year. At first Hamilton's attempts to recruit him had been unsuccessful, for Jeremy had been firmly set against fighting his own family; but the death of his best friend, Lieutenant Richard Weston, under circumstances that pointed to rebel murderers, had finally pushed him over the edge.

Jeremy thought about this as he stared out the window. There had been another reason he had joined the army: he liked and respected Hamilton, who had done his best to restrain the Indians. The northwest tribes would have caused bloody mayhem in the past two years had Hamilton not skillfully managed them. Jeremy hoped the officer would be able to do the same this year, but he was not so confident now. The British were out for revenge after the humiliation of having an entire army captured at Saratoga last autumn, and such revenge might include orders to wage a wider Indian war—a war that Hamilton could not prevent from becoming wholesale massacre on the frontier.

Gwen called sleepily once more, "Dearest, why don't you come to me? It's too early to be up. This is your first day of rest in such a long time."

Jeremy strapped on his regimental sword and scabbard. "Gwen, I forgot to tell you last night," he called, speaking in flat, restrained tones. "I must go across to the fort on . . . on military matters."

Silence followed. Jeremy brushed his sleeves and wasted a few more moments, but when his wife did not speak or appear, he went to her, Cape following. They crossed the hall to the master bedroom, which also overlooked the straits, past a young apple orchard on the side of the hill. The curtains had already been opened; Gwen must have risen to draw them and then gone back to bed. Now she lay awake in the large four-poster, her golden hair spread on the pillows, her lovely blue eyes intent on Jeremy as he stood there, fully dressed in his uniform.

"Military matters . . ." she said quietly, and gave a wry,

resigned smile. "You do look handsome." She reached out one hand, and he took it and sat down on the bed, kissing her fingers.

"And you look beautiful."

She caressed his cheek and sighed. "But not beautiful enough for you to dare wrinkle that lobster coat."

He pinched her hard, and she yelped, laughing, and they wrestled—although, indeed, Jeremy was careful not to rumple his uniform. Cape yelped and jumped on the bed, licking and pawing them both. Jeremy grabbed Gwen's wrists and held her down, kissing her roughly, and she struggled, giggling, trying to get free, and to avoid Cape's tongue. Finally she bit Jeremy's ear, and he had to let go. Then he swept her from the bed and carried her across the hall to the common room.

Gwen Bently was fair and slim and graceful, light in his arms, and Jeremy could not love her more. He loved her so much that he was certain they would always be happy— even though he was a loyalist in king's uniform and she a rebel supporter. Also, she loved him enough to live with him here in loyalist country.

As Jeremy set Gwen down at the table, where a teapot, cups, brown bread, cheese, honey, and apples stood waiting, he said, "When we go to live down at Vincennes this summer, there won't be any military matters to trouble us, and I promise I won't wear this lobster coat at all!"

She drew his head down and kissed him. Jeremy well knew that his wife was eagerly awaiting the day when they could leave Detroit. Hamilton had offered him an assignment at Fort Sackville, on the Wabash River at Vincennes, and he and Gwen planned to live there quietly for the duration. Since practically all of the residents of Vincennes were French—neutrals for the most part—Gwen would not be reviled as a rebel supporter, as sometimes she was here. Also, Jeremy probably would not be obliged to fight rebels, living so deep in Indian country. Jeremy had held out this arrangement to Gwen last autumn, when they had decided to marry. It was a compromise, not a solution, but both of them were tired of living with the burden of civil war always between them.

Gwen poured the tea, and they sat in the morning sunlight

for some time without speaking. Cape lay down by the door again, still hopeful of a long walk. Jeremy and Gwen enjoyed these quiet moments together, and had them all too rarely. Much had happened since December 1775, when Gwen had first arrived at Detroit from New York Town. She had come by way of Montreal, traveling with her uncle and her cousin. For a year Gwen had lived with those two at Valenya as Jeremy's guests, and in that time he had fallen in love with her.

As Jeremy drank tea, he gazed at his wife, thinking of how well she had managed under the circumstances. He knew how it pained her every time a party of Indians arrived with miserable captives from the frontier settlements to the east. It was not easy for her to tend those wounded, to soothe orphaned children, to comfort distraught widows. He knew what she went through, for he felt much the same.

Gwen spoke as if she knew his thoughts. "What military matters must you attend to, then? Does Henry Hamilton expect his raiders to deliver another load of wretches today?"

Jeremy felt that prick him; he did not look up from his tea. "No, the spring campaign against the settlements won't begin in earnest for another week or two." He was reluctant to say more, for he never liked it when Gwen allowed her bitterness to become sarcasm.

She said, "Perhaps he wants a medical opinion on some scalps, to determine whether they're rebel or loyalist, and whether he should pay or—"

One look at Jeremy's suddenly angry expression was enough to still Gwen. Her gaze dropped, and they both sat there in silence, not touching their breakfast. Then she said, more gently, "I know—I promised to remain calm about Hamilton's war." Gwen's face was flushed, and her lower lip trembled slightly.

Jeremy reached across the table and gripped her hand. "Soon we'll be away from all this. The war will never come to Vincennes, and before long Parliament will have to make terms with your Congress."

"Make terms?" Gwen's eyes were on him, searching, as if she found it hard to believe what she had just heard. "Do you mean that?"

"I admit times have changed." He knew now the rebels could not be beaten—he had known it ever since news had come of Saratoga and a possible French alliance.

"Jeremy . . . I never realized you . . ."

He got up and went to the fire, thinking of the disaster last year, when Burgoyne's entire army had been captured at Saratoga, and how the French would soon have troops and war materiel in America, on the side of Congress. He had thought it absurd in 1776 when the colonies had declared themselves independent, but it appeared now they would have the military and financial support to make their declaration stick.

He leaned on the mantelpiece, looking down at his polished boots. "I've been thinking about the coming campaign, and all the Indians who've come to Detroit this spring." He slowly shook his head. "Hamilton mustn't let them loose. The war must be brought to an end before the killing gets any worse. It's up to the British government now, and I'm sure cooler heads in London will make terms this year."

Turning to Gwen, Jeremy saw the hope in her, like a light. He smiled. "Another year in this lobster coat, Gwen, and I'll have fulfilled my promise to Henry Hamilton—I'll have served the loyal cause as I promised—and then we'll put the war behind us."

She finished his thoughts, voicing the hope they shared so often. "And then your family can come back to Valenya! Oh, Jeremy—how I have longed to hear you speak so!"

She rose, and he took her in his arms.

"It must be so," he whispered, but did not add the bitter words he was thinking: *The loyalist cause is beaten.*

After a moment, Gwen again asked why he had to go to the fort this morning. Though it troubled him, he had to answer. They were still embracing as he said, clearing his throat, "There's to be a flogging."

Gwen tensed. "Oh, no!" She did not draw away, but he heard the hurt in her voice, for they knew every one of the hundred or so men of the Redcoat garrison. "Who is it?"

"Corporal Bates."

Gwen released herself from his arms, pain and dismay on her face.

"Oh, no, Jeremy—he's just a boy! He's the one with the pet monkey, isn't he? The Welshman who sings so—"

Jeremy nodded.

"What did he do?"

"He insulted Mark Davies . . . threw a mug of beer in his face."

Gwen drew a slow breath, closing her eyes. They both knew it would go hard for Bates; Davies was not one to spare the cat-o'-nine-tales.

When Gwen asked why Bates had been so rash, Jeremy replied that Davies had seduced the soldier's young wife and was living with her in a house outside the fort.

Gwen shook her head. "It's no wonder they call Redcoats 'Bloodybacks.' Ah, dear heavens . . . poor Bates." She came to Jeremy and leaned her forehead against his chest. "Are you the duty surgeon?"

"No, but I have to be there . . . all the soldiers must. You know—regulations."

Sluggishly, Gwen went to sit back down at the table. "Regulations. Yes, how I know about Redcoat regulations. Redcoat honor, Redcoat punishment, Redcoat war-making."

She put her hands over her face and tried not to cry. Jeremy stood behind her and caressed her hair.

He said, "Not much longer, my darling; not much longer and we'll be away from here, where we can do some good for folk who don't have anything to do with this damned war! No rebels, no loyalists—just folk trying to live in peace. Until then . . ." He leaned over, took her hands, and kissed her cheek, tasting the tears. "We'll live for the day when peace comes and this country is settled, and it'll be the finest country anyone has ever seen!"

Closing her eyes, Gwen kissed his hand and whispered, "I long to go away, Jeremy. I can't endure another summer of suffering prisoners and . . . and . . . and your Redcoat regulations!"

He knew she was approaching the breaking point. Something had to be done, not only for the sake of their marriage, but to protect Gwen's health of mind. She surprised him by abruptly standing up straight, taking a deep breath, and saying firmly that she would come along to the fort.

"If you're to go a-soldiering today, then I'll work, too!" She began to clear the table. Cape, sensing a journey, stretched in anticipation, her slender tail wagging. "I'll make a bed in the hospital for poor Bates and do what I can to ease his suffering at the hands of that monster Davies!"

Jeremy saw the fire in Gwen's eyes, and it made him all the more sure of why he loved her. Had she been a man, and circumstances slightly different, she would be carrying a rifle for the Continental army. He touched her shoulder, and she came into his arms. He was proud to be her husband, happy to share his life with her.

By nine o'clock, with a warm breeze blowing in from the western woodlands and prairies beyond the fort, Detroit was filled with the curious, both red and white, who had come to see the flogging. Indians of all tribes and descriptions mobbed the perimeter of the parade ground, and many had to be ordered off ramparts by sentries and cried down from the roofs of buildings. For all their severity when it came to torturing prisoners or punishing unfaithful squaws, Indian warriors simply could not understand flogging. They never would succumb to such degrading punishment, preferring exile or even death, and it puzzled them that nearly every Redcoat, especially seasoned veterans, bore scars from the lash.

The white onlookers were far fewer, and they kept apart from the Indians. To them the flogging was less a matter of fascination than it was grimly inevitable—especially since Mark Davies was behind it. Davies had few friends among the sixteen hundred whites at the straits, and was almost universally hated by the troops. The Indians may have been in a festive mood, but few of the whites looked cheerful as the battalion drummer boy, tapping a slow march, led the punishment procession from the guardhouse and along the promenade inside the fort's palisades.

Except for the ominous drumming, everything grew silent. Even the most boisterous Indians became hushed as they stared intently at the young prisoner, paraded between two pairs of guards. Stripped to the waist, hands manacled, he looked frail and slender, though his bony shoulders were thrust back bravely.

Billy Bates had been in the army and America for less than three years. In that time he had been promoted to the rank of corporal and saved enough to bring over the girl who had become his wife. The young woman had been unhappy from the start, however, unused to the rough, lonely life of an army post. She had been easy prey for the unscrupulous Davies. Last autumn Davies had hired her as a private nurse to tend wounds he had suffered in the disastrous Mohawk Valley campaign; she had lived with him ever since.

The affair had caused a minor scandal, particularly since Bates was well liked by nearly everyone at the straits. Especially at this time of year, when the fort was busy, Bates would earn a few extra pennies by playing his concertina and singing, while his pet monkey performed acrobatics and held out a tin cup. This morning, as the corporal was drummed around the fort's perimeter, the monkey was tethered to a barracks porch, chattering and squealing in distress.

The procession reached the parade ground, and the drumming stopped. Bates was led into a hollow square formed by the men of the garrison, all of them turned out immaculately, brass and firearms shining in the sunlight, hair powdered white, scarlet tunics brilliant in the April sun. In the center of the square stood the dreaded triangles—three tenfoot poles lashed together in a pyramid, upon which the punishment would be administered. Bates was led forward, his hands quickly tied to the top of the pyramid, his feet spread and tied to the bottom, and a heavy cartridge belt draped over his thin shoulders to keep his head from moving during the lashing.

At one side of the square of soldiers stood Jeremy Bently, in the group of officers ranged beside Henry Hamilton. Hamilton, hands behind his back, seemed impassive. He was a tall, fine-looking man, fair and slim, with keen blue eyes and a firm mouth that made the features of his long, narrow face seem that much more refined. He wore the fulldress scarlet-and-white uniform of the king's Fifteenth Regiment, with the gold, crescent-shaped officer's gorget hanging high on his chest.

Above the hush of the crowded parade ground rose the slow tap-tapping of the drum that would beat time for each stroke to come. An enormous sergeant, a cat-o'-nine-tails dangling from his hand, stepped toward Bates. There was sadness in the sergeant's eyes, though he had no choice but to lay on, and lay on hard, or the drum major would come up with a cane and beat him mercilessly. If the drum major held back, then a senior officer would wield a cane to beat leniency out of the drum major. Mark Davies was the officer in command of the punishment.

The drum major ordered the sergeant to do his duty, and immediately the lash rose, then fell with a ripping whack that made the onlookers wince. The Indians muttered and shook their heads.

As the drum tapped out time, the whip rose and slashed. Corporal Bates was trying not to scream. With a lead bullet clenched between his teeth to protect his tongue, he hissed and his eyes went wide with every stroke.

Jeremy could already see the blood running down. He wished he were the surgeon on duty, with the right to call an early end to the punishment; but Surgeon Lawrence Sennet, an aging veteran, was assigned that responsibility. Sennet must be somewhere nearby—though Jeremy could not see him—for the punishment was not allowed to proceed without him. Jeremy was sure the slender Bates would not take more than fifty lashes before bone was laid bare, and perhaps lungs exposed as well.

Jeremy gritted his teeth with every stroke. After what seemed an eternity, twenty had been laid on. The prisoner's head hung, and he was whimpering. The distant, frantic screams of the tethered monkey seemed loud. Jeremy knew this was more than enough. Mark Davies was standing at the far side of the hollow square, eyes glittering, savoring the punishment.

Jeremy had the urge to leap out and pummel the man but refrained from showing the slightest emotion, for that would only give Davies more pleasure. Davies no doubt had demanded full punishment to satisfy his own cruelty, but he was not beyond increasing the punishment simply to rankle Jeremy.

Jeremy stared at the ground, unable to ignore the lash and the groans of the victim. He tried to imagine Gwen's lovely face, her large and soft eyes, but knew she, too, must be suffering to be aware of what was going on at this moment.

After thirty lashes, Bates's legs gave way and he slumped down, hanging by his arms, the bullet slipping from his teeth as he cried for his mother. The flogger stopped and glanced about him; the duty surgeon should have come to look the poor wretch over. Finally Jeremy saw the surgeon step into the square. The elderly Sennet was a gangly, drooping figure in a disheveled old uniform and a dirty wig. His tricorne was askew, as was his wig. He had been drinking too much again.

Sennet clucked, bent over the corporal, and in a creaking Maryland voice cried out thickly, "The poor lad's had all he can take, suh!" He gestured to the drum major, who nodded and turned to Davies. A look of annoyance came over Davies's thin face. He shook his head, idly waving a cane.

"Carry out the penalty, drum major. I daresay Mr. Sennet's not in any condition to deem whether the corporal can withstand his just punishment."

At that moment, a soft sound began running through the paraded Redcoats, a sort of whisper that Jeremy recognized as sniffing. Every soldier must stand straight, and none could show his anger or compassion, but there was a time-honored method of expressing sympathy with a prisoner, and that was to sniff. A hundred men began to sniff, and the sound rose like air whistling through trees. Davies stiffened and angrily called for Sennet to step back and for the flogging to resume.

Jeremy hoped that Lieutenant Governor Hamilton would intercede, but he feared Davies would be allowed free rein for the sake of overall discipline. Davies was Hamilton's most effective liaison with many of the eastern tribes, and Hamilton would not alienate him or embarrass him in front of the men if he could help it. Jeremy's anger surged, and blood pounded in his head. Sennet had retired, embarrassed and indeed too drunk to make more of a stand against Davies.

The lashing went on, stroke after stroke, Corporal Bates howling and groaning. The soldiers were sniffing loudly, and the Indians had taken up the sound, probably because they thought it funny. Davies stood erect, mouth turned downward, hatred on his face. The lashing reached fifty. The corporal's skin was flayed, ribs red and showing.

The drum major called a halt, and as Sennet again swayed meekly into the square, the sniffing stopped. But Davies immediately strode forward, commanding the drum major to step aside. Davies motioned with his cane. "I'll call on you, Mr. Sennet, when the time is appropriate."

Sennet tried gamely to hold his own, saying, "This lad's had enough, suh! Anyone can see that!"

Davies moved briskly between Sennet and the prisoner and waved with the cane for the sergeant to continue. The sniffing started again, and Davies folded his arms, the cane sticking up as a reminder of his right to beat the sergeant. Sennet was weaving, hardly able to stand, but his own spunk was up, and he tried to push past Davies, who blocked his way. In the clumsy encounter, Sennet's hat and wig fell off.

Davies shouted, "Keep out of this, you drunken sot! Stand back, I say! Don't interfere with the king's justice."

"I'll interfere, Mr. Davies," Jeremy shouted. He moved past the startled Hamilton and made right for the corporal, who had fainted. "If Mr. Sennet is discomposed, I'll take his place, at his request. Thank you, Mr. Sennet." Jeremy was pale and furious at the sight of the corporal's bloody back. "Cut him down, drum major, and take him to the hospital."

Davies slashed the air with his cane. "You have no right! Lay on, Sergeant, or I'll put this cane across your own back."

"I say hold!" Jeremy bellowed, stepping toward the sergeant.

Davies cut the air again, cowing the burly sergeant, who raised the cat to strike—but Jeremy grabbed his arm at its height. The sergeant tried to yank away, but strong as he was, he could not overpower Jeremy. Stubbornly he continued to struggle, glaring at Jeremy as they swayed back and forth. Davies was ranting, and the Indians shouted for glee as Jeremy and the sergeant silently wrestled with their arms. Then, abruptly, the sergeant relented.

Lowering his arm, he whispered, "Forgive me, Dr. Bently." Jeremy released him, and the man turned away, his head bowed. Davies hurried to strike him, raising the cane high.

"Captain Davies, hold!" Henry Hamilton was walking toward them, and Davies hesitated in the middle of the blow. Hamilton had every reason to be angry at officers bickering in the presence of the troops, and at the sight of his black mood, Davies quickly tucked the cane back under his arm.

Composing himself with obvious difficulty, Hamilton stopped a few paces from them and took a deep breath.

"Captain Davies," he began, almost casually, absently rubbing his forehead as he spoke, "I think it prudent in this case to accept the judgment of Dr. Bently." He nodded to the big sergeant, whose ruddy face lit up. "Cut the prisoner down and take him to the hospital."

Hamilton sounded utterly weary. Jeremy, still panting from his exertions, felt slightly embarrassed; he knew how burdened Hamilton was with the repugnant duty of sending Indian raiders against the white settlements, and no doubt the man had more important problems on his mind than a blow-up between two subordinates.

"Gentlemen," Hamilton said with a sigh, "I demand that we have no more of this." He had a troubled look as he glanced at Corporal Bates being untied; then he spoke curtly, in a clipped voice. "Captain Davies, dismiss the troops, if you please. Be so good as to come to my quarters directly; we have plans to make for the campaign."

Davies was livid but managed to restrain his fury. He clicked his heels in salute, spun, and called shrilly for junior officers to dismiss the garrison by companies.

But before his command could be repeated by the subordinates, a burst of riflery and raucous shrieking turned everyone's attention toward the water gate. A gleeful babble of Indian voices drew nearer, and the crowd parted to let in a large war party of grotesquely painted Senecas who surrounded a group of white women and children.

Jeremy tensed, and so did Hamilton. How sorry these miserable captives looked! Four of the women were carrying a man on a sling, his head bound in bloody bandages, and even from this distance Jeremy could see he was as pale as death. No other men were to be seen, but there were plenty of scalps on the belts of the Indians. The children were filthy, barefoot, clothed in rags, and bruised from their long ordeal.

Jeremy was about to dash away to them but saw that Surgeon Sennet was already arranging with the Senecas for custody of the captives. The other Indians in the fort were chattering and shouting in praise of the Senecas, but most of the whites, Jeremy noticed, were quiet, soberly watching a scene that had become all too familiar of late.

Just then Mark Davies spoke cheerfully to Hamilton in a high-pitched, nasal voice: "After we send all these braves against the settlements this summer, we won't have any- where to put these dogs of rebels, Your Excellency!"

Jeremy ignored a mocking glance directed his way. Davies rarely missed an opportunity to take revenge for all Owen Sutherland had done long ago to humiliate him, and Jeremy, even with his uniform and rank, was not exempt from the man's spite.

Hamilton did not reply, and Davies spoke again.

"I'll wager that my Senecas will outdo even the Shawnees in the coming campaign, sir. Why, by the time we're done, there won't be a god-rotting rebel west of the Appalachians, save for those we've interned up here!"

When Davies still got no reply from the somber Ham- ilton, he lost his smile, turned, and once more ordered the regiment dismissed. As drums beat and voices shouted com- mands, Jeremy looked at Hamilton, whose face was wan, almost sickly.

Jeremy bluntly said, "So new orders have come from London, sir? Is it all-out war now?"

Hamilton clasped his hands behind his back and stood there, shoulders hunched, jaw set. He was watching sentries and the duty officer escorting the jubilant Senecas toward the council house, where payment for the captives would be arranged. The lieutenant governor did not reply, but Jeremy understood that his own worst fears had come to pass: London was ordering Hamilton to unleash all the Indians this summer.

Then Hamilton looked darkly at Jeremy, his head lowered, bushy brows concealing his eyes. He spoke softly but clearly through the hubbub of the fort.

"Do not let your hatred for Captain Davies embarrass me again, or you'll soon learn that our friendship will not override my duty to maintain discipline."

That touched a nerve, and Jeremy stiffened. This was the first time Hamilton had placed rank between them. They had long been on best of terms, from before Jeremy had joined the army, but now Jeremy could not find words to reply. Once more Hamilton began to rub his forehead, then abruptly turned and started back to his quarters.

With a sinking heart, Jeremy watched till Hamilton disappeared into the trim, whitewashed commandant's house, where Jeremy himself had spent several months as a child. His own uncle, Colonel Henry Gladwin, had once been commander of Fort Detroit, a position that made him protector of the American frontier. How it all had changed since then, since his happy boyhood. How he hated this war!

Abruptly remembering the suffering corporal and the man who had been brought in on a sling, Jeremy hurried toward the hospital, hoping Gwen would not be so shaken that she would accuse him of condoning such brutality.

chapter 13

BENJAMIN'S FATE

The hospital was a long, low, square-timbered building that had formerly served as a trading house for the Frontier Company. With the decline in the company's business after the departure of Owen Sutherland and the Morelys, the building had become available to Jeremy, and with Gwen's help he had turned it into an efficient, clean hospital.

He strode from the busy street up the porch steps, coming in behind two privates who were carrying the unconscious Corporal Bates on a stretcher. Inside, the air had the scent of dried herbs mingled with the strong smell of bayberry-and-lye soap. Sunlight filled the room, which was furnished with twenty cots, about half of them occupied—one with the captive settler, Jeremy noticed. It looked as if Gwen had already treated him.

Bates was laid face-down on a cot that had been spread with an old sheet. Gwen was not there, and Jeremy assumed she was in the surgery room next door. He took off his tunic and quickly rolled up his sleeves, kneeling beside the corporal. With a groan, Bates turned onto his side, his legs curled up, face white. The two privates moved back and watched wordlessly as Jeremy administered a strong dose of laudanum paste mixed with water. Soon Gwen appeared at the bedside. She was wearing a crisp white apron, her hair tied up under a linen mobcap. Her face was drawn, and the corners of her mouth twitched down involuntarily as she looked at Bates's back.

Without a word, she set to dressing the wounds, first washing them with a warm herbal solution. As she worked, Jeremy dismissed the lingering soldiers, who said as they departed that they would care for their friend's monkey.

When she had finished, Gwen sat down in a chair and released a long sigh. Jeremy saw that the patient had fallen asleep under the laudanum. He looked at his wife and took her hand. Her eyes were full of tears.

Jeremy said, more bluntly than intended, "Don't think your rebel army is any different—" She turned away, taking a handkerchief from her sleeve and blowing her nose. "They use the cat for discipline, too, just like the British army and the loyalist regiments. . . . Gwen, dearest, I just mean to say—" He broke off, clenching his jaw. "Ah, what's the use?"

After a long silence, Jeremy went to inspect the other new patient, and Gwen followed. She said he was a Pennsylvania farmer who had been scalped by the Senecas and, having survived, had been brought back as a captive. She did not have to explain what Jeremy already knew: the warrior who had caught this man would claim rewards for both prisoner and scalp. There was no official payment for a scalp, but taking one to Detroit proved victory against rebels, and that earned payment. The man was babbling deliriously as Jeremy inspected then rebandaged the ghastly wound; clearly he would not last the week.

Gwen knelt on a stool at the bedside, hands clasped, her forehead upon them. Jeremy went to her and put a hand on her shoulder.

She said, "It's all become so much bigger than anyone expected." She put a hand on his, and he squeezed her fingers.

She whispered shakily, "You say that we'll leave this place for Vincennes, where there is no war, where it's peaceful. But we can't go; we're needed here!" Looking pleadingly at Jeremy, she asked, "Do you believe the British can break the rebellion by allowing Indians to destroy the settlements?"

"You know better." Jeremy stared down at the dying Pennsylvanian, anger welling up in him.

Gwen pressed: "How many folk like this have we treated in the past two years? How many more will there be? How many will die in the name of the king, in the name of

Redcoat honor, in the name of an empire that's been rejected by the will of a strong people?"

"Enough, Gwen!" He glared at her. "I don't need a lesson in scruples! Parliament must end it, but don't forget it's rebels who began this war!"

He moved to a window away from the cots. Outside, in the bright and sunny fort, scores of capering, bragging young Indians were prancing about in anticipation of the warpath and the night's festivities. Gwen came to his side, lightly touching his arm as she, too, gazed at the warriors.

"They're like children," she said softly. "Like great big spoiled children, mean and bullying, and dangerous—"

"Hush," he murmured, taking her hand.

"It's all just a game to them, a magical, bloody celebration, a childish rite of manhood—"

"Gwen! I know who they are and what they're capable of!"

She was breathing faster, as if something was driving her to speak. "Just as this war's a rite of manhood for the lords overseas! Ministers and Redcoat generals will refuse to make terms, refuse to admit that Americans will never again be subjects to a king who's just as much a spoiled, dangerous child as those savages out—"

"Silence!" He swung around and shook her roughly. She wrenched away from him, eyes flaring. "Gwen, you mustn't be heard to speak so here!"

"It's true! You know it's true, Jeremy, and each day that your loyalists and British and Redcoat generals refuse to admit it, the more suffering comes down on the heads of Americans!"

Jeremy strode away, turned and walked back again, then attempted to examine Corporal Bates. All the while he was white with anger, but had no reasonable answer. Some of the patients had been awakened by their arguing and were staring at him.

All of a sudden Gwen relented, and with a cry she came to embrace him. He put his arms tightly about her, though her harsh words still rang in his ears.

Gwen whispered, obviously trying to control herself, "It will stop only when loyalists and rebels both see that nothing can be gained from further slaughter."

He stood back. "Tell that to your Congress, then."

"Tell it to your commander!"

"He knows—no one needs to be told we're all mad and proud and stubborn, and that this war's hell for all of us! Everyone knows!"

"Not everyone! Mark Davies loves the killing! And there are others like him on both sides who'll keep on killing as long as they're allowed to!"

"We've said enough." Jeremy moved away again, but swung back. "I've told Hamilton the Indian war's all wrong. But he's a soldier—he has his orders."

"Like you?"

"Damn it all, Gwen!" he hissed. "For now, I'm a soldier, yes!" He collected himself and eyed his scarlet tunic hanging near the door. "I thought that by putting on that coat I could have some influence, that I could help prevent Hamilton from letting loose mad dogs like Davies." He did not say aloud that he had been wrong, but he thought it, felt it, like an ache in his mind.

Gwen made no reply.

More quietly, Jeremy said, "I never imagined I'd be ashamed to wear a British uniform." He gazed at the floor. "Now I understand why my uncle refused to accept a general's commission to return to America and fight rebels. I understand only too well. . . ."

Gwen caught her breath, as if waiting to hear him say he had changed his mind completely—but he did not. He was not certain what was right anymore. Nearby, Bates rolled onto his back and moaned, even though under the laudanum. Jeremy went to him and spoke softly, turning him onto his side and propping a pillow behind him so he would not lie on his wounds.

Outside, Indians whooped, and there was a burst of shouting and cheering, accompanied by a distant fusillade of gunfire. It was the familiar sound of another triumphant war party coming in.

At last Benjamin Sutherland had hope. He was less than a day's journey south of Fort Detroit, camped on the western

slope of Lake Erie near the river's mouth. The land here
was familiar to him, and even the scent of the evening spring
breeze spoke of home. By tomorrow night he would be
safe with family friends at Detroit—maybe even home at
Valenya with his half-brother Jeremy.

He sat on a low bluff, looking eastward across the darkening water, the sun setting orange behind him. His hands
had been left unbound, but he was still closely watched,
especially by Amaghwah. He had no intention of escaping,
of course, though he probably knew this country better than
any Shawnee. He had been within a mile or two of here
many times with his family, fishing and picnicking, sometimes trading with the Sandusky Hurons. The western end
of Erie had always been a place of rest, and even now
Benjamin felt that way.

On a scrub oak above him Punch was pecking at insects.
A little farther off, in a Huron apple orchard, Wabete's men
were huddled around a cooking fire, finishing their evening
meal. They were laughing and joking, in the best of spirits
now that Detroit was near. Blackfish and his men had already departed for the fort, in a dozen long canoes borrowed
from the Hurons. They had left early this morning, after
painting their faces yellow and green and donning new shirts
purchased from the local tribe. The Kentuckian prisoners
had looked relieved, aware that their ordeal would soon be
over. A few of them, including Boone, had shouted and
waved good-bye to Benjamin, saying they would see him
in Detroit. Benjamin had wanted to go with them, but he
knew that Wabete's men would wait another day before
leaving. If they arrived with Blackfish, there would not be
enough praise left for the smaller, less successful war party.
Wabete's Shawnees wanted their own grand entrance, their
own traditional fire of joy, as the triumphant musket salute
was called.

Suddenly Benjamin heard raised voices, and he looked
back at the camp; Wabete and Amaghwah were in an ani-
mated argument, which was not unusual these days. Benjamin could not hear what it was about, nor did he care. It
was obvious even to him that Amaghwah hungered to be
the leader of Wabete's men. The warrior seemed to object

to Wabete's every decision, ever since the old chief had refused to sell Benjamin to Mark Davies. Certainly the two would come to blows before long, though Benjamin was sure Wabete would prevail in any fight. He had a grudging respect for Wabete, who had at least treated him fairly, if not kindly. Oddly enough, even Punch now came willingly to Wabete, hopping on the Indian's shoulders and hand— a sight that amused the other warriors, though it disgusted Amaghwah all the more.

Eventually the argument ended and Amaghwah strode off. The campsite grew quiet, and Benjamin left the bluff to rest in the blanket Wabete had given him. As a captive, he was not permitted near the fire and slept some distance from the others. Punch squawked and fluttered onto a bush beside him; Benjamin curled up and tried to sleep.

Through the early evening he slumbered fitfully, for he was both tired and excited. Once he was roused and ordered to collect firewood, and after being handed a few scraps of food he went back to his blanket. Half asleep, he watched the moon rise and heard the fire being built up against the chill of the wind.

For the first time since being taken captive, Benjamin was certain that tomorrow his life would change for the better. It was a comforting thought, and he drew the blanket up over his head to shut out the shining of the moon.

A shrieking noise woke him violently. Heart pounding, he sat up and blinked at the moon, a glare of white. Against it a shadowy form was writhing, as if in battle with an unseen ghost. With a shock he realized it was Amaghwah, trying to hold on to Punch, who was fluttering and squawking. The bird must have seen Amaghwah stealing up on Benjamin; but whatever had happened, Punch was getting the worst of it as Amaghwah knocked him down in a flurry of feathers.

"No!" Benjamin sprang up and shouldered into Amaghwah, who fell to hands and knees but kept scrambling after the flapping, hurt jay. Again the Shawnee had Punch, this time by one wing, and again Benjamin thudded against him—so hard that he, too, fell to the ground. Amaghwah snarled and stood up, but seemed determined to kill the jay before dealing with the boy.

Benjamin quickly regained his feet, but Amaghwah had Punch firmly now, and the bird squawked as the laughing Indian held him up to the moon and slowly began to squeeze the life out of him.

Benjamin sprang again but missed as Amaghwah stepped nimbly aside. Stumbling to a halt, Benjamin whirled to attack once more, fearing he would be too late.

Then someone else was there, and Amaghwah's shriek was cut off abruptly, followed by choking and strangling sounds. Benjamin moved forward, gasping, and in the moonlight he saw a man fighting with Amaghwah, who crashed to the ground with such force that he lay there, feet slowly sliding back and forth, as if running in a dream. Wabete, like the great elk that had given him his name, stood silhouetted against the moonlit sky.

"Peshawa." His large hand held out, Wabete took a step forward. In the dimness, Benjamin could make out the bird's limp body, unmoving.

Sorrow overwhelmed him, tears running down his face, and for once Benjamin did not care about showing weakness to a warrior. The chief gave the jay to him. Punch's eye gleamed, and Benjamin knew there was yet a spark of life there.

Sobbing, he whispered the bird's name and carefully rubbed the jay all over, talking words of encouragement. The beak opened and closed, but no sound came forth. He kept caressing the bird. He could feel no broken bones, and once the wings flapped. Punch had lost some feathers and was stunned, but he was alive.

"Make him well, Wildcat," Wabete said. "Keep him warm inside your shirt."

Benjamin nodded and laid the bird on his blanket. Too late he saw a quick movement behind Wabete; he sprang up, throwing himself viciously at Amaghwah, who was stabbing for the chief's back. Wabete spun, but the knife caught him in the upper chest, and with a grunt of pain he dropped to his knees. Benjamin's charge had deflected the thrust and prevented a worse wound, but already Amaghwah was drawing back to strike again. Benjamin shouted, lunged for the man's knife arm, and with all the might he could muster yanked Amaghwah away.

Benjamin was strong, but Amaghwah was a mature warrior, and he heaved Benjamin hard to the ground. Amaghwah turned for Wabete again, to finish the assassination before the other braves interfered.

The wind knocked out of him, Benjamin struggled to his feet as the dazed Wabete looked helplessly up at Amaghwah. The blade came down again. Wabete diverted the blow, and the knife slashed the back of the chief's neck. Wabete was too stunned to rise, but he blocked a third quick strike with his forearm. He was off-balance now, and Amaghwah had him at his mercy.

With a groan, Benjamin threw himself on Amaghwah's back, wrenching the man's head around by grasping his face and clawing at his eyes. Amaghwah tumbled to the ground, snarling in rage, digging the knife at Benjamin, stabbing the boy again and again on the legs and arms. Finally the others were awake and shouting, trying to find out what was happening. Benjamin heard them, but he could not call, for he was using all his strength to keep Amaghwah down. But the man fought free again, took a slash at Benjamin that just missed, and looked up to see the rest of the party coming at him. With a mad cry he sprang right into their midst, bounding through them and off into the darkness.

At Fort Detroit, the arrival of Blackfish's party caused great excitement. Jeremy and Gwen went to the porch of the hospital to watch the Shawnees approach down the muddy street, which was lined with throngs of clapping, jeering Indians and loyalists.

Jeremy had heard of Daniel Boone and looked on with curiosity as Indians running in advance shouted out the man's name, crying that Blackfish had taken the Kentucky fighters without a shot. Surrounded and goaded on by the Shawnees, Boone and the tethered Kentuckians trotted into sight, and although they were dirty, tattered, and exhausted, their heads were held high. There was a fire in their eyes that made Jeremy sorry to have such men as enemies.

Gwen pressed against his shoulder as the white captives filed past; in their wake ran more Indians and some boys and dogs from the settlement. If this were an Indian village and not Detroit, the Kentuckians would have had to run the gauntlet between two long lines of people armed with sticks and switches. Even so, some of the squaws now lining the route ran out to strike or kick the prisoners, before they were driven back by Redcoat sentries.

Jeremy was about to comment that none of the prisoners appeared seriously injured, when a middle-aged man standing nearby made the same observation as he greeted the couple. He was a short, portly, well-dressed merchant named Dawson Merriwether, a longtime friend of the Sutherlands. Today he looked unusually stern, however, and Jeremy quickly guessed the reason: Merriwether was a native Virginian and no doubt knew some of these Kentuckians, many of whom were originally from Virginia.

"Henry Hamilton's waging this dirty war as best he can," Merriwether declared, mopping his red face with a silk handkerchief. "No man can do more . . . and hasn't old Blackfish here proved we can employ Indians humanely?"

Merriwether was carefully avoiding Gwen's eyes, though at the last moment he glanced sheepishly at her, as if in appeal to her common sense. Her troubled expression gave him no comfort, however, and she did not reply. Jeremy wished she would say something polite instead of staring so intently at the prisoners being herded toward the parade ground. He cleared his throat and bade Merriwether farewell as the Virginian moved off to his own trading house a few streets away. When Merriwether was gone, Jeremy turned to Gwen.

"You see, there is some civility and honor to this frontier war after all."

Still she did not reply, and was about to go back into the hospital when she gave a cry of surprise.

"It's Tamano and Mawak! They've returned at last!"

They had been trailing the Shawnee party, and both looked spent and hollow-cheeked from their long journey. Now they came directly to Jeremy and Gwen, who ran down to the street and embraced them enthusiastically. Tamano had not been heard from in months, since he had sent word to his wife at Detroit, saying he was searching for Owen Sutherland. Jeremy could hardly restrain himself, sure that Tamano would have news of his family.

As the four of them mounted the steps to the hospital, Tamano said he had come to see Jeremy even before going home to his family.

"There is something to tell, brother," he went on, following Gwen and Mawak into the back room, where there was food in the kitchen and a private place to talk. Mawak sat down heavily in a chair, and Tamano helped him lay his rifle and pack on the floor. "It is about Benjamin, who is a prisoner of the Shawnees."

Jeremy stopped short, the blood draining from his face. "Prisoner of Blackfish? I didn't see him!"

"No," Tamano replied. Gwen, too, was listening, her eyes wide. "Benjamin is with another party downriver, Blackfish says. Blackfish told me this when I met him, only an hour ago. Benjamin will be coming in tomorrow."

That relieved Jeremy, and after closing the door, he pulled up chairs for the rest of them. Hamilton would buy Benjamin's freedom, and the boy could stay at Valenya.

"What on earth happened? Is Ben well?"

"Blackfish says the boy is strong and healthy. Shawnees caught him four moons ago. They will demand great payment from Hamilton or perhaps from you before they hand him over."

"They'll get whatever they ask. It will be good to see him again!" Jeremy had so many questions that he didn't know where to start.

It was Gwen who remembered Indian politeness; she rose, saying, "Husband, let us properly welcome our guests with food and drink and a pipe; we can talk later."

Jeremy smiled at her and, apologizing to his friends, quickly rose. As Gwen busied herself preparing bowls of whitefish stew, bread, and mugs of beer, he fetched a pipe, lit it, and passed it to Mawak.

After smoke and food, questions began, and Jeremy absorbed everything Tamano and Mawak told him. He learned to his astonishment that Owen Sutherland was on the way to Detroit and wanted to arrange a meeting.

Mawak said in Ottawa, through a mouthful of bread, "Your father will send word to you when he gets here; he has something important, only for your ears."

Jeremy accepted that without question, but he was worried. Sutherland would not seek him out in loyalist country unless there was something extremely important to discuss. Surely it must be about Benjamin. Though Jeremy longed to see Owen, he knew his stepfather would again try to persuade him to spurn the loyalist cause.

He took a deep breath. "I will gladly meet with him, but only if he will swear not to spy on the fort while I know of his presence here. My honor demands this much."

Mawak and Tamano nodded once to signify their agreement. Behind them, Gwen listened as Jeremy occasionally translated whatever was said in Ottawa. Her hand went to her heart, and Jeremy wondered what she was thinking. He guessed she was hoping that Sutherland would finally prevail on him to resign his commission. He held her gaze a moment; if Sutherland had something worthwhile to say, he would of course hear him out. He would listen to reason, but he would not shift with the political breeze.

Gwen took her eyes from him and offered the Indians more bread and stew, which they hungrily accepted. As she ladled the stew her hands were shaking, and a little spilled on the floor. Jeremy sensed that even Tamano and Mawak knew why she was nervous; a rebel supporter at Detroit had good reason to be afraid.

Tamano said casually, as if to calm Gwen, "It will be good for your man to hear something of the other side now that the world has changed and things are not as they once were."

She nodded and went back to the stove.

Mawak burped and said the food was good, adding in English, "Donoway want to see Valenya, lady. He want tell his woman how you keep it home."

Gwen turned and said, "He will be welcome, Mawak. Valenya will always be his home."

Jeremy gave a small smile. "Always. And home, too, for Benjamin, who will stay there until Owen comes. If he wants, he can take the boy away to safer country."

Gwen looked at him questioningly. As a rule, rebel captives were resettled on the straits and not imprisoned, as long as they promised not to fight for the rebellion again. They were not, however, allowed back into rebel territory. What Jeremy had suggested would be strictly against regulations, even though Benjamin was too young to fight.

Jeremy gave a shrug. "So you see, Gwen, when it comes to my brother and stepfather, I can be more than just another Redcoat marionette."

She smiled and came to his side, putting an arm about his waist. The Indians chuckled, then rose and thanked her, in white-man's fashion, for the food. It was agreed they would all meet again when Benjamin was purchased.

Tamano said, "We are both in need of a celebration. My uncle here was ill for some weeks, and we could not travel until he recovered."

Mawak hefted his gear, grunting loudly. "Now strong as bull moose! Ready to sing!" He thumped his chest. "Need more 'n beer, though."

Jeremy grinned. "We'll all sing, and we'll make Valenya dance once again! It's been too long since we rattled those fine Philadelphia windows! Let's give Benjamin something to remember us by before we send him on his way!"

The Indians loudly agreed, and Jeremy felt the almost-forgotten rush of good cheer, a lust for living that always had been the lifeblood of fur traders, Indians, and soldiers who dwelt at the straits. There would be a party, with all their friends invited.

"Everyone not in the army, at least," he declared, putting his arm around Gwen, who hugged him to her. "Pa will be glad to know we haven't forgotten how to laugh and dance, even though so many of our folk have left us. A party, whether any fur came in this spring or not!" He glanced at his red tunic and grinned. "And I promise—no damned lobster coats or lobster regulations to dampen our spirits!"

Benjamin Sutherland watched canoe after canoe of Indians paddle northward to Detroit. It was morning, and he sat leaning against a tree at the edge of the campsite, the helpless

Punch cradled on a blanket in his arms.

Nearby Wabete lay half conscious, while his warriors rested or milled about, waiting for their chief to show some sign of change. Benjamin looked down at the jay, who seemed more dead than alive, and tucked the corner of the blanket over its fragile body. He did not know whether any bones had been crushed or if the bird had suffered other serious injury.

Benjamin had already inspected and bandaged his own wounds; none of them seemed very deep. He was not in too much pain, though he would have trouble walking any distance. He gazed back at the old chief, who was wearing his precious scarlet coat and was covered with blankets, lying on a bed of balsam and leaves. Wabete's men were sad, especially because they had failed to catch Amaghwah, whose tracks had led down to the water's edge, then vanished, as if he had taken a canoe. Yet no one remembered a canoe being drawn up at that spot last night; it was as if someone had been waiting for him, anticipating his arrival, and had helped him escape.

Benjamin wished he could get on with the journey to Detroit, which was so maddeningly near. Yet for some reason he felt sorry for old Wabete, even though the chieftain had led a raid against his family's settlement. Benjamin still knew little about the casualties among the whites and was aware only that the Indians had been driven off with great loss. He was almost certain Susannah and James had managed to escape, for the Shawnees had not taken any scalps from the Wyoming; and surely his parents were all right. In any case, it all seemed so long ago, and even though he was eager to get to Detroit, he hoped Wabete would recover.

Suddenly the old chief uttered something, and the men rushed to his side, some of them kneeling. Benjamin got up, his wounds smarting, and moved closer. He heard Wabete speak in a breathy, soft voice.

"Where . . . where is Peshawa, my wildcat?"

The Indians parted, one of them pulling Benjamin forward. Wabete looked up, his eyes half closed and his expression inscrutable, although it was clear he was enduring great pain. His bandages were concealed under his clothes, but apparently the bleeding had stopped.

The chief nodded slightly, then asked Benjamin, "And our fierce jay?"

Benjamin cleared his throat. "He yet lives, but I know not how long."

Wabete closed his eyes, saying in almost a whisper, "Wabete, too, lives...." He opened his eyes and said, "Wabete lives because Peshawa is brave." He gave a little smile and coughed once, pain wracking him, but he fought it down and looked once again at Benjamin. The boy could not help but notice affection in the man's dark eyes.

Wabete sighed and spoke to his men. "If this old Indian is to die, it should be in his own lodge, not in the lodge of Henry Hamilton."

He glanced about at the warriors, whose concern showed in their faces and was evident in their voices as they nodded and agreed to take Wabete back to Chillicothe. When one warrior asked what should be done with the prisoner, Wabete coughed noisily, causing them all to look anxiously at one another.

"It is your right," he said, "to demand the full spoils of victory in exchange for him at Detroit."

Benjamin felt tremendous relief, and his heart pounded fast. The Indians began talking among themselves, deciding who should go to Detroit with Benjamin and who should go southward to Chillicothe, carrying their chief on a litter.

Their talk was interrupted as Wabete coughed again. Then he said—in a voice unexpectedly strong and clear—"But think of this, my brave warriors...." He coughed, and Benjamin saw a sidelong glance escape his slitted eyes, as if he were calculating something. "... you would greatly honor this dying chieftain, my warriors, if you considered matters most deeply before taking away his captive, the son of Donoway..." He coughed and coughed, and when he spoke again they hung on every word.

"... for at the door of death, Wabete thinks it would be a last pleasure, a final remembrance, to keep the boy—" That sly glance escaped again.

Benjamin caught a breath. The Indians, too, were startled

at this remark, and once again Benjamin thought Wabete was eyeing them too calculatingly for a dying man. Benjamin's heart was racing as Wabete's unexpected appeal began to be absorbed by the others, evidently without objection.

Wabete weakly raised a hand, saying dramatically with eyes closed, "It is the madness of a dying one, perhaps... but, brothers and nephews, there is something in my old heart that says life will remain in my body for a time, if only I have the hope... the hope of final glory... the capture of Donoway himself!" He sighed and waved limply. "But I leave it to you whether this captive white boy should be exchanged or left with me."

The Indians began to chatter among themselves. Benjamin was in a cold sweat, chilled to the bone to think Wabete might actually get his wish. Valenya was just hours away! Yet he knew better than to say anything. He looked down at Punch, who seemed less alive than ever.

A tear welled in Benjamin's eye, and though he felt suddenly weak and was still breathing hard, he refused to yield to emotion. He stood up straighter, his chest stuck out. To his surprise, Wabete was looking intently at him. The old Indian had an expression of approval on his face, which was now quite alert.

"It is as I expected, Peshawa. You do not beg for freedom!"

Benjamin's mind grew cold, his eyes hard, but the more resolute he tried to be, the more Wabete softened, as if admiring his courage.

Wabete said, "I am pleased, Peshawa, that you do not grovel. That is why..." He coughed, but it seemed forced. "That is why this... dying old man... is not prepared to give you up. Not yet."

Wabete's eyes took on a strange light, and suddenly Benjamin recalled what the chief had told him about an eldest son having died at the age of fifteen. And had Wabete really said that the boy's nickname had been Peshawa?

chapter 14

HAMILTON'S WAR

When Benjamin did not appear at Detroit, Jeremy grew worried. He and Gwen had stayed overnight at the hospital, and all that day they had anxiously awaited the Shawnees' arrival. By sunset, however, no Shawnee parties had appeared, and Jeremy could wait no longer.

As soon as the fort's gates closed for the evening, he went to see Hamilton at the commandant's house and informed him of the situation. Hamilton advised patience, saying that nothing out of the ordinary had been reported downriver and that surely Benjamin's Indians would be in soon.

The next day, however, only three of Wabete's men arrived, with a sack of scalps they said had been taken from the Fort Pitt militia. They told Hamilton that Wabete and the boy captive were well on their way back to Chillicothe.

When Jeremy was sent word of this, he flew into a rage. Storming into Hamilton's office, he was in no mood to be put off with assurances that his brother would be exchanged soon enough—yet that was precisely what Hamilton first said.

The lieutenant governor sat at a polished table cluttered with papers, pens, an inkstand, and belts of colorful wampum beads. Maps of the eastern frontier were spread open before him, showing settlements, Indian tribes, and rebel strongholds. On the wall beyond were several pen-and-ink landscapes of Detroit and the vicinity, done by Hamilton himself. Jeremy stood impatiently at attention, cocked hat under his arm, his face flushed with anger.

"I respectfully request permission to follow those Shawnees and recover my brother, sir, before something happens to him."

Jeremy's jaw was clenched tight, and he was doing his best to govern his anger. Hamilton methodically laid aside his quill, pushed back his chair, put the tips of his fingers to his lips, pondering. In that silence Jeremy realized Hamilton was allowing him time to compose himself, for the sake of avoiding heated words. Hamilton was a wise, dedicated professional whose coolheadedness was widely respected, but right now Jeremy was almost beside himself, wishing he could throw off his uniform, don a frontiersman's outfit, and get on the trail before the Shawnees were too far away.

Before Hamilton had replied to his first request, Jeremy remarked, "Anything might happen, sir, especially if they get hold of rum. You know—"

"I know!" Hamilton said gruffly, rubbing his forehead, taking a long breath. "I know what you are thinking, Jeremy, so please allow me a moment to consider matters thoroughly before you go charging out of here half-cocked, ready to knock some redskins on the head and stir them all up against us!"

Hamilton rang a bell, and an orderly entered the room and waited at attention. Hamilton paused a moment before addressing him.

Impetuously, Jeremy said, "I'll get the boy without any trouble."

"Surgeon Major! If you please, sir!" Hamilton spoke sharply to the orderly. "Fetch Captain Davies, and ask that he attend me immediately."

Jeremy recoiled but for the moment said nothing. Davies had just been with the Shawnees, and it was normal that Hamilton would consult him in this. At Hamilton's request, Jeremy took a seat. He held his tongue while the lieutenant governor called for brandy.

Hamilton rose to pace slowly, glass in one hand, rubbing his head with the other. "I don't have to tell you, Jeremy, that one misstep with the savages might cost us dearly; and in your distraught condition I won't allow you the chance to start trouble."

Indeed, Jeremy knew that the thousands of Indians gathering around Detroit were like gunpowder and must be handled carefully; if they wavered in their allegiance and thought the rebels might be the side destined to win, then one serious mistake by Hamilton could touch off slaughter that would obliterate Detroit, Michilimackinac, and perhaps even Niagara. Indians suddenly abandoning the French in the last war had changed the balance of power and won an empire for the British. Hamilton would not risk so turning Indians against the king's forces, and especially not the powerful Shawnees.

An uncomfortable silence hung in the room, but after a second glass of brandy was poured, Captain Davies came in, trim and military, clicking his heels, holding his narrow chin high. He had a look of arrogance about him, as if he already knew what Hamilton wanted and could do it. Jeremy rose and greeted him correctly, and Hamilton offered a brandy, then bade them all be seated to consider how best to recover Benjamin Sutherland without causing trouble with the Shawnees.

"I regret to tell you, gentlemen," Hamilton said, "that I am not always able to recover every prisoner." He glanced from Davies to Jeremy. "This very day Blackfish absolutely refused to give up Daniel Boone, though I offered him a hundred pounds sterling. It seems he has some foolish notion of adopting the man."

Jeremy was astonished. A hundred pounds was more hard cash than an Indian might see in his entire life! He asked, "Do they know whose son Benjamin is?"

It was Davies who replied. "They do." He sat more erectly, adding with cool confidence, "My agents among them say they have already refused a large offer to give him up, apparently because their leader intends to use the boy as bait to snare Owen Sutherland."

Jeremy's heart sank. This news made him all the more resolved to go out himself, in full uniform, and demand Benjamin's release in the name of the king. If that failed, there would be no other way but by force.

He bluntly said so, which caused Hamilton to become exceedingly grim.

Davies cleared his throat. "You well know, Your Excellency, what the consequences of such rash behavior would be to the king's interest. Why, it would play right into the hands of the damned rebels—"

"I'll take that chance!" Jeremy declared.

Hamilton spoke sharply. "I won't!"

"It's my brother, sir!"

"It's my duty to keep order and—"

"Blast order!" Jeremy was on his feet. "I'm talking about my brother's life!"

Hamilton was flushed. "And I'm talking about an empire, and about the lives of a thousand loyal folk!" He half rose and leaned over the table, glaring at Jeremy, but his voice became low, almost soft. "Be seated, or I'll order you to your quarters immediately and deal with this without you at all."

Jeremy stood there with fists clenched at his sides, aware of the smug mockery on Davies's face. The captain was behaving perfectly, as cool as could be, playing the part of Hamilton's dependable right hand.

Hamilton spoke again, his voice almost a hiss. "Be seated, Jeremy—please!"

Jeremy obeyed. More calmly, they discussed what had to be done, and Davies made it clear that the Shawnees had to be handled with care and respect.

"They fear the Longknives as much as they fear losing the king's favor. But it's the Longknives who might kill them, while our troops are too few to offer any real threat. Therefore..." He turned his hat over in his hands, appeared to be thinking most seriously, and said with wrinkled brow, "...therefore it's my honest opinion that an officer whom they know and trust should be sent down to deal with this delicate matter. Naturally, Your Excellency, I accede to your wishes, since you know far more than I in regard to the overall perspective."

Hamilton was quiet, thinking. Jeremy was in control of himself by now, but his instinct was to hit the trail and do what had to be done without further agonizing.

After a long sigh, Hamilton sat back, fingers tented to his lips. "The safest course of action for all concerned, including your brother, Surgeon Major, is to have Captain Davies carry out this mission alone—amply supplied, of course, with gifts to exchange for the lad."

Jeremy did not like this one bit. "Let me go, sir, with Tamano and Mawak. They're known by the Shawnees."

Davies began to cluck his tongue and shake his head, the way an older boy might rebuke a child.

"Your Excellency," Davies said in a tone of amazement and disappointment, "surely you well know those two scoundrels have just been to rebel country! They might be spies, for all we know. And who can say what mischief they'd do against our cause?"

Jeremy could have picked him up by the scruff of the neck and thrown him through a window, but Hamilton was listening intently and apparently took the man seriously.

Davies went on. "The one's a drunken sot, and the other is Owen Sutherland's favorite. Surely, sir, we can't rely on them to carry out the king's business." He clucked and sighed.

Jeremy pleaded with Hamilton. "Sir, trust my judgment in this!"

Davies clucked again, and Jeremy swung on him. "Hold that oily tongue or I'll stuff it down your throat!"

Davies paled, hatred visible in his face, but he was not the man to challenge the likes of Jeremy Bently. Hamilton stood up.

"Surgeon Major Bently, the matter is decided! You will—" He stopped himself, as if restraining anger that might have sent Jeremy to his quarters under arrest for insubordination. He started again: "Now, attend my words, Jeremy. It is you who must trust me in this matter. You must be patient, and you must await the success of Captain Davies."

Jeremy was livid with rage, but he knew Hamilton would not change his mind. He said nothing as Hamilton curtly explained that Davies would set off immediately to recover Benjamin.

When Hamilton finished, Jeremy rose, asking to be dismissed. Before leaving, he looked at Davies and said, "The lad's life is in your hands." Davies faced toward Hamilton, who was staring at the tabletop as Jeremy went on. "And your life, Davies, is in mine."

In the following weeks, more and more of the northwestern Indian chiefs and warriors began to arrive in Detroit in response to the great spring council called by Hamilton. Jeremy had witnessed large councils before, but never one quite like this.

He remembered the huge peace council at Niagara after the defeat of Pontiac's uprising, and over the years since, scores of meetings had strengthened ties between the tribes and the British. But no council ever had been convened on such precariously unequal terms, calling up the combined savage might of thousands of northwestern Indians to join Hamilton's scant white forces.

Indians eager to fight the rebels arrived from every direction: Sioux came on horseback from as far west as the Great Plains, and Christianized Iroquois traveled in whiteman's whaleboats up the lakes from New York; hundreds of warriors from distant northern forests paddled down the straits in birchbark canoes, and spokesmen from the southern mountain tribes arrived in elm-bark craft and dugouts. Lodges had sprung up thickly on both sides of the straits, along the tributaries, and next to established villages, leaving hardly a birch or elm tree with its bark as Indians stripped them to fashion makeshift shelters. The dense blue smoke of hundreds of cooking fires hung over the straits from dawn to dark.

It was like a rising tide of fighting men surging at a floodgate that only Henry Hamilton controlled. Jeremy knew and feared that after this council Hamilton would open that gate, releasing five thousand bloodthirsty Indians in hundreds of war parties that would be impossible to manage.

This morning, the final day of the council, Jeremy stood on the ramparts of the fort, watching the Indians assemble on a grassy field just downriver. A large council fire was being hastily built up by some soldiers, and Hamilton's speech would begin there within the hour. Thus far Mark

Davies had not returned from Shawnee country, so there
had been no word about Benjamin. Jeremy was almost sick
with worry.

He thought of springs past when the fort and settlement
would become a crowded and muddy, colorful, swirling,
noisy and gay place. This spring it was still muddy and
crowded, but the mood was no longer lighthearted like the
heady trading festivals of past years, when two hundred
thousand pelts would change hands, rum would be drunk
by the kegful, and for three weeks thousands of rowdy folk,
both red and white, would sing and dance day into night.
Now it was the ominous war songs of boastful warriors
dancing around blood-red poles. Henry Hamilton was feeding these hordes, and he had seen to it that not enough rum
circulated to cause real trouble. He did not want drunken
arguments, brawls, or killings among the warriors who this
summer were needed to fight rebels.

Jeremy watched as painted warriors of more than a dozen
nations arrived before the fort, beaching canoes, leaping
out, and with a shriek darting up the long slope to the council
ground. Most of the tribes he could identify, though he was
unfamiliar with the mighty nations of the distant south—
Chickasaw, Choctaw, and Creek. They had sent their representatives to parley with Hamilton, although their warriors
would remain in the south, to be supplied by British agents
operating out of loyalist-held strongholds on the Mississippi
and the Gulf Coast. Their representatives had come, Jeremy
knew, to learn how Hamilton would set all the warriors in
motion at one time to fall upon the rebel rear in a single,
devastating campaign.

It was almost the moment for the final council, the beginning of a last day of speeches, feasting, drinking, and
singing the war song. Jeremy made his way down the ladder
to the promenade inside the palisades, and at the river gate
he joined several other officers to walk toward the council
ground. The Redcoats moved through swarms of laughing,
sporting Indians and past a few score French residents who
had set up stands to sell food, trinkets, paint, beer, blankets,
and some hardware. The noise increased as Jeremy approached the circle of dignitaries and took his seat a few

yards behind Henry Hamilton's large chair. Hamilton was part of the innermost circle with the leading chiefs, and he was wearing his best uniform, complete with medals, a gold sash, and belts of Indian wampum. Compared to the painted and feathered Indians, he was the picture of precision and civility, though he looked as proud as they, and every bit as grave. As he nodded to acknowledge Jeremy's presence, strain was apparent on his face.

By now the council fire was a long blaze of huge logs, at least a hundred feet from end to end. Near it at intervals hung several large kettles in which bear meat bubbled. This potent stew would ceremonially nourish the fighting men, and each tribe had one of its own men in attendance at the cauldrons. Every person in the inner council circles, including Hamilton and Jeremy, had a plate of pewter, wood, or simple bark to hold the meat, which was soon ladled out all around but left uneaten for the moment. Ranged beside Jeremy and his fellow officers were a dozen or so important British and French officials deemed worthy of joining the feast. Jeremy had not wanted to be here at all, but he had been ordered to attend, and in any case he was curious to know what Hamilton would tell the warriors before sending them against the frontier.

Hamilton leaned back to Jeremy and said, "I hope you've finally calmed down from our last meeting."

Jeremy nodded curtly. "As calm as I'll ever be, sir."

That did not particularly satisfy Hamilton, who frowned, then faced the council grounds, where an important medicine man was now standing. Half-naked, he was holding the head of a bear upon his own head, part of the skin draped down his back. The speech-making began with this tall, wiry fellow calling upon the Maker of the World, the Master of Life, to bless their meeting. Then he prayed to the lesser spirits, the lower manitous, the spirits of the forest, trees, and mountains, asking for protection in future undertakings.

Everyone was silent, though Jeremy estimated there must have been well over a thousand men now gathered around, seated on gently rising ground so that all could see the proceedings. When the medicine man—the master of the feast—came to the end of his long harangue, he swung the bear's head down, holding it suspended from a thong of leather for all to see.

He cried, "This is the head of the Longknife enemy!"

The Indians growled loudly, seemingly as one man.

"This is the enemy who will feel our wrath, who will be driven away by the united force of the red nations joining with the sons of the great white father across the sea. One day we shall hold the severed head of the enemy—like this!"

He raised the bear's head, then swung it on the thong, beginning to dance and to chant his war song. The Indians shouted and grunted in accompaniment, with a sound like the short expiration of breath: *Ho-ho-ho! Ho-ho-ho!*

The faster the man sang and danced, the more frenzied the others became. Jeremy saw that many of the whites were chanting along, most just to humor the Indians, though a few seemed genuinely caught up in the pulsing, rhythmic din and wild dancing of the medicine man. Even Hamilton looked unusually passionate, which troubled Jeremy. There was no doubt that at this moment Hamilton was the mightiest man on half the known continent, and these enthralled savages represented his power.

The master of the feast danced with the bear's head all around the long fire, coming at last to Hamilton and laying the head at his feet. The bear's mouth hung open, its tongue cut away, eyes put out, brutalized as a symbol of the enemy. Jeremy knew it was time for Hamilton to rise and, with the head, dance and sing his war song before the massed, chanting Indians.

This Hamilton did without reservation, and Jeremy's heart beat faster as his commander loudly sang a soldier's tune, adding his own words, telling how the Longknives must be punished, driven out of Indian country, and how there had never before been so mighty a rising of the Indians at one time. He lauded them, exhorted them, and in the name of the king blessed their war-making. He called on them to spare noncombatants and promised greater reward for prisoners than for scalps.

As Hamilton finished his dance, he raised the head of

the bear for all the cheering, whooping warriors to see, and with a yell hurled it into the crowd, which pounced upon it and began to tear it apart with their teeth.

Jeremy sat there glumly as Hamilton came back to sit down, sweating and red in the face, obviously pleased with the excitement he had caused; he had promised that tonight the Indians would be armed.

The master of the feast gave the signal for the bear meat to be devoured as symbolic sustenance, and everyone fell to eagerly, including the whites. Jeremy, who normally had a taste for bear stew, sat there motionless, staring into the crackling fire while everyone else gobbled the food with their fingers.

The skinny medicine man wolfed his down and grinned at Hamilton. Then he caught Jeremy's cold eyes and saw the meat untouched on the plate. The Indian seemed perturbed, staring hard. Hamilton took note of this, glanced over his shoulder, and tensed as he saw Jeremy was not joining in.

"I suggest, sir," Hamilton began with a hiss, "you eat, or depart at once!"

Jeremy did not look at Hamilton but rose abruptly and, dropping the plate, strode out of the council circle. He had to step through Indians less important than those devouring the meat, all of them obviously wondering what was wrong with this white man.

When he was almost out of the crowd, Jeremy bumped into a Redcoat and, hardly looking at the man, began to push past. Then he realized it was Mark Davies, who was trying to join Hamilton.

"Where's my brother?" Jeremy demanded loudly, grabbing Davies by the arm and almost lifting him off the ground. "Where is he?"

"Steady, Bently," Davies said quietly, but seemed genuinely upset. "Your brother's still with the Shawnee, but I believe he's safe . . . for the moment."

Davies tried to pass, but Jeremy's powerful hand did not let go. "You were supposed to get him out!"

"Unhand me!" Davies grunted, trying not to cause a scene in front of all these Indians. "Your brother can't be got out as yet, and if I'd tried any harder, he'd have been slain on the spot! You must believe me! Here—this letter proves it!" He pulled a letter from his tunic and offered it to Jeremy.

Jeremy took it but was almost blind with anger at Davies and fear for his brother. Without releasing Davies, he flipped open the letter.

Davies said nervously, "They wouldn't let me have him because he's to be adopted."

"In the name of—!" Jeremy saw the letter was indeed in Benjamin's handwriting.

"Maybe in a year or so he'll be given enough freedom to be able to walk out of there, but believe me, Bently, no one can do anything until then!"

Jeremy broke away, dashing through the mob, heading for the fort. He meant to saddle a horse immediately, equip himself, and gallop down to Chillicothe. He would get the boy free one way or the other.

But Henry Hamilton had other ideas. Within the hour, Jeremy had been confined to quarters, Davies evidently having warned Hamilton of what was happening. At first Gwen had tried to reason with her husband, but she had been unable to move him. Before Jeremy had finished packing for the trail, however, Hamilton had put a guard on the hospital door. After the council, Hamilton came in, boiling with anger. Bear grease stained his splendid uniform.

Gwen was listening at the half-open door to the back room as her husband stood before Hamilton, who was pacing back and forth, declaring, "This is the last time you'll defy me, Jeremy! For your own good I'm demanding a promise that you'll not try to go after your brother, and in turn I'll post you to Vincennes immediately."

"We're more needed here, to tend your captives." Jeremy's voice was flat, disinterested.

"Surgeon Major! If I say you'll go to Vincennes on the next supply boat, you go! And that's what I do say! You will give me your word to stay close to Vincennes. I'll do all I can to rescue your brother, but it must be done my own way, in my own time! Now, you leave in two days.

Any other response on your part will constitute insubordination, and you'll be . . . you'll—"

Hamilton fought for composure, spun away, and threw his arms up in a gesture of helplessness.

"Can't you see, Jeremy? Can't you see this is for your own good and for Gwen's good?" He turned, imploring. "I don't want to lock you up, but by the Lord I'll do that if you imperil my campaign! Now, you'll take yourself and your rebel wife down to—" Hamilton caught himself, obviously sorry to have said that about Gwen. He clenched his fists. "I regard you highly, Jeremy . . . surely you understand that . . . and because I value your service and friendship, I'm arranging that you'll finally get away from Detroit, as you and your wife have wished all along."

Jeremy said in a low voice, "Not in this way, Henry. Not because you're forcing me."

Hamilton reddened, leaning forward as he said, "I am *ordering* you, Surgeon Major! You're a soldier first, and you'll obey orders. There's no need for force unless you require it, sir! Now, good day!"

Hamilton departed, leaving the door open, and as he passed Gwen he told her to talk some sense into her husband. She hurried in, closing the door before embracing Jeremy. She was trembling.

"Let's just go," she said. "Let's just forget all this!"

Jeremy held her close. "We'll go, but I can't forget any of it. We'll go, but I'm afraid this damned war won't let us get away so easily."

Although Jeremy and Gwen had no inkling of it, there would be a party at Valenya after all. They spent a quiet Saturday afternoon preparing for the long journey to Vincennes, Jeremy busy packing medical supplies downstairs in the clinic, and Gwen up in a bedroom, sorting clothes she would take. At first they did not hear the voices singing in the distance. Out on the straits, several boats filled with their friends were rapidly approaching, every paddler, oarsman, and passenger singing loudly if not tunefully and enjoying the sunshine and the coming surprise.

In the dim room upstairs, Gwen held up a pretty beige and brown riding habit that had belonged to Jeremy's first wife, Penelope, and a sad nostalgia came over her. Jeremy and Penelope had not been married long—not even a year—and Gwen thought of how suddenly and drastically death could change the lives of those who survived. Losing Penelope at the hands of brigands who attacked her ship on Lake Erie surely had much to do with making Jeremy a loyalist. He blamed the rebel Congress for destroying stable government and permitting the lawlessness that allowed such pirates to pillage almost at will, and she certainly understood how he felt. In some ways she even agreed with him.

Gwen sighed, recalling those first days at Detroit. She had met Jeremy soon after Penelope's death, and from the start she had seen how deeply he had loved his wife. Penelope must have been special indeed, very strong and courageous to forsake her family's comfortable estate for a wilderness that was being swept into war.

She knew it would take a long time for Jeremy to get over his loss, but he was too fine a man to be beaten down by it. Soon they would start anew, where there would be fewer memories to haunt him. For that reason she would not take the riding habit, though it suited her and she loved to wear it. Perhaps in a few more years...

Suddenly Gwen heard singing and yelling outside and hurried to the window, looking down to see nearly a hundred folk in canoes, whaleboats, rowboats—even a small sailboat—coming toward the landing. As she watched, the men of the flotilla raised and discharged their guns in a *feu de joie*, and she thrilled to see that her departure would not be a sad one after all. She heard Jeremy shout her name from downstairs and saw him stride out of the house with Cape, who barked and bounded about. Then Jeremy raised two pistols and fired them into the air to return the salute, and whooping loud and long, raced down the path to the landing, throwing himself into the arms of his friends. While the first ones ashore hugged him, others kept on singing and fired a few more rounds for the fun and the noise.

Gwen arranged her hair quickly, then scampered downstairs to greet them as they moved up from the water's edge.

Kegs of ale and rum were being rolled up the beach, while
a side of beef, already spitted, was lugged on strong shoulders, and women carried covered dishes, bottles of wine
and brandy, and baskets of food.

Gwen waved from the front door, and several of her best
friends began to sing a song she loved called "Drum Major,"
about a young woman who enlists in the Redcoats to be
with her sweetheart soldier. She knew they were poking fun
at her willingness, for Jeremy's sake, to live among loyalists
even though she was a Congress supporter. They had even
changed the words:

> Young men and maidens and bachelors sweet,
> I'll sing you a song that is new and complete,
> Of a brave rebel damsel that followed the drum,
> For the sake of her true love to Detroit she
>   has come!

Gwen's loyalties might have been a touchy subject to
others across the straits, but these friends were determined
to let nothing spoil their fun, and they sang lustily, making
her laugh, though tears were in her eyes as she embraced
Annie Ross, her dark-haired cousin and best friend. Then
came Angélique Levesque, petite and full of life, who helped
out at the hospital; her husband, Jacques, the scout; Jean
Martine, a portly storekeeper, longtime Frontier Company
partner, and Angélique's father; Dawson Merriwether, who
was a little drunk and sang as loud as anyone; and the Irish
seafarer Simon Clancy, a brawny, good-looking young man
who had courted Gwen before Jeremy won her heart. Now
Clancy had a pretty half-breed girl on his arm.

And there was Tamano and his Ottawa wife, Lela, and
their two children; Mawak and his many wives; even Corporal Bates, who had brought his concertina and his monkey, General. As Gwen waved to Bates and called out that
she was glad he was recovering, he released the playful
monkey, who ran up and leaped onto her shoulder, chattering excitedly, making the children laugh and try to get
his attention. It was a glorious send-off, and though Gwen
had a hard time keeping the tears from her eyes, soon she

was too busy greeting friends to be sad. It was a perfect ending to their former life, she thought, and an appropriate beginning to their new one.

Valenya's lawn soon became a rowdy, uproarious place, even more so after the greetings ended and the feasting and dancing began, then went on for hours. Gwen could not remember ever having a better celebration.

Later in the day, as the sun was setting, Jeremy and Gwen strolled away from the company, Cape joining them as they walked hand-in-hand along the beach. Behind them, the party was in a lull; a bonfire was being built up as a lone fiddler, a Frenchman, played a gentle tune that left everyone, including the children, quiet to listen.

Jeremy picked up a stone and tossed it into the shimmering water. Even the straits were placid tonight, as if resting for what was to come.

Gwen said, "I'll miss it here."

Jeremy tossed another stone, took her hand again, and walked on without speaking. She knew he was reluctant to leave Detroit; but just as she had remained in loyalist country to be with him, he would willingly leave here to start again in a place where she would be safer and happier. Not everyone at Detroit was a friend like the folk at the party. Many people made snide remarks, just loud enough for her to hear, and men like Mark Davies were always ready to cause trouble. She could not even voice her opinions, for speaking out against the king could result in her arrest.

For just a moment Gwen thought of Davies, who had gone eastward a few days earlier with a band of painted Senecas. They had been bragging about a combined Tory and Indian assault on New York or Pennsylvania settlements this summer and had deliberately paused in front of the hospital to make certain she had heard them.

Though the breeze was warm, she shivered to recall their gory boasts, and Jeremy put an arm about her. How strong and good he was, she thought. The world must have gone mad, for surely she and Jeremy Bently would have been enemies had circumstances been slightly different. That made her press against him, and she closed her eyes to listen to the plaintive fiddle music in the distance.

They stopped and gazed across the straits toward the setting sun, and Cape sat at their side. The fiddle ended its tune, and after a long silence, voices started singing an old favorite that even the French and Indians knew. It was titled "I Would That the Wars Were All Done."

In the meadow one morning when pearly with dew,
A fair pretty maiden plucked violets blue.
I heard her clear voice making all the woods ring:
Oh, my love's in America to fight for the king,
And I would that the wars were well over,
Oh, I would that the wars were all done.

chapter **15**

CONTINENTAL DOLLARS

At dawn it was dark in the Sutherland cabin, even after Susannah had opened the loft window. This morning, like every morning, she had unlatched and pushed back the shutters, taking care not to expose herself, in case some Indian marksman was hiding out in the woods, waiting for a chance target.

Downstairs, Ella was preparing the cooking fire, and the table was already set for Sally and Tom Morely, who were to come over for breakfast before attending Sunday service in another hour.

After making her bed, Susannah went to the overhang above the door and peered down through a peephole in the floor. Just last week a family a few miles away had been too casual, and now they were gone. There had been hardly any Indian trouble in the Wyoming since the New Year, but those people should not have let down their guard. They had unbarred and opened their cabin without thinking, and several Indians had been hunched near the door, waiting. Only a young boy had escaped to tell the sad story, the rest either being killed or carried off to Detroit or Niagara.

When Susannah reported everything clear, Ella opened the front door, letting in the cool air of a cloudy morning and the sound of birds chirping. Heera had been lying near the stove, and he padded outside ahead of the women. Standing near the door and breathing in fresh, invigorating air, they heard the comforting, steady whack of an ax on firewood and saw Hickory Webster tramping back from the well with a bucket of water. She waved good morning, and Susannah and Ella waved back. Ella looked healthy and rosy-cheeked from frequently exercising outdoors of late. She was nearly well, the head wound having healed cleanly.

A few minutes later the Morelys arrived, dressed in their Sunday best. Their eighteen-month-old Timothy Owen soon was scampering about the cabin like a rabbit, constantly bothering Heera, who had come back inside but seemed to be wondering about leaving again. Susannah adored the baby, and she wrestled him onto her knee to share some maple sugar.

As Susannah tickled Timothy, who giggled and squirmed, she said to Sally, seated across the table next to Tom, "This critter likes Indian sugar as much as you do. One of these days we should take him to Albany and let him taste some real ice cream."

Sally exchanged glances with Ella, who was taking pancakes from a sizzling and smoking frying pan. Susannah noticed the looks and guessed what they were thinking. She said to Timothy, "They believe I want to go to Albany just to see your uncle James, but you know better, don't you? We all just need a visit to the city to cure our cabin fever."

Timothy gurgled and reached for more maple sugar. Susannah teased him with it before handing it over, then looked at the others. They were smiling as if sharing a secret, and that annoyed her.

"Really," she said to Sally, "we need a trip to Albany, where the girls don't laugh and call you a boy if you say it's fun to read books, or call you uppity if you tell them there's more to life than sewing, spinning, cornhusking, and cabin cleaning!" She appealed to her mother. "When I tell them my brother's an Edinburgh-trained doctor, they think I'm boasting! And when I try to take care of my skin with a bonnet or a sun hat, they say I'm vain! I'm tired of their endless, dreary talk."

Ella smiled and sat down, and they bowed their heads for silent grace, Timothy tugging away at Susannah's curls, she occasionally tickling him.

As they sipped coffee—rationed for Sunday breakfasts—Tom said that he was not having much success selling his cabinetwork in the valley, because few people had money to spend.

"I've already taken more chickens in trade than we could eat in a year, and I'm tired of eating chicken anyway."

Through bites of pancake he said, "Maybe if we went to Albany I could work there for a while and learn a few things from those Dutchmen. There's a market there for good cabinetwork, according to what James writes me."

Susannah looked up with interest, and Sally said, "How I wish we could just go home to Detroit."

It became quiet, as if they all would rather not think about that. Immediately Sally apologized for bringing up so tender a subject, and Tom touched her hand, saying they would get back home soon enough.

"War can't go on forever; been three years and more already." He accepted another pancake from Ella, who agreed with him.

She said cheerfully, "I expect a letter from Owen any day now, saying everything's fine with Benjamin and Jeremy, and . . . and so on." She took a deep, forced breath that ended with a smile. Picking up her fork, she said, "In my heart I long to be home again, but as a substitute, a journey to Albany would be a pleasure; still, I'll not leave this valley willingly unless Owen knows where I'm going, or he writes me to come westward to him."

"Now, that," declared Tom, "would be fine with me. To travel westward, closer to Detroit! There's talk about a campaign starting from Pitt . . . but I reckon it's just that: talk."

Sally said she had heard the Illinois country was peaceful and still prosperous enough for traders, because the Indians were not especially hostile to Congress supporters. "If Congress ever takes that region, it might be a sensible place for all of us to go and await the peace or the fall of Detroit."

Ella looked downcast, and Susannah was sorry she had brought up the whole subject with talk of Albany. Intentionally changing the mood, she whispered something to Timothy and let him down to the floor, where he scampered right at the sleeping Heera and leaped onto the stout husky's back. Laughing and wrestling with the dog, the child soon found himself plumped down on his bottom, while Heera patiently licked his face.

Just then the sun broke through the clouds and slanted warm, bright light into the cabin. Susannah had the sudden urge to rush outside, grab a skipping rope, and make a circle of the entire settlement. When she was excused—until church began—she eagerly did just that, Heera also taking the chance to escape, loping along behind. Thoughts of Albany, delicate skin, and handsome young men were put from her mind happily, and completely.

That afternoon Mel Webster was the first to see the arrival of the packtrain from Albany, and he laid aside his needle and thread and rose to shout a greeting. He had been seated at the door of his cabin, stitching a new fabric balloon to replace the one that had been destroyed, and he was glad for an excuse to pause in his tedious work.

Mel and the bearded master of the train stood talking in the sunshine, joking that had this been Connecticut or Massachusetts, the master would have been fined for traveling on Sunday. Susannah was in her cabin reading *Robinson Crusoe* when she heard Mel's halloo. She rushed outside as her mother came around the corner of the cabin, pausing to wipe her hands on her apron. Ella had been weeding in the flower garden, and she watched as her daughter hurried to the packtrain master, who was already distributing letters. A troubled look crossed Ella's face as she noticed a knot of men accumulating around a man on horseback who did not look as if he belonged with the packtrain. The men were all grim, and after a moment they moved off toward the blockhouse, obviously in a hurry. Something was wrong.

Ella was distracted as Susannah got the package and came running back, her blond hair streaming behind.

"There's a letter just for me!" Susannah cried, excited that James had actually written directly to her instead of only to Ella. "And it's got something in it!"

Once they were in the house and seated at the table, however, they found that the envelope for Susannah held only a brief note—plus three shiny brass buttons, each marked with the letters *FC*, for Frontier Company. Susannah loved them from the start, thinking how thoughtful James had been. The accompanying letter took away some of her joy, however, for it explained that Jeanette Defries had thought up the idea to send the buttons.

"He must be seeing a lot of Jeanette," Susannah said with a sigh, as her mother opened another, much longer letter from James. "And she must feel quite sure of herself to suggest he send me pretty buttons."

Ella seemed to be hardly listening, and Susannah noticed a look of concern on her face. At Susannah's request, she read aloud.

It was the bad news of the gunpowder shipment, and after Ella finished the story, then read on silently, Susannah was left utterly depressed. James was failing despite all their high hopes! She turned the three buttons over in her hands, staring down at them, tears beginning to come.

"Wait!" Ella declared, her expression changing to amazed delight. "Wait—listen to this:"

> . . . but we persevere, and we think of other ways to counter ill fortune, spies, and Bradford Cullen. With much of our remaining sterling we have bought up great quantities of Continental dollars, and by affixing the stamp of the Frontier Company, and my personal endorsement as well, we promise to pay the bearer on demand, thus making those bills worth almost their face value.

Ella marveled aloud at the boldness of the scheme, and Susannah quickly forgot her depression when she saw how much her mother admired James's ingenuity. In effect, Ella explained, James had backed thousands of dollars of Congress's paper money in a way the underfinanced Congress could not. The Frontier Company's assets and good name would stand behind those stamped, endorsed bills, and whoever accepted them in payment would be assured redemption in sterling at any time.

"And if someone in turn uses the bills to pay his own debts," Ella went on, "and the next person does the same, and so forth, those endorsed continentals might circulate for years!"

Susannah was not sure she understood it all, but it certainly sounded clever.

James admitted in the letter that he did not yet have

enough sterling to cover the notes if they were all redeemed immediately—an eventuality he thought unlikely—but in a week or two he would have resold at tremendous profits whatever goods he had initially purchased, and then would be able to meet the company's obligations. Indeed, if all went as expected, he would start a profitable chain of transactions that would put the Frontier Company back on its feet.

Ella laid the letter aside. "Sounds like he's made the most of the one advantage we have—hard money. I do believe he's finally on his way to reestablishing the company. Well done, James!"

Susannah could not have been more thrilled, except for the nagging knowledge that lucky Jeanette Defries was so close to James.

Just then there was a hubbub outside, and Tom Morely came breathlessly to the door, rifle in hand, shot pouch and powder horn slung over his shoulders. At first Susannah thought he was going hunting, but his expression told her that something was very wrong.

"Militia's got to go!" he declared, breathing hard. "Injuns 'n' Tories . . . Butler's Destructives, a lot of 'em, coming down to the Susquehanna. They left Niagara two weeks back, and they're raising more Injuns as they go. Express rider just came in."

As if to confirm his words, the bell on the blockhouse began clanging, calling everyone to council. Tom said the entire valley's militia would be raised, with some placed in garrisons at the strongpoints, forts, and blockhouses, others sent out as scouts, and the rest to go on with the work necessary to keep the valley communities fed. When Ella nodded that she understood, he dashed away to the next cabin to spread the warning.

Before they went outside, Ella faced Susannah, taking her shoulders and saying, "We might not have much time, dear. Think now what you'll take . . . and what you'll have to leave."

There was cool resolve in her mother's face, but Susannah saw the pain behind it. She nodded, the corners of her mouth tugging downward against her will. They went quickly out the door to join the mingling crowd of settlers making for the blockhouse, where the leaders would explain everything.

What should be taken, and what left? Susannah clutched the three buttons and closed her eyes, ready to face the worst that might come.

In Albany, James Morely was carrying through his latest scheme with far greater finesse than he had the gunpowder deal. He had spent a thousand pounds sterling to purchase fifty thousand Continental dollars in hundred dollar bills from many individuals, and by laboriously signing his name and affixing the mark of the Frontier Company to each bill— a prodigious task—he had made those continentals worth ten thousand pounds of purchasing power in British sterling.

Acting quickly, with the aid of Peter Defries, he had secretly sent out agents to purchase livestock, flour, and more gunpowder. He had impressed on the agents that no one in Albany was to know for whom they were working. Naturally, Bradford Cullen would be aware of everything immediately, and that was what James counted on. Once the commodities were contracted for, but not yet delivered, James set in motion the next part of his plan.

Defries was also his confidant in this, and the two of them met one evening in James's small apartment in a neighborhood just below old Fort Frederick, the stubby fortification on top of the city's hill. Defries could not keep from chuckling as he watched James complete and sign a letter to a leading loyalist officer, purportedly from a British commander downriver near New York. Using a forged seal and a bit of official scarlet ribbon, James turned the letter into a persuasive-looking British military dispatch, then smudged and creased the whole thing as if the courier had met some evil fate. Defries wanted to add some drops of blood, but James thought that was going too far.

He tied the ribbon, saying, "I hope your Oneida Indian friends are able to get this to someone who'll put it into Cullen's hands—and I hope he'll believe it's from an intercepted British express."

Defries took the letter, grinning with delight. "Don't

worry about that. By the time this gets back to Cullen, it'll have gone through so many hands that he'll never know exactly how his own people got hold of it. And once we spread our little rumor and watch it grow, it'll convince him all the more that this letter's the real item!" He pocketed the letter and asked James to read the preliminary draft again.

James cleared his throat, held up the paper to the light, and read:

My Dear Sir:
    In haste I must inform you that our previous sus-
picions have been confirmed. Montreal will once again
be the rebels' target, and you must accordingly prepare
to counter an army the exact size of which we have
yet to determine. We have reason to believe that
Frenchmen will be the core of this invasion, which is
scheduled to take place by summer. Rebel contingents
are already secretly on the move to Albany, and their
maneuvers are so confidential that even their leading
men in that city have yet to be informed of the strong
forces soon to appear at their door. Troops will arrive
overland from Boston, up from New Jersey, and even
from Pennsylvania, Rhode Island, and Connecticut—

Defries cackled. "Whyn't you say Virginia, too? It scares the hell outa Redcoats when they hear Longknife riflemen'll be after 'em!"

Defries listened to the rest of the letter, then departed, still chuckling. James felt sure the Dutchman would carry out his own role without a hitch. Through the waterfront grapevine, Defries would spread rumors that French agents were already in the city; then he would tell woodsmen he knew to prepare to go northward on a scouting mission. Furthermore, he would mention the possibility of a French invasion fleet in the mouth of the Saint Lawrence that sum-mer—a fleet that would eventually have to be fed from Albany.

James was certain Defries's rumors would fall on fertile ground, for no other city in America compared to Albany when it came to profiting from war. Over the past hundred years the city's merchants had prospered outfitting one British force after another against the French and Indians, and whenever a rumor started about a possible expedition, it spread like wildfire.

Sure enough, within a day James saw his plan working. Merchants were scrambling to make contracts for military commodities, and everywhere the coffeehouses were filled with entrepreneurs attempting to profit by buying and selling contracts. But to their dismay, most of what an army needed had already been bought up by several agents who seemed determined not to sell until the army came and paid them hard cash. These, of course, were men employed by James. Offers flew at his agents, and the opportunity for quick profits was ripe.

But James waited. He stayed alone in his apartment for forty-eight hours, sending messages to his people and receiving news in return. Speculative fever swept Albany, but Bradford Cullen had not joined in. James was anxious for word from Defries that Cullen had done the expected and tried to buy out James's agents at any price in order to corner the market. Cullen did nothing, however, even after two straight days of steadily rising prices on what few goods remained available. Profit-hungry speculators rushed frantically through the city, but no one controlled an amount of goods anywhere near the vast quantities contracted by James's agents. James had even sent his own men to bid against other agents of his, thus further upping the price of war materiel and supplies. The third day came and went, but Cullen did not take the bait. There were several rich merchants willing to buy from James's men, but James craved to lure Cullen to his hook, to get even for the gunpowder humiliation.

James felt dizzy more than once in that small room, where he stayed cooped up with cold food, flat ale from the noisy tavern downstairs, and piles of reports from nervous agents whose hurriedly written letters came in hour after hour through various couriers. He was sicker than he would admit, but the sheer excitement of the challenge facing him kept him up nearly around the clock. He knew that if he failed and truth of the sham campaign got out, he would be stuck with enormous quantities of goods that he could never sell at a profit.

So James worried and waited, growing more irritable with every passing day. The fourth day arrived, and he found he had scarcely bothered to change his clothes. He had slept without undressing and by now had lost his appetite. He felt dizzy almost all the time, and once had actually fainted, waking up to find himself on the floor, a nasty bruise on his forehead.

Still no word from Cullen. James's contracts required him to take charge of the goods within a few days from now. He had to sell, or he would indeed be ruined. Where was Cullen?

Late in the morning, just before lunch, he heard footsteps on the stairs, then a hurried knock on the apartment door. At his call, Jeanette came barging in, a bundle of reports in her hands, her eyes ablaze.

"It's working!" she cried, hugging him. "Cullen's offering a price that can't be refused, and Father says it's time for our people to sell!"

Mouth dry, heart beating, James leafed through offers and corresponding reports from his agents, all of whom were itching to sell. It was a small fortune in profits for the company. James laughed aloud. He had done it. He embraced Jeanette, spinning her around, but then stopped and eased her back.

"Not yet," he said, licking his lips.

"No, James?" She was dismayed, and that amused him. "But at this price we'll cover our endorsement of all those continentals, and make a handsome profit, too—"

He pulled away and went to the window, feeling a storm of excitement and power erupting within him. It was a glorious feeling, a wonderful feeling, a sense of finally knowing one's own strength. Jeanette spoke in appeal, but he cut her off, hissing in a harsh voice:

"Not yet! We can do better! We'll hold on . . . a little longer." He shook a fist at her. "That'll convince old Cullen all the more that there really is a campaign on the way, and that our agents know very well how much our goods will be worth when the right time comes!" He saw the admiration and awe in Jeanette, and he felt strong, important, a match for anyone. This time he was sure Cullen was outwitted.

His tone became confident, commanding. "We'll wait until Cullen makes one more offer, and then . . . then come to me, and I'll decide."

Jeanette began to back out of the room, and at the last moment James realized she was unnerved by his behavior.

"Jeanette," he called, and she stopped; he smiled benevolently, and that also was a good sensation. "I intend to change our company's affairs once and for all, Jeanette, and those strong enough to face what must be done will respect my seeming aggressiveness."

Jeanette said nothing, but he could see she had been moved by the gentleness in his voice and the warmth that had come over him, a warmth he actually felt within. She smiled back.

"Don't worry," he said. "You'll get used to these things. After tomorrow, nothing will ever again seem too great for our company to undertake."

James was right. Cullen made another offer, this one even higher than expected, and everything James had accumulated was sold to Cullen and Company at tremendous profit, and for pounds sterling. For James Morely, it was a feat of willpower, genius, and guts.

Just a few days after his triumph, James received an unexpected message from Cullen, inviting him to another meeting. He was surprised at first, but did not think Cullen could already have learned there was no secret plan for a rebel invasion of Canada.

That evening, James was again in Cullen's office, seated before the large table, bathed in the yellow light of the two oil lamps. He was tense, yet sure it did not show. Cullen seemed even more jovial than on their first encounter and made interesting small talk, sharing excellent brandy and even mentioning that Linda had been quite pleased to have met James in person.

"My daughter knows a worthy gentleman when she sees one," Cullen wheezed, closing his eyes as he sipped his brandy. "Have a care not to wink at her, young man, or she'll command me to raise her dowry and offer her to you posthaste!"

Cullen was chuckling, but James saw no humor in the thought of being wed to Linda Cullen, no matter what the dowry. He clumsily muttered that he already had his eye on a girl or two.

"I'm flattered, of course, that Linda should show interest in me, especially when so many other men must see a great future as your son-in-law."

Cullen scoffed and set down his glass with a click. His eyes narrowed. "Useless pack of rascals, most of them. Few could make their way in the world even if I handed them everything I had—which is what I would do to the right man, mark you." He grunted. "Those that might make decent heirs are all too squeamish about . . . let's say about false idealism. You know what I mean about false idealism. You and I share something of the same standard when it comes to false idealism."

James licked his lips. He was about to say he knew just what Cullen was getting at, when he noticed a massive map of North America on the wall behind the table. For some reason he had not seen it before. Illuminated by the lamplight, it was covered with symbols indicating Cullen and Company trading posts—obviously from before the war—as well as places where Cullen now had offices, plantations, manufactories, docks, and shipping. James was astounded by what he saw; the man who inherited such an empire would control wealth rivaling any man's. Cullen had power that could change the world.

Cullen seemed not to notice the astonished expression on his visitor's face. He began speaking idly about all the men who had craved Linda's hand but whom he had rejected because they were not the right sort.

"But a man who understands the correct use of power and who prudently distinguishes between righteous honor and false idealism . . . now, that's the man who would be right for my child."

With force of will James returned to the present and tried to shut out the visions of opulence and influence that swept through him when he looked at that amazing map. If only one day he could be master of such an empire!

Cullen poured another brandy and wheezed, "No doubt a young man like you, a fellow from our new, earthshaking, aggressive generation, well understands what I mean by the correct use of power. Why, this war couldn't be waged by Congress or Parliament if it weren't for strong men who understand the correct use of power, and what has to be done to keep armies and navies chasing one another around the world!"

James nodded and drank some more brandy, which was beginning to go to his head. "It takes a bit of genius and a practical attitude."

"Precisely!" Cullen said with a chortle. "Genius, hard work, and the practical sense of when to use power to do the right thing . . . such as, let's say, create a favorable business climate, or bend the truth to make them see what we want them to see, and do what we want them to do!"

He snorted and leaned back, laughing heartily. "I must admit, young man, you've proved yourself worthy to me! I'd feared there were too many false idealists in America, and not enough practical geniuses left."

James realized what Cullen was getting at. The man had found out who was behind the campaign rumors. He knew everything! Yet there was no sense of threat, as James had expected after all Owen Sutherland had said. Instead, Cullen's flattery was quite generous, and James presumed he truly was amused to have been outwitted in this relatively small matter—small to him, at least.

James sat up, his chest thrust slightly forward, and said, "My motto is take opportunity when you can, and *make* opportunity when you must."

"Not bad." Cullen nodded, smiling. "Admirable motto, indeed." He leaned over and picked up from the floor a small, leather-bound chest, which he laid on the table. Wheezing with the effort, he said, "There's nothing better for making opportunity than creating rumor . . ." He held up a finger. "Nothing better, except having adequate funds to do whatever you wish, without fussing with elaborate schemes or rumors, whether opportunity rears its fickle head or not."

Cullen unlocked the chest, but did not lift the lid. James wondered what was in there.

The merchant said, "And there is also a graven rule that says one must face the consequences of boldness, when that boldness offers someone else the fickle opportunity of which you speak." He looked closely at James, a twinkle of humor in his eyes. "I believe, Mr. Morely, you will immediately honor this—"

Opening the lid, he revealed thousands of Continental dollars—the very ones James had endorsed and promised to redeem in pounds sterling.

James was stunned. He could not speak. His heart contracted, and he took a long breath to steady himself. Cullen was demanding hard cash in return for these Frontier Company continentals, and that payment would wipe out all the profits James had just made by the war rumor. But if Cullen had expected James to melt, or to beg for time, he was not to be gratified.

James did not even bother to examine the bills, saying coolly, "Certainly, Mr. Cullen; please have them sent along to our office in the morning, and your agent will return immediately with pounds sterling at the face value to which we committed." James was not even breathing hard.

He saw that Cullen was deeply impressed with his reply. No doubt Cullen was surprised that so young a man had not buckled in a moment of extreme stress.

Cullen let the lid softly drop, then sat back, fingers knitted at his massive stomach, where a sparkling ruby pin was attached to a watch chain. Cullen's eyes half closed, as if he were examining James even more closely. James rose and bowed.

"If I may take my leave, sir—I've a busy day and an early start tomorrow, counting all that money."

James was amazed that his heart had slowed down. He no longer felt nervous. He even smiled. If he had been set back once again, at least he had achieved something that would one day bear fruit—he knew he could confront Bradford Cullen.

Cullen said quietly, "Perhaps, when the differences between our companies are less vexing, Mr. Morely, you and I will put our heads together—old and young—and see if we can't set the world on its ear now and again, eh?"

Cullen stood up for the first time, and he was a vast bulk of flesh. He reached across the table and offered James his pudgy hand, which was dry and strong, despite his ogreish appearance.

James looked into Cullen's beady eyes. "Perhaps . . . when our differences are not so vexing."

James left, and when he reached the street, where it was raining, he felt like leaping for ecstasy—just as much as he felt like kicking himself for not buying back all those endorsed continentals sooner. No doubt many of their holders, when offered instant cash, would have been glad to sell for half of face value in these uncertain economic times. Surely, he realized, Cullen had made just such deals himself!

Jamming the tricorne on his head, James decided he should go out tomorrow and purchase an entire new suit of clothes. Then he thought of that map of Cullen's empire and what it all might mean to him. It was too much to contemplate, and his mind was whirling so fast that he had to walk. Telling his carriage driver to go on without him, he cried, "I've thinking to do!" As the whip snapped and the carriage rattled away, James pulled up his collar against the rain and strode off briskly. To himself he said, "Thinking to do, and a world to set on its ear!"

He saw that map of Cullen's domain, and against it was Linda's homely face. How tumultuous his life was just then, and how intriguing were the possibilities for a man of boldness and brains—if he had money. He was splashed by a passing carriage, but he hardly cared. Absently he took out a handkerchief to wipe the mud from his face. It was the handkerchief Susannah had given him, and as he rubbed his cheek the sprig of mistletoe fell out, unnoticed.

chapter 16

HOME

Long shadows reached back from the seven standing stones to a grove of white birches that shone in the rosy light of sunset. The straits at Valenya glittered as if on fire. Soon, the waters were transformed, slowly darkening as the sun went behind the horizon. The last rays lingered on the big house, which seemed to glow, then to cool, and fade to ashen gray, hushed and empty.

Before full darkness came, a tall wraith slipped out of the birch grove and moved slowly, deliberately, toward the great stones, passing between them and stopping in the center of the space formed by their arc. Here the wraith stood over a stone that was small by comparison, and with bowed head went to one knee. Owen Sutherland was paying his respects to the grave of the Ottawa woman who had been his wife. It seemed so many, many years ago.

After a moment he looked up at the house, which was silent and appeared uninhabited. He presumed Jeremy and Gwen were still living there, but perhaps they were on a prolonged visit to the fort. Still, there should have been someone taking care of the place in their absence. Sutherland moved away from the grave, put his tattered hat back on his head, and drifted through trees and bushes toward Valenya, the place he called home.

No one was in sight—not even a single animal—yet it appeared the house and grounds were being well kept. There was a new hay barn, and when he tried the door he found it barred and the windows shuttered up. Silently he moved to the corner of the barn. The shore was not far off to his left, the house fifty yards away. Could it be a trap? Had the British heard he was coming? But then it would have been a better trap to make everything seem natural, not so empty.

Sutherland was weary, his face gaunt and eyes hollow. His buckskins were nearly in shreds, but his weapons were still clean and oiled, the long rifle ready in his hands as he knelt to watch for some sign of life. Darkness settled down. His heart was pounding to see his beloved home once again. How he wished he could simply step out onto the white pebble path, whistle to Ella, and see the door fly open, the children bounding toward him with outstretched arms. But that was almost a lifetime past. Valenya was as magnificent as he remembered it, but without the familiar signs of his family it had lost something. Where were Jeremy and Gwen?

When he felt sure no one was in hiding, Sutherland crossed the lawn, moving naturally so as not to arouse suspicion in case someone happened to be passing on the straits or hunting within sight. He circled to the back door and, using his key, went inside. The house was dim and smelled like it had been closed up for some time, the air musty, cold, and dreary. Closing the door behind him, he moved in the half-light from one room to the other, seeing that the place had changed little, although most of the furniture was draped.

He had the urge to light a fire and sit down in his hoop-backed chair with a pipe, but the fireplace had been swept clean of ashes, and no firewood was in sight.

There came a faint sound outside, a clump, as of a footstep on the path. He tensed, an eternity of lonely travel having honed his senses, drawn his nerves taut. Silence. Perhaps it had been the wind.

Then the sound came again. Someone was opening the front door and entering the hallway. Was it a trap after all?

Sutherland moved noiselessly, taking a place near the door of the common room. Someone was fumbling with a tinderbox. Finally he saw the light of a candle drifting closer, though he did not recognize the step. It was not Jeremy, that was certain, nor could it be Gwen, for it was a man's footfall.

Sutherland drew out his dirk and readied. When the figure came in the door, he grabbed it roughly by the shirtfront, causing the candle to jump and sputter. The fellow struggled and cursed, but Sutherland had him.

"Thief!" the man grunted, punching futilely with one hand while trying to keep the candle lit with the other. "Get out of this house, rascal, before I—"

Sutherland released him and stepped back. Dawson Merriwether was rumpled and shaken but unhurt save for a scald of candle wax. When he saw who had grabbed him he stopped short, his eyes opening wide and then narrowing, as if he could not believe what he was seeing.

"Owen, by God!" He took a step toward Sutherland, and they gripped hands, for they had been good friends before the war. "I should have known you'd come back!" They embraced roughly, glad to see each other again.

Sutherland said, "I'm looking for Jeremy, and for Benjamin." He saw his friend had aged considerably, had become more stooped, no doubt in part because the war was going so badly for the loyalist side. "I'll not spy on the fort, Mr. Merriwether, so you needn't feel I'll compromise your honor while I'm here."

Merriwether resettled his wig, which had been knocked askew in the struggle. "Of course, of course . . ." He pursed his lips and looked at Owen closely, saying, "I see you've come far, but I'm afraid you'll have another long journey ahead of you, my friend. Your sons are not in Detroit."

Sutherland sighed and gazed at the floor. For the first time it seemed as though going on with this quest might be beyond his power, for he was worn out from living with little to eat and being in constant danger. This latest news was such a jolt that he laid down his gear and let himself collapse in his chair before the cold hearth.

Merriwether fetched a flask of Sutherland's own fine Scotch whiskey and poured them drinks. Sitting down, Merriwether quickly explained that Jeremy had been ordered to the Illinois weeks ago.

His words made Sutherland close his eyes and lean forward, hand on his head. The Illinois was a long, long way from here. It was also a bad place for Jeremy to be. Again he felt the urgency that had driven him on for Benjamin. Jeremy would be directly in George Rogers Clark's path, and Longknife rebels were brutal with loyalist Americans in Redcoat uniforms. When he heard that Benjamin had been taken back to Shawnee country again, Sutherland became angry and felt weakness turning as if by some willed process into raw power. A new fire raged within, fueled by something more than mere physical endurance. He would not give up this chase. He would not go back. He would go on, no matter how far, how long.

Merriwether sat forward in his chair and said softly, "I have food and clothing for you—"

"I must go! Now!"

"You must be equipped, Owen." Merriwether's voice was firm. "I'll go back across the straits, and by morning you'll find all you need at the doorstep of this house."

The elderly merchant stood up, and Sutherland did the same, saying, "We have much to talk about, you and I . . . much to tell." He was grateful to this man, and once again could not grasp that they could be enemies.

Merriwether smiled, his eyes lit by the flickering candlelight. It was now full dark outside. "We'll talk after the war, here, in these chairs. Yes, Owen, we have much to talk about, much to wonder. Perhaps by then we'll understand how our differences came to this."

Sutherland saw tears in Merriwether's eyes as he turned away; the merchant still had the limp received some years back when ruffians posing as Congress supporters had cruelly ridden him on a rail and burned down his house, killing his wife. Partly because of that, Merriwether would never be disloyal to the king, although his daughter had died as a rebel's wife, murdered by loyalist Indians. Dawson Merriwether was as fine a man as Sutherland could want as a friend.

Merriwether paused before leaving the room and from the dimness said, "You know you can trust me, Owen?"

Sutherland's voice was weak, and he was very sleepy. "Mr. Merriwether, we will never drift so far apart that I won't trust you; I'll be here in the morning, sir."

Then Merriwether was gone, and Sutherland was alone. He sat down, illuminated by the candle, listening to the familiar sounds of the house. He might simply be resting after a normal day's strenuous work, here in his comfortable old chair. But he was in enemy country. He did not belong here. He heard, unexpectedly, the big German clock ticking away in the hallway, and that made him smile. Merriwether was caring for the house in Jeremy's absence, and was even winding the clock regularly.

When morning burst through the eastern windows, bright light struck Sutherland where he lay hunched in the chair. He sprang awake, feeling he had slept too long, uneasy that he might be discovered. He hurried to the front window, expecting to see the pile of gear and food promised by Merriwether; but there was nothing. Not only that—he sensed he was not alone.

Moving back slowly from the window, he was unable to see anything outside that told of the enemy at hand. Then he heard someone in the house. Merriwether? He turned quickly, drawing his dirk, listening. At first all he heard was the clock ticking loudly; but then there was a clink of glass, and he knew someone was in the back room.

That was where Ella had kept her loom, and he tiptoed down the hall and peered through the door, which was partway open. Now the room was far different. He saw shelves of bottles, medical books, a cot against the rear wall. This, he realized, was Jeremy's clinic. Someone was here. Pushing the door wider with his foot, Sutherland was ready to strike.

"So you've finally awakened," Tamano said in Chippewa and came into sight from behind the door, a smile on his face. Sutherland laughed and hugged the Indian, who said Merriwether had come to his lodge last night. "He already sent over everything we'll need for the journey, and it's packed in our canoe."

Sutherland stepped back, suddenly feeling tremendously hungry and happy to be with his friend once again. He sheathed the dirk.

"Good for Merriwether," he said, then looked in question at Tamano. "What do you mean, 'our' canoe?"

Tamano turned back to what he had been doing, putting some of Jeremy's medicines into a traveling pouch. "Have

you been in the woods too long, white man?" he said.
"Forget human talk?" He looked back at Sutherland and
grinned. "I'm going with you, after we have a feed. I've
had my fill of loyalists and soldiers. I don't like Longknives
much better, but these British deserve to have a revolution
and lose their American empire."

This answer did not satisfy Sutherland, and he said so.

Tamano shrugged. "Maybe I just want to be back on the
trail with Donoway. Or maybe I just want to be on the side
that wins, for I know that this time the Redcoats will lose."
He looked unusually serious. "At least that's what my dreams
tell me . . . and my dreams are never wrong."

He told of a dream in which great wagons full of settlers
were marching westward, past forts bristling with cannon
and manned by rebel soldiers.

"The British are finished, Donoway, but if they fight on
they'll drag the Indians down with them." He shook his
head. "I will not let that happen without trying to help my
people make peace terms."

"I am glad," Sutherland said.

He took his friend by the forearms. At least this was as
it ought to be. Owen Sutherland and Tamano were going
on the trail together once more, and whatever might confront
them, they would face it as brothers.

The closer Benjamin's party came to Chillicothe on the
Scioto River, the better Wabete became. It might even have
been described as miraculous the way the aging warrior
recovered from his stab wounds, although Benjamin had
noticed when the bandaging was being changed that none
really seemed potentially fatal.

Benjamin's own wounds had been nearly as bad, though
thanks to Wabete they had been treated and bound and now
were healing. It also helped that he was able to rest often
as they stopped at many villages along the way.

Punch fared not so well. Though he could stand now,
he could not fly, and made not one squawk during those
weeks on the southbound trail. Benjamin kept the bird in
his shirt, feeding it morsels of ground corn, suet, and whatever he could scrounge from lodges where they stopped on

the way. Wabete, to Benjamin's surprise, followed the bird's progress closely and even went so far as to call upon a local medicine man for help. The grizzled old healer had no sympathy for blue jays, however, saying they were useless troublemakers who warned game of the hunter's approach. His gruff recommendation was to relieve the jay's misery by wringing its neck.

That got him in trouble with Wabete, whose injuries seemed suddenly to vanish as he threw the man bodily out of his camp, even refusing to pay the fee of wampum beads for the consultation. It cheered Benjamin somewhat to see Wabete so concerned about the bird.

They made the last leg of their journey by canoe, and when they finally reached Chillicothe, Benjamin almost immediately found himself surrounded by a large crowd of onlookers curious to see the son of Donoway. From scattered comments it began to dawn on him that his father had been here not too long ago, searching for him, and had somehow escaped unharmed.

Wabete, while glorying in all the attention his captive received, was himself warmly welcomed by his many relations. His younger brother, obviously very fond of Wabete, invited him to a feast the next day in honor of his return. As it turned out, this brother had several children, one of them a slim, pretty girl of Benjamin's age, named Evangeline. The first time Benjamin saw her—she was serving food to Wabete—he thought she must have some white blood, perhaps French, for she was lighter than the other Shawnees, as were her brothers and sisters.

Evangeline's family's lodge was a ways upriver, isolated from the main village, and Benjamin could not figure out why, until he learned that her folks were Moravian Indians—converts to a form of Christianity brought to the wilderness more than twenty years ago by German missionaries. Some of these courageous, devout missionaries still lived in Moravian communities to the east, places with names like Gnadenhutten—Mercy Village—and Salem. Benjamin had heard of the Indians there, who were known for their skill at white crafts. Many of these Indian families had been converts for a generation, but Evangeline's folk were new, having become Moravian Indians eight years earlier. Though they had chosen to remain in Chillicothe, many of the Shawnees in the village regarded them with suspicion.

They treated Benjamin kindly enough, but after the feast had gone on for several hours, he slipped outside the smoky lodge to get some air and check on Punch, whom he had left under a bush. As he sat in the sunshine, feeding the bird from his own plate, coaxing its beak close to the food, he suddenly realized Evangeline was kneeling at his side. She was looking at Punch, concern on her face.

She spoke passable English, asking him first if he could speak German, which she said she had learned in the church school. He said he could not.

"No matter!" she declared in Shawnee and bent over Punch, who at her very touch seemed to take interest. "May I see?" Benjamin handed the bird over and sat back to watch her caress it and talk soothingly, feeling the bird's wings and tail, moving its neck slightly.

Benjamin said glumly, "Nothing's broken, far as I can tell. Seems shocked or something . . . guess I would be, too, if some Shawnee tossed me about—"

The sound of jubilant whooping and cheering distracted them, and they turned to see several canoes coming swiftly downriver, warriors raising and shaking paddles and firing their muskets into the air to herald their arrival. Benjamin was surprised to discover that it was Blackfish and his men, and in the chief's canoe was the dour Daniel Boone, still a prisoner.

Wabete, wearing his new red tunic, came out to greet the arrivals. As the canoes drew nearer, Blackfish boasted that Hamilton could not buy Boone even for a hundred pounds sterling.

With that, Boone roared in annoyance, "There ain't an Injun in all Americay worth that much money!"

Blackfish laughed loudly, crying out that Boone earned his price every time he made another joke. Flashing a gloating grin at Wabete, he leaned back in the center of the canoe as it drifted past the lodge where Benjamin's party was watching.

"You be Injun soon, Boone!" Blackfish declared in Eng-

lish; then in Shawnee he said to everyone, "Big white man
snaps like a turtle! That is what I will name him when I
make him my son: Sheltowee, Big Snapping Turtle!"

Hearing this, Boone looked even more defiant. He spotted Benjamin as the canoe went by.

"Hey, Sutherland!" he shouted. "When they adopt you,
boy, make sure they give you a good name, see?" As the
canoes floated out of sight, Benjamin heard him call out in
Shawnee: "Do not forget, chief, snapping turtles snap at
black fish, too!"

That got a rousing laugh from all the Indians, Blackfish
loudest of all. Benjamin was not feeling cheerful, however,
not when he thought that he, too, might be adopted. A
captive who tried to escape after being adopted was doomed
to instant death if recaptured.

When Benjamin turned back to Evangeline, he was
amazed to see that Punch was hopping spryly about. Excited, he sat down beside the girl, saying, "Punch looks like
he might recover! What did you do? What did you give
him?"

Evangeline smiled and shook her head. "They say I am
good with sick creatures... but I just care for them, you
see—"

She pointed toward a number of pens and cages behind
her family's lodge. There were all sorts of small animals:
raccoons, bear cubs, squirrels, a few chickens that seemed
ill, and even a skunk asleep under a large rock. Benjamin
smiled, then saw with amazement that Punch was ruffling
his feathers.

"Punch!" he cried out, and the bird cocked its head,
jumped onto Evangeline's palm, and began preening himself
vigorously, as if to say he wanted to look good for this
Indian girl. Benjamin laughed, "You're handsome enough
to fly! Can you?"

Evangeline held Punch up. The bird fluttered its wings
weakly and opened its mouth to squawk, but nothing came
out. Still, Punch was game, and with effort sprang from
Evangeline's hands. She anticipated what would happen,
and as the bird fluttered out of control to the ground she
deftly caught it.

Punch preened again, shook himself, and tried to squawk. Still nothing. Benjamin figured he had probably lost his voice, but suddenly that did not matter, as Evangeline gave Punch a slight boost into the air and the bird flitted away, zooming awkwardly at first. Unable to direct himself, he barely managed to land on a bush not far from the youngsters. Benjamin cried out, and Evangeline laughed with glee. The adults came to the lodge door, and Wabete hooted to see Punch fly again, this time lifting to a tree branch, then darting downward to land on Evangeline's hand.

Benjamin took the bird, who hopped on his hands and shoulders. Then he threw Punch up, to soar high, all the way to the treetops. Everyone was chattering about how remarkable this young Evangeline was.

Benjamin was astonished, wondering how the bird had so quickly recovered, when he saw an Indian boy, about twelve years old, standing not far away and watching Punch fly about. The boy had just come back from hunting, for he held a bow in one hand and a dead rabbit in the other. He was a stout lad, handsome and alert. He was also completely unsuspecting, and Benjamin could not resist such an opportunity. When Punch was in just the right position, Benjamin whistled sharply in command.

The Indian boy did not realize what was happening until it was too late. Punch whirred down, pecked him on the forehead, and flew away, leaving the boy staggering with amazement.

Benjamin stifled a laugh as Evangeline gasped, asking why the bird had done that. Punch flew down to Benjamin, who said he had no idea. Then the bird hopped onto Evangeline's finger, and she walked toward the boy, whose eyes were watering from the pain.

"Come on, blue jay, be kind to my cousin," she said sternly. She motioned the boy to come nearer, but he backed off and strung his bow with an arrow. "Have no fear, Tecumseh! He will be nice if you are! Have no fear!"

"I am not afraid," Tecumseh declared, brandishing the bow. "But if he does that again I will make an arrow flight out of him!"

Tecumseh stood there defiantly, but when Punch fluttered

his wings and tried to squawk, the boy backed off slightly. Benjamin came alongside Evangeline and said to Tecumseh, "I'm sorry, but he won't do that again—if you're a friend of mine."

At that Tecumseh seemed to calm down, and his dark eyes darted from Benjamin to the bird. He nodded, gave a grunt, and turned away. Before he was gone, he glanced once over his shoulder, as if to make certain the bird was not about to attack, then vanished along the path to the main village.

"He's really a good boy," Evangeline said. "But his twin brother is a troublemaker. He will be a sorcerer, the medicine men say!"

Benjamin said Moravian sorcerers were unheard of, and Evangeline laughed lightly, saying those two were certainly not Moravian Indians. They were true Shawnees, worshipers of the old religion, and already sworn enemies of whites who tried to take their country. Then she became more serious, and her eyes were distant as she said:

"The wise ones say that these two are destined to be war leaders one day, leaders of many Indian nations. . . ." Her gaze fell. "But it is not said if they will triumph or die."

chapter **17**

MASSACRE

Not long afterward, Benjamin learned to his joy that Daniel Boone had escaped. The Shawnees were furious and searched everywhere for him, but a few weeks later Benjamin heard that he had reached the stockade at Boonesborough in four days, traveling an astounding hundred and sixty miles. The Indians talked often of this feat, and one of them who had since parleyed with Boone had been told everything: how the man had stolen a horse and reached the Ohio, floated across on a log, then run the rest of the way to Boonesborough, deep in the Kentucky woods.

Benjamin was inspired at first, but found it hard to remain optimistic when several young warriors began to make a habit of harrying and insulting him, warning that if he dared try to get away he would be slain. Benjamin knew they were probably right, for he was no Daniel Boone.

Nevertheless, as time passed he was given the freedom of the village and was even allowed to compete with the young men at shooting, wrestling, running, and riding. He won the grudging respect of the Indians for his remarkable abilities, and Wabete beamed every time he did well.

Benjamin made few friends, though. There was Evangeline, whom he saw often; and her cousin Tecumseh was friendly enough. But Tecumseh's twin brother, Tenskwatawa, a sly, skinny fellow, was seldom to be seen. As an aspiring medicine man believed to have rapidly developing powers, Tenskwatawa was often in the company of wise men who were his teachers in the magic arts. Evangeline, Benjamin soon learned, had little respect for him; she said he was cruel to animals and hateful. In any case, Benjamin was in no hurry to meet Tenskwatawa. He couldn't afford to have an enemy with such influence among the Shawnees.

For her part, the pretty Evangeline was always kind to Benjamin, and he grew very fond of her. One day, in front of her lodge, she surprised him by saying that she knew Jeremy. As Benjamin stood there dumbstruck, she explained that her family often traveled for trade and to visit relatives up at Sandusky, where Jeremy and Gwen had held a clinic two years ago.

Stirring a pot of stew that hung over the fire, Evangeline laughed and said, "I exchange small secrets with Dr. Bently. He teaches me ways of cleaning wounds before binding them, and I tell him about my ways of healing animals." She said the Bentlys had invited her to Valenya whenever her family was in Detroit. "They say maybe I can be a doctor like them, and they will teach me someday!"

It was strange to hear his brother being spoken well of in an enemy village where he himself was a prisoner; Benjamin felt a lump in his throat and had to look away to regain his composure while Evangeline diverted herself tossing a small ring in the air, which Punch caught in his beak and brought back to her.

Benjamin longed with all his heart to get away, to be home again, but he was deep in dangerous country, and it would be foolish to attempt an escape until he had no other choice.

Absently, he sat down by the cooking fire and murmured, "I wish I had wings like Punch."

Evangeline looked at him with sympathy; she forced a gentle smile and went back to her cooking.

Benjamin shook off his sadness and said, "Maybe I can't fly away, but one of these days, I'll find a way to—"

He held his tongue when he saw Evangeline's twin cousins come shambling out of the trees, hunting bows in their hands, arrows stuck in their thong belts. They were naked except for loincloths, and both had turkey feathers in their hair. Other than that they could hardly have been less alike.

Benjamin had not observed Tenskwatawa closely until now, and he marked the contrast as the two brothers looked intently at Punch, who was hopping on Evangeline's hands. Tecumseh, tall and erect, with a fine physique, was good-looking in an alert, confident way. Tenskwatawa was stooped, so skinny as to seem half-starved, though his muscles were stringy and his hands large and nimble as he tried unsuccessfully to coax Punch onto a finger. For the first time Benjamin noticed that he was missing his right eye.

Tenskwatawa quickly lost interest in the bird, his sulky mouth turning down sharply at the corners, but Tecumseh appealed to Evangeline to throw the ring up again for Punch to catch.

As she and Punch repeated the trick, making Tecumseh shout with delight, the other boy strolled toward the seated Benjamin. He stopped only a couple of paces away and poked his bow down at Benjamin's chest.

In Shawnee, he said, "How could this white dog bring much reward at Detroit? Uncle Wabete should have scalped him and sewn the scalp to a horse's tail—then it might look like a man's—"

In an instant Benjamin was on his feet, and with a savage shove he sent the boy sprawling on his back. Tecumseh slashed his bow at Benjamin's face but missed, and in the next moment found his feet yanked out from under him and held off the ground as his naked buttocks were swatted with his own bow. Tenskwatawa was up swiftly, bow in hand, a hunting arrow fitted to the string, but Benjamin used the other boy, squirming upside down, as a shield.

"Go on, shoot!" Benjamin snarled in Shawnee. "Put that arrow in this whelp's tail, and then I'll turn you upside down, too!"

Startled, Tenskwatawa hesitated. When he did find the presence of mind to aim, it was impossible to get a clear shot. Benjamin was so much taller and stronger than either of the younger boys that he surely could have taken them both on if not for that arrow.

The elders came to the door of the lodge, but it was Evangeline who stopped things from getting worse. Holding the bird from attacking, she sprang in front of Tenskwatawa and then backed toward Benjamin, calling for him to let Tecumseh down.

Benjamin did so—fairly roughly—but held on to the boy's bow. Evangeline shielded Benjamin and kept a grip on the fluttering Punch as she declared to the adults, "Tenskwatawa started this trouble! He insulted the white boy! Don't blame the white boy!"

Benjamin knew that if she moved away, the one-eyed brother would shoot.

There was a tense moment until Wabete appeared and growled, "Do not interfere with my captive without my permission!" He shook a fist at the sullen boys. "Begone, or I'll let this wildcat teach you both a lesson!"

The youths backed off, and Benjamin tossed Tecumseh his bow. Without a word, the brothers turned to leave, but before they were out of sight Benjamin noticed Tecumseh rub his buttocks and glance angrily backward.

Evangeline could not help but giggle, and as Wabete grumbled and went back inside, she said, "Tenskwatawa was in need of a lesson, but his brother did not need the spanking you dealt him!" She giggled again. "Though it was funny to watch!"

Just then Punch tried to squawk and flew into the air, darting straight at a nearby bush, as if on the attack. Benjamin thought Tecumseh's brother might be there with an arrow, but the sudden crashing of someone hurrying away sounded more like a full-grown man. Benjamin rushed to the edge of the clearing, whistling for Punch, who came flitting back to his hand. Through the trees he could just make out a lean, hunched figure slipping away. The man glanced once back over his shoulder, and Benjamin felt a jolt of fear. It was Amaghwah.

For July it was not a very hot day, but tramping for the past hour or more in bright sunshine made the four hundred and fifty jaunty militiamen of the Wyoming Valley talk loudly of cold ale and spruce beer. The younger ones called for a swim in the broad Susquehanna, which flowed past just a hundred yards to their right, beyond a wooded marshland. That set up laughing and joking as the men tried to overcome their nervousness.

Tom Morely was as thirsty as any, and just as confident. These were good men, though few knew much about soldiering. They had been called up for the past several weeks and now were on their way to make short work of what was reported as a smaller number of loyalist rangers and Indians marauding through the northern end of the valley. No one doubted the courage of the loyalists, many of whom had lived in this same valley before the rebels had driven them out, but Indians did not favor pitched battles unless they had the advantage of cover or greatly outnumbered their foe.

Tom shifted his rifle from one shoulder to the other and removed his hat to wipe away sweat. Butler's Destructives would need a good many brave Indians to turn back this strong force of rebel fighting men, he thought. These men and boys would not quit easily, for they were protecting their homes. Many valley farms had already been destroyed during the frustrating cat-and-mouse game of the past weeks, as Butler's men struck here and there almost as they chose, killing farmers, burning down cabins, and cutting off militia scouting parties. Always they had slipped off before the rebels could send reinforcements.

Now, with a decisive clash just hours away, all that would end. Word had come that the Destructives were on the march down the valley, heading right for this main militia body. The enemy had massed its raiding parties and was looking for a major engagement.

"They'll get more than they've bargained for!" cried big Joshua Jenkins, the Congregationalist settler from Tom's small community. He tramped alongside Tom through the meadow grass left bent in a long swath behind the marching column. "This time they won't slink up on us! We'll be there waiting, to give 'em fire and brimstone!"

"Tell 'em, preacher!" someone shouted.

"Say a prayer for their lost souls, the Tory dogs!"

"Murdering swine!"

As he marched, Tom was quiet. He was watching the dense marshland to the right, about fifty yards from the main column of troops. It was a tangle of trees, swamp grass, and thick bushes, good cover for an ambush, even though the scouts had said the enemy was massed and coming this way out in the open. On the left were more trees. Tom was becoming uneasy.

Then he was distracted by a shout, and looking forward saw a column of black smoke surge into the sky from about a quarter of a mile away.

"That's Wintermoot's fort!" Jenkins yelled. "That's where they say Butler made his quarters after he took it!"

"That means he's pulling out!" another called, and the shout was taken up angrily by other soldiers, who surged ahead. "Stand and fight, Butler, you low dog!"

"We're coming to settle accounts, Butler!"

"Cowards! Let's catch 'em!"

The troops moved more quickly along the open fields, and their officers smoothly formed them from a column into two wings, ready for battle. Soon word came back that skirmishers had run into enemy scouting parties, who had fired and run like rabbits toward a larger body of men who were hastily withdrawing. Although the rebel leaders were trying to restrain their men, the militia were eager to come to grips with the hated Tories and Indians. Yet Tom felt less and less confident as the meadow narrowed and the woods on each side hemmed them in ever closer. He wanted to say something, but the officers were too busy organizing the battle lines. Dry-mouthed and sweating, he sensed that the killing was about to begin. He checked his rifle's priming as he moved, and though others were laughing and singing, he became edgy—not afraid, but very suspicious.

Suddenly a group of forty or so Indians sprang out of longer grass a hundred yards ahead and opened scattered fire. The rebel militia gave a shout and let off a massed volley as the Indians spun and fled, none falling wounded. The rebels cheered and advanced in formation, certain the battle was as good as won. It was simply a matter of catching and punishing the enemy before they got clean away.

Then another party of the enemy leaped up, these mostly green-uniformed rangers, with faces painted as grotesquely as any Indian's. They, too, fired and retreated, and the rebels quickened the pace almost to a run, cursing to see the loyalists spring across an overgrown fencerow and vanish. After a moment a defensive line rose from behind the same fencerow, and the enemy fire became more heavy. Men on either side of Tom fell wounded.

"Have at 'em!" Jenkins yelled, and Tom could not help but think that the man was no Indian fighter, for all his courage. Overconfidence was a fault, and Jenkins was not alone. Earlier that afternoon the older officers had wanted to wait for better information about the enemy before taking the field, but other, younger, men had accused them of cowardice, forcing them to go out against their own best judgment.

The militia ranks advanced steadily toward the fencerow, every other man moving five paces forward, firing, then reloading as his neighbors advanced and fired. Smoke was sour and dense. Cries of the rebel wounded were heard more now. Tom's rifle jumped, the bang loud, the flash spreading a black powder mark on his check. As he reloaded, ramming home the bullet, he noted that the loyalist fire was growing hotter and that quite a few of his fellows had fallen, making the others even more angry and impatient to finish the assault with hatchets.

Just as Tom aimed again and fired, a sudden, tremendous blast of gunfire erupted from both sides—the woods and marshland. With horror he realized that hundreds more of the enemy were concealed there, waiting for the rebels to enter the trap, as they just had. Bullets thudded into bodies. Men groaned and fell all around. Blood splashed Tom, who loaded and fired, knowing his force was outnumbered. Confusion took hold of many, and a rising gale of Indian war cries told that a fatal mistake had been made.

Mounted officers rode back and forth, shouting, trying to maintain order, but the left wing of the rebel army began to crumble and retreat under the brutal fire. On the right, however, Tom and his fellows held on. They fired, loaded, fired again, until their muskets and rifles were almost too hot to hold. Then Tom saw Indians rushing toward the open end of the field to cut off retreat. Others saw it, too, and fear gripped many. They began to huddle and run, some dropping their guns. The wounded were hauled back by friends and family, but often the men trying to save them went down, too. The enemy came out in small groups to attack stragglers or fugitives who tried to escape. The screaming and war whoops were terrifying, the Iroquois in their warrior skullcaps and wooden chest armor looking like devils.

Tom kept cool, and he loaded and fired, staying close to other men who would not break and run. They were too few, however, as instinctively they tried to find one another in the hazy, smoke-covered field, which was littered with dead and dying. They closed ranks and withdrew slowly, dragging their wounded, firing and loading.

Then the wind gusted and cleared the smoke, and Tom had a good view of what was coming at him. To his dismay the entire field seemed filled with the enemy, whose weapons and bodies glittered and glistened in the sunshine. Instead of a few hundred, as once thought, there were well over a thousand against the remnants of the original rebel four hundred and fifty. Guns were volleying on every side, and rebels were steadily falling, whole families of men going down together—brothers with fathers and grandfathers, uncles and cousins, all wiped out in that fierce nightmare of slaughter and hellish noise.

Tom and his dogged companions withdrew toward the narrow gap fast closing behind them. They might have battled through, but then the enemy surged forward in a great mass, closing in on the survivors, overwhelming and cutting down the fugitives, and hammering against those few who, like Tom, stood bravely to fight and die.

It was Joshua Jenkins who escaped to warn Ella's settlement. Having barely made it to the river, he had swum across while many other men drowned or were shot down in midstream. Jenkins was a strong man, and after reaching the east bank, he ran from cabin to cabin, warning the womenfolk to flee, that everything was lost, and that the Indians would be coming soon.

It was early evening when he reached his own people. Susannah saw him first; she had been standing guard by the trail and nearly shot him as he came running wildly through the gathering gloom of the forest. Mel, who was not especially a fighting man, and some of the boys gathered around Jenkins, who told them of the disaster. Hearts pounding, Ella and Susannah came to the midst of the frantic people in the clearing as the gasping Jenkins was given water and whiskey. Susannah wanted to cry. She nearly collapsed on her mother, who held her up and listened intently as Jenkins breathlessly related the terrible news.

"It was a scourge of hell!" he moaned, while his wife swabbed his dirty, sweating face. "Hell descended upon us! I can't . . . I can't bear to tell you, but near all the men . . . near all are lost! We must flee!"

He gave way to exhaustion, and the people of the community became painfully silent for just an instant; then many began to cry and wail, while others ran to their cabins, to ready what they could for their escape.

Ella's eyes were wet to think of Tom and so many friends, but she kept her composure as she stared hard down the trail into the woods. It was as if she were making plans to fight back somehow.

Susannah saw this and tried to be strong. "I . . . I'll tell Sally," she gasped, and her mother gripped her hand. Sally had not been feeling well and was sleeping in her cabin. "But what shall I tell her?"

Ella patted her hand, wiped her own eyes, and said, "We'll both go and make her listen to reason, for she won't want to leave here until she knows for certain about Tom."

Just then a rider came thundering down the trail, and folk who had been scurrying about, loading wagons and collecting children, abruptly stopped, some of them bringing guns to bear. But it was Hickory, who had been off visiting some Oneida friends upriver, not far from the battle scene. She leaped from the horse, and Mel caught her as she panted out all she knew.

"Iroquois and Tories burning valley! Ella, they got Tom! He lives!"

Ella came and gripped her arms as Hickory explained that she had seen the few surviving militiamen being taken to a grove of trees on the west bank of the river.

"I hear Injuns say they kill 'em all! Kill all tonight!"

There was a wailing moan, and they saw Sally at the door of her cabin, hands clutching the doorframe, her face white, eyes blank. Then her little son toddled out and called for his daddy. Susannah ran to Sally to keep her from fainting.

"Spare me nothing!" Sally cried to Hickory, fighting away from Susannah and past a weeping Lettie Grey, who had come to hear what Hickory was saying about her son. "Tell me all, quickly! Can he be saved?"

Hickory embraced Sally but did not immediately reply. Meanwhile the people resumed their hurried preparations for escape. The only fighting man among them other than Jenkins was Jeb Grey, who took charge of organizing a convoy of small carts to carry the old folk and the sick. They would head eastward, away from the enemy, in the hope that the marauders would not range too far into the foothills in search of more victims and booty.

Sally was shaking, and tears were streaming down her face as she turned to Ella. "There're not enough men to go after Tom, are there?"

Ella looked at the ground. Hickory declared, "I know just where he be! Just where he be! Need a boat . . . I wish there was time! Gotta move fast! Move fast!"

People were running past, carrying belongings. Joshua Jenkins had already sent some armed boys down the trail to watch for the enemy's approach.

"We only got a few hours!" Jenkins cried, swiftly organizing people, grouping them into traveling parties, and sending them off on different trails up into the hills. "Come on, Sutherlands, Greys, Mrs. Morely! Got to go!"

Ella ignored him and said to Hickory, "Do you know where we can get a boat to cross the river?"

Hickory knew, and suddenly Sally and Ella had become like warriors themselves, fear and sorrow gone from them. Susannah listened, nervous and excited as her mother and Sally made hurried plans to send Timothy with Lettie, Jeb, and herself and then to go with Mel and Hickory down into the valley and make a wild attempt to rescue Tom.

Susannah was shocked that she was being left out. "I can handle the boat!" she insisted. Ella stared at her. "I'm going, Mother. You can't stop me."

In the depth of night, the western bank of the Susquehanna was dotted with roaring blazes for three or four miles as cabins and small forts burned, lighting up the sky wherever one looked. Indians and some of the more bitter Tories had sated themselves on blood and booty. In one brief, fierce battle they had dealt a disastrous blow to the rebels. Fewer than a dozen of their own men had been lost, while more than three hundred rebels had been killed in the immediate fighting or later as captives at the hands of the Iroquois.

Tomorrow the destruction would continue, until the last pockets of resistance were wiped out. So far, most of the women and children had been spared; Colonel John Butler, the loyalist commander, had sent them packing into the dismal forests and swamps, as much to get them out of his sight as to keep them away from the Indians. Older males, however, were turned over to the Iroquois to do with as they chose, and not far from the battle scene, Tom Morely sat in darkness, waiting for death.

He had been knocked down and taken with twenty others that afternoon, and was bruised but unwounded. Now he was bound and seated behind some bushes, his face painted the black of a condemned man. Not far off, around a great bonfire, were several hundred Indians, and in their midst was a large, flat rock that ran with blood. The other men captured with Tom had been taken to that rock and killed with the blow of a war club, and their mutilated bodies lay on the ground in a grotesque heap. Tom had seen some of them die, and sick with horror had turned away and sat down, waiting to be called by the three Seneca guards who stood nearby. They were busy watching a blood-spattered chief complete a long speech about victory. Earlier, Tom had seen the same man drinking the blood of slain rebels.

Tom knew he was near the river, and he had thought about escaping. Dense cattails were just behind him, and he could hear the ripple of the water above the droning Indian voices and the guttural chanting of the chief. He sat with knees up, hands and feet tied with rawhide. He had tried to work the thongs loose, but the more he struggled the tighter they became, numbing his hands. His guards mostly ignored him; they seemed impatient to join the rest of the Indians, who were drinking great quantities of captured rum and hugely enjoying this bloody celebration.

Tom heard someone approach and looked up to see a shadowy white man standing above him, staring down. It was a loyalist ranger in a dark green uniform, his face painted black with streaks of red. Tom expected no help from him; no one could stop the Indians once they had a condemned prisoner in their hands. He thought of little Timothy, and of Sally, and his heart turned. He drew a slow breath.

The ranger spoke in cultured English that told of some breeding, and the voice seemed familiar to Tom.

"I arranged it so that you would be last, Morely. Among redskins that's quite an honor, you know. I like to take care of my old neighbors from Detroit." He laughed softly.

Tom suddenly felt fury course through him as he recognized the voice. "Davies! I might have guessed you'd be here to see this, you hellhound—"

Davies lashed out with his boot and caught Tom hard on the face, knocking him over. When the Indian sentries came to see what was wrong, Davies angrily ordered them away, saying he would guard this prisoner until his time came. The Iroquois moved off a little, to listen to the speech, waiting for the signal to bring the captive out to the flat rock.

Davies knelt over Tom, who sat up and sullenly looked away.

"This is what'll happen to all you rebel scum! This is what you brought down on yourself. It's no more than you deserve, and I won't rest until I see you all in hell at the hands of these savages!"

He grabbed Tom by the hair and yanked his head back. Tom saw a blade come out. He expected to die right then, but fiercely spat blood and spittle into the officer's face. Davies cursed, pulling back to wipe away the muck. Just then someone else was there, standing between them. The din among the Indians was rising, and they obviously were ready for their next victim. Davies growled at the newcomer, a squaw.

"What do you want? Get out! Get, woman!"

The squaw bent over, hands appealing, and spoke in an Iroquois tongue. She said she had something for the condemned prisoner.

"He needs nothing! Be off!"

Davies had wasted enough time. He grasped Tom's hair, pressing the blade against his throat. "Nice meeting you again, Morely. Too bad you can't stay—"

The squaw was there again, very agitated, begging Davies for something, clutching at him. When Davies tried to brush her away with his knife hand, she caught it in both of hers, talking fast. She was so remarkably strong that he could not easily pull his arm away. At the same time, Davies seemed reluctant to alert the guards that he was about to murder their prisoner. He cursed and fought to get free, releasing Tom and standing up awkwardly. In the tussle his hat was knocked off, making his head a perfect target for the club that came out of the darkness. There was a crack, and he slumped down heavily into the bushes.

Ella threw down the club, and with Sally cut Tom free as fast as she could. No one spoke. Hickory placed herself to intercept a guard who was coming just then, for the chief was calling for Tom's death. It was too dark for the Indian to see Tom being unbound, and Hickory blocked the way, talking softly and laughing. The man pushed her aside, but by now Tom was free. He would have killed Davies right there had not the guard seen him and called out in surprise. The call was short-lived, for Tom drove Davies's knife into the warrior's throat, then quickly grabbed the man's tomahawk.

The second guard was immediately upon them, but Hickory dropped him with a blow from a hammer, and Tom tomahawked the astonished third guard before he could give a warning.

"Come on!" Tom ordered, dragging them away. He had no time to finish Davies, for some of the Indians sitting around the bonfire were rising to see what was going on.

Ella and the others rushed with Tom through the dark trees and cattails toward the waiting canoe as a shout of anger arose behind them. In the canoe, Mel and Susannah held the paddles ready. Also in the boat was Heera, sitting in the bow, perfectly still. More Indians were shouting, not far away in the darkness.

Tom's group crashed through brush and into the water as Susannah and Mel pushed the canoe to meet them. Tom yanked a rifle from the stern as the others piled into the craft. He heard Indians thrashing about in the reeds, searching for them, shouting and whooping in their drunken excitement. Then he, too, was almost aboard, but as soon as he laid his gun down, an Iroquois splashed into the shallows directly ahead of them, musket in hand. The Indian whirled, saw the boat, and gave a chilling yell, bringing up the gun from just a few yards away. Before he could fire, however, Hickory threw her hammer, hitting him squarely on the chest, and Heera was on him like a phantom, splashing, snarling and biting, driving him to his knees in the shallows. Tom leaped through the water and quickly finished the man off, then pushed the canoe out into the fast-flowing channel as Susannah pulled Heera back aboard. Two other Indians appeared through the reeds and got off quick shots that zipped narrowly past.

Before the canoe had reached the middle of the stream, a blood-chilling wail of fury pierced the night, like a madman's anguished cry. It was not an Indian voice, though many Iroquois were ranging up and down the riverbank in search of their escaped prisoner. It was a white man's eerie lament, haunting and evil.

As he paddled, Tom answered the others' unspoken question. "It's Mark Davies. He's lost again, and it's driving him insane."

chapter **18**

VINCENNES

By comparison with Detroit, the small fort at Vincennes was a rickety hovel, its haphazard palisades showing gaps that a fist might pass through. Called Fort Sackville, it was protection to no one, and all its buildings were in poor repair.

The sleepy French village huddled next to the fort was not much more imposing. Its few streets, running up from the east bank of the broad Wabash, were rutted and uncared-for, and most of its hundred or so buildings were small, rude dwellings of squared timbers, though a few had puncheon walls. The majority were whitewashed, in the French manner, with brightly painted front doors and rough picket fences. A few of the best houses were of stone, with porches winding around them, and as in every French frontier community, there was a stout log church in the center of town.

The seven hundred or so residents were a carefree lot, just as strongly influenced by their Indian neighbors as they themselves influenced the local tribes, who were their main source of trade. Here, even the passage of time was still marked Indian style: the time of berries, the time of potatoes, the time of floods. Little was known of the world beyond New Orleans to the south or Detroit to the north. Indeed, Vincennes was as backward as any white community in America could be, and its people had long been content that way. The men were all good boatmen and woodsmen, the women sturdy and wise in the ways of the frontier, and the children ran free like Indians.

And it was peaceful here. Few Vincennes natives had fought in a war since the early Indian-French conflicts at the beginning of the century, and even the more recent British wars against the French and Indians had never reached this remote village. Many of its family names, however, were of respected wilderness fighters, for Vincennes had been a refuge for them at the end of the last war. Rather than submit to British rule, these proud Frenchmen had drifted here from Canada and Detroit, to forget and be forgotten. They had taken the oath to Britain only grudgingly, for they were too French to admit defeat. Like the Indians, they harbored a hope that the French king would someday send armies to reconquer the land.

From the start Jeremy and Gwen had taken to these lusty folk, who were always ready to have a party and loved to laugh and dance. The Bentlys in turn had been quickly accepted, and their medical skills had endeared them to whites and reds alike in the region. They had set up their clinic in a rented stone house and already made several trips to outlying Indian villages and the more isolated French inhabitants.

Jeremy soon discovered he was the nearest thing to a symbol of British authority within six hundred miles. He was the only Redcoat at Vincennes, for Fort Sackville was maintained and guarded exclusively by local French militia. The man who had been the king's lieutenant governor here and who had built the fort was gone. He had left months earlier, embarrassed and afraid because British colonial officials had not supplied him with funds to buy the usual presents expected by Indians when they returned from their winter hunting grounds. Such shortsighted stinginess, Jeremy knew, was typical of the disregard with which the British government managed the northwest. He had not been surprised to learn that one lieutenant governor, supposed to have been posted southwestward in Kaskaskia, had not even bothered to leave England.

Ignoring such dismal precedents, the Bentlys set to work every day with enthusiasm. No one seemed to mind that they were British Americans, and people did not inquire about Gwen's politics. Jeremy, as he had promised, seldom wore his scarlet tunic, and that was to Gwen's liking. They were far from the military stronghold of Detroit, and out here it seemed that most troubles could be put aside for the future.

Near sunset on a soft July evening, Jeremy and Gwen finished work at their clinic in the village and took Cape for a stroll to the river. Fort Sackville flew the Union Jack, raised by a militiaman on duty, but otherwise the stockade showed little sign of habitation. Its rough palisades ran along the riverbank, and as warm sunlight fell in shades of red and purple on the pickets, the fort seemed more like the edge of a dense wood than a military post.

Gwen and Jeremy borrowed a boat and, with Cape bounding aboard, put out into the placid river. The horizon was low on every side, and the sun was almost down, leaving the world shadowed and tranquil. They hardly spoke as Jeremy rowed upstream; they listened to birds in the swamps, frogs and crickets on shore, cattle lowing in lush meadows. A flight of ducks fluttered down to one of the many ponds in the lowlands along the river, and Gwen said she could not wish to be anywhere else in all the world just then.

Immediately Jeremy's thoughts turned to Benjamin, and it seemed Gwen read his mind, for she said she knew how difficult it was for him to be happy, things being as they were.

He replied, "I can't go on waiting and waiting for Hamilton to save my brother." He watched his hands as they stroked the oars. "But let me worry about it, Gwen. Trust me that when I do what I must, I'll consider carefully..." He found it useless to say more. He knew that when he could wait no longer, he would go for Benjamin, and that was that. No one, not even Hamilton, would be able to stop him. First, however, he would give Hamilton more time to carry off the business in a formal way.

Recently he and Gwen had heard from some Shawnees that Benjamin was not in immediate danger and that the chief who held him intended to adopt him. That knowledge was some relief, but not enough, and the Shawnees had been intentionally vague as to where the boy was being kept. They did not want to be blamed if Jeremy caused trouble with their people.

Forcing a smile, he gave his attention to Gwen, glad to see her looking so healthy and well rested. She smiled, too, then lay back, letting her fingers trail in the water, with Cape's head on her lap.

After a while she spoke, and her voice was unexpectedly tense, although it was apparent she was trying to sound casual. "Do you think these French children are as wild as they are because of being so far from civilization?"

Jeremy had not thought about that, and replied that the influence of Indian children certainly had a lot to do with the French being so rambunctious and heedless.

"But perhaps we British can learn something about happiness from them," he said as he turned the boat, the left oar holding back while the right worked in the rippling water. "If a child is well influenced by civilization, yet knows the ways of the wild, then that child can be something special, it seems to me."

Gwen was half sitting up, staring at him, her eyes colored by the setting sun. Jeremy guessed she was wondering whether their children would grow up here, far from eastern culture. Gwen turned to gaze at the fort and village, which now lay in shadow.

He said, "I've noticed you regarding the children very closely of late."

She sat all the way up, elbows on her knees. Nervously, she began to stroke Cape, who snuffled and nuzzled against her.

Jeremy held the boat steady and said softly, "Our children will know more of the world than just the wilderness, or just civilization. That'll make them stronger and wiser . . . and happier, too."

He began to row toward shore, but Gwen looked at him so intently that he had to pause. He held the oars out of the water, the boat giving way in the current.

With eyes full of emotion and excitement, she said, "I'm with child, Jeremy."

Such a rush of joy coursed through him that he nearly lost the oars overboard as he reached for her, and the startled Cape struggled to get out of the way of their happy embrace. They began to spin slowly downstream as Jeremy hugged

Gwen, who sighed and held him, her tears running down.

"I was so hoping for this!" he said as Cape resumed her comfortable place, head in Gwen's lap. "How I was hoping! It's a new start! And we'll be the happiest family in the emp— Anywhere!"

Gwen said the baby should come in November and that a certain Frenchwoman had already agreed to be midwife. By now the boat was well below the fort, and Jeremy had to return to the oars to keep from having too long a pull back upstream.

They were home by full dusk, passing arm in arm through the village as their dog padded on ahead. They greeted villagers carrying lanterns, nodded to a ragged Indian wrapped in a trade blanket, and strolled on home, looking absolutely carefree.

Owen Sutherland watched them. It was he, not an Indian, disguised by the blanket, and by now he had discovered that several other men wandering through the village in blankets were not Indians but spies from Colonel George Rogers Clark. He would have been amused by the coincidence had he not been on such a vital mission.

Sutherland stood in the shadows of a public house, where a group of Frenchmen and a couple of Indians were drinking and singing. His heart was still beating rapidly from his joy at seeing Jeremy and Gwen, but he dared not approach them on the street. Word might already be circulating in the village of his presence in the region, and the French or some bold Indians might risk trying to capture him for a reward. It was essential that he speak with Jeremy soon, however, for the rebel spies he had encountered had told him that Kaskaskia to the south had been seized by Clark's men not long ago and that Vincennes would be next. If Jeremy was taken as a loyalist prisoner, he would be in danger of execution, as an example to the wavering French. Sutherland himself might not be able to intervene, for Clark could be a hard, ruthless man.

Sutherland pulled his blanket closely about him, keeping his face averted from the group nearby. He hoped Tamano would be safe among Clark's Longknives; the Chippewa warrior had gone southward to make contact with Clark, and if all went well, he would be back tonight.

As the Bentlys entered their house Sutherland set off along the street, going around to the darkened back door and knocking. Within, the dog barked, and Sutherland heard his stepson's voice for the first time in almost a year, asking who was there.

"A friend," Sutherland replied, and a moment later the door opened, letting out the soft light of candles and lamps and revealing his stepson's astonished face.

Awkward at first but excited to see his stepfather, Jeremy offered food and drink and asked him to sit at the plain oak table in the middle of the room. In the candlelight Jeremy noted how drawn and thin Sutherland looked, and after hearing of the journey from the Wyoming Valley, he well appreciated all that his stepfather had been through. Sutherland's voice was unusually soft—not weak, but seeming to come from deep within, as if every word spoken had been carefully considered and had significance.

Sutherland looked older but still strong, perhaps even harder than Jeremy remembered from the days when he had been a brawny, muscular man, handsome and vigorous. Like his voice, his strength seemed seated deep within, for outwardly he conveyed a quiet humility, as if he had endured and conquered great hardships.

Before the conversation began in earnest, Sutherland filled himself with Gwen's leftover stew, cornbread, and apples. Gwen had nervously wanted to whip a pie together for the occasion, but Sutherland said he was more than content. Jeremy saw how tense Gwen was, and he felt much the same, wondering what this visit meant. While Sutherland ate, Jeremy read a letter from his mother, which caused such welling up of emotion that he had to go out into the backyard for a time, just to be able to breathe. When he came in, Gwen was bustling about with the dishes and Sutherland was standing before the fire, filling a pipe.

Jeremy went to clear the table and sat down, lighting another candle and saying, "Shall we talk now?"

Sutherland nodded and sat. Gwen was being unusually

clumsy with her work, dropping things, unable to stop her hands from shaking. Jeremy finally asked her to let the dishes be and to sit with them, for it was important she hear what was to be said.

Sutherland was casual, puffing on his pipe, and began the conversation by asking all Jeremy knew about Benjamin. When the involvement of Mark Davies was revealed, however, Sutherland's anger was like a flash of lightning.

Staring hard at Jeremy, he said, "Since when did you put your trust in that dog Davies? Did you think he would serve us and try to save the lad? How could you agree to letting him go for Benjamin?"

Jeremy became angry himself. "We'll not get far if you blame me for something that was beyond my control! Hamilton would not let me go along, and I warned Davies clearly before he went out...."

Gwen sat motionless, her hands clasped on the table. Her lips were pale with anxiety, her eyes downcast.

Jeremy began to explain further, but Sutherland sighed and shook his head. "I was a king's soldier once myself, son, so you don't have to go on. But that time is long past, and I don't understand why you're a British soldier, when your country has need of you."

Jeremy flared, barely keeping his voice down. "We should speak of rescuing the boy, not of my opposition to your tyrannical and bloody rebellion! Yes, I admit my cause is faltering, and for that very reason I won't abandon it until the honor and interests of the loyalists are upheld, even if it must be done on the battlefield!"

Sutherland nodded slowly. "You had best win that battle yourself, for it's little enough honor or support your king gives you loyalists. He won't arm or supply you well enough to win your own battles, he doesn't trust you, and the British army sneers at Americans as much as ever it did. They'll never give loyalists a real chance to fight for what they believe in, except for those who lead Indian raids—men who'll sacrifice women and children in the name of loyalty!"

Jeremy got up and walked to the door and back again, saying, "Did you come here to enlist my help to save Benjamin, or to argue yet again about my loyalty and your treason?" He glared at his stepfather, though the pain of their separation clawed at him. Yet he could not deny that Sutherland was right to say loyalist Americans were treated poorly by the British; and matters were getting worse in that regard.

In the ensuing silence Sutherland took Richard Weston's journal from a carrying bag. "I came to save Benjamin . . . but I also have the hope you'll listen to reason."

Jeremy took the journal and gave a start when he read Richard's name. He sat down, eyes wide, and Gwen touched his arm. He turned to the passages Sutherland indicated, then read aloud, for Gwen's sake. With every page he grew more furious, his voice more strained.

When he had finished, he was red in the face, his heart pounding. He slammed the book down on the table, got up, and threw open the back door again. This time, however, he could not walk away from his emotions, could not let the night air settle his turbulent mind. Davies had killed Richard, or had ordered it done. From that moment Jeremy knew he would have no rest until the man had been punished. He swung back to Sutherland and stood staring at him.

At last he said, "Justice will be done!" Hatred consumed him as he repeated those words.

With that, Gwen got up, tears in her eyes, and said she was going to bed. "I can listen to this no longer. It is not for me to decide." She moved to Jeremy and took his hands. "I have made my decision already. I'm yours, husband, wherever we are."

Not even taking a candle to light her way up the narrow steps, she bade Sutherland good night and left the room. For some time, the two men did not speak. Jeremy sat down at the table, reading the journal once again, becoming all the more certain of Davies's guilt.

Sutherland let his pipe go out, then said, "I would not ask you to resign your commission because the loyalist cause is lost, son, but because your king and Parliament have failed you, have failed all America. Their time is past. We're already a new country, and you should join us to be part of it."

Jeremy stared sullenly at the tabletop, only too aware of how the British had bungled their affairs in America. But the next step for him was not as clear as Sutherland had made it.

Sutherland pressed. "Remain neutral, and go on with your profession for everyone's sake. But don't stubbornly deny the evil that your eyes tell you is corrupting your cause in the northwest! Your mother and I never expected you to lie to yourself, and your father would have felt the same."

Jeremy sat back in his chair, feeling weary, the inner turmoil conflicting with his sense of duty and honor. He said hoarsely, "It's my hope . . . my belief . . . that Lieutenant Governor Hamilton will restrain the Indians this year." He spoke without emotion, as if trying to convince himself. "The only way loyalists will protect their rights in this war is to hold their own and to negotiate firmly at the peace table. Pa, for as long as I'm able to support the effort leading to that end, I'll not resign my commission."

Sutherland looked at him, and unexpectedly it was as if the separation they had put between themselves did not exist. Their love, their lifelong bond, made differences vanish for a moment, and they gazed at each other unselfconsciously, speaking feelings without words. Jeremy wished with all his heart that it had not come to this.

Finally Sutherland stirred, saying in a whisper, "I understand, son. Aye . . . I understand." He cleared his throat, and Jeremy saw new resolve come into his eyes. "Then let's get on with another plan, a way to work together to get Benjamin to safety. . . ."

As Gwen lay in the darkened upstairs bedroom she could not help but hear the voices below. It was clear to her how deeply these two men loved each other, and it gave her pain to see the gulf between them. She had long known that Sutherland wanted Jeremy to resign from the army, and felt the same way herself. She had deliberately stayed out of the discussion, however, even though the words of Richard Weston's journal had clutched at her heart. She had known young Weston well, and the knowledge that Mark Davies had been behind his murder bewildered her. She knew it had nearly shattered Jeremy, though he kept it inside.

"Justice will be done!" was all he had said, but he had said it with a cold resolve that made her shudder, fearing that her husband, too, might become a murderer.

Justice will be done. She lay there, praying that justice would indeed be done, and that Jeremy would see at last that the cause he so nobly supported was wrong. In tears, she prayed silently that he would come upstairs to her and say he had been wrong. She wanted him to say there was a new world to build, a world that repudiated men like Mark Davies and misguided warmakers like Henry Hamilton.

The familiar queasiness that had come over her so often of late made her turn on her side, and she closed her eyes. The voices below were slow, with long spaces between what was said and what was answered. The wind was blowing gently outside, and through the open window wafted the sound of the mighty Wabash, eternal and unchanging. Were rivers like men? Was the Mississippi a father of waters, as the Indians said, and all the tributaries sons? Rivers rolled on and on, though sometimes they dried up and weakened, at other times overflowed. But they always rolled on, in the same stubborn direction, much like men.

Jeremy, too, was like a river. Gwen knew he was not meant for a uniform, but that joining the army was his idea of honor, his way of offering sacrifice to . . . to justice! He had decided what was right, and like the river moved stubbornly in his direction—a direction that to her seemed impossible to change. One did not reason with the Mississippi or the Wabash. One loved them, and lived with them, and kept them from becoming so overwhelming that they destroyed things without meaning to.

Gwen felt the inner sensation that told of life within, life that was more than she, that was she and Jeremy together, and more than both of them.

To herself, she whispered, "For the child, Jeremy . . . won't you do it for the child?"

Perhaps she had dozed off, or perhaps no time had passed at all, but when the door opened, Gwen sat bolt upright, feeling something had happened. Jeremy came in and closed the door. He sat on the bed in darkness, and it seemed he was bearing a heavy load. She knew he had made a decision.

Gwen took his hand, and he kissed hers.

"We're leaving Vincennes for a while," he said quietly. "If it's all right with you, that is. Owen wants us to come with him to a nearby Shawnee town to make a try for Benjamin—a week or so away. I'll be in uniform, and we can go out as doctor and nurse, as we always do, so Hamilton can't complain too strenuously if he finds out."

Gwen was enthusiastic about the idea, though she knew it could be dangerous. When Jeremy asked whether she was fit enough to travel, she assured him she was.

"When we get my brother out, you and I will go up to Detroit, and I'll present Richard's journal to Hamilton." He rubbed his eyes and sighed. "It's pretty strong proof, and I'll confront Davies with it to see how he reacts. If there's the slightest suggestion he's guilty..."

Gwen gripped his arm. "In your heart, what do you believe?"

"He's the one who killed Richard, or had it done!" He ran his fingers through his hair, head bowed. "I should have known."

Gwen squeezed his arm comfortingly. She longed to remind him that one of his strongest reasons for joining the British army was his belief that rebels had murdered Weston, but she said nothing. He was suffering enough. Let time and common sense do their work now ... and justice. Justice would have its way somehow, of that she was certain. Jeremy could not delude himself forever.

Faith kept her spirits up. She took his hand and placed it against her tummy, then kissed his cheek.

"You won't feel me as slim as this much longer." She felt a rush of happiness, and when he kissed her, she hugged him tightly, then held him away, saying, "Your pa will need to be given blankets, and—"

Jeremy kissed her again. "Don't trouble yourself. He's gone out of the village on some business of his own. I didn't ask."

• • •

About a half mile outside Vincennes, on higher ground, Owen Sutherland met Tamano as planned. Sheltered from sight of the village by dense trees, they crouched before a fire as Tamano related what he had learned. Clark and a hundred and seventy-five Longknives, he said, were in possession of Kaskaskia, a few days' march away. The few hundred French militia there had to a man declared themselves on the side of the rebels, and the folk here at Vincennes would no doubt soon do the same.

"Even their priests want to be rebels," Tamano said, "and maybe I cannot blame them when I see how fierce Clark's men are. The Indians of the Kaskaskia, Illinois, and Wabash are to be summoned to council with Clark and told that if they stay loyal to the king they will be cut off and destroyed when the rest of Clark's great army comes up from the Falls of the Ohio."

Sutherland nodded and smiled. "There's no great army, and there won't be for a long time, from what Clark's men told me in Vincennes. But as long as Clark can keep the tribes here afraid of him and keep the French and Indians unsure of which side to back, he'll capture the whole country hereabouts. Hamilton won't be able to challenge him until next spring."

Tamano asked how far into Shawnee country Sutherland intended to take Jeremy and Gwen. "It will be dangerous for you, Donoway, even if you are with a Redcoat officer."

Sutherland knew that was true. "I don't intend going more than a few days from here before telling them everything. Clark's men should be here in a day or so, but Jeremy will have a good start for Detroit."

Though the fire played over his ruddy, thin face, his expression darkened. "Once they're safe, I'm going back into Shawnee territory alone." He looked at Tamano, who was staring at him. "I won't rest until I get Benjamin out."

The next afternoon Sutherland and Tamano met Jeremy and Gwen on a low hill east of Vincennes. From here they could see the fort and settlement clearly as they rested before departure. Sutherland would have preferred to go immediately, but Jeremy was worried about Gwen, although he said nothing about her being pregnant.

Finally they set out, leading two packhorses, Gwen riding one. She was in high spirits, for she enjoyed traveling to Indian villages with Jeremy, though she had never been to a Shawnee town. There was always much they could do to help, for most Indians in this region had never seen a white doctor.

As they moved down the side of the hill, they heard distant shouting, and Jeremy turned absently to see what appeared to be a large hunting party marching raucously up the road and into the fort. He would have thought nothing more of it, but before he had gone much farther he noticed the Union Jack being hauled down swiftly. He stopped short, wondering what drunken shenanigans were going on.

"I've a mind to go back there and thrash someone!" he said angrily. Sutherland quickly made a casual joke about it, trying to urge them out of sight of the fort, for these obviously were Clark's men or their French allies, though he had not expected them so soon. But Jeremy was still watching the fort when the red and green flag of the independent state of Virginia went up and snapped insolently in the breeze.

"It's an attack!" he cried and grabbed his rifle from its scabbard on the packhorse. Gwen and Sutherland both called for him to stay, but he declared, "The rebels—they've taken the fort! I've got to go back there!"

"Son, there's nothing one man can do to stop what's coming." Sutherland spoke decisively, touching his arm. "You're out of this now, and your first responsibility is to take Gwen to safety, not risk your lives with futile heroics!"

Jeremy shook off his stepfather's arm and stepped back, abruptly realizing that Sutherland had known this would happen. In his anger and without meaning to, Jeremy almost brought the rifle to bear on Sutherland's heart. "You betrayed me! Dishonored me, Pa! You did this full knowing I'd be leaving my post at a critical time! Did you lie to me about Benjamin being near? No doubt!"

Sutherland's riled expression showed how that tore at his insides. He shook his fist at Vincennes. "I just kept you from dancing at the end of a rope as an American in a British uniform!"

Jeremy was ablaze and said to Gwen, "So this is your rebel cause, full of lies and dishonor!"

"Enough!" Sutherland cried and stepped forward, shoving the rifle aside. "I'll say no more about this! You've enough provisions and two good horses! There's folk along the way who'll help you get back. Now, either speak civilly, or we part here without another word."

"I would have it so!" Jeremy swung his horse's reins, then pulled Gwen's mount along with him. Gwen looked pained, and she reached down to touch Sutherland's hand in thanks. Jeremy strode rapidly away, down the trail that would take them northward to Detroit.

Sutherland stood there, Tamano sadly waiting nearby, and for some time they watched Jeremy and Gwen, until they were nearly out of sight behind some trees. Gwen had turned to wave a last time, but Jeremy just marched on, leading the first packhorse, pulling the reins so that its neck stretched forward. He did not look back.

A week later, Sutherland and Tamano joined George Rogers Clark down at Kaskaskia, a clutter of French and Indian communities as poor and outcast as any in the northwest, yet which were key to control of the Mississippi, Kaskaskia, and Illinois rivers.

Clark had them firmly in his grip, and through guile, boldness, and incredible courage proceeded to convince the Indians and French that he was the mightiest power to come this way since the valley was made. He said he was the vanguard of a great Virginia army, the man who would here and now decide who was the enemy of Congress and who was a friend. The Indians were numerous and glum and at first skeptical, but with the well-known Owen Sutherland on Clark's side, they soon came to believe that they should make peace terms. They were persuaded, for now, to stay out of the white man's war and even ignore the fact that Clark had no gifts with him to carry through the correct wilderness diplomacy.

When Clark uncovered a Winnebago plot to kidnap him, he laughed with scorn and dared them to try. He threatened to destroy anyone who stood in his way. Soon the Winnebagoes and many other Indians felt menaced by his every move, the more so when he laughed in their faces. For years, the very name Longknife had struck fear into their hearts, and Clark played that for all it was worth. More than once Sutherland left one of Clark's Indian councils shaking his head and chuckling at the man's brilliant, fearless audacity. Clark knew just when to threaten, when to soothe, and when to offer the hand of peace, and he did it all without the traditional gifts, without rum, promises of alliance, or the high-blown phrases of adoration Indians loved to hear.

Clark alternately reviled and appeased them. He exhorted them to come and fight him, saying it would be a great pleasure, though no honor, "to rub them out," as the Indians put it. Later, when the intimidated Indians—who outnumbered him ten to one—needed some comforting, he said he might be able to speak in their favor with Congress, but that they had better stay quiet while he considered whether they were worth his effort.

At times, Clark's speeches were absurdly heavy-handed, and he explained the cause of the revolution in terms that made even Tamano smile. Clark said the forefathers of Americans had been driven out of England by an oppressive king who had then tyrannized and robbed them in America, making them pay tribute to the extent that "we got poor and were obliged to go about naked." If Americans killed a deer, they were allowed to keep only the meat and had to turn over the valuable skin to the government. When Americans complained about such treatment, the king sent troops to kill them and burn their villages. Clark went so far as to say that the British intended to tax the Indians if the rebellious colonists were brought under control. When Tamano had heard this, he had begun to laugh. Sutherland had been seated next to him in a great throng of whites and Indians, and seeing his friend chortling, he had leaned over and asked why.

"This," Tamano had replied with a nod, "is what you call shit of the bull, Donoway, but these Indians want to believe it. They don't know what else to think of this brave Longknife, and believing shit of the bull makes it honorable for them to do nothing until they see what Hamilton and his Redcoats will do."

Illinois, Winnebagoes, Piankashaws, Miamis, Cahokias, Chippewas, Ottawas, Missisaugas, Potawatomies, Osages, Iowas, Sauks, and Fox all came in to parley with Clark and his small army of rowdy Virginians and Kentuckians. None knew that the men he had sent homeward one day had refused to reenlist and that his army was actually cut in half. Few guessed how weak he really was.

There were moments when Sutherland thought a spark would set off an attack and that the Longknives would be massacred, but Clark held the Indians in check, even challenging one of their greatest war chiefs to come back on the morrow ready to fight. The chief was so impressed that he threw off his British medals and declared himself a friend to the Longknives, whom he was "happy to meet and to see what they were made of."

And, indeed, Clark's men would not have shirked such a contest, for after a lifetime of fighting Indians they hated them. In fact, few things would have given these backwoodsmen more pleasure than a sharp fight with one of the tribes that had for decades marauded the frontiers—and no doubt the confused Indians sensed this reckless bloodlust.

Clark also had great effect on the French, who were amazed to hear for the first time of the Franco-American alliance. The British had suppressed news of the treaty in order to avoid trouble, but now, once again, the French had the hope of being redeemed by their old monarch.

As for Owen Sutherland, he still longed to go off for Benjamin, but soon learned that the Shawnees had been stirred up like angry hornets by Clark's invasion. They had sent few delegates to the councils and had kept up their raids against Clark's small base camp on the Ohio. They had not been cowed like the tribes to the west.

Frustrated by this turn of events, Sutherland decided to stay with Clark and wait a few more weeks before going in for Benjamin.

chapter **19**

DANGEROUS DUTY

When James Morely received Ella's grim letter about the tragedy in the Wyoming Valley, his first urge had been to assemble a packtrain and travel down there to help them recover. But on reconsideration, he had decided he would be more valuable working for the Frontier Company in Albany.

He did organize a packtrain, however, and Peter Defries, himself a former teamster, headed it on the mission to succor their friends and relations. James had hoped Defries would bring the survivors back to Albany with him, but Defries had written that they all were resolved to leave their ruined homes and go westward to Fort Pitt, where a campaign against Fort Detroit was planned. The massacre had roused bitter anger at Indians and loyalists, and word was out that a large militia army was to be formed at Pitt.

Hearing this, James thought that some wealthy rebel would have to spend large sums to equip and supply such a force. Congress was too poor, its credit almost nonexistent—at least it would be until France began sending enough loans and gifts to prop up the revolution. Had he been sure Congress could pay well enough, he would have headed west himself to profit by acquiring what the army needed. That would be difficult, of course, because any goods out at Pitt would have been shipped by Bradford Cullen's agents, who firmly controlled most inland transport. Considering the number of armed guards, boatmen, and laborers needed, and the expense of acquiring boats and animals, anyone wishing to challenge Cullen's commercial grip on the frontier would have to invest a huge sum, far more than James had available.

For now, he decided, he would stick to Albany, where he was doing quite well using sheer daring and brains to outmaneuver Cullen time after time. His small victories—winning a military contract with the lowest bid, or having ten thousand spears manufactured soon after General Washington ordered them for the troops as substitutes for bayonets—were heartening, though little more than pinpricks in Cullen's leathery side. There came a day in late August, however, when Cullen once more took notice of his upstart rival, for again James was urgently called to the elegant brick mansion overlooking the Hudson.

When he was in Cullen's presence, James wondered how this old, tired man could ever be considered the personification of evil that Owen Sutherland claimed he was. Sitting in the dim room, with heavy curtains drawn against the sunlight and heat, Cullen looked pale and flabby, totally harmless.

His fat fingers thrummed on the tabletop as he wheezed and said, "Mr. Morely, as you can imagine, I'm at the age when I begin to feel the need to leave something worthy behind . . . a legacy if you will, a token to my memory—something more than just a great trading company that bears my name."

He mopped his brow, and James thought he looked pathetic. He felt almost sorry for the man, who seemed so near to death.

"In other words, I have the burning desire to do something lasting for . . . for my country."

He looked straight at James, who wondered whether Cullen meant loyalist or rebel America.

"To that end, Mr. Morely, I need a gentleman upon whom I can depend—one who knows the wilderness, who knows the trade, who understands military supply, and who, above all, is daring and bold." Cullen paused, putting the handkerchief away, still gazing at James.

Wasting not a moment, James said, "If these complimentary descriptions are meant to refer to me, sir, I'm honored and flattered. But it has been made clear that my company and yours cannot do business together after all the conflict that has passed between them. . . ."

Cullen nodded and wheezed, knitting his fingers over his belly. Slowly, he said, "This answer is what I expected. I realize you will not go against the orders of Owen Sutherland."

James bristled. "Sutherland has nothing to do with my stand, sir! I'm my own man, and what's past is past between our firms as far as I'm concerned. But I have a certain responsibility to the Frontier Company, and as long as I'm entrusted with that responsibility, I am reluctant to make separate arrangements with you, Mr. Cullen. Though . . . I must admit, I have some regret about that."

"Quite," Cullen muttered, pouting. "Quite." He mused a while, then stiffly turned to the map of his empire behind the desk. He gave the bottom a tug, and it came off the wall, sliding neglected to the floor and showing another, this one a regional map of the Illinois, Wabash, and Mississippi rivers, as well as part of the Ohio.

James immediately noted that instead of British flags on the settlements at Cahokia, Kaskaskia, and Vincennes, there were flags of Virginia. How was that possible? He looked questioningly at Cullen.

"Yes, the world is changing, Mr. Morely, and for those who can accommodate that change there will be glory and honor, not to mention profit!" He laughed as if he had thought of some private joke. "For those who are enslaved to the past, to old conflicts, and who will not allow old wounds to heal, there is no future . . . no hope! Not unless one can think of the country's need, of a cause that is bigger than petty quarrels."

With a pointer he touched the three posts that Clark had taken and said, "These are now in the possession of Virginia." James listened closely to this amazing news. "There are a couple of hundred Kentucky troops with authority from Virginia who want to march all the way to Detroit and claim the country for . . ." He guffawed. "Not for Congress, but for the independent state of Virginia! Congress hasn't a farthing to spare for those brave lads out there—lads who're setting the British on their ear! But Virginia hasn't a farthing for them either, even though those rebels control thousands of square miles of the finest country in all America. Fur country, timber country, farmland—you know it well! They control the Mississippi, and they are masters of the Illinois, the Missouri, the Ohio, and the Wabash!" He laughed again. "Quite a feat; quite a triumph!"

James knew this area was one of the most strategic spots in all the continent, and whoever possessed it at the end of the revolution would not only command much of the northwest fur trade, but would dominate the gateway to the unexplored interior of America, including the fabled, undiscovered water routes to China. The possibilities for commerce, land speculation, and exploitation of natural resources were endless.

Cullen cackled, as though he read James's mind. James listened, awestruck, while Cullen told the full story of Clark's invasion, a story no one else in Albany had heard of yet. Cullen believed the British could do little to drive Clark out before next spring.

"Clark's problem is supplies. You see, Mr. Morely, the British control the lower Mississippi, and as I said, Virginia and Congress are too poor to send him much by the Ohio." He leaned forward. "Whoever succeeds in supplying Clark in his hour of need—and that most dire hour will be next spring—whoever succeeds in this will be in the government's debt and can name his reward, whether it's a million acres of the best land, governorship of the territory once Congress reorganizes, or both." His voice became nearly a whisper. "And for a clever, daring man in such a position, there will be much, much more!"

Indeed, James could see that a strong man with the right commercial ties could wrest control of the region and hold it against all latecomers, profiting enormously. If the British empire were defeated, this would be the future of America, the beginning of an American empire! Perhaps even a whole new independent country!

After further absorbing discussion, Cullen laid his proposal before James.

"Let's begin anew, Mr. Morely. Let bygones be bygones for the sake of our country, and for the sake of our . . . your future!" He again leaned forward, an intensity coming into those piercing eyes. "Would that I were young like you!"

He smiled genially, saying, "I can arrange the boats, pack-trains, and the necessary supplies if you will take charge of an expedition this spring. It's a dangerous duty I'm asking of you, and I also will request that you put up as your investment in the partnership twenty thousand pounds sterling. . . ."

James stayed cool as Cullen continued, but he was troubled as well as intrigued. He estimated the total expedition would cost nearly one hundred thousand pounds sterling, most of that money being Cullen's. What Cullen was asking the Frontier Company to contribute was James's leadership plus twenty percent, but even that sum was far more than he had available. Cullen offered to lend the difference and in return would split the profits equally. It was a generous offer, James thought. If something went wrong, however, and the goods were lost, the Frontier Company would suffer a setback that might be impossible to overcome. And, as Cullen said, it would be dangerous. Surely loyalists and Indians would be guarding the Ohio, the only route to reach Clark. Still, James well knew that great success required great daring, and he was excited to think of what success might mean. The notion that Cullen and Company and the Frontier Company might be kept from carrying out this grand undertaking simply because of old feuds was galling.

Cullen said, "I have come to you with this proposition, Mr. Morely, because you've proved yourself to be the best man available. Were I young, I would undertake it myself, because I know that in generations to come Americans will look back and say that the supply of Colonel Clark was the key, the final move, the brilliant tactic that won the northwest! This expedition will make all the difference, and no American will ever forget it!" He closed his eyes, as if savoring the fame and honor that would surround him after such a triumph. "I will be proud to lay claim to some small part in the enterprise; and when I die, my soul will rest more easily." He sighed, eyes still closed.

James wanted to believe Cullen. He, too, understood the dream, the ambition for power and unsurpassed wealth.

They sat in silence a little longer, then James said softly, "To prove once and for all that I am nobody's servant, Mr.

Cullen—" He offered his hand, and Cullen reached across the table to take it. "Let us, sir, together, set the world on its ear!"

"Well said, Mr. Morely!" Cullen laughed. "Well said, indeed!"

As soon as James left the room, a door in one corner opened, admitting a ragged, stooped figure in dirty buckskins who could easily have been mistaken for an Indian. With his scraggly beard and black, flashing eyes, the fellow was a marked contrast to the puffy, cultured merchant.

"Sit down, Mr. Girty," Cullen said amiably, offering a glass of whiskey, taking brandy for himself. "We'll make short work of completing our plans!"

Simon Girty had been well paid by one of Cullen's agents to bring news of Clark's accomplishments directly here. He had moved faster than rebel expresses from Pitt and Kentucky; even loyalist spies in New York knew nothing yet about Clark in the Illinois.

Girty drank his whiskey in one gulp, and as his host poured him another he said, "Won't be no trouble cutting that expedition off, Mr. Cullen. My men'll watch it float all the way down from Pitt. Easy as pie. But losing 'em supplies to the Injuns means you're gonna pay a pretty penny, I'm thinking." He gulped the whiskey. "You must want to rub this Morely out pretty bad."

Cullen slammed his own glass on the table, and Girty was startled.

"Not Morely! I want him spared. Instruct your Redcoat and Indian friends I want Morely unharmed and held at least a few weeks, then sent back to Albany. At the right moment, you'll tell him I personally have paid his ransom." He began to chuckle and poured more brandy for himself. "You can do what you will with the booty and the other passengers." He toasted. "Now the Frontier Company will be smashed once and for all!"

Girty licked his lips, staring at the whiskey until Cullen pushed the bottle across the desk. Girty poured and muttered, "Don't worry, Mr. Cullen, I'll see that the lad keeps his hair on. Don't worry about this hoss doing his duty one bit! Time I'm done, Morely'll be praising you to high heaven for saving his scalp!" He snorted. "You'll ransom him— that's slick!"

Cullen drank brandy, stared hard at Girty, and said, "I depend on you to protect him, Simon. Nothing less will be acceptable. Nothing."

Even the indomitable Girty was uneasy before that scathing glare, but he slid under it to pour another drink.

"Got a awful dry!" he hissed, and downed the whiskey, the best he had tasted in years.

Autumn came, and Clark was still on the Mississippi, now busy preparing his men for winter. In early October, Owen Sutherland heard from Tamano that a force of thirty Ottawas was on its way to a small stockaded trading post north of Vincennes. Clark had not taken this post, and Tamano said the Ottawas were going there to meet a loyalist agent who would supply them to fight Longknives. Sutherland advised Clark to cut off trouble before it started.

Lately there had been many rumors of a strong enemy invasion army being assembled by Hamilton up at Detroit; if that army got quickly through to Vincennes, and if the Ottawa advance party were able to rouse other Indians to take up the hatchet, it could be a fatal winter for Clark's men. Sutherland persuaded Clark to lend him twenty Kentuckians, and with thirty additional French volunteers, he and Tamano headed north to the trading post.

Sutherland had won the allegiance of many young Frenchmen at Vincennes and Cahokia by reminding them of the Franco-American alliance. He had convinced them Clark was the man of the hour and the rebels the cause to support before it was too late. Showing the utmost respect for their superior knowledge of the area and their fighting qualities, Sutherland made the French feel worthy, and knowing his reputation, they regarded him highly in return. By the time Sutherland had marched them brutally hard through the wilderness for several days, they were even more proud of themselves and eager to prove further what sort of men they were.

As it turned out, Sutherland's force arrived just a few hours after the Ottawas got to the post. Swiftly, silently, they surrounded the small stockade, where the Indians were already feasting in preparation for speeches and gift-giving by the British agent, a prosperous French trader. Local French and Indians who had seen the arrival of Sutherland's group made no attempt to warn the Ottawas, and that told Sutherland much of the changing mood of the people here.

The Ottawas, as usual for Indians, put no guards on the gates, and the loyalist spokesman was just as overconfident. They were stunned when the two unbarred gates at opposite sides of the fort suddenly were thrown wide and in streamed the fighting men. Kentuckians and French dashed around the inside of the fort's walls, surrounding the astonished Indians, who leaped to their feet. The portly Frenchman had been standing in their midst, about to deliver a speech from a scroll he was holding out before himself. Before the man could destroy the scroll, Sutherland walked confidently through the Indians and politely took it away. Then he addressed the angry, sullen Ottawas, telling them to be seated. They obeyed, for rifles were at the ready on every side. Sutherland raised a hand in welcome to the Ottawas, the tribe that had adopted him and among whom he was well known.

"Donoway speaks for the leader of the Longknives, who has been sent here by the great council fire of Virginia, which is a free country at war with the British king. The Longknife leader Clark is angry, and I, Donoway, am sorry that the Ottawa have come here with war in their hearts, for to fight us will mean their destruction. . . ."

Sutherland's tone was harsh, but his words were respectful, and the warriors listened in glum silence as he explained that the Longknives, not the British, now made law in the western lands, and that any Indians who did not learn this lesson fast would pay a heavy penalty. He continued:

"It is not our way of making war to capture sleeping men, and so we will not say we are victorious in battle this day. Let us simply say we have spoken together and it has been made clear that the warriors of the Ottawa may leave this place and join the army of the king, if that is their desire. You may all leave, with your weapons, this very moment."

The Indians were surprised and glanced at one another,

then at the Longknives and French, as if to assure themselves they were not being taken prisoner.

Sutherland spoke again. "But I warn you that if Ottawas who fight for the king should again fall into the hands of the Longknives and their French friends, there will be no mercy. Donoway has spoken."

It did not take long for the leading Indian to rise and solemnly profess innocence. "Our purpose in coming here," he finally announced, after much digression, "was only to find high ground from which to watch the battle between the soldiers of the king and the Longknives."

After the Ottawas hurried off—Sutherland first having presented them with the food and drink of the sulking British agent—the Frenchmen and Kentuckians burst into laughter. Sutherland was satisfied, for he knew the Ottawas would have something amazing to tell others of their nation about the generosity and confidence of the Longknives, who had invited them back to make war if they so chose.

After ordering the French merchant locked in the guardhouse, Sutherland went with Tamano to a cabin in the fort to read the speech that was to have been delivered in the king's name. With a mug of ale in his hand, he sat before a roaring fire while Tamano stood at the door watching the rest of the men make a bivouac in the courtyard, then begin to divide up the British goods piled high on the porch of a trading house.

Sutherland read quickly through the standard, flowery speech, which promised the moon and lauded the Indians to the very heavens. But then he read something that stunned him, and he leaped to his feet.

"Tamano!" he cried. "The Wyoming's been destroyed! This bastard's boasting that the whole valley's been wiped out! I've got to go back now!"

Sutherland immediately rejoined Clark, who was reluctant to see him go. There was no stopping him, however, for he had received no word from his family in almost a year. He had sent a few letters with Clark's couriers, but no one knew if a courier got through until months afterward. Many did not get through.

Sutherland parted with Tamano—who agreed to remain as Clark's scout—and set off alone by canoe. In two days' time he had reached the Ohio and begun the long paddle upriver. This was extremely dangerous country. Roving bands of Indians were everywhere, and the region beyond the mouth of the Wabash would be even worse. Still, the weather was fine and cool, and Sutherland paddled hard day and night against the Ohio's current. He made good headway, keeping close to the southern shore, where the chance of meeting Indians was less. He usually camped in late afternoon, ate, then traveled until long after dark. He slept in the canoe when he could, with the craft lashed to trees or tangled driftwood. Days passed, and he met no one at all. The air turned much colder and damp, the bite of winter in the wind.

All the while his worried mind turned over and over thoughts of his family. They might have received his letters and know he was with Clark, but he had no idea where they could be, or even if they were alive. He pressed on, hardly sparing himself time to rest, for it was almost a month to Pitt, and weeks further to the Wyoming. Even Benjamin's rescue had to be put from his mind. At least there was a good chance the boy was still alive.

He passed the muddy, swirling mouth of the Wabash River, whose waters flowed down from the north and mingled with the wide Ohio. So far he had not seen the slightest danger; but had danger stalked him, he probably would have sensed it. Sutherland had always counted on his intuition to tell him when he was in peril, and one late afternoon on a drizzly, gray day, he obeyed that instinct and pulled the canoe into shelter under some overhanging birches. There he waited to see what would happen next, his rifle resting on his knees.

He did not know what was wrong, but things were too quiet. The sound of the river and wind in the trees seemed loud, but birds were still, and there were no creatures to be seen scurrying along the riverbank. He sat there silently, waiting, gazing upstream, peering into the thickets on the near bank and listening for whatever might reveal something. Danger was lurking here, but where?

Soon he saw a canoe with a lone white paddler coming downstream close to his side of the river. It was one of Clark's men, a Virginian Sutherland recognized as a courier who had been sent eastward months ago, obviously on his way back to Clark. He was a quick-eyed, bearded fellow, anxiously watching the trees and perhaps feeling Sutherland's presence near the wooded shore. Then Sutherland realized, too late, that the birds were not still because of this one man.

A musket shot rang out, then another, followed by war whoops and rustling in the thickets not more than thirty yards away. Shawnees had been lying in wait. The courier was down in the canoe, which spun once or twice and began to drift slowly toward Sutherland. He could make out at least six Indians wading into the cold water, trying to snare the canoe.

He leveled his rifle at the lead Shawnee and fired. The man leaped into the air and fell thrashing in the water. The others hesitated, bewildered, looking about. Sutherland loaded so quickly that before they could get their wounded friend back to shore he shot another one, whose hands went to his head as he collapsed in the water.

Now the Shawnees were more concerned with taking cover than with getting the boat and the wounded Virginian. Sutherland reloaded and watched for them to show themselves. When the courier's canoe came almost level with his, he laid aside the rifle, took up the paddle, and stroked hard, shooting out into the current to intercept the craft. He was exposing himself to enemy fire, however, and muskets cracked on shore. Sutherland hunched low as bullets zinged past. Hauling the boats together and steering them out into the stream, he was surprised when the bearded Virginian suddenly sat up, rifle coming to bear. Sutherland ducked as the weapon barked, and he heard an Indian gasp and fall into the water. The warrior had been wading into the shallows to cut off Sutherland's boat. Now he sank in a pool of blood, just yards away.

The Virginian groaned, "Get me outa here, friend, afore them smokeskins get our range!" Bullets splashed into the water, and several thunked against the boats. "Smokeskins can't shoot worth a damn, but one cuss got lucky with me!" He groaned, blood smearing his belly. "Guess I pushed my luck too far this time. The woman wanted me to stay home . . . but I got dispatches for the colonel. . . ."

Sutherland told him to be still and worked quickly to lash the two canoes together by the thwarts, Indian bullets singing past all the while. The man was bleeding badly, and Sutherland paddled with all his strength to get them far out into the stream. It would be too difficult to cross the river here; he would have to steer downstream and find a safe place to put ashore and tend the man. The musket fire soon stopped, but Sutherland waited until he was several miles downriver before he pushed into a cove. It was too late. The man was dead.

It would not be long before the Shawnees came down this far to look for their prey, and Sutherland barely had time to scratch out a shallow grave and lay the fellow to rest. He covered the grave with brush and stones, hoping it would not be found and opened by Indians, who would scalp and mutilate the body. Then he hid the extra canoe in thick bushes and stove in its sides with his tomahawk. He planned to cross the river and stay concealed there until things quieted down; then he would set off homeward again. Taking the dead man's personal effects, which would have to be sent to the family, Sutherland also quickly examined the dispatches for Clark. There were letters from Virginia leaders Thomas Jefferson and Patrick Henry, men who had helped plan the Illinois campaign. The courier's satchel also held dispatches from Clark's officers at the base camp upriver near the Falls of the Ohio. All of it was extremely important, because Clark needed to hear about reinforcements promised from Virginia that winter—enough men to storm Detroit itself.

Then Sutherland was startled to see among the letters an envelope for himself, from Ella. Hurriedly tearing it open as he sat there in the canoe near the fresh gravesite, he was forgetful of all else, and read with heart pounding.

. . . we are well, although our bereavement at the tragedy will be long with us. My dearest, do not worry for us, for we are living safely at Fort Pitt. We have heard of Col. Clark's astonishing success and are proud that you have played some part in it. How we wish you were with us or we with you, but it is best that you go on seeking Benjamin and aiding Col. Clark to pacify that country in the name of Congress. . . .

Ella's letter made it sound as if Clark's war had been won and that folk in the East were ready to journey by the boatload to the Illinois and settle down and farm. Sutherland smiled to think of how Clark's modest successes had created such a stir back in the states. Ella wrote that the following year would see great migrations of settlers over the Alleghenies and into Kentucky. That might indeed turn the tables on the enemy, Sutherland thought, putting enough rebel fighting men into the region so that the Indians and loyalists would have to sue for peace.

Something crackled. Shawnees. Slowly, Sutherland laid aside the letter, casually leaned forward, and from the corner of his eye saw movement in the trees. A musket was being aimed. At the perfect instant, Sutherland threw himself flat, and the gun went off harmlessly. When he came up, the rifle was in his hands, and a young Indian dashing with a tomahawk into the shallows suddenly stopped short, finding himself staring into the muzzle.

The warrior looked with dismay at death. He might have thrown the tomahawk and done some damage, but before he could recover, Sutherland rasped in Shawnee, "Next time, don't miss! Now turn away, and thank the manitous that you have another chance to learn how to fight. Turn now!"

The youth turned. Putting up a brave enough appearance, he walked stiffly out of the water, but when Sutherland yelled for him to run, he bolted into the trees. Then the Scotsman drove the canoe out of range, far into the middle of the wide river.

Sutherland hardly thought twice of what to do next. These dispatches had to get to Clark. Ella and Susannah were safe, thank God, and now he could renew his search for Benjamin. He headed the prow westward. It was much easier going downriver, with the powerful Ohio current behind his canoe. It was good to think he would soon be back with Clark and able to get on with all that had to be done.

PART THREE

Triumph

chapter 20

HAMILTON MOVES

Autumn brought a glory of color to the straits at Detroit, but Gwen Bently hardly noticed. As the days grew shorter, she grew cold within whenever she thought about Jeremy's duty. He would not shirk that duty, and would go with Hamilton's expeditionary force that was readying to leave for Vincennes and an attack on George Rogers Clark.

To complicate matters, Gwen had her unborn child to think about. In her condition it would be foolish to travel with the army, so she would stay at Valenya. She and Jeremy had spoken of the coming campaign often during the months since their return from Vincennes, and Jeremy was determined to go. At her urging he had finally relented somewhat in his bitterness at Owen Sutherland, but he still smarted from having been induced to leave his post at a critical moment, and Gwen knew it was partly his pride that moved him to volunteer to join Hamilton for the march that autumn. He needed to vindicate himself in Hamilton's eyes, and in his own.

Hamilton, of course, wanted him along, and Jeremy felt an obligation to the soldiers, who would need his doctoring if the fighting was heavy; besides, he was still determined to help Benjamin. At Vincennnes there might yet be an opportunity for him to journey eastward to Shawnee country, or a chance that Hamilton would be more persuasive with his Shawnee allies.

On a cold, blustery October morning, Gwen stood near the fort's crowded landing, along with scores of others waving good-bye to the soldiers and militiamen. The fort could spare only thirty-five regulars for the expedition, so nearly a hundred reluctant French militia had been pressed into

285

service. Loaded into fifty-two small craft ranging from sleek whaleboats to clumsy barges, the expedition and its thousands of pounds of equipment and supplies floated out into the straits. A fleet of Indian canoes paddled alongside, even though the wind was in the northeast, spitting snow and gusting, making the water unsafe for birch boats.

Gwen waved to Jeremy, who was in a barge that carried a wagon and a six-pound cannon along with its crew. He stood on the wagon seat, lifting his tricorne to her and their friends nearby. Although her cousin Annie Ross was there, Gwen felt very alone just then. Her legs were tired, for she was big with the baby, which was due in a month.

She waved until the boat drifted so far off that she could no longer make out Jeremy. The weight of the baby was bearing down, and she heard Annie say she looked pale and should rest. Gwen was sad, but tears would not come. She would not let them, not now or later. She was determined to give birth in joy and hope, for that was what life was all about. The certainty of that had made it possible for her to live here with Jeremy. He had to do what he must, and so did she.

Gwen had known it might one day come to this, that Jeremy would go off to war and leave her here. She was as ready as ever she would be, and not afraid. Head raised, her resolve giving her strength, she began the long walk to the whaleboat where Dawson Merriwether was waiting to take her and Annie Ross across to Valenya; they both would live there until Jeremy's return. Annie tossed back her long, auburn hair and chattered lightly, trying to be encouraging, but Gwen saw a tear on her cousin's cheek.

She gave Annie a little shove, saying with a laugh not to be so glum. "I can't take care of you and a baby at the same time!" Gwen smiled and felt much better for it. "It's easier to be happy!"

"Not for me!" Annie tried her best, but sniffed. "I'll cry for both of us, then, and you can be distracted by cheering me up!" By now Annie was smiling in spite of herself.

Gwen cast a final glance at the flotilla disappearing around the bend in the river. She thought, *I have a duty, too, husband. And honor to keep*.

Annie was wiping her eyes, steering Gwen around muddy puddles. Gwen turned and felt the baby move. She longed to sit down and rest.

She was distracted as some men in the dispersing crowd began to grumble loudly that the rebels in the Illinois would soon pay for their insolence.

"His Excellency and the Injuns'll roast a few of 'em afore this is done, and chase the rest all the way back to Philadelphee!"

Another man, a vagabond, sometime-trader, and known rascal, cackled and called for them all to drink Hamilton's health in the alehouse. "Scour the whole country of them vermin rebels," he said, staring sidelong at Gwen, who stared back at him in defiance. "Run them all out on rails! God-rotting rebels!" The fellow might soon have said something directly to Gwen, but a couple of Redcoats came between them—friends of Corporal Bates—and suggested they all go and have a drink, guiding the complaining man away. One of the soldiers, a middle-aged, cheerful fellow, touched his hat to Gwen.

"You've got friends here," he said, blushing in apology for the other man's insolence. "We're all grateful for what you do at the hospital, ma'am." He touched his hat again. "You've got friends, ma'am."

He walked off following the others. Annie pushed closer to Gwen, saying, "And there's plenty of us who will help with the hospital, even after you give birth." She forced a smile, and Gwen was glad for her company as they strolled away, arm in arm.

For Hamilton's small army, it was a grueling, hard journey from the moment they first disembarked on the Maumee River, unable to proceed farther without portaging. Encumbered by large boats, cannon, stores, and great quantities of Indian gifts, they moved at a crawling pace for weeks, following the Maumee toward the headwaters of the Wabash.

Rain, snow, cold, rapids, ice, carrying-places that were meant for canoes, not flatboats, all impeded progress. Furthermore, since Hamilton's plans were to raise Indians as he journeyed—enough, he hoped, for an army of eight hundred by the time they met Clark—he stopped at nearly every sizable Indian village along the way. At each he would make a tedious speech, dance and sing the war song, and hand out gifts enough to please a Turkish vizier. Then he had to sit and listen to lengthy speeches in return.

Jeremy was there all the while, and he grew tired of it. He knew Indians well enough to realize that some tribesmen were less than wholeheartedly committed to the king. They were worried about Clark, and often they passed on to Hamilton wild rumors about a thousand or more Longknives advancing up the Wabash to oppose him. They complained they needed British protection, and only pretended joyfulness when Hamilton removed old French medals given years ago and replaced them with images of George the Third. During feasts and gift-giving the Indians promised to hold their great father Hamilton by the hand and to oppose the Longknives, but for all the bluster and brave talk, Jeremy often sensed an undercurrent of fear.

Nevertheless, all along that tedious, plodding route, Hamilton won the promise of support of the tribes, and Jeremy came to believe that after Hamilton defeated Clark, there could yet be a great Indian outbreak that spring.

Finally, in December, Hamilton's expedition was floating down the Wabash, and by the middle of the month they surprised undefended Vincennes, taking Fort Sackville without firing a shot. The local French militiamen, who had sworn allegiance to Virginia, offered no resistance, and five Kentuckians—all Clark had left there—knew better than to fight there after being surrounded by such a large force. The only trouble came when a group of young Indians broke into the fort after the surrender. Hamilton's troops had already prevented them from attacking the hapless residents of the town and pillaging their homes, and the stockade itself had been quickly secured by regulars posted at the gates, but the Indians slipped through the cannon ports. Once inside, they made straight for the small herd of horses the Kentuckians had kept there.

The frightened horses began thundering around the courtyard, the shrieking Indians in wild pursuit until Jeremy

alertly opened the gates to let the animals out. Most of the
Indians kept chasing them, hoping to capture a prize, but a
few decided to break into a storehouse, no doubt in search
of the garrison's supply of rum. Jeremy saw what was happening and knew that if the Indians became mad on firewater, they would surely try to kill the Kentucky prisoners
or the French who had taken oaths to the rebels. Drunken-
ness might even cause trouble among the various tribes,
which were always bickering over some real or imagined
slight. Rushing into the dim storehouse, he ordered the
warriors out and, when that didn't work, wrestled one after
another away from the rum keg, throwing them head over
heels out the front door, and more than one through the
window. Finally they gave up, sullen, battered, and angry
to be denied the pleasure of a good drunk.

Emerging from the storehouse, uniform tattered, bruises
on his head, Jeremy stood there panting, while from the
opposite end of the fort Hamilton waved and nodded in
gratitude. Seated on a chair on a gun platform above the
rickety palisades, the lieutenant governor was in the process
of calling out the Frenchmen, the church bell tolling as a
signal. Many of the townsfolk were already gathered below
the walk, their heads bowed, eyes furtive. Finally, when it
appeared they were all present, Hamilton began giving them
a severe tongue-lashing.

Jeremy wished he would be more tactful. Many of these
people were his own friends, and their good favor could be
just as important to the British as the support of the Indians.
Yet Hamilton spared them nothing. Addressing them in their
own language, he said they had lied before God by spurning
their oath to the king; then he proceeded to insult and harangue them until many blushed with anger and shame.
Jeremy felt a sinking feeling as he listened.

"Until you recant your sinful oath to the rebels, I cannot
promise you the protection of the king! I want to believe
that your base conduct was the result of bad advice given
you by a few dishonorable persons, but honest men whose
word is their bond should never have heeded such advice.
Be assured those dishonorable persons will be punished, as
must all traitors! But the mercy of the king is so great that

those of you who genuinely ask forgiveness and willingly submit to an oath of allegiance to your God-given sovereign—those will be forgiven and taken into royal protection!"

There was a sudden surge forward as the Frenchmen heartily agreed to take the oath. Hamilton glared down at them, shaking his head in disgust.

"Think seriously of what it is you will do!" he cried with upraised hand. "Hear! Think upon this oath, so that you will not again perjure yourselves! Disobedience will mean severe punishment!" He shook his head again, as if repelled by the sight of these people.

Soon two hundred and fifty Frenchmen were crowding into the log church to sign their names to the oath. First, however, they were required to kiss the silver crucifix at the altar to solemnize their promise. As this was taking place, Jeremy joined the lieutenant governor at the door of the church; Hamilton did not stop grumbling as he returned Jeremy's salute.

"Pathetic dogs, wretches! I won't trust them an inch. Even my Detroit Frenchmen are not to be trusted, for they're all kin to these base rogues."

"Sir," Jeremy said, "many of these men fought against us in the last wars, and they were known to be brave—"

Hamilton waved that off and turned to watch his regulars organizing hired French laborers into parties, unloading military cargo from boats in the river.

"I'll never trust them. I'd trust Indians first! It'll be Indians that take Clark's knaves, not timid, turncoat French militia. No, I'll be glad to see the last of these scoundrels, except for one or two who know how to lead Indian parties."

The mention of men who led Indians put Jeremy in mind of Mark Davies. That subject had been tender with Hamilton ever since Jeremy had put forth Davies's possible complicity in Weston's murder. Jeremy spoke carefully:

"Do you still expect Davies to report back soon, sir?"

Hamilton tensed, his jowls working. "For the time being I want to hear no more of Captain Davies, do you understand?" He glared at Jeremy, who nearly gave way to rising anger. For weeks after his return to Detroit, Jeremy had tried to convince Hamilton that a court-martial should be convened either at Detroit or back at Montreal headquarters. Yet every time he had suggested this, Hamilton had become annoyed.

The lieutenant governor gruffly added, "Captain Davies is of great use to me right now at his post guarding the Ohio River. I won't recall him until this Clark business is cleared up. At least Davies is a man I can depend upon. Such men are few and far between, these days!" He obviously wanted to drop the subject, but the resentment in Jeremy's eyes must have prodded him to speak on.

"Dash it all, man! Let it lie until the campaign's over! For all that you hate the man, there's no hard proof Davies is guilty of anything."

"Proof enough for me, sir."

"Not for me!"

"Then I'll bring charges personally down at Montreal—"

Hamilton threw up his hands. "As you wish! But do not again mention this subject to me." He turned away and said curtly, "Unless I bring it up first! Now please be about your duties opening a hospital. We're at war here, not conducting court-martials!"

Jeremy touched his hat in salute and began to walk away. He was disappointed, more bitter than ever about Hamilton's protectiveness toward Davies. The man was allowed absolute free rein and had not been back to Detroit since well before summer. Jeremy knew Davies had been fighting as an Indian leader along the eastern frontier, one of the few regular officers permitted to do so. Usually only French and American loyalists were employed with the Indians, but Davies relished such fighting so much that he had volunteered to patrol the Ohio River with the Shawnees. Still, perhaps it was better Davies had not shown his face back in Detroit, for Jeremy surely would have called him out and killed him then and there, regardless of the law.

A cheerful shouting arose from near the fort's gate, and Jeremy saw it was Corporal Bates, the man Davies had ordered lashed for insubordination. Bates had not been with the expedition; apparently he was just arriving from Detroit with dispatches for Hamilton and letters for the men. Soldiers thronged about him, asking whether he had news from home, and in response he gave his pet monkey a handful of letters, sending it scampering among the men to hand them over. The Redcoats, Indians, and French laughed, but all Jeremy could think of was news from Gwen. By now the baby should have been born.

The monkey grabbed another letter from Bates, then bounded toward Jeremy, springing into his arms. Like the other men, Jeremy handed over a penny, which the monkey insolently bit, as if to test it, then double-timed back to Bates, who was presenting the dispatches to Hamilton.

Jeremy tore open the letter, then gave an exultant yell, most unbecoming of a British officer. As he whooped, the monkey screamed in answer and the soldiers of the expedition turned to watch.

"It's a boy!" Jeremy announced. "A fat, healthy boy!"

The soldiers gave three cheers, led by the sergeant who had flogged Bates. Jeremy raised his hands above his head in happy response.

Hamilton gaily shouted, "An extra gill of rum for every king's soldier!" He doffed his hat to Jeremy, who nodded in thanks. "You're a lucky man, Surgeon Major, and I envy you!"

With everything at Vincennes well under control, and Clark apparently unable to strike back from Kaskaskia, Jeremy soon became restless. When he had first set out on this campaign, he had expected to be laboring to save wounded men; but by late December, with snow setting in, it was obvious there would be no campaigning until spring.

Jeremy felt as though he was wasting time. Hamilton did not need him now; in fact, these days the lieutenant governor bothered little about the war, spending much of his time at an easel or making pen-and-ink renderings of charcoal sketches he had done along the way. Jeremy was itching to go into Shawnee country after Benjamin—and perhaps on the way confront Mark Davies, though he did not admit this openly. When he asked permission to go, however, Hamilton put him off, obviously wanting to avoid any possible quarrel with the powerful Shawnees.

So Jeremy did nothing, even though he knew he could be in and out of Shawnee country several times while Hamilton pursued his hobbies and waited for spring. As the days passed, Jeremy learned from a Frenchman that Benjamin was in the Shawnee town of Chillicothe, on the Scioto River. The idea of rescue became more and more of an obsession. He had to do something to save his brother.

When he went to see Hamilton again, he was bluntly refused permission to go. Once more they argued, and once more Jeremy wondered why he had put on a Redcoat uniform at all.

chapter 21

TOKEN OF WAR

Warm weather came early to the Illinois country, and by late January the village of Kaskaskia was a muddy quagmire. Rain fell instead of snow, filling low ground with water and slush that made roads almost impassable. Everyone stayed home, marooned by floodwater and mud, able to travel only on the rivers, which were unusually high for this time of year. Any more rain would inundate the entire region, hampering the movement of Clark's patrols, who were watching the approaches from Vincennes.

It was a clear, windy morning when Owen Sutherland was called to a meeting with the other rebel officers in Clark's spartan quarters in the old French stockaded fort. Word had come that Vincennes had been retaken by Hamilton, and it was common knowledge that strong parties of Indians under French leaders were roving the countryside, trying to intercept Clark's spies and couriers.

Sutherland was sure that Hamilton was preparing for a springtime assault on Kaskaskia and Cahokia. The French sensed this, too, and were growing increasingly nervous, although the local Indians still did not know what to think or do. Clark had fewer than a hundred men of his original force left with him; the others, their enlistments up, had gone back to Kentucky to protect their families.

Clark kept up a show, pretending these men were only on leave and would garrison his base fort at the Falls of the Ohio. He still claimed there was a major army massing at the Falls, one that would soon join him on a march northward to "prevent Hamilton's retreat to Detroit." Few French knew whether to believe him, but he was so audacious, so haughty, and at times so charming, that they did not challenge him openly.

Yet there was no way to stop the rumors that thousands of Indians were already on the move to join Hamilton. It was said that six forces of more than a dozen nations, along with groups of whites, were approaching from the north— one from Michilimackinac, coming down the Mississippi; another skirting the western shore of Lake Michigan; a third on the Wisconsin; the fourth raising Indians from the eastern shore of Lake Michigan; the fifth massing at Detroit; the sixth at Sandusky. With his accustomed nonchalance, Clark detailed these reports to the seven officers assembled in the fort's main room.

He was bareheaded, his red hair like fire in the bright early morning sun pouring through the windows. Standing at one end of a table around which the officers and Sutherland were seated, he indicated the routes of the enemy on a homemade map tacked to the wall.

Sutherland more than anyone realized the danger implicit in what Clark was saying. He was also aware that more Indians were gathering at villages east of Vincennes, including the Shawnee towns of the Scioto. And to the south were the Cherokees, Creeks, and Choctaws, with thousands of fighting men.

Clark went on: "Already there are six hundred Indians at Detroit, preparing to come south to Hamilton at Vincennes." He touched several points on the Kentucky and Pennsylvania frontiers. "All these posts together have fewer than six hundred men on militia duty, and if they are attacked, they can muster no more than a thousand able-bodied men to meet the enemy."

He indicated Kaskaskia. "The bulk of the enemy will strike us here first, and however long we can hold out, that is how long our people at home will have to prepare for the next attack."

He said couriers had been sent east to warn the settlements, but so many people were emigrating westward over the mountains that there was a mood of overconfidence back on the frontier.

"They seem to think we've already won out here, that

the country's firmly in our hands. . . ." He gave a dry laugh
and shook his head. "The fact is, no matter what they think
or do at home, they can't be ready for the storm that's soon
to break on them."

Sutherland knew Clark and the Longknives could not be
better prepared than they already were; but even if they sold
their lives dearly, perhaps delaying the enemy by a few
weeks, it would not be enough.

Clark said, "If we pull out now, abandon the Falls of the
Ohio, withdraw into Kentucky, we still won't save our
homes. Even those who run back over the mountains will
be in for a surprise if they think this storm will pass them
by."

They all knew it would not pass by. Even Fort Pitt, where
Sutherland's family was now living, would be unable to
hold out against the onslaught Hamilton was building. Cold
anxiety haunted Sutherland as he sat listening. He wished
there were a way to get Ella and the others to Albany . . .
and surely Benjamin would soon be in the midst of hundreds
of excited warriors collecting at Chillicothe. Even if Clark
attempted to withdraw eastward up the Ohio, the Shawnees
would be waiting. His men would never pass without a
vicious battle against heavy odds.

Clark said, "Hamilton's been receiving Indian delegates
for the past weeks, and he's tried to make the Vincennes
militia into a garrison force, but"—he grinned confidently—"since my reports are from spies who are to a man
Vincennes Frenchmen, you can well imagine that the Hair-
buyer doesn't have the backing of those people."

Sutherland agreed with Clark's assessment. Unlike the
Frenchmen of Cahokia who had marched with Sutherland
and formed a soldier's bond with the Longknives, the militia
in Vincennes might quickly desert Hamilton in the coming
struggle.

Clark paused a moment, giving his men time to digest
what he had said; then he asked, "Do any of you have a
better plan of action than immediately attacking Mr. Hamilton at Vincennes?"

Every officer stirred; they glanced at one another, at first
surprised, then smiling and nodding.

Sutherland was as excited as any of them at this brazen idea, and he spoke up: "We do have certain advantages, Colonel. First, the country between here and there is completely flooded—two hundred and forty miles of water, most too shallow for boats, the rest too deep to wade, so no one can cross it."

The officers chuckled quietly as Sutherland continued, "And until his Indian guests arrive, Hamilton won't have much to defend himself with, especially when we surprise him by swimming through his front gate."

One of the officers put in, "However we get there, a hundred Kentuckians won't be enough even to surround the fort, considering that Hamilton has plenty of Indians in the villages near Vincennes."

Clark nodded, suddenly becoming serious. "We're building a gunboat out of a Mississippi bateau, and that'll carry what artillery we have; but I'd bind myself seven years a slave to have five hundred fighting men right now!"

"Would near two hundred do, sir?" Sutherland asked.

Clark's expression did not change. "Depending on the sort of men."

"I'll wager that a hundred French from Cahokia and Kaskaskia will join us, if we handle them right."

"You mean call up their Gallic pride, Mr. Sutherland?" Clark grinned at that. "I've been thinking the same and have had a number of flags made for just such an occasion. What do you say we invite the Cahokia militia to a shindig and start passing those flags out—to honor them for going with you against the Ottawas on the Wabash."

Not long afterward, what began as a rousing party at Kaskaskia turned into a pompous ceremony honoring the delighted Cahokia militia. Clark presented them the elegant banners, which they marched around and around the town and fort, accompanied by lusty, robust singing. The young men of Kaskaskia watched quietly from the side, as envious as could be.

Sutherland knew the *habitants* well, understood their fierce pride and explosive temperament; he laughed and drank and sang with them, all the while lauding the Cahokians and

consoling the Kaskaskians, saying they were unfortunate to
have missed the fun against the Ottawas. The Kaskaskians
drank less, sang less, and laughed less than either the Cahokians or the Longknives. Then Sutherland and Clark persuaded the girls of both Cahokia and Kaskaskia to join in
the march around the town, taking the arms of the bold
Cahokians — and that was almost more than the Kaskaskians
could bear.

A little while later, when Clark gathered the leading men
of the militias together at the fort to explain his plans, the
Kaskaskians actually pleaded for permission to form a company and go along. Clark, of course, was overjoyed, though
he did not show it. More than a hundred Frenchmen volunteered to march with him through two hundred and forty
miles of icy water. No one asked if it was possible, or what
would happen if they failed. They enthusiastically swore
allegiance to Clark, and Sutherland could tell that the fire
of New France blazed in their blood as it had not done in
the fifteen years since the British conquest.

"We can do it!" Clark declared to Sutherland as they
stood at the gate of the fort watching the laughing, cheering
Frenchmen of both villages march around the walls, waving
their new standards and sporting with the admiring girls on
their arms. Kaskaskia was no longer a sleepy village, but
a staging area for a determined army that believed in George
Rogers Clark, because he believed in them.

On the morning of departure, the little town of Kaskaskia
was festooned with garlands and ribbons. Banners of every
sort hung from ropes suspended above the streets, and feasting and singing filled many a house as families bade their
young men farewell.

A wooden platform had been raised in the courtyard
outside the Church of the Immaculate Conception, a square-
timbered building that commanded the village. The men of
the expedition assembled there casually at first, along with
friends and relations, enjoying an unusually balmy day for
the fifth of February. When Clark arrived they fell into
ranks, the Frenchmen close to the platform, the Kentuckians
behind. This was the moment for the priest, Father Gibault

to bless the Catholic French, but Clark's Presbyterians and Anglicans were in the assembly as a token of respect and unity.

Gibault was a short, droopy, long-nosed man with a bald spot on the back of his head. He was greatly revered by his parishioners, and from the beginning had done much to persuade them not to resist the rebel takeover. As he stood there on the platform, looking small and frail, his eyes reverently to heaven, he called upon the Frenchmen to honor the alliance between the newly independent states and France.

Sutherland knew Gibault's cooperation was critical if Clark was to have an army at all, and as he stood there listening, he thought that the priest could not have been more persuasive.

Gibault's nasal voice was strong, full of emotion.

"Colonel Clark has come to us with the olive branch of peace, and with the solemn promise of Virginia that we may live as always, worship as always, and be respected far more than the British government ever respected us. . . ."

He called on his people to remember the mercy Clark had displayed after capturing the region, when the Long-knives could have plundered every French village. "Be faithful to the Virginian who has avoided shedding your blood," he said, "yet who has the courage to walk into Indian towns that even I, a man of the cloth, fear to enter.

"Because of my spiritual calling, I can play no part in worldly affairs. But the welfare of my people is close to my heart, and I advise you all to think of the changing world, and to remember the justice and honor already shown us by Colonel Clark."

With that, Gibault prayed for the men, told them to treat with kindness any French of Vincennes or Detroit who might be captured as the enemy, and wished them a swift and joyous return to their families.

Sutherland looked out across the prairie, at the many pools of water in low spots, and at the rising streams flooding fields and roads. He would have appreciated a prayer for dry weather.

After the "Amen" the troops fell out for the last good-byes, and the forty Cahokia militia and a few Kentuckians boarded the stout bateau, which carried seven small cannon. The boat would descend the Mississippi, travel up the Ohio and then the Wabash, eventually to rendezvous with Clark's force slogging overland.

The army departed with enthusiasm, Sutherland and Tamano moving out front to scout, along with a couple of Frenchmen. As soon as Sutherland had gone a hundred yards, the road sank into three feet of water for as far as he could see. He and the others waded in, the chill like bands of steel drawing tight on legs and thighs, numbing the crotch until it was painful.

Glancing at the stoic Tamano, Sutherland said, "Indians know better than to wage war in weather like this."

Tamano grunted. "Perhaps we do not take war seriously enough, unlike the whites." He shivered, raising his rifle and powder horn above the water, wading ahead and looking up at the cloudy sky. "When I was young, war was a game of honor, but back then this country was the Indian's. Soon it will belong to a new race . . . a hard and hungry race that does not care about miserable cold!" He shivered again. "Ahh, I'm sure I'll have no more children after this journey's done!"

From the very beginning the tramp from Kaskaskia was bitterly hard. Every road and trail of that low-lying country was covered with at least several inches of chilly water. Trudging hour after hour in mud and freezing cold was brutal for the one hundred and seventy-five men, but no one complained, and they made rapid progress, as much as twenty miles a day at times. Men joked about the weather being warm for February, saying that Colonel Clark had ordered the southerly winds to blow and melt the snow so that Hamilton would see the flooding and think himself safe, surrounded by an immense moat.

They watched Clark closely through those tough first days, and Sutherland wondered whether the Virginian also was feeling the pain, the numbness, the ache that rose through the legs to the thighs and plagued a man's hips until the spine itself seemed as cold as an icicle. Clark plodded ahead, refusing to ride as befitted an officer—in fact none of his officers rode their mounts, but trudged on through the slush just like the men.

Sutherland admired Clark's strength and good judgment. The men kept up behind him, pushing themselves hard, because they would not let him think them weak. They walked on day after day, often through rain or a cold mist, seldom putting a foot on dry land. Always Clark was in the lead.

More than once Sutherland recalled his lonely journey to Chillicothe last winter. That, too, had been a sore test of strength, but here in the drowned lands—where there was hardly a spot to make a fire, seldom anywhere to sit down and rub numbed feet back to life—this march was proving even more difficult. He was very tired by the end of the first week—more tired than he had ever been. It was not simply that he was growing older, for he saw the drawn and sunken expressions of younger, hardy men and knew that even Clark was feeling the drain and the ache that would not go away. Even when the sun came out to dry their clothes, their feet and leggins stayed wet and cold. Still they sang and joked and goaded their fellows into an extra effort, challenging one another and laughing if a man slipped and fell into the muck.

To cheer them, Clark allowed each company in turn to hunt for the day's food and gave them horses with which to bring in game. For many nights during that first part of the march the troops feasted like Indians—indeed Tamano thought no Indians on the warpath had ever eaten so well. Game was plentiful in the region, and dry firewood was bundled and carried for miles until the evening campsite was found. Then the singing and eating would begin, and the day's suffering became part of ribald jokes and hearty teasing. There was plenty of talk about better ground to come.

Sutherland knew, however, there was no better ground between here and Vincennes. With Tamano he had ranged well in advance of the main body, discovering that the Little Wabash—actually two overflowing streams three miles

apart—was a real barrier. For several miles there the wate
was three or four feet deep. When Sutherland told Clar
this, he saw that the Virginian was troubled.

They stood on high ground while the rest of the me
took a break, falling out to rest on tree limbs and rocks
Looking out over that dreary landscape, not a leaf in sight
they saw the expanse of gray and muddy water slowly drif
ing southward. Naked trees thrust up out of the water, an
dead, rotting cattle floated in tangled clutters of driftwood
The men were also staring at the water, and they wer
unusually quiet. Clark said to Sutherland that the huntin
parties should go out and that extra rum would be distrib
uted.

Without a moment's hesitation, he added cheerfully
"We'll make a dugout and load it with our baggage. We'l
ferry these two rivers directly, carrying every pound o
baggage and every man. It'll be an interesting diversion, ¿
pleasure trip!"

Clark gave orders to subordinates, men who a momen
earlier had been gloomily contemplating the broad lake be
fore them, well aware that the two deeper channels coul¿
suck a man down for good. With Clark's jaunty commands
the men leaped into action, as if he had instilled anothe
dose of confidence and the river crossing would be a mer¿
lark.

Sutherland could not help but grin, and Clark noticed
saying, "Let's have some wrestling contests, some knife
throwing! And how about some singing, to see who's better
French boatmen or our Kentucky Virginians!" At that Clar¿
laughed heartily, then spoke so that Sutherland alone coul¿
hear: "Keep their spirits up, Mr. Sutherland, at least unti
we cross this flood. By that time they'll be so dismaye¿
that they'll never want to return this way in retreat! They'l
have to go on! They'll have to win!"

The spirits of those brave Kentuckians, Virginians, an¿
Frenchmen did not falter. All day they were floated across
the swollen rivers by piling a dozen at a time into that rough
dugout. The packhorses were unburdened to swim across,
then loaded at the other side.

Though the rivers were passed without mishap, Sutherland feared that much of the rest of the way would be through waist-deep water. But there were no complaints. The more a man shivered, the more he was the brunt of jokes; the louder one sang, the more his friends were impressed and encouraged. When a French drummer boy floated for a while on his drum, playing a tattoo as he passed them all, the men took great delight and pushed on as if it were a hot summer day and the water a welcome amusement.

By nightfall, after Sutherland had found a half-acre knoll of trees that was fairly dry, the men were camped around roaring fires, laughing and joking, proud of their accomplishments. Sitting with Sutherland, who was puffing a long-stemmed pipe, Tamano gnawed on the last of some deer meat and listened to a man translate a Frenchman's joke to the Virginians, who whooped and slapped their thighs at the ending.

Tamano chewed, then said in Chippewa, "Already they're talking about the big Wabash as if it were just a creek. It seems that nothing daunts them."

Sutherland chuckled. "By the time they go to sleep they'll have taken Vincennes and Hamilton, divided the spoils, and be halfway to Detroit."

Tamano tossed the bone into the darkness, where it splashed into the water that was all around the campsite. "Clark is a man, Donoway, and without him this march would not happen. But it is a long way to go, and the Wabash is no creek, nor is Vincennes ours until it is taken."

Sutherland lay down and covered himself with his blanket for a few hours' sleep before Clark would call on him to resume scouting. "A week and we'll be there, my brother," he yawned. "Be glad you're an Indian and don't often have to follow mad Longknives on the warpath."

Tamano sat listening to the men laughing around the fire. He was thoughtful, serious. "It is true, the Indian does not go to war in bad weather, for bad weather is an omen of failure, a sign that the manitous are not with us. But perhaps, Donoway, that is why we have not defeated the whites, and never will."

• • •

Lingering, wasting time, sitting in muddy Fort Sackville week after week while Benjamin was a prisoner was beginning to get to Jeremy. Just as irksome was the way Hamilton was fawning over the Indians, especially the Shawnee delegates. The lieutenant governor had all but rejected the local French militia outright; his treatment of them had been so callous that by February he was unable even to mediate the many irritating disagreements that arose between the Frenchmen of Detroit and those of Vincennes.

Finally, after a brawl between the Detroit militia and some townsfolk, the Detroiters asked permission to go home, promising to return in the spring. They felt unwelcome among their own people, who they claimed were rude, inhospitable, and not at all enthusiastic about being loyalists.

Hamilton was so disgusted that he scarcely attempted to maintain the discipline a commander must exercise over troops in such situations. To Jeremy's astonishment, he let most of the Detroit militia, nearly a hundred men, go back— but only after chastising them, then adding to the insult by disarming half their number. Even the French of Vincennes thought this far too shameful a way to treat the Detroiters.

In despair, Jeremy gave up trying to counsel Hamilton on the politics of frontier campaigning. At least there were still many hundreds of Indian warriors within a few days' travel who had promised to rise and support Hamilton in the spring campaign. Jeremy was as certain as ever that Clark could not stand against Hamilton's army, yet that thought caused him a different worry. He was sure Owen Sutherland was still with the Kentuckians; Hamilton's Indians had confirmed this. In two months there would be all-out war between the two forces, pitting Jeremy against his own stepfather.

That caused him endless distress. Henry Hamilton was well aware of it and more than once had suggested he go back to Detroit to be with Gwen and his son. Jeremy was tempted by the offer, but he was determined to be here when the crisis came. Perhaps he could do something to prevent wanton slaughter of the rebels. Besides, once victory was assured, Hamilton would be less fearful of offending his Indian allies. Surely then he would allow Jeremy to go for Benjamin.

One February morning Jeremy sat in his small cabin writing a letter to Gwen. Bright sunlight fell onto the table—sunshine that was welcome after several rainy days. He smiled to think of the baby, who had been named after his friends Richard Weston and Tom Morely. *Richard Thomas Bently*—that sounded good, and gave him something to think about besides the war.

Jeremy glanced out the room's one small window. Hamilton was on the parade ground, preparing to feed and flatter another pack of boastful Shawnees. In the distance, from beyond the palisade, came the roar of firearms: the Shawnee delegation arriving, no doubt. It was time for him to attend his commander.

Sighing, Jeremy signed, sanded, and folded the letter as in the background the fort's guns let off seven blank rounds in salute. The cabin shuddered with the concussions, dirt sprinkling down from the roof. Jeremy idly wondered whether the rickety stockade would ever be made as stout as the new blockhouses under construction. Months of work were still needed to rebuild walls, plank up the gaps between palisades, and erect the needed shooting platforms that the fort's builders had neglected to install. That meant the fort would not be defensible until March or April. It was no wonder George Rogers Clark had made no attempt to hold this place against Hamilton.

Going out into the chilly air, Jeremy joined the few Redcoat and French militia officers sitting on chairs alongside Hamilton. There was much drum-beating as the sixty Shawnees came striding in to take their places around a large, roaring council fire. Though it was midwinter, the weather was mild enough for the ceremony to be held outside, and Hamilton had furnished each Indian a balsam pine cushion spread with a fine trade blanket as a gift. Hamilton himself sat on an ornate chair set on a puncheon platform.

Food was brought to the Indians, and Hamilton instructed that ale be served all around—except to the regulars, who were expected to stand at ease while the Indians gorged themselves. This council was extremely important for Hamilton, who needed the Shawnees armed and ready to strike hard at Clark in Kaskaskia, while a mixed white and Indian force attacked from Vincennes, and a third army came down the Mississippi. After Clark was destroyed, the combined forces would move against Kentucky, joining with the powerful Creek, Cherokee, and Choctaw nations to make an army some three thousand strong. The rebels would be hardpressed to stop them from crossing the Appalachians.

Hamilton wanted these Shawnees—most of them headmen or war chiefs—to carry his war belts to the southern Indians and the Delaware and Iroquois to the east. Thus the Shawnees would help coordinate the assault, which would be reinforced by tribes of the distant northwest. Last year Clark's unexpected invasion had intimidated the Indians here, foiling Hamilton's original plan for a frontier campaign; now the tribes awaited on Hamilton to see what he would do to Clark. These Shawnees were here to learn firsthand of their great father's resolve, courage, and strength. If Hamilton appeared weak, if he was not a convincing orator, the offensive might falter once again.

Jeremy thought Hamilton looked unusually tense as he stood to address the Shawnees. Again and again he promised them victory, assuring them that the might of the British king would be behind all their undertakings. He tried to belittle the influence of the Longknives and said their recent successes had been mere luck, possible only because of the treason of certain French individuals.

Once again Hamilton was laying the blame at the feet of the Illinois whites. Jeremy thought him wrong, even foolish, to say this, because the Indians had long been closely tied to the French and were greatly influenced by how the French responded to British policy. Sullen French meant confused Indians. Hamilton was losing his grip on the situation, it seemed, not taking the importance of the French into account. Nor did he impress the Indians as once he had, as an omnipotent commander. Proof of that came when a skinny, wizened Shawnee chief rose to speak. He was introduced as Catahecassa, war chief of the Shawnees at Chillicothe.

"...our French brothers have been counsels to us for many years, and it gives us pain to hear them accused of cowardice and disloyalty when they were given no support from the British king, our great white father across the sea."

Jeremy saw Hamilton stiffen as he heard this. The war

chief closely observed the lieutenant governor's expression before going on.

"But we Shawnee have no love for the Longknives, and we mean to fight them to the death. We will fight at the side of the great white father's young men, who will supply us with food and ammunition and will repair our guns when they go bad from killing so many enemies."

Catahecassa reached under a blanket on the ground and picked up what seemed to be a scalp stretched on a frame, but he did not show it clearly, holding it behind his robe as he spoke.

"The Shawnees make war against the Longknives, and we will fight them until our final breath. We expect no mercy from them—no mercy for our men, for our women, or for our children. So also will we treat them, and in the time of the Green Moon we will take up the hatchet and attack them wherever they are to be found!"

The other Indians shouted in agreement. Jeremy saw that this was exactly what Hamilton wanted to hear, for the officer became relieved, obviously pleased with Catahecassa's promise.

The Shawnee chief waited until the shouting died down, then stepped forward, saying, "With the support of the great father in Detroit, we will destroy all Longknives. This is a token of what we will do, a symbol of what the triumph of the king's Indians will mean to our enemies!"

Catahecassa offered the stretched scalp, and Jeremy paled in horror to see it was the scalp of a white baby. The other whites were visibly shaken as the Shawnee chief stared hard at Hamilton, who hesitated rather than accept the scalp. Everyone fell silent. The scalp was held out. The Shawnees were forcing Hamilton into a tight spot, testing him to see whether he would condone their traditional ways of warmaking, their all-out slaughter of men, women, and children.

Jeremy prayed that he would not yield. He must not take that scalp! Hamilton's face was set, his eyes blank.

Jeremy was on the edge of his chair. The entire fort was absolutely silent, save for a crying French baby in the crowd. Mouth dry, heart racing, Jeremy thought of his own son, who could not be much older than the infant whose scalp this was. To Jeremy's dismay, Hamilton began to reach out—

"No!" Jeremy shouted and sprang toward him. "Don't do it!" His fellow officers moved to block the way, but Jeremy shoved them aside. "Don't let them do this to us!" Hamilton was bewildered, the Indians angry.

Jeremy broke away from the last man trying to stop him and was but a few feet away when Hamilton turned and confronted him.

"Silence, Surgeon Major! Return to your place!"

Jeremy stopped short, seeing to his horror that the scalp was already in Hamilton's hands. Jeremy shuddered. *It has come to this!* he thought, and then said it aloud, twice. The Indians grumbled and began to complain. Catahecassa's eyes were half closed, but he seemed pleased.

Hamilton motioned for soldiers to surround Jeremy, and several bayonets were brought uncomfortably close. Jeremy stood there, gaping at the baby's scalp, hardly hearing as, in a shaky voice, Hamilton ordered him put under arrest and taken to his quarters. An officer who knew Jeremy well spoke quietly, pleading that he cause no more trouble, lest Hamilton press serious charges.

Jeremy just stood there, swaying, eyes on the scalp, fists clenched. It was a nightmare. He imagined the son he had never seen, and he heard Gwen's voice in his mind—heard how she wanted him to come back to her. He was breathing heavily, anger and regret flooding him. The officer was speaking in more urgent terms, and that brought Jeremy partly to his senses. Shrugging off the man's hands, he glared at Hamilton and hissed, "I have not come to this, sir!" Then he spun and began to leave the council. At the last moment, just to see whether this was really happening, he turned to watch. To his inexpressible revulsion, he saw Hamilton thank Catahecassa, who backed away, a sly grin on his face.

As if he could not help himself, Hamilton suddenly looked at Jeremy, then to the scalp and back, his lower lip thrust out, face red.

Then Hamilton turned abruptly away, and in a voice that

cracked at first, began speaking. "Our honored Shawnee guests..."

Jeremy left the council, many eyes on him, as they had been that day at Detroit when he had refused to partake of the ceremonial war feast. But he did not care, and before he reached the cabin he was yanking off his scarlet tunic. Inside, he threw it onto his cot and began pacing the small room, back and forth, thoughts racing in an agony of sorrow, shame, and anger.

Then, as if clouds had cleared, there was no longer any doubt about what he had to do. He stopped pacing, took a deep breath, and closed his eyes. At last, he was finished with it. Before a soldier, he was a doctor—and a man who could not be driven or beaten down. He would never obey unless he believed completely in what he was doing. He had made the crucial decision, and a great weight seemed to leave him, a rush of inner peace filling his heart. For the first time in far too long, he was a free man!

chapter 22

CLARK'S MARCH

That evening, as he had expected, Jeremy was called to his commander's presence. When he entered the modest log headquarters building and saw Hamilton slouched in a chair by the fireside, he thought the man looked broken. Hamilton hoarsely offered a seat but did not rise in greeting. He was holding a charcoal sketch loosely in one hand, as if he had been looking at it.

Jeremy carried the envelope with his written resignation. He felt awkward as he took a chair beside Hamilton, who was staring into the fire, his eyes bleary and dark.

After a lengthy silence, Hamilton raised a finger and apologized for neglecting to offer something to drink. Jeremy said a drink was not desired.

Suddenly Hamilton sat forward, elbows on knees, the firelight playing on his haggard face. "In times of war, men do what duty compels them to do." He licked his lips and swallowed, rubbing his forehead. "Of course, I don't have to say that to you, do I?" He cleared his throat and laid aside the sketch. Jeremy saw that it was the rendering of a magnificent chalk bluff on the Wabash, where he and Hamilton had spent some enjoyable hours looking for fossils during the long journey south.

"Perhaps, though, I just need to say that to someone . . . someone who'll remember me as a man who tried to do his duty, who tried hard to prevent unnecessary bloodshed. A man who . . . wanted peace with honor, and who stood up for what he knew was right. Just as you have done, and are doing now."

He glanced sidelong at Jeremy. "I can guess what's in your letter." He sat back, looking limp and defeated. "I'll not stand in your way. When you get home, give your wife my regards and offer my blessings on the child." He smiled wistfully. "You're a lucky man, Jeremy. One of these days, when my affairs are simpler, I'll marry, too, and I hope I have a son like you."

It hurt Jeremy to hear this. Clearly Henry Hamilton was basically a decent man, a minor government official whom circumstance had burdened with tremendous responsibilities, but who had little support from his leaders to carry out those responsibilities. A small regular British army with loyalist volunteers could easily have overwhelmed the rebel settlements in the northwest with minimal bloodshed; but Parliament would never pay for such an army.

Hamilton did not raise his head when he spoke. "I had hoped this Illinois campaign would change things for the better. Perhaps that was foolish of me." He closed his eyes, as if he wanted simply to go to sleep; then he sighed and said, "I came down here to be a soldier, not to be the 'Hair-buyer' at Detroit, the man who heartlessly sends bloodthirsty savages against innocents." He shook his head. "Will I ever be understood?"

When Jeremy did not reply, he went on, his voice steadily rising. "I came down here to fight open war on a field of honor, against men, not to direct a dirty campaign against women and children." He took a long breath. "But I have not the troops to wage even this campaign. I cannot depend on the French, and all I have are thirty-five faithful regulars, a few scouts, and whatever the Indians decide to send me!" His eyes lit. "But the Indians will send me considerable strength. They, no one else—not Detroit, not Niagara, not Montreal, not London—*they* can send me fighting men, just like that Shawnee chief today can send me fighting men!" His face was flushed, fists clenched on his knees.

"That Shawnee will fight rebels to the death because he must! And if I can get him to fight the way I want him to fight, then we can crush this ungodly rebellion once and for all!" He gestured grandly at a map on the wall above the hearth. "We can sweep the frontiers clean of the enemy and wage such a war on the rebel rear that we will compel Congress to surrender!"

He shook a fist, then seemed to think better of it and instead sighed once more, waving his hand as if to ward off Jeremy's objections, which did not come.

"Don't tell me I'm right or wrong—that's yet to be proved! But nothing will be proved if we don't march eastward this spring—and we won't march unless the Indians are assured of my unwavering support. This is a desperate gamble on their part! They rightly fear the Longknives, and they must be convinced that I'll be at their side."

He paused, as if still waiting for Jeremy to voice an opinion. Jeremy was silent, however. He was sick of this war and wanted no more rationalizations, no more explanations, no more grand strategies that justified the scalping of babies.

Finally Hamilton looked at him directly, with eyes shadowed and bleak, as though the soul had been driven out. Jeremy felt profound compassion.

In a voice that suddenly wavered, Hamilton said, "You wish I'd never taken that damned scalp!"

Jeremy bowed his head and fumbled with the letter. He could stay no longer. Rising, he said, "I hope you will accept this without further ado, sir."

Hamilton reached for the envelope with shaking fingers, then let it fall into his lap as he stared blankly at the fire. Suddenly he raised his head, chin up in an attitude of firm resolve.

"Jeremy, I'll not accept this resignation."

Annoyed, Jeremy was about to say it did not matter, for nothing would keep him in Vincennes now; but Hamilton spoke decisively.

"I know you intend riding into Shawnee country for your brother, and for that reason I'll not accept this resignation until I hear you're safe and sound back at Detroit." He stared hard at Jeremy, who understood now what his commander was getting at. "Keep that lobster coat on your back, my friend, for it'll get you through to Chillicothe. Without it you're a dead man."

Jeremy offered his hand in thanks, and Hamilton stiffly rose, both of them standing erect and proud, uniform brass glittering in the light of the fire.

Jeremy said, "Until we meet again, sir."

Hamilton nodded. "In a better world."

As Jeremy went to the door, Hamilton sat back down, looking dejected and alone. Jeremy said a last good-bye, but Hamilton was oblivious. He was speaking softly to himself.

Before closing the door, Jeremy thought he heard him whisper, "Perhaps...perhaps I was wrong." Hamilton leaned forward, putting his hands on his face, and that was the last Jeremy saw of him.

Owen Sutherland was asleep, although it was dawn. During the past two weeks on the march, he and Tamano had been out scouting nearly every day, traveling almost twice as far as the others, and he needed rest. The troops were stirring in the camp; a few were able to get fires going with wet wood, and soon the higher ground that the army occupied was dotted with fourteen small, smoky blazes.

In his half-slumber, Sutherland heard their voices and smelled the smoke, but his troubled mind saw Benjamin wearing Indian clothes and looking downcast. He reached for the boy, tried to draw him close, to get him away from Shawnees who suddenly appeared like shadows between Benjamin and him.

The thud of a distant cannon woke him, and he sat up, listening. Every man in the camp was alert, and there came a jubilant cry. "Morning gun! That was Vincennes's morning gun! We're there!"

Sutherland was wide awake, and nearby Tamano was also sitting up, excitement showing in his eyes. Sutherland shook off the haunting dream and got to his feet, feeling his belly rumble, for like the others he had not eaten in two days. The continually rising flood had driven the game away, and all that the men had caught was a fox that had been treed by the water. The sun appeared, gray and cold, and Sutherland stared ahead into the shimmer that lay upon water, water, and more water, as far as he could see. Somewhere before them was the turbulent Wabash, and beyond it Vincennes.

"Not quite there yet," he murmured.

They set out again, into the water. The men began to talk about the gunboat that had been sent off from Kaskaskia; they asked aloud whether it was already ahead on the Wabash, waiting to rendezvous. Sutherland hoped so, for the boat could get them across quickly, and it had cannon and another fifty men, as well as desperately needed gunpowder and food.

Clark had ordered one more dugout canoe built, and the two small boats now carried sick men, equipment, and what little powder had not been damaged by the water.

By now all the men were weakening, and when they stumbled, it was hard to get up. Yet on they went, feeling their way with each step, until shortly before noon, when they mounted a rise and finally faced the broad Wabash. Sutherland estimated they were several miles downstream from Vincennes. No rebel gunboat was in sight, but after a few minutes they spotted a party of five French hunters, whom they easily surprised and captured.

The hunters turned out to be from Vincennes. They had some provisions, which did something to ease the hunger of the weakest of Clark's men, and their canoe could be used to hold the gear of men no longer able to carry their own.

Standing in a copse of trees while the troops rested, Sutherland listened to the hunters nervously tell Clark about Vincennes. They said Hamilton had strengthened Fort Sackville, and added that there had been rumors of Longknives being in the vicinity. When Clark asked how long it would take to march to Vincennes, one of the Frenchmen laughed ruefully.

"*Monsieur,* you cannot *march* to Vincennes from here! It is several miles, and you must have boats . . . many boats for such a strong force! The water is too deep!"

Clark glanced at Sutherland, who saw in the colonel's dark, angry look that nothing would stand in his way. Even if the gunboat did not arrive, Clark would go on.

Sutherland smiled and said, "This French gentleman doesn't know what our men have come through." To the hunters he said, "Ask any of your fellow Frenchmen here how they managed to come well over two hundred miles through this flood, when you say it is impossible to finish our journey."

Hearing this, the hunters looked astonished, and Clark sent them to talk with their Kaskaskia and Cahokia acquaintances. He and Sutherland watched as the various stories were told—spiced with humor but little exaggeration—and received in openmouthed awe by the hunters. With each episode related, the militiamen seemed to be instilled with new strength and courage. They began speaking of the incredible trek as if it were nothing much, quite normal for men such as they. Although at first the hunters had been loudly complimentary and admiring, they soon became very quiet to hear what these footsore, wet, and starving soldiers had achieved in the past two weeks. Some of the soldiers even began singing, others stretching arms and legs, calling for a resumption of the march, saying they could cross the Wabash in the canoes.

"They're ready now," Sutherland said to Clark, who nodded, intense emotion evident in his expression.

"I could not have asked for better troops."

"Nor they a better commander, sir."

Uncharacteristically, Clark blushed and rubbed his nose, clearing his throat and looking around at his gear as if seeking something to do. All the while the men were stirring, ready to push on immediately. Clark ordered them to rest, however, saying they would begin the crossing tomorrow.

In the morning, Clark's hungry army left its horses and baggage in camp and, canoe load by canoe load, crossed the swirling Wabash. They battled floating logs and debris that thudded against the boats, and it required the great skill of the Frenchmen to handle the craft in the turbulent current, paddling over and back, again and again until every man had been ferried to the other side.

Once across the main channel, the men were still in three feet of water, and they pushed off on foot, though the flood sometimes rose to their chests and they had to hold their weapons above their heads. Always they were careful not to stumble and ruin what little remained of their dry powder.

In this country, a surprise counterattack was always possible, and Clark's scouts had spotted several distant campfires that morning. The enemy might be on the lookout for them, and if Hamilton attacked in boats, the rebels would be virtually defenseless. Those not killed immediately would be tortured by Hamilton's Indians.

The weather had turned sharply colder overnight, and now when Sutherland pushed on ahead of Clark and the others, he had to break a thin sheet of ice as he went. Pain and cold were oppressive, but he put them from his thoughts and drove onward, one sluggish foot before the other.

The army traveled in rough file, two or three abreast, a long dark column of men against water that reflected the grimy sky. Sutherland recalled what the French prisoners had said about the fort having been strengthened, and he wondered how tough it would be to crack. Pondering the coming assault helped him to keep from feeling his belly contract and cramp. He was starved, as were they all. There was little joking or singing to be heard now.

That afternoon they rested on a small knoll called the Mamel, or breast. The whole company crammed onto that little island and huddled together, coughing, teeth chattering, some shivering so hard that friends had to make them walk around and exercise their limbs to prevent them from going lame. Grim and worried, Clark sent Sutherland and Tamano ahead in a canoe to sound the route to the next high ground, a maple-sugar camp a mile or so away. The report was not good, for Sutherland found the floodwater six feet deep in places. Most of the men were shorter than that.

Standing to one side with Sutherland so the men would not hear, Clark said, "To ferry all of us over there in boats would consume the entire day or more!"

Sutherland agreed, saying that to lose that much time might break the men's spirits.

Staring at the gray water, Clark asked, "Six feet at the deepest, you say?" He thought a moment, then looked back at the men, who were quaking with cold and hunger, some complaining that to go on was madness. Under Clark's glare they became quiet, and soon every eye was on him. To

Sutherland, Clark said with desperation, "They mustn't doubt for one minute! Not one!"

With that, he poured gunpowder from his horn into the palm of his hand, mixed it with water, and blackened his face, as Indians did before going into battle. Everyone was silent, watching. Then he raised his rifle and screeched a bloodcurdling, ringing war whoop, and they rose to their feet, still silent, but with one accord. Clark turned and strode into the water, and the men fell in behind, heads lifted, hollow eyes hard, trusting him completely.

"Sing," Clark shouted. "Sing, you warriors!"

Sutherland was close behind with Tamano, and they sloshed into the freezing water and raised their weapons with weary arms. Exchanging glances and a tired grin with Tamano, Sutherland lustily broke into the old soldier's tune, "The Girl I Left Behind Me," and the others took it up. The French hummed brassily, and when the verses had run out, they started their own well-known tunes. The deeper the water became, the louder everyone sang—except for the short ones, who soon found themselves up to their necks and struggling for breath.

After a while, Clark called for a rearguard to be formed, to "put to death any man unwilling to march." Whatever his actual motives were, the order resulted in a mighty shout of agreement from the men. They drew on their failing strength, making the final effort as a unified force, forged in hardship and suffering.

Still the water became deeper. Smaller and weaker men had to be carried by stronger, taller ones; others clung to floating logs, paddling along. On they went. Exhausted men stumbled, went under, and were yanked up by comrades. Then, amidst it all, the insolent joking started all over again, and the singing went on as if they did not care who heard them coming. The canoes passed back and forth to help those who were too small or were flagging, ferrying them ahead to the sugar camp. But most of the men doggedly pressed on, aching arms holding rifles and equipment high.

The water became so deep that at one point no one had more than his head above the surface, except for those who were being carried. Sutherland's arms were sore, his body almost without feeling. With every step his feet sought for solid ground, though the water seemed to thicken and hold his legs from moving. Even Clark would soon be out of his level. Yet Sutherland knew the Virginian would cross or drown trying.

Then Sutherland felt something familiar underfoot. Could it be possible? Excited, he probed and tested with his toes, looked at the distant sugar camp and a flooded line of trees leading to it, then cried out, "I've found a path! Here, everyone, this way, and we'll get on high ground! This way!"

He was right. The feel of smooth, worn ground beneath his moccasins told that a path was there, and in this country most paths followed the highest land. Sutherland and Clark paced ahead with new strength, and the men whooped for joy. The path went right for the sugar camp, where canoes were discharging weary men. The water here slackened and became more shallow, steadily dropping until it was only at knee level. The men laughed and cheered, urged themselves to the limit, and when they made dry land, many fell forward, bodies half in, half out of the water, as if unable to go farther.

Those strong enough dragged the others out of the water, and the most alert men began to light fires. Once again the benumbed were stood on their feet and forced to exercise, for even the heat of the fires would not revive frozen legs and arms.

Clark's eyes glittered in that smeared black mask as he said in a croaking voice to Sutherland, "We're almost there! But what we need most right now is food! Food to lift spirits before we attack—"

"Look!" Sutherland exclaimed, and pointed across the water at a canoe being paddled upstream. In an instant he and Tamano took one of the canoes and set off in pursuit. It turned out to be a frightened squaw and her children, who had a half quarter of buffalo and some corn and tallow. Sutherland brought her back, paid her in trinkets, and in no time the men were eagerly boiling up the meat.

There was little more than a small bowl of broth for each man, and far more was needed for survival and strength, yet again many a soldier refused his own ration and gave it instead to a weaker man.

That little food was enough to encourage them all, and soon even the sun came out to shine warmly. By late afternoon they were rested, refreshed, and instilled with new life. They were not quite at Hamilton's door, but it was just a matter of hours.

"Nineteen days," Sutherland murmured to himself, watching the haggard, grizzled men sleeping in the sun. "Through two hundred and forty miles of water..." Then he thought that Jeremy was probably inside Fort Sackville. He closed his eyes and prayed the battle would be brief and that Jeremy would not be hurt. It would have to be brief, for if the British held out even a week, the Indians would learn that Clark was not strong. The tribes would rise, surround the besiegers, and wipe them out.

Sutherland's thoughts were interrupted as Clark strode past at the water's edge, calling for men to assemble their standards and company colors.

"Put 'em on long poles, boys, and we'll go in there like an army of ten regiments—so long as we stay behind the high ground and just let 'em see our flags!"

Vincennes had six hundred fighting men in the village, fort, and nearby Indian towns, though just how many of them Hamilton could count on no one knew. But then, no one in Vincennes knew how large Clark's army was. Clark's spies had already told him much about the enemy's defenses and about the reluctance of the French militia to back Hamilton, but if the British appeared to be winning, the French would likely stick to them.

Clark had to bluff. He immediately sent a letter into the French village, stating in politely confident terms that those who were "friends of liberty" should get into their houses and stay there, and those loyal to the king should "instantly repair to the fort and join his troops and fight like men." Anyone found under arms when Clark's force marched in, the letter said, would be treated as an enemy. He even sent greetings to villagers from Kentuckians the French knew had gone home, thus giving the impression that the attackers were a fresh army up from the colonies.

From higher ground east of the village, Clark and Sutherland observed the commotion the letter caused in the town, as scores of people rushed outside to gaze across the rolling prairie, looking for the invaders. From where Clark and Sutherland stood, the houses of the village obstructed the view from the fort, and when Clark sent his men marching back and forth in sight of the villagers, he knew the Redcoats could not see them from the ramparts. As soon as the enemy was warned by French sympathizers, the fighting would begin.

Sutherland enjoyed watching Clark's false display of strength, which must have been impressive indeed to the Vincennes folk. Clark's men paraded back and forth, officers on captured mounts, the dozen flags fluttering bravely. Because of intervening swells of land that blocked parts of the view from Vincennes, the marching and countermarching must have made the attackers seem to number at least a thousand.

The men were impatient to attack, but when they had finished their demonstration, Clark marched them swiftly out of sight. At dusk, however, they reappeared on high ground behind the town, closer to the fort. Watching from the trees, Sutherland was troubled that no activity could be seen inside the fort. It was understandable that the French village was quiet, hardly a stray dog in sight, but why did the fort seem so unprepared? Clark's spies had told him that Hamilton had called out the local militia to garrison the fort because there were rumors that Longknives were in the vicinity; but no apparent defense had yet been organized, with only a couple of sentries in sight.

As darkness fell there was an ominous stillness. Sutherland looked back at the men readying their weapons for the assault and saw on their faces the grim expectation of a fierce battle. He thought the garrison must be lying in wait; worse, Clark had told him that a party of twenty French and Indian scouts was reported out somewhere behind the attackers. If they could stir up the tribes in time, things would go badly. And there was still no sign of the gunboat and its men and artillery.

At the order, Clark's force moved swiftly. Most of the men rushed through the village to occupy it and find food. A small party took up firing positions near the closed main gate. This second group, including Sutherland and Tamano, opened fire with their long rifles, peppering the fort. At first there was no response to these blasts of gunfire.

Sutherland continued to wonder what was happening, until Tamano reminded him that the local Indians often saluted the fort as they passed at night. It was possible Hamilton still did not realize he was under attack! Sure enough, when the first sentry dropped wounded, the warning finally went up, and the British and French in the garrison sprang to the ramparts.

From then on, the night crackled and flashed with heavy gunfire, punctuated at first by the deafening roar of cannon from the fort. Clark's men spread out around the palisades and concentrated their fire against the cannon ports. Whenever a port was lifted, twenty rounds were sent into it. Soon it became impossible for the British to stand to their guns, although Longknife shouts and insults angered them sufficiently to make them try a few more times. They were not fast enough, however, for the instant a port opened, a hail of gunfire met the man aiming along the cannon barrel, and he went down.

Clark's troops whooped and shouted, the reserve companies milling about in the village, sometimes returning to the firing line for a few volleys. They withdrew after a while to the village again, laughing uproariously, behaving as though their numbers were five times what they actually were.

Sutherland stayed at Clark's side, following him around and around the fort. It soon became apparent how well Clark had planned this assault, for there were Frenchmen from the village who seemed to have been awaiting the Virginian, and they offered hot food and drink, as well as precious gunpowder from hidden stores.

The night was long and noisy, and the air grew foul with sour gunsmoke, but after several hours only two of Clark's men had been wounded. The rebels were well concealed by houses, strong fences, and earthworks and barricades hastily thrown up within easy range of the fort. After firing, men would roll away to shoot from another spot, making it seem there were far more of them than in actuality and avoiding return fire that was aimed at the flash of their guns.

Most of the French in the village stayed indoors. During the night, Sutherland heard that Clark's letter had so awed the townsfolk that no one had given the slightest hint to Hamilton of the rebel approach. The fort had been still because it was unprepared. Sutherland was gratified to hear that nearly every Frenchman believed Clark had at least a thousand men out there.

The biggest danger now was if the scouts Hamilton had sent out raised hostile Indians. Clark asked Sutherland and Tamano to find this party and trail them in preparation for an ambush. As it turned out, Sutherland discovered them hiding just behind rebel lines, waiting for the first chance to break for the fort and scale the walls to join Hamilton.

Clark soon ordered all rebel firing to cease, and a large gap was made in the lines as a few companies noisily withdrew to the village. In the hour before dawn, Sutherland watched Hamilton's scouting party make their desperate dash. No one fired a shot, even as the scouts nervously called for ladders to be let down to them. As soon as the ladders were dropped the scouts went scurrying up as fast as they could, frantic to get inside.

Just as the first men were clambering over the pointed palisade, Sutherland and a gang of Virginians rushed back into nearby bushes and let out a mighty shout, heckling and taunting the scouts, who were so startled that those at the top of the wall dived headlong over the pickets, dropping all the way down the other side. Others tumbled back to the ground, ladders falling over, men crashing into one another.

The laughing Virginians shouted congratulations to the scouts for getting inside—as all eventually did—adding that it was good they were trapped in the fort instead of out making a war in the rear of the attackers.

When daylight came, Sutherland saw that every cannon port, every firing loophole had been shot to pieces. Wherever as much as a shadow had passed across an opening, e fire it had drawn had been devastating and accurate.

That morning Clark sent in a demand for unconditional
urrender. Hamilton refused, but requested a truce for three
ays in order to carry out negotiations. Clark declined, and
e rebel firing was redoubled, hotter than ever, while hardly
shot could be sent from the fort in return. As long as
Hamilton did not know how weak Clark really was, he had
o feel his position was hopeless.

At last, in the afternoon, Hamilton sent out a flag of
uce, and soon afterward Clark and Sutherland met him
nd another officer in a small, unadorned room of the church,
ot far from the fort's front gate. The two leaders took seats
t opposite ends of a table, sunlight warmly falling upon
hem, while Sutherland and a British captain named Hay—
veteran Sutherland knew from Detroit—sat nearby, lis-
ning. Hamilton was immaculate in his scarlet uniform,
hough the awful strain showed on his face. He was wan,
is eyes bloodshot, but he displayed no fear and was every
it an officer as he again rejected Clark's demand for un-
onditional surrender, scorning the Virginian's warnings of
tter annihilation. The thought of massacring the garrison
aunted Sutherland, who believed Jeremy to be inside.

"Should the battle continue and I be compelled to storm
ou," Clark said, "many good men will be slain on both
des. I must warn you that if my force should suffer such
ss, none of my officers will be able to hold their men back
om killing every last defender in their rage." He leaned
ack and said, "You know what Kentuckians will do to men
ho've sent redskins against their families!"

After a moment Hamilton replied in cool, gentlemanly
nes. "My men have declared they will die rather than
urrender at your discretion, sir." He stared straight at Clark,
hose color rose. "If you have no other terms to offer,
olonel, further discussion is in vain."

Clark shook his head, then spoke in a soft, slow voice.
I know to a man how many you can count on, sir. Your
rench are all against you, and your thirty-five regulars—
x of them wounded, I understand—can do no more than
e well, I assure you."

Hamilton's eyes narrowed, but he said nothing.

Clark went on. "It is pure folly to think of making a defense with so few against my own great numbers!" He leaned slightly forward. "Surrender unconditionally and trust to the generosity of Virginia, and you'll have better treatment than if you hold out to draw up terms."

Hamilton remained expressionless, but his words were sharp, full of fight. "I will never take so disgraceful a step."

Clark was quiet for a while. After a moment, he continued the conversation, which turned several more times around the point of unconditional surrender. As they talked, Sutherland leaned over to whisper to Captain Hay, a portly, dark man, and a native of Pennsylvania. Sutherland asked him about Jeremy.

Hay waited for Clark to begin speaking before he whispered in reply, "Dr. Bently is gone, Mr. Sutherland, and resigned from the army, too; left a few days back for Chillicothe, after your other lad."

This struck Sutherland like a shot, and he nearly sprang from his seat. At that moment, Hamilton rose, refusing to surrender unless the garrison was allowed to go on parole to the British base at Pensacola.

Clark stood up, saying, "We will not begin further hostilities until one minute after your drum is sounded."

Hamilton was pale, mouth set, but his distress was lost on the anxious Sutherland, who knew Jeremy would need help to get Benjamin free. As far as Sutherland was concerned, Henry Hamilton's fate was sealed.

As Hamilton and Hay departed from the church, Sutherland told Clark about Jeremy. Clark was sober, but a fire of enthusiasm was in his eyes as he no doubt contemplated the great victory at hand.

Sutherland said, "You don't need me, Colonel, but my sons do."

The Virginian assessed Sutherland a moment, then held out his hand and said, "I'll arrange for a horse to speed you on your way, Mr. Sutherland. When you return, we'll have a feast together in honor of our success—yours and mine!"

chapter **23**

RESCUE

Benjamin had never seen anything as horrible as the
~~day~~ ay the Shawnees burned an accused witch at the stake. It
~~was~~ as said the unfortunate young woman hated her own people
~~and~~ nd had used black magic to cause last year's poor harvest.

Forced to sit in attendance among the young men in the
~~outer~~ uter circle, Benjamin had looked away when the fire was
~~lit~~ t around the frantic, screaming girl. To drown out her
~~shrieks~~ hrieks, the Shawnees had sung a mournful song, with witch
~~doctors~~ octors prancing and capering around the stake, sounding
~~rattles~~ attles and banging drums to drive out the evil spirit pos-
~~sessing~~ essing her. It seemed forever before the screaming had
~~stopped~~ topped.

Benjamin felt sick. He had known the girl, a friend of
~~Evangeline's~~ Evangeline's. Like many others in the village, Evangeline
~~was~~ as griefstricken but had been helpless to do anything, for
~~the~~ ne accuser was said to be a prophet: Tenskwatawa, the one-
~~eyed~~ yed twin of Tecumseh.

In just the few months since Benjamin had been brought
~~here~~ ere, Tenskwatawa had grown in social stature, until several
~~weeks~~ eeks ago he had been formally declared a seer of great
~~powers~~ owers. Almost immediately afterward he had used his new-
~~found~~ ound influence to condemn this poor, defenseless girl.
~~Evangeline~~ Evangeline hated him for it, and she had warned Benjamin
~~to~~ o stay out of his way.

Still keeping his gaze averted from the stake, Benjamin
~~could~~ ould not ignore the awful stench that hung over the gath-
~~ering~~ ring. After a while, when a medicine man began making
~~a~~ speech, he was able to look around at the faces in the
~~crowd~~ rowd. The village was packed with newly arrived warriors
~~massing~~ assing for the spring warpath, and somewhere among them,

Benjamin knew, was Captain Mark Davies. Davies had
arrived yesterday, reportedly to recruit braves, and so far
Benjamin had managed to avoid him.

Tenskwatawa . . . Davies . . . Amaghwah. Benjamin was
finding life in Chillicothe extremely precarious these days.
In fact, he had enjoyed few peaceful moments since the day
he had spotted Amaghwah in the woods near Evangeline's
lodge. He had warned Wabete, of course, but nothing had
come of it, even though Wabete had ordered a search.
Amaghwah had been declared outcast ever since the attempted assassination last year, with a sentence of death if
ever he was caught near the village of Chillicothe. According to Wabete, Amaghwah had fled south to join Davies,
who now led a band of hard cases and outcasts based near
the Ohio. These men recognized no tribal authority and
obeyed only Davies, who kept them well supplied with
British goods, arms, and rum. Outcasts such as Amaghwah
would not dare enter Chillicothe, but they might be camped
nearby, waiting for Davies.

As soon as he could, Benjamin slipped away from the
appalling ritual, making his way toward Evangeline's lodge.
Feeling glum and lonely, he paused near the dwelling of
one of Wabete's relatives, petting the family dog, who had
come to greet him.

Benjamin gazed at the darkening river. The sun was
almost down, the sky a blaze of orange. Everywhere groups
of strutting fighting men were making their way from the
ceremony back to their lodges for the evening meal. Benjamin's attention remained on the Scioto River. To him it
was a highway to freedom, cutting through the Shawnee
hills toward the Ohio River and the Kentucky settlements.
Yet to go that way would be a dangerous journey. Perhaps
it would be more prudent to flee toward Vincennes, where
he had heard his brother was posted; but what would the
British do to an escaped Shawnee captive these days? Probably send him back.

His adoption was not far off, he knew. He was strong
again and healthy, looking like an Indian, dressed well in
good buckskins and a fine red trade shirt. Already he was
being treated like a young warrior and seldom had any work
to do.

Suddenly the dog growled and backed off, and Benjamin felt a chill of fear. He whirled around to stare straight at Mark Davies, standing a few yards off. He was wearing a green uniform and was flanked by a dozen or so well-armed warriors. Casually, Davies waved his companions on toward the village council ground. Putting his hands on his hips and grinning, he spoke in that shrill, refined voice that Benjamin so hated.

"You'll have some interesting company in a few days, Sutherland. There's a rebel convoy coming downriver, and those who survive our welcoming party will be brought to Chillicothe for some . . . festivities!" He laughed and, touching his hat, strode away, shouting back, "They won't last as long as you have, though . . . but have a care that you continue to last! Have a care, Sutherland!" He laughed almost giddily, like a madman, then he was gone, trotting to catch up with his band of Indians.

Benjamin became cold with dread for the people in that doomed convoy. He knew suddenly that if he must risk his life, then it should be to warn those people. If only he could get away and move fast enough, he might reach the Ohio before pursuers caught him.

His heart was beating fast. If he were successful, the convoy might take him to freedom. He hungered to get away and return to his family.

He began to head back toward the council ground, intending to mingle with the people and find out all he could about the approaching boats. If he stayed close to Davies's Indians, listening to them boast of their plans, he would learn what he needed to know of the ambush. All he had to do was stay away from Davies, who might become suspicious. As for the others, he looked so much like a Shawnee boy now that he probably would not be noticed eavesdropping.

An hour later it was nearly full dark, and Benjamin hurried to Evangeline's lodge to fetch Punch. By now he knew the plans of ambush, including the place the Shawnees would prepare the attack. He was excited and nervous as he thought of all he would need to take along on his escape. He would go that very night.

Just as he reached the clearing in front of the lodge Evangeline appeared, running toward him from the dark woods, and Punch flitted overhead to land on his shoulder. Evangeline was breathless and looked disturbed. At first Benjamin thought she was still grieving at her friend's execution, but he quickly sensed something else was on her mind.

"Someone has come to see you," she whispered anxiously, gripping his arm and looking about to see if anyone was listening. Her family's lodge was dark, everyone apparently still at the village.

"Who wants me? Are you all right, Evangeline?"

She was obviously afraid, her eyes darting about, and she whispered for Benjamin to wait here until she called for him. Punch stayed on his shoulder, which pleased Benjamin, who lately had thought he was losing the bird to Evangeline. She had even renamed him—a long Shawnee word meaning the "jay without a squawk." With one finger Benjamin was stroking the bird's feathers when suddenly he heard an angry shout from beyond the lodge, and the jay flew into the air. Benjamin ran toward the sound, recognizing Evangeline's voice.

"You're a fraud!" she cried. "A murderer and a fraud!"

Benjamin darted around the lodge and in the dimness saw her struggling with Tenskwatawa, who had her roughly by the wrists as she tried to kick and scratch. Punch was pecking at Tenskwatawa, but he shook off the bird and twisted Evangeline from side to side until she was almost on her knees. His painted face with its missing eye made him look like the devil himself.

"I am a prophet, born under the shooting star! I have smelled a witch, and she has been destroyed before she could again injure our people!"

"You lie—"

"It is you who lie, Moravian unbeliever! I know who you really are, animal charmer! You cast spells over the creatures of the woods, and you will soon cast a spell over us if I do not prevent—"

Tenskwatawa gagged as he was yanked hard from behind and hurled to the ground. Benjamin stood over him, fist clenched.

Benjamin pointed, "Your time will come, evildoer!"

Breathless, Tenskwatawa scrambled backward and went for his knife. Then he saw the fierce look in Benjamin's eyes and thought better of it. Instead he got up quickly and stood there, trying to catch his breath.

"I have the second sight, paleface!" he hissed madly, and spat. "And I see you are in mortal danger!" He grinned like a death's-head, bending forward at the waist, but ready to flee if Benjamin made a move. "Death stalks you! I have seen it!" He cackled, looking all the more hideous.

Suddenly Benjamin sensed the Indian was looking past him, but to turn might give Tenskwatawa an opening with that knife. Suddenly Evangeline screamed, and Benjamin whirled. It was Amaghwah, ugly and fierce, coming from the woods. Three other Indians were with him, all with weapons drawn. Benjamin was unarmed, surrounded. Evangeline gave a shout and sprinted away past Tenskwatawa, who slashed at her but missed.

"Let the brat go," Amaghwah snarled as he closed in, knife and tomahawk in hand. "This won't take long." He waved his friends back. He wanted to be first. The others would ruin what was left.

Benjamin had nowhere to run, and it was too far from the village to call for help. He tensed, crouching. Into his racing mind came the unexpected thought that no one would warn the convoy now. Fright gave way to anger. He was breathing faster, chest heaving, strength surging through his body.

Tenskwatawa moved closer than he should have, perhaps wanting first blood, and Benjamin whipped around, kicking him hard between the legs. The boy went down with a howl, dropping the knife, and before Amaghwah could react, Benjamin grabbed the gasping Tenskwatawa and hurled him. Amaghwah was knocked backward, and Benjamin picked up the boy's knife, making a move to slip into the woods.

But the other Indians were there, grinning, knives threatening. Tenskwatawa went limping off toward the village, whimpering in pain. Again Amaghwah closed in, his knife glinting in the darkness. Benjamin was prepared now.

With a thud and a groan, one of the other Indians abruptly went down. Benjamin's heart jumped as he saw a shadow

move from the trees. He thought he saw a sword gleam
Another Indian shouted, and in that moment Amaghwa
turned. Benjamin hurled Tenskwatawa's knife, which struc
Amaghwah high on the left shoulder. The Indian shrieke
and spun around and around, clutching the knife, droppin
his tomahawk. Benjamin heard savage grunts and the clas
of steel. The other Indians were being attacked. Benjami
dived for the fallen tomahawk and turned to face Amagh
wah, who was whining, yanking at the knife and backin
away.

The two other Indians gave a shout to retreat, but on
crumpled. His fellow ducked and scrambled for the woods
but as Benjamin closed on the writhing Amaghwah he hear
a grunt and from the corner of his eye saw the second India
go down. Amaghwah was backing up quickly, unable t
get the knife out, panting in dismay. Benjamin would hav
been satisfied to drive him off, but Evangeline emerge
from the woods just then and could not get out of Amagh
wah's way fast enough. With a screech he grabbed her hai
and yanked her toward him.

Benjamin raised the tomahawk. "Let her go!" He ad
vanced, but Amaghwah laughed in spite of his agony.

"She will die!" He jerked the girl toward him—but a
that instant Punch dived and caught him hard in the face
and he staggered, roaring in fury. That was enough fc
Evangeline to break loose, and Amaghwah reeled away
finally yanking out the knife. He bolted into the bushes wit
a crash of branches, then was lost in the darkness. Evange
line cried out, rushing into Benjamin's arms, shaking wit
horror. He drew her close.

Someone else was behind him, and Benjamin swun
around.

"Jeremy!"

The brothers threw their arms about each other, holdin
Evangeline, who was still weeping. In the dimness Be
jamin saw that Jeremy was in full uniform, a bloody swor
in his hand.

"Evangeline was going to help me free you," Jerem
said, roughly tousling his brother's hair, as if to make sur
the boy was really there. "She was coming to me when tha

dog tried to kill you. . . ." He stared at the trees where Amaghwah had fled.

Just then a great hubbub arose in the direction of the village, and the three of them turned to listen. Benjamin could make out what sounded like women wailing, as if in mourning. He looked questioningly at Evangeline, who seemed just as puzzled.

Jeremy said hurriedly, "We've got to get out of here, Ben."

Benjamin frowned. "Let's wait until Evangeline goes down there to find out what's happening."

Jeremy nodded, and after he and Benjamin dragged the bodies into the woods, they followed Evangeline away from the trail to a dense thicket on a ledge overlooking the village. In the lights of the many distant campfires they could see people running back and forth, as if in panic. Evangeline called for Punch, who lighted on her shoulder.

"Keep quiet here," she whispered to Jeremy and Benjamin. "I'll have food for your journey when I return, but let no one see you!"

With that she hurried away, and the brothers again embraced, both speechless with joy and relief. As they rested on a fallen tree just inside the bushes, Jeremy quickly explained that he had decided to resign from the army and remain neutral for the rest of the war. Benjamin could hardly restrain himself from shouting with glee.

"Ma'll be happy, brother! How she's suffered over you. . . ." He grinned. "I wish you could tell her yourself."

Jeremy said, "It's still a long way to home."

Benjamin nodded. "Yours and mine."

Abruptly they realized they wanted to go in opposite directions—Jeremy north to Detroit, Benjamin southeast to rebel territory.

Jeremy looked troubled. "My wife and child—I have a son now, Ben—they're at Detroit. I'm going there . . . to Valenya."

Benjamin lowered his head; then he looked up, saying, "I'm glad for you, Jeremy . . . but I've got to go to the Ohio." He did not speak of his plan to warn the convoy, for he did not know whether Jeremy would object, considering it an act of war against the king. It pained Benjamin to think that although his brother had risked his life to rescue him, the whole truth could not be told to him just then. "I'll go alone," Benjamin said.

Jeremy sighed, and after a moment he replied, "I'll take you to the Ohio before I turn back to Detroit, Ben. Another few days down here won't cost me much." He stood up to stare at the noisy village. The screaming had not abated and, indeed, seemed to have become more general, as if every woman were lamenting some loss or crying out in fear.

Benjamin gripped Jeremy's hand. "It's wonderful to see you again! More wonderful than I ever imagined!"

It was not long before Evangeline came running back, slipping into the bushes where they waited, dropping a basket of food at their feet. Out of breath and obviously in much distress, she panted, "Hamilton is defeated and taken prisoner! The great father has been tricked by the Longknives, believing they had ten times as many as attacked him! He has been shamed, and now even the French of the Illinois are rising against the British! My people are afraid, and they talk of a coming attack!"

Jeremy and Benjamin looked in amazement at each other as Evangeline told them the rest. Apparently Hamilton had surrendered only two days after Clark had begun the assault. It was a stunning disaster for British and loyalist arms.

In the faint light, Benjamin saw that his brother was shocked. As Jeremy sat down on the log, Benjamin tried to keep from exulting that the Hair-buyer had been whipped. He understood why the Shawnees were so shattered by the news, for they had considered Hamilton almost undefeatable, the right hand of the king.

Benjamin asked, "Will it be safe for you at Detroit now, brother? The Longknives will surely march there next."

Jeremy had no immediate answer. Shaking his head, he said, "I don't even feel sorrow at this rebel triumph. Strange, but perhaps I've known that one day it would come to this."

The chaotic sounds from the village continued as they listened in silence, Evangeline and Benjamin gazing at each other, knowing this might be their last time together.

Jeremy rose, saying, "I meant what I said, Ben. I'll take you to the Ohio."

"But your family at Detroit—if they're in danger, you must go to them. I'll be all right, as long as I'm on the trail before Davies and his men set off. I'll outrun a rabbit to warn those . . . to reach the Ohio—"

Jeremy looked at him sharply. "Warn who? Is Davies here? What are you talking about, Ben?"

Benjamin was self-conscious and shuffled his feet; he attempted to change the subject, saying that Jeremy should get north before the Longknives cut off the trails to Detroit.

Jeremy spoke firmly. "You have a plan that you won't tell me—your loyalist brother." He nodded slowly. "I see."

Benjamin stared blankly toward the noisy village. People were busy emptying lodges, gathering up crying children, and leading out packhorses to be loaded for a hasty departure. Benjamin did not know what to say.

Jeremy shook his head. "Yes, it has come to this, Benjamin, and you're afraid that I might not care about whose blood Davies spills in the name of . . . in the name of the king!"

Benjamin looked at the ground, saying in a whisper, "I don't know who you really are anymore, Jeremy."

Evangeline was at the edge of the trees, sobbing as she watched her people hurrying away from Chillicothe, loading canoes or starting on foot up the river trail, fleeing the expected wrath of the Longknives.

She said, "The Longknives have already punished a village of Delaware near Vincennes. Many were killed . . . everyone is afraid now! The British have lost, and the Indians will also be destroyed!" She gave a shuddering sob and put her hands to her face.

Benjamin laid his arm over her shoulder. "Your family has nothing to fear, as peaceful Moravians. . . ."

She shook her head and leaned against him. "They have everything to fear, from both Indian and white! Each side believes that Moravians aid the other, and there are bad men, red and white, who will slay us just for the taste of blood! It has always been so with my people. Benjamin, I . . . I must go back to my lodge. My people will be looking for me."

Jeremy was taking off his tunic. "This red coat will do me no good with the Indians now; they'll have little regard for a British soldier after Hamilton's demise." He turned to Benjamin and said, "I've a horse and pack not far from here, and I'll put on some comfortable gear. . . ." He clapped his brother on the shoulder. "For the first time in years I'll do something right! I'll come with you to stop Davies, whatever he's up to. We have a reckoning coming."

Trembling with excitement, Benjamin shook his brother's hand.

Jeremy looked from his brother to Evangeline and put a hand on the shoulder of each. "Farewells need not mean it's forever; not if your hearts refuse to be parted."

Benjamin took Evangeline's hand, and Jeremy left them alone, except for Punch, who landed on their clasped hands, and did not try to squawk.

Early in the morning, two days later, Jeremy and Benjamin trotted swiftly southward along an upland trail, following hunting paths Benjamin had learned about in his time with the Shawnees. They had left Jeremy's horse with Evangeline, who had assured them she could explain away its presence.

By now the entire valley seemed empty, for nearly every Indian had fled northward, struck with fear by Henry Hamilton's defeat, expecting hordes of Longknives to march up the Scioto at any time and fall on Chillicothe. Benjamin wondered whether the warriors with Davies had been as intimidated. Although both he and Jeremy understood the Indians' fears, they reasoned that the Shawnees were not yet in danger of attack by Longknives, especially since additional loyalists and Indians might yet arrive from Detroit and farther north.

By the time the two runners drew near the Ohio River, they were convinced that the Valley of the Scioto was indeed completely deserted. From their vantage points on higher ground it was a dismal, forlorn sight—village after village lying in silence, lodges empty, many possessions left behind. Everywhere were starving chickens, stray dogs, and even beef cattle left to wander along the flats.

Seeing these things, Benjamin thought about Evangeline and old Wabete. For all he had suffered as a prisoner, Benjamin regretted not having seen the chief one last time. He had asked Evangeline to write a letter in farewell to Wabete—she would write it in German, of course, but Wabete would not know the difference—and to say Benjamin had left it with her. Benjamin wondered whether the old chief would be very hurt. He told himself it did not matter, that all he wanted was to get away from the Shawnees forever, but he could not deny that it would be good to see Wabete again. He had grown to like and respect the old man, and as he ran along that narrow, wooded trail, he hoped that one day the two of them would meet again, in time of peace.

Then there was Evangeline. Parting with her had been painful, a hurried, awkward farewell that had ended with him shoving Punch into her hands and telling her to keep the bird caged for a few days. Had he really kissed Evangeline? Perhaps, but it all had been so emotional, and so rushed, that he could not remember clearly.

As Benjamin ran on, these thoughts coursing through his mind, he regarded his brother. Jeremy led the way down the trail, lean and graceful, looking at last like the older brother Benjamin had always admired. He was dressed in plain buckskins and linsey, his officer's sword at his side, and wore a narrow-brimmed felt hat with a feather in it. Benjamin thought the sword and feather unlike the normally unshowy Jeremy; perhaps he had become accustomed to adornment, having spent so much time in a brilliant scarlet-and-gold uniform.

Jeremy glanced back over his shoulder. "The Ohio's not far now, I'll wager." He grinned. "I'd like to think you're managing well to keep up, brother, but I've got the feeling you'll tread on my heels if I don't keep pushing myself harder than I like."

Benjamin smiled, glad for the compliment, and watched his footing as they dropped down a long grade toward a swampy lowland. He said, "Too much time doctoring for you and not enough time in the woods, bro—"

A shot rang out, then more, and Jeremy spun, stumbling heavily, crashing head over heels down the slope, with Benjamin frantically shouting his name and bounding after him. Suddenly the trees all around were filled with Shawnees, whooping and yelping, and Benjamin was cut off from his brother. He shouted in fury, yanking his tomahawk free, desperate to get to Jeremy. But neither of them had a chance. He chopped with the tomahawk as the first Indians came in, followed by Amaghwah, painted like a fiend, face black with three red stripes on each cheek. Then he saw Mark Davies, laughing with a terrible joy, and abruptly he saw nothing more.

chapter 24

THE TRAP

Benjamin sat in a campsite surrounded by dense trees. He was bound hand and foot and gagged, his face bruised and battered, a nasty gash running down the left side of his head.

He hurt everywhere after the beating Mark Davies and Amaghwah had given him. Every time he tried to turn his head, pain smote him like a hammer blow. The only consolation was that Jeremy was still alive, although he had been shot in the left shoulder and arm. Davies had bound him, too, and done nothing to ease his pain, although the wounds had been roughly bandaged.

Benjamin looked over at his brother, who sat leaning against a tree, his lips cracked and dry, blood crusting his clothes. Jeremy's eyes were half open, and when he saw Benjamin gazing across the fire at him, he winked and gave a little smile, as if to say they were not beaten yet.

Benjamin stiffened, seeing Mark Davies approach with Amaghwah. Davies stopped before Jeremy and gave him a wicked kick, cursing him for a turncoat.

"You'll soon be brought back to Detroit, Bently, and there you'll be hanged as a traitor for all to see, including your rebel wife!" Jeremy kicked futilely at Davies, who stepped back and laughed. Jeremy said, "Justice will be done, you scum! You killed Weston!"

Davies sneered. "Who'll believe you, turncoat?" His eyes narrowed, cold and glittering. "That fool was no loss to us, and he got what he deserved. Just as you will, turncoat!"

Benjamin felt as if he were going mad with anger, and he strained against his bonds to free himself and attack Davies.

337

Seeing him struggling, Davies laughed and came to stand over him, a long hickory switch in his hands.

"As for you, Sutherland, I have a worthwhile use for you!" He snickered as Benjamin battled to get at him. "Listen well, knave, and I'll give you good cause to want to kill me." He slashed Benjamin on the side of the face. The pain was searing, but Benjamin kept his head up.

"Listen well, and I'll tell you who it is on those boats coming down the river." He laughed mirthlessly, and Amaghwah, standing behind him, aped him, even though he could not understand a word Davies was saying. "On those boats—"

Just then a stocky man in ragged buckskins burst into the camp, sweating from a hard run, and Davies rose to meet him. Benjamin recognized him at once; it was a face he would never forget.

"What is it now, Girty?" Davies demanded, his tone of voice revealing his contempt. "Speak up, fellow!"

"They're coming!" Girty panted, and glanced at the two brothers. "They're coming, sure—three wallowing flatboats, slower than sunnin' turtles. If'n they leave the channel, they're goners." He looked at Benjamin, who glared back at him. "And when they spot this 'un, they'll think about coming in all right, Cap'n." He spat tobacco juice on the ground and wiped his beard, muttering, "You done some slick work here, real slick."

"Right," Davies said, not looking at Girty. "You stay here, fellow, and guard Bently." He rudely waved the scout away with the switch and called for Amaghwah to rouse the war party and assemble at the place of ambush. Girty spat again and moved reluctantly, obviously disliking the officer's arrogance. Then Davies knelt beside Benjamin, grabbing him by the hair, to finish what he had to tell him.

Out on the Ohio River it was brilliant and warm, with a southwesterly wind gusting the water into whitecaps, covering the surface with froth.

Ella Sutherland sat on the roof of the deckhouse enjoying the sunshine, grateful for a peaceful stretch of river. For almost two weeks they had journeyed down the twisting, rain-swollen Ohio, having started at Pittsburgh in three newly built boats that were more like barges, scarcely manageable in the current. Squat and sturdy, they were built to carry heavy cargoes through shallow water. All had similar large deckhouses, with walkways along the sides from bow to stern protected by thick plank gunwales. There were firing loopholes at intervals along the gunwales, and each deckhouse had shuttered windows as well as a mud-and-stick chimney aft to vent a cooking fire. Ungainly as these craft were, they were a comfortable way to travel.

Ella stared at the two other boats a few hundred yards ahead. She loved the beauty of this wild country and could easily imagine how peaceful it would feel here if it were no longer dangerous. So far there had been no trouble with Indians, but she would be glad when they reached the safety of the Falls of the Ohio, a few days away, where Colonel Clark's fort had a strong garrison.

The common wisdom back at Fort Pitt was that Clark had so intimidated the Indians of the region that it was now possible to migrate to the Illinois country without fear of attack. Surely the Indians were also aware of the thousands of settlers streaming over the Alleghenies, seeking to settle new lands and avoid the conflict back east; soon there would be too many for the tribes to resist.

When James Morely had come to Pitt last winter, Ella and her family and friends had eagerly joined him, exhilarated to know they soon would be resettled in a land closer to their homes at Detroit. Ella did not underestimate the dangers of this journey, but they were worth the risk if she could be reunited with Owen. In any case, there were twenty brave armed men in the other two boats, which, like this one, were laden with the supplies, munitions, and equipment James had collected for George Rogers Clark's advance force.

Ella glanced back at Jeb Grey, who stood at the other end of the deckhouse, leaning against a huge steering sweep that extended over the stern and trailed thirty feet behind in the water. Jeb, too, seemed to be enjoying the sunshine, and he grinned and waved.

"Beautiful day," he said. "Too bad Lettie's still on her

back down below. She's still seasick, though I reckon she'll get over it by the time we reach the Falls . . . then she won't know how to walk on land anymore!" He laughed and shaded his eyes against the sun, gazing at the distant southern hills. "Wish this current'd take us over to that side; we're a mite too close to the Injun shore for my comfort."

Ella looked to her right, at the bright green bluffs of Shawnee country, where the trees were already in full leaf. It was hard to imagine that an enemy might be lurking amid such beauty. Jeb was right, she thought; they were drifting farther and farther from the safer southern shore.

She glanced around at the others on deck, to see whether they, too, were uneasy. To her left and toward the stern, Mel and Hickory were seated in the sun, chatting quietly as they sewed away on Mel's latest levitation machine. This one was bigger than ever, and Mel had draped it all along the port railing to air and dry while he continued sewing. His latest wild notion was to inflate the fabric bag over the deckhouse when they reached the Falls of the Ohio. Normally boats had to unload their cargo before being laboriously guided and hauled around the Falls—actually a series of rapids—but Mel figured his levitation machine, when attached to ropes run beneath the hull, could provide the extra few inches of draft needed. Ella was skeptical about this scheme and doubted that the boat's pilot would go along with it, but she thought that the colorful fabric with its reds and yellows and blues gave the rough-hewn, unpainted flatboat a cheerful holiday appearance.

As for Susannah and James, they were sitting in the bow, deep in conversation, with Heera asleep at their feet. Ella had spoken privately with James a few days ago and knew he was trying to discourage Susannah's infatuation. Though James was very fond of Susannah, he was not in love with her, and now he was trying to let her down gently.

Ella released a long sigh and closed her eyes, the sun and wind so soothing. She knew how Susannah must feel. Perhaps the change of scene would do her good. Perhaps it would do them all good. Ella did not know how long they would be in the Illinois, and she still held out hope that their ultimate destination would be Detroit. Lately she had even more reason for optimism, for they had heard from a passing canoeman—a Kentucky courier—of Clark's astonishing victory over Hamilton and of how the Indians were abandoning the warpath. Surely the British and loyalists could not hold Detroit or the northwest much longer.

Ella's thoughts were distracted by the sound of someone climbing through the hatch between her and Jeb. The man stopped halfway out to sniff the wind, then clambered onto the deckhouse. He was a tall, lanky fellow of middle age, missing his front teeth but clean-shaven and neatly dressed. This was the pilot, John Gaffney, a Pittsburgh resident who had made this journey several times and often reminisced about steering the first flatboats ever sent downriver. That had been many years ago, and they had carried gifts for negotiations with Pontiac in the Illinois.

Gaffney peered at the water, removed his jockey-style cap, and scratched his gray hair as he considered their route. Only then did he acknowledge Ella, nodding politely and saying, "Best not spend too much time on deck for a while, Mistress Sutherland. This is the heart of Shawnee country, and you never know when 'em redskins will take a notion to throw some lead our way."

He pointed to a low, dark mass far downstream, where the river began to curve to the left. Those were floating islands of driftwood, he told her, and to pass them the boats must stay in the main channel, which was close to the right-hand shore.

"Current's strong enough to run us by safe if'n we're smart with the steering oar, but it ain't good to give 'em Injuns any extra targets on deck, ma'am."

Ella agreed to stay below while the convoy passed the floating islands, which Gaffney said would take them an hour. He tipped his cap to her, then went to relieve Jeb, who followed Ella down the hatchway.

Inside the dim cabin it felt cozy and secure, with the aroma of cooking making the room seem much like any well-kept cottage—although the slight but constant rising and falling of the floor took some getting used to. Poor Lettie Grey had not managed that yet and remained abed in one of the small, curtained-off sleeping areas. Ella greeted

Tom and Sally Morely, who were busy setting the table.
They told her that Mel and Hickory, who had been on watch
most of the night, had already eaten, and that Lettie was
still unable to keep anything down.

Sally took a pan of apple fritters from the galley fire and
said sympathetically, "She hasn't the will to go on deck,
poor thing. The only way we can take her mind off sickness
is to let Timothy Owen stay with her and cheer her up."

While Sally filled plates and Tom drew mugs of cider,
Ella peeked inside the curtained chamber near the bow where
Lettie was asleep with her grandson. Timothy was a beautiful boy, with long lashes and dark curly hair; he sucked
his thumb as he cuddled close to Lettie, one hand tangled
in her hair.

Ella smiled, wondering whether Gwen Bently would give
her grandchildren soon. Then the voices of Susannah and
James came from beyond the door to the deck. Ella went
to call them in for the meal, but the door was stuck, and
as she tried to force it, she could not help but overhear them.

Susannah's voice caught as she spoke: "I know I'm far
too young for you, James, and that Jeanette's already almost
a woman, but I thought perhaps you meant to...
to wait... until—"

Ella felt awful hearing this and was about to shout through
the door, but James quickly answered:

"You must understand that in life, one never quite knows
what will happen next. I'm too caught up in company affairs—in the Albany business, as well as in important ven-
tures like this one. I can't say what I'll be doing or where
I'll be tomorrow. How can I promise anyone I'll wait?"

Susannah sniffed. Ella cleared her throat and shouldered
the jammed door to let them know someone was there, but
James was too intent on what he had to say and did not
hear.

"Jeanette means... means no more to me than... you
do, Susannah, but you must not give your heart away to
someone who is not fit... yes, not fit to take care of it...
in... in a way that's... fitting!"

Ella kicked and pounded on the door, calling brightly
that food was ready. Then she turned back to the main room,
where Sally was standing, watching her.

Sally said, "They've been talking like that for days now. James is kindly trying to change her heart, but Susannah's not to be consoled."

Ella smiled, actually more relieved than worried that the relationship had taken this turn. It would all settle down in time. She went to the table, where Tom and Jeb stood waiting for her to be seated. As James wrenched the door open and he and Susannah came in from the bow, Ella said quietly to the Morelys that everything would be better with the youngsters after they reached the Falls.

She whispered, "James will go back to Albany, and Susannah will turn her thoughts to boys her own age, in a whole new, exciting country."

Susannah and James sat down a bit self-consciously as Tom warmed to the notion of settling in the fabled Illinois.

"Folks talk about the Kentuck as being all git and no give for settlers, but the Illinois's even better, a land where the soil's so rich that all a man need do is put a plow to it and what he wants'll sprout right up behind him afore his day's work is done."

James smiled. "You, a farmer, Tom? You're a cabinet-maker, and the French out there are too poor to buy your work. Who are you going to sell your cherry hutches to? The Indians?"

"It ain't French and Injuns that interests me, but the American folk who'll follow after us to the Illinois. You heard all the talk back at Pitt from them who wants to come down the Ohio when they know it's safer."

Ella cleared her throat and bowed her head, and they all sat in silence a moment. As food was served, the conversation continued. Tom said he was sure the Illinois would be well settled by people from the colonies before five years were out.

"Tell you what, Tom," James said with a smile as he ladled gravy onto his meat, "you make your cherry hutches, and I'll sell them in New Orleans to those rich Spaniards! Or maybe you should build a Mississippi boat—a strong, big keelboat with plenty of cannon, and we'll go down there with an army and capture New Orleans for ourselves and make our own empire!"

James chuckled, but no one else thought the idea especially funny, particularly since the possibility of a frontier war between Spain and America was all too real. Both countries claimed the upper Mississippi that Clark had just wrested from Britain.

James sensed the disapproval and said lightly, "Don't be so gloomy! Anyway, you must admit this new homeland you're setting out for might require you to fight to keep it." He looked at them, and Jeb shook his head, while the others attended to their food.

Jeb said, "If we got to fight and build empires, son, we don't need to think about it over food."

James shrugged and fell silent.

Ella thought James had changed markedly since he had left the Wyoming; he seemed unusually confident, almost cocky. He had spoken of ideas for his future that were indeed grand, yet no one, including Ella, had been told how he had raised the money for this expedition, or how he had managed to organize the men and equipment and find the scarce essentials now packed into the holds of all three flatboats. When asked, James had become evasive, promising to reveal the details in due time. For the moment, he insisted, they should turn their attention to reaching the Illinois.

Just then there was a shout from Gaffney above, alerting them that the first boats were not far from the narrow channel between the floating islands and the shore.

"Best finish yer meal, gents," he called through the hatch, "then ready some firearms in case there's redskins waiting to give us a salute!"

With that, the men bolted down the rest of their food. Mel and Hickory joined the others, and soon everyone was at his station, with James in the bow, Tom at the stern, Jeb on the roof of the deckhouse with Gaffney, and Mel at the port side near his fabric bag, which he tied down to keep it from falling overboard. The women rapidly cleared the table and secured everything that might be damaged by gunfire or rough water. Ella's heart quickened as she made sure the shutters on the windows were closed, further darkening the cabin. She told Susannah to douse the cooking fire with water, and that sent smoke and steam up the chimney, some into the room. Little Timothy toddled out, barefoot, rubbing his eyes and asking for the potty, which Sally brought, setting him in a corner before going back to her tasks.

When she had the chance, Ella took Susannah to one side and said, "Don't think so seriously about James, dear. You're not yet a grown woman, so why trouble yourself with a woman's heartache?"

Susannah's eyes were red, and not from the smoke. She nodded, her mouth twitching, and said, "You may be right, Mother, but I can't help feeling the way I do. Common sense tells me I'm wrong, but I . . . I just can't ignore my deepest feelings." She looked at her mother, as if wishing she could explain herself better. "I don't know what will happen next for James and me, and neither does anyone else, so . . . I mean to go on as always, simply following my heart. Is that so very wrong or foolhardy?"

Ella smiled and touched her daughter's cheek. "There's no other way to go about it." She gave a little laugh. "We're here on this boat, in this country, because I'm determined to rejoin your father. I'm following my heart, too. Some people would say that's foolhardy, I guess—but I know it's not wrong!"

Simon Girty was glad enough to stay behind in the camp to guard Jeremy, who lay in a feverish agony from his wounds. Girty was no glutton for hot lead. He would be satisfied to share the plunder after the attack; let the others have the scalps and the glory. Anyhow, he knew why Davies had chosen him to stay behind: he was the only one who could be trusted not to kill and scalp the prisoner. For some reason that Girty could not fathom, Davies was set on bringing this man back to Detroit for public execution.

Girty spat out his tobacco wad and licked his gums, thinking it was as well that he stayed out of the way. Though he disliked Davies's arrogant treatment of colonials and felt uncomfortable with the man's hysteria when things went wrong, a job was a job. As long as Davies kept his promise not to kill James Morely, Simon Girty would obey him.

As Girty lazed about the camp, eating Indian popcorn

and drinking whiskey, he wished he had some fresh meat to roast. He also wished he were back at Detroit, to see just what the British were doing about the defeat of Hamilton. Girty shook his head, still finding the whole story hard to stomach. He had heard that Hamilton's first words to Clark after the surrender had been, "Where's your army?" Truth was, there was no army, not yet, so the British and Indians were not beaten by a long shot. Still, Girty wondered where he would go if the British gave up the northwest. Perhaps it was as well he had made a deal with the merchant Bradford Cullen, a man who would always fall on his feet—if he didn't die of old age first. He considered again how to get James Morely back to Albany. . . .

Girty's head cocked as he heard movement in a thicket a little distance down the trail. He tensed, brought up his rifle, and got to a crouch. Eyeing Jeremy, he satisfied himself that the prisoner was asleep and well bound. The noise came again. Girty listened, his senses sharp. Was it an enemy trying to slip up on him?

After a moment, the sound came once more, like some creature walking through the woods. No enemy would make such a racket if he was trying to be stealthy.

Then Girty heard the call of a wild turkey, and his eyes lit. Before the others came back to eat it, he would have had his fill of a savory meal. He moved off slowly along the trail, glancing back once to make sure Jeremy had not stirred.

The gobble sounded again. Girty was so skilled a hunter that he could tell it was a young and tender bird, its succulent meat just what he needed to pass the time waiting for Davies to return. He licked his chops. He could almost taste it.

The gobbler moved away slowly, obviously unaware it was being stalked. Girty drew closer, moving soundlessly, listening to every rustle and cracking twig as the gobbler scrabbled for food. Any moment he would have it in his sights. No turkey ever got away from—

Something lashed about Girty's legs and yanked his feet out in a tremendous lurch that turned him upside down, his rifle and gear clattering to the ground and his head cracking on a rock as he was jolted up into the air. He swung back and forth, dangling helplessly, caught tight in a snare, the loop around his ankles leading up to a springy sapling.

Girty bounced, twisting, shouting in anger, but the next thing he saw made him stop jerking and writhing, for it was Owen Sutherland, a broad grin on his face.

"Gobble, gobble," Sutherland said, slipping the knife from Girty's belt. "It's an old Indian trick against whites, and it works every time when the prey's a slick hunter like you."

Girty was suspended, arms down, face red, helpless and speechless. He realized Sutherland had snared him like this to avoid a gun battle that surely would have alerted the Shawnees. And there was likely another reason Sutherland had snared him instead of killing him.

Sutherland voiced it: "I owed you my life. Now we're even." Just then Tamano came along the trail, and limping at his side was Jeremy, who obviously had not been sleeping at all. Sutherland put an arm about his stepson's waist and led him out of earshot, then proceeded to examine his wounds.

Girty was furious with himself, and embarrassed. He grumbled as Tamano picked up the fallen rifle, powder horn, and ammunition pouch, and, rejoining Jeremy, headed back to the camp. Then Sutherland approached. He stuck Girty's own knife into the ground nearby.

"You bounce up and down long enough and hard enough," Sutherland said, "and you'll be able to get hold of that knife and cut yourself down—if I leave it there." He let Girty think about that, then said, "But I'll take it with me unless you tell me a few things."

Even upside down, Sutherland looked cold and ruthless to Simon Girty, who eyed the knife and knew that without it he could easily die hanging here.

"Ask," he said hoarsely. "But . . . give me one promise in return."

Sutherland said he would consider it.

Looking more flushed than being upside down might justify, Girty whispered, "Don't never tell nobody how you got advantage of me!" He grinned awkwardly. "A prime woodsman's gotta take care of his reputation, you know."

chapter **25**

BATTLE ON THE RIVER

Benjamin Sutherland watched the flatboats approach, horror and fear sweeping him as he struggled helplessly against his bonds. His arms and legs were roped securely to a tree submerged in four feet of floodwater, twenty yards from shore.

He was naked to the waist and gagged so he could not cry out. He would be clearly visible to the boats in another minute or so. Behind him, hidden in the trees, were Davies and thirty Indians. Over in the tangle of the floating island were another thirty Indians, waiting beside their canoes. Benjamin stopped fighting the ropes and stared at the scene. The boats would have to pass through a channel less than a hundred yards wide. The current would push them through but at the same time bring them within a stone's throw of the shore. Davies himself was on high ground that jutted out from the land and gave him a clear view of his men's positions and the river. Benjamin could make him out, about thirty yards downstream, his green uniform a dark patch against the new leaves.

Benjamin was sweating, though the water was cold. He was exhausted from wrestling with his bonds, approaching despair with every moment that passed. He had chewed at the gag until it was shredded, but it would not come off. He gnawed fiercely, wanting to shriek that the boats should keep away from the shore and not come for him; but the gag was still too tight, and he could not get out a sound.

The boats drifted closer, until he could clearly pick out men on the deck. He could not see his family, or anyone familiar on the first two boats, and few people were visible on the third, which was much farther off, perhaps four

348

hundred yards, and partly obscured from sight by over-hanging branches. But all three craft were now in the strong current of the river bend and could not get across to the other side even if they tried. Their only chance was to take cover and steer through the middle of the channel, letting the river drive them past the Indian guns. They had to ignore him and not come in any closer to shore.

He wrenched and tugged until his wrists were raw and stung. He must warn them! He could not cause others to die—his mother, sister, friends. It was bad enough that Jeremy was doomed back in the camp, waiting to be hanged for treason.

Half blinded by tears of rage, he fought against the ropes, bit at the gag, cursed Davies. From the shore he heard Davies laugh softly, saying, "Struggle! That's right, Sutherland—let them see you want to live! Let them see!"

The front boat was close now, and Benjamin heard the voices of men laughing and joking on the deck. He stopped his writhing, breathing hard while still gnawing at the gag, even swallowing shreds of it. Perhaps they would not see him if he were still.

Then Davies called loudly, "Help me!"

Benjamin gasped, tormented.

"Help! Hail there on the boat! Please save me!"

No! No! Benjamin longed to cry. He convulsed, his lungs aching, but all he could do was make a muffled screech behind the gag.

The boatmen clambered onto the deck, pointing and waving at Benjamin. They numbered at least ten, most of them armed. They must have been confident of their strength, for they steered nearer to shore, attracted by Davies's pleas and by the sight of a white boy in mortal danger. Their tillerman was careful, however, and directed the others to take cover along the plank sides of the craft, leaving only himself exposed. He shouted to Benjamin, asking whether Indians were around.

It was Davies who answered, "No! They left me here to die! Save me!"

The tillerman turned the lumbering vessel slightly out of the current, and others tossed out a couple of anchors, while three armed men put off for shore in a rowboat that had been tied up alongside. Filled with terror, Benjamin heard the Indians readying themselves, rifles being cocked. Over on the floating island he saw movement; the canoes were being loaded with warriors. He worked frantically at the gag. The second boat was closing now, its men also on deck and armed.

Benjamin fought to scream a warning. He feverishly wriggled, biting the gag. Then it fell free! He gulped a breath, and at the top of his voice howled, "Trap! Trap! Go back! Go back!"

The rowboat's crew was confused but had only an instant in which to think about rescue or flight. Davies screamed a command, and the woods burst into gunfire, obliterating the small craft and blowing the three men into the water. Benjamin moaned, and wrenched his eyes from them. The Indians unleashed volleys at both flatboats as the defenders ducked for shelter. The man at the steering oar of the second craft was immediately hit, and his boat began drifting free with the current. The first flatboat, held fast by anchors, was directly in its path, and when a man on board tried to hatchet one of the hempen cables, he was shot and fell into the water.

The whites were being cut to pieces, their wounded groaning in agony on the decks. Now the third boat was approaching the Indians' range, the current too strong to allow it to escape. The gunfire and savage whooping from shore suddenly subsided, as if they all were readying to fire at the third boat.

Benjamin writhed to get free, but it was useless. Then he saw three canoes full of Shawnees from the driftwood island come slicing into the channel, making for the anchored flatboat, whose men were busy firing at the shore. Benjamin screamed a warning, and a half dozen of the whites regrouped near the bow. They were badly outnumbered. The Indians stormed aboard, surrounding them, chopping several down with tomahawks and war clubs. The rest of the whites went aft, where they fired with effect from behind crates and barrels. The Indians, too, quickly took cover, some of them rampaging into the boat's cabin.

Benjamin's screams had been heard by Mark Davies, who shouted, "You annoy me, Sutherland!" Davies fired, and a bullet splintered the bark near Benjamin's ear. Shaken, he wrenched himself around the tree to gain some shelter, but Davies still had a target. With a cheerful shout, he fired again. The bullet cut Benjamin's left shoulder, and the searing pain made him slump down, stunned, expecting the next bullet to be the last.

Jeremy Bently took a deep breath, steadying his rifle as he got Davies in his sights. Lying in the shelter of bushes not twenty yards from where Davies was reloading, Jeremy took careful aim. He hardly heard the other gunfire; he saw nothing but Davies's back at the end of his rifle. He watched as Davies brought his rifle up to aim at Benjamin, who was just visible in the water beyond. Davies would never get the shot off.

At the last moment, Jeremy could not kill him from behind and shouted, "Over here, Davies!"

The officer swung, staggering backward in astonishment, bringing his rifle around but unable to spot Jeremy, who held him in his sights. In that instant, Davies froze, helpless, terror in his eyes. Jeremy began to squeeze the trigger, but suddenly there came a noise to the right, very close, and a Shawnee sprang from cover, rifle aimed.

Jeremy rolled away, hearing the warrior's shriek of victory, but the Indian did not fire immediately. Jeremy expected the shot and kept rolling over and over toward a thicket. He sensed more than saw the Shawnee leap closer to him, eager for a better target. Abruptly Jeremy stopped his roll, firing at the Shawnee without aiming, slamming the Indian backward, the man's rifle going off harmlessly but very close to Jeremy's face. Jeremy staggered to his knees, the sting of a powder burn dazzling and half blinding him.

He thought of Davies and Benjamin and struggled to his feet, trying to see, the ache of his wounds making him woozy. He found himself still in sight of where Davies had been concealed, but the man was gone. Out on the water the battle raged more fiercely, but to Jeremy's amazement,

Benjamin also was nowhere to be seen. Where was he? And Davies? Jeremy quickly reloaded, then took to the brush. Davies must be somewhere nearby.

A moment earlier, Benjamin had been so shaken that he had thought he saw Punch flitting by. Then there had been someone behind him, a blade underwater, slicing his hands and feet free. Taking a deep breath, he had ducked below the surface, amazed to find Wabete, half naked, beckoning him to follow.

Now Benjamin struck out, still underwater, following Wabete toward shore as bullets zipped into the water.

He wanted to swim toward his mother's flatboat but somehow felt he should follow Wabete. He went on behind the Indian, who finally broke surface under the cover of willow bushes. Panting and blowing, Wabete dragged himself out of the water, so exhausted that he tossed the knife onto the muddy ground and lay there, breathing heavily and chuckling.

Benjamin crawled to his side, looking anxiously about for the enemy. At that instant, while the sounds of battle raged around them, Punch hopped onto his shoulder. Benjamin felt a rush of joy and gratitude for Wabete, and he blurted out, "I'm sorry I could not say good-bye to you!"

Wabete sat up and laughed, saying softly, "Peshawa, a man escaping captivity need not say good-bye to his captors!" Then his leathery face fell, and he looked closely at Benjamin. "I wish you had not known me only as your captor; I followed you here because I still hoped to make you my son. I could not let you die out there!"

Benjamin was moved, and he groped for something to say, all the while knowing he could not linger. "My mother is out there, Wabete, and I must go to her."

The Indian became somber, though Punch bounced lightly onto his shoulder. Then, unexpectedly, he reached over and gripped Benjamin's forearms. "I knew you were one who would pick his own day to die, Peshawa." He released his grip. "Go then! And be brave!"

Suddenly Punch opened his beak and sprang up. The bushes parted, and an enormous Shawnee pushed through,

his rifle directed at Benjamin, who scrambled back, reaching
for Wabete's knife. Hatred was on the Indian's face as he
cocked the rifle.

"Go!" Wabete shouted and leaped to block the man.
Startled, the warrior tried to shove the chieftain aside. In
that same instant, Benjamin whirled and dived into the water.
Wabete held the angry Indian back, but he fought free,
knocking Wabete down with the rifle butt. Then Amaghwah
was there. He coolly aimed his weapon and fired at Wabete,
who collapsed, shot in the chest.

Out on the river, the second boat spun out of control and
crashed into the first with a splintering crunch. The Indians
were swarming aboard from their canoes, fighting the defenders hand to hand as the whites still alive on the first
boat scrambled over the rail to join their fellows. The two
vessels were locked together, stranded in the middle of the
channel. The third flatboat was coming on steadily, riflemen
aboard accurately picking off the Indians attacking the two
marooned craft. This gunfire enabled the badly outnumbered
whites to hold on, but it was only a matter of time before
more warriors came out to board.

Panting for breath, Benjamin Sutherland surfaced near
shore, some distance from where he had been with Wabete.
To his amazement he saw Indian war canoes—ten of them—
drawn up on a sheltered strip of beach, with not a guard in
sight. He knew what Davies would do next, and this was
his chance to prevent it. Scrambling out of the water, he
dashed at the boats, knowing that once spotted he would
be finished.

At the first canoe he slammed his foot through the side,
but then noticed to his surprise that the bottom had already
been stove in. He ran to the second canoe and saw the same
thing. A glance told him someone had destroyed every one
of the canoes, all down the line. And where were the guards?

Benjamin heard the war party coming along the shore
trail toward their canoes; they were shouting, eager to come
to grips with the whites on the flatboats. He bounded off
and jumped into a clump of bushes, to his shock landing
on someone lying there. Gasping, he rolled away and saw

it was a dead Shawnee. Then he saw two other bodies, laid neatly alongside this one, rifles and ammunition at their sides. These must be the guards. Benjamin was not fighting alone.

The warriors appeared, painted and feathered, glistening with sweat and bear grease. They were so close he could smell them. He lay perfectly still, watching their fury as they found the boats destroyed. Shrieking and shouting for their sentries, they ran up and down, calling for Davies, who was nowhere in sight.

Benjamin did not move a muscle, not even closing his eyes. Legs went back and forth, just yards from him. Then, high above, he saw Punch hopping about on a branch, cocking his head and trying to squawk. He hoped the bird would not land on him. Out on the water the third flatboat was drifting toward the other two as though it meant to ram and join the fight. Benjamin wondered how many fighting men it had on board to dare take on the Indians like that.

He watched, suddenly full of fear as he spotted his mother moving about on deck, carrying rifles to men in the bow. He wanted to scream for her to take cover, but the Indians were all around, some of them still searching the bushes for sign of the missing sentries. The battle was not going the way they wanted, and they were angry.

Three more canoes suddenly shot out from the driftwood island, fifteen Indians paddling straight for the third flatboat. They paused long enough to fire a volley and then, as one man, paddled hard to bring them alongside. Benjamin despaired to see them clambering up the bow, getting over the planking. He saw the tillerman shot down and recognized James Morely, leaping up to take his place.

Near Benjamin, the Indians on shore gave a shout of encouragement, howling and screeching, hopping about, frustrated that they might miss the final kill. Amaghwah came running up, calling for the others to dive into the water and capture the first two boats. Amaghwah threw down his rifle and sprang into the water, and the rest of the Indians followed, almost thirty of them. Benjamin longed to join his family out there, but his gaze moved to the abandoned rifles. Many of them would be loaded.

And then an unexpected thing happened on his mother's boat.

Owen Sutherland, Tamano, Tom Morely, and Jeb Grey rose up with a fierce shout and, armed with sword, tomahawk, ax, and even Jeb's old Redcoat musket with its bayonet, went at the boarding Indians like demons.

The first attackers were all cut down, toppling back into the water, one crashing onto his canoe below and tipping other men overboard. The whites were shrieking as wildly as the Indians, who kept on coming up, chopping with tomahawks and war clubs.

Two got over as Jeb skewered a third but could not pull his bayonet free. One leaped on his back and another struck at him with his tomahawk. Jeb let go of his musket, grappling with the warrior on his shoulders and kicking at the other one, who dealt him a solid blow on the thigh, laying open the muscle. Yet Jeb did not go down. He bellowed and spun around, hurling the first Indian overboard, and when he turned to face the other, Sutherland was attacking with his claymore, driving the man toward the stern. Jeb yanked his musket free, then saw two more Indians come over the side and spring at Sutherland. Before he could charge to his friend's aid, he found himself facing three Shawnees, who scrambled over the planking and whipped out tomahawks and knives. Though bleeding badly, Jeb presented his bayonet and stood his ground—then with a shock realized that his grandson, little Timothy Owen, had somehow got out of the cabin and was sitting between his legs, howling in fright.

That made Jeb wild, and he lunged and swiped at the Shawnees, Tom Morely suddenly at his side, and then Heera, too, beside them, growling and biting, dragging down one Indian while Jeb and Tom fought the others. From the deckhouse roof James jumped down beside them, swinging a musket butt at a warrior who was half over the side, pistol coming up.

The musket handle hit the man squarely in the head, but the pistol went off and James staggered, falling heavily, blood pouring from his upper chest. Timothy kept howling until Sally reached out the cabin door, dragging him back in and slamming it closed.

Meanwhile, Sutherland cut down the first Indian, then leaped onto the cabin roof, slashing with his claymore and making the other two duck. Before they could recover he crashed down feet-first on the one, at the same time stabbing the other, who staggered back into a club wielded by Mel Webster.

The remaining Indians hesitated a moment but did not retreat, for they saw that two other canoes had skimmed out from the island and were drawing up at the far side of the flatboat. Only Ella and Hickory were there, armed with rifles and occupied more with the action in the bow than with watching their side of the boat. At the last moment, Ella looked through a loophole in the planking and screamed that Indians were climbing the side. She shoved her rifle out to fire, but a strong hand grabbed it and wrenched it aside as it went off.

Ella screamed Owen's name, and Hickory fired her gun, but it only flashed in the pan. In another moment the Indians would clear the side and be on deck. A few had already grabbed onto the mass of heavy fabric Mel had draped atop the rail, for Ella saw it shift and sag. One warrior kicked his leg over the side, pulling himself up. Ella picked up an ax and swung at him, but he was too quick and sprang away, landing on the deck. Hickory pushed past her and clubbed him on the head, felling him in a heap, but there were others, and more hands and feet were grabbing the top of the rail.

Suddenly Ella swung the ax at a rope securing the heavy fabric, which was already slipping over the rail from the weight of the Indians. Hickory did not have to be told what to do. As Ella axed another rope, Hickory pushed at the whole mass with her musket butt. It all gave at once, and the astonished Indians found themselves sliding back into the water, the massive fabric smothering them, dragging them down into the river and capsizing their canoes.

Immediately Mel was there and fired two pistols through the loopholes, wounding one of the floundering Indians and taking the fight out of the rest, who either struggled to get drowning friends free of the sinking fabric or swam away out of range. Ella and Hickory hastily reloaded, but the few remaining Indians in the bow had lost the urge to fight and quickly sprang overboard, joining the rest in the water.

Sutherland had already leaped back onto the roof to grab for the abandoned steering oar. The body of John Gaffney lay at his feet, and the wounded James Morely had been dragged into the cabin, where Susannah could be heard wailing in fright. Sutherland quickly took in the situation, glancing at the hard-pressed defenders on the first two boats, then at the Indians swimming from shore. In a matter of seconds his boat would sideswipe the other two and the main body of Indians would be upon them.

Roaring a Highlander's war cry, he heaved at the oar, steering the flatboat away from the first two craft and straight into the midst of the thirty Indian heads. The Shawnees went wide-eyed at the sight of the massive, blunt prow bearing down on them, with Sutherland whooping like a madman at the oar. When riflemen in the bow began picking them off with well-aimed shots, some began turning back, while others dived underwater.

Then someone on shore began shooting at the swimming Indians with deadly accuracy, and a desperate, confused clamor went up as the warriors realized they were surrounded. In the middle of it all, Amaghwah shouted for them to make for the trapped boats and join the warriors fighting there. Immediately Sutherland yelled for Tom and Mel to drop anchor. The men on the other boats would need help.

Just as the anchors splashed into the river, a howl of terror arose from shore, and Sutherland saw Mark Davies frantically trying to defend himself with his sword while backing along the crest of a knoll. Jeremy was attacking recklessly, hacking and battering with his own sword, although his wounded left arm hung limp at his side. Sutherland noticed that Jeremy was swinging wildly, as if he could not see clearly.

In that moment, even the most fearless Shawnees hesitated, seeing Davies hard-pressed above them. Sutherland heard Ella gasp in fright, but like her, he could not take his eyes from the duel, as Davies desperately parried and blocked, unable to stop Jeremy's mad assault.

Then Davies stumbled back, falling to his knees and screaming for mercy, but Jeremy kept pounding at him, almost deliriously. Davies blocked blow after blow, but he was finished. The Indians began to flee, diving from the stranded flatboats, those already in the water striking out downstream.

Sutherland cupped his hands to his mouth and shouted for Jeremy to hold off, but Jeremy seemed not to hear.

"I yield!" Davies screamed. "I yield! Mercy! In the name of God, have mercy!"

Steel rang against steel, and Ella rushed to her husband's side, horrified by what had come over her son, who was raging at Davies, cutting, thrusting, and stabbing, just missing his victim, who kept begging to surrender. Then Davies threw down his sword and ducked, hands over his head and whining in terror. Jeremy's sword rose for a killing blow.

With all her might, Ella shrieked, "Jeremy! No! Don't do it!"

Jeremy wrenched his head around toward Ella's voice. He paused, panting and swaying, his sword still high; but then, slowly, he lowered it and dropped to one knee, close to his shivering enemy.

"Thank the Lord!" Ella moaned, collapsing into her husband's arms, shaking as she repeated, "Oh, my son! My son!"

Sutherland took a long breath, looking at the exhausted Jeremy. The Indians were in full flight now, being picked up by others in canoes before they were sucked away by the powerful current. Sutherland held Ella close to him, a tremendous weariness welling up inside.

The brief calm was shattered by a shout of fury, and Sutherland looked up to see Davies thrust a knife into Jeremy's ribs. Ella screamed. Davies was wide-eyed, howling like a maniac. Jeremy did not fall, even as Davies yanked out the knife with a shriek of joy. Before Davies could thrust again, Jeremy rammed home his own blade, so hard that it lifted the man off the ground. Davies staggered away, blood pouring from his stomach. He stumbled, then fell backward, vanishing over the edge of the knoll.

Ella screamed, and Sutherland dived overboard, stroking furiously for the shore. Heera leaped in after him, and seconds later Tamano and Ella launched the canoe Sutherland had used earlier to come out to the flatboat. In a few minutes they all were with Jeremy, who lay on his back, gasping for breath.

Ella felt faint with shock as she kissed her son's sweating, dirty face. His eyes were red from the powder burn, but when they flickered open, they were clear and full of love. Sutherland tore away Jeremy's bloody coat and shirt to find the wound. As he did so, Jeremy struggled to look at it, asking Tamano to hold his head up so he could see better. With a torn piece of petticoat Ella wiped away what blood she could, and Jeremy coolly touched the gash, pressing his fingers against it to see how bad it was.

With a grunt of pain he said, "Good thing there's a doctor around." Ella bit her lip, pushing the cloth against the wound to stop the bleeding. Jeremy looked at her and smiled. "The patient will live, Ma. . . . Don't worry, I don't have much more blood to lose—"

He lay back unconscious, and with a moan Ella put her head against his chest. Even so, she felt that his heart was beating strongly.

Sutherland said, "Let's get him to the boat. He won't die as easily as that."

As Tamano and Ella paddled Jeremy back to the flatboat, Sutherland went with Heera in search of Benjamin. He was sure Davies had taken a fatal wound, but if he were not dead, he would not go far. Sutherland would get him later. First he wanted Benjamin; he knew it was his son who had fired at the Indians from shore.

The riverbank was strewn with dead and dying Shawnees, a doleful sight. Sutherland and Heera hurried along, watchful of any enemy with fight left in him. Then Heera disappeared into a clump of willow bushes.

There Sutherland found the boy, kneeling over an old Indian's body. Heera licked Benjamin's face, and with a cry the boy hugged the dog close before jumping up and rushing to his father, embracing him fiercely, tears rushing down both their faces.

"It's over," Benjamin gasped.

"Aye, laddie. Thank heaven!"

After a while Benjamin pulled himself free. He looked down and whispered, "This is Wabete, Pa—the one who wanted to adopt me." He knelt by the chieftain, whose eyes were closed, as if he were asleep. "He saved my life." Punch flitted down, and Benjamin took him on his finger. "Not only mine, eh, good friend?"

A little ways off, at the foot of the knoll where Davies had fallen, a hunched, nervous figure pushed through the bushes and stopped at the officer's body.

Simon Girty crouched down and turned Davies over. To his surprise, the officer was not dead, although he was in shock, the sword having passed through his left side in a nasty, jagged wound.

Girty glanced anxiously out at the flatboats and saw that the whites there still appeared busy tending their wounded. He would have time to get the man away.

Davies groaned and tried to move.

"You gonna live?" Girty asked, propping him up.

Davies gasped, breathing with difficulty. He coughed hard to see whether blood would come into his mouth—a sure sign of a fatal wound. It did not.

With great effort, Davies got to his knees and said, "Get me back to Detroit ... and I'll live! Get me ... back there, Girty, for I've reason to survive!" He glared at Sutherland's people on the flatboats and saw Jeremy being carried below. He hissed, "I've reason to survive, Bently. ... You'll pay yet, turncoat. You'll pay!"

Girty moved to the officer's good side and pulled him to his feet. Calling softly, he signaled to Amaghwah and a couple of gloomy Shawnees, who came out of the bushes and helped carry Davies away.

For Girty, a handsome reward was in store, if the officer lived. That was some consolation for losing Bradford Cullen's business.

In the flatboat's cabin, Jeremy soon regained consciousness and guided his mother and Lettie Grey in cleaning, stitching and binding his wounds. He would live, it was clear, and

Ella was filled with a joy that was doubled when Owen brought Benjamin aboard. She could scarcely believe it possible to have both her sons back after so long without them. She wiped away her tears of happiness, for there was work to do caring for the wounded.

Jeb Grey had taken a tomahawk blow that had sliced off the tip of his left thumb and slashed his thigh. He was bound up and laid in bed, with a dose of laudanum to put him to sleep. As for James Morely, his wound was painful but not lethal, the lead ball having broken his collarbone on the right side. Soon Jeremy found the strength to supervise work on both of them, with Susannah paying special attention to James. Poor Gaffney was dead, as were half the men in the first two boats, with most of the others wounded.

By late afternoon, the survivors got the three flatboats back into the channel. Once far out on the river, they waited for a quiet stretch of water, where they buried their dead in weighted sacks, so that the Indians could not get to the bodies.

As the flatboats drifted into the evening, Ella sat in the bow with her two sons. She was smiling, for she had just learned she was a grandmother.

Seated across from her, on a bench with Benjamin, Jeremy adjusted the sling on his arm and put a hand on hers. "I've got to get back to Detroit soon, Ma."

Ella knew he was thinking of Mark Davies, whose body had not been found. She grasped his hand and said, "How I want to see that grandson, and my daughter-in-law!"

"She's a stubborn rebel just like you," he said. "And she'll be just as happy as you when she learns I've resigned my commission."

Ella's eyes lit, and Jeremy quickly explained that he intended to take a neutral stand for the duration. "My fight against Davies is a personal battle," he said. "I'd fight him no matter what uniform he wore."

Ella knew Jeremy would face trouble at Detroit, where his combat with Davies would soon be reported. Yet he must go, for Gwen and his son.

After a while the dose of laudanum Jeremy had taken made him drowsy, and he went into the cabin to sleep. A little later he was joined inside by Benjamin, who curle up on the floor, content at last to be with his family.

As Benjamin lay there, he heard the familiar sound o Sally's and Mel's violins from out on the deck. It was slow, mellow tune, and Benjamin thought that music ha never sounded so sweet.

Now and again he heard Timothy Owen scampe around the boat's walkway, giggling as he chased Heera Tom, Hickory, and Lettie talked softly nearby. Benjami knew now what home meant, and that it was wherever hi people were. Before falling asleep he thought of Evangelin and wondered how she would feel in company with his folk He recalled her face, smiling and beautiful. . . . Then Punc fluttered onto the sill of the cabin window, trying to squawk Benjamin thought again of old Wabete. Perhaps, he decided it was better not to remember too much just then—espe cially Wabete, and how he missed Evangeline.

After all he had gone through, Owen Sutherland needed t be alone, and he took a canoe and set out downriver. H had to think, settle his emotions, and let the battle-madnes soak from him in the rush of wind and water. He was don at last with his long quest, and thanks to George Roger Clark, the rebellion had won a mighty victory in the north west. Never again would the British have the unswervin allegiance of the Indians.

He bowed his head and laid the paddle on his knees a the boat drifted downriver. Though his body ached all over he felt relieved, spent, as if a great burden had been lifted He was overjoyed to have his sons back and to be reunite with Ella, yet . . . there remained one troubling question— a question that only James Morely could answer.

Before sundown, Sutherland paddled back to the boa Everyone was watching him as he entered the cabin an went directly to James's curtained-off alcove. He called t James, and noticed Susannah sitting nearby with Timothy She was staring at her father with an anxious, questionin expression.

James bade him come in, and Sutherland picked up

candle and entered the dim room, placing the light on a crate by the bed and sitting down. James looked sweaty and pale but not overcome by his hurt. Without wasting words, Sutherland complimented him on all he had achieved in Albany, saying Ella had explained almost everything.

James did not reply. The boat creaked, gently rising and falling, and the candle flickered as the two men sat awhile without speaking. The sound of the river was a constant low roar, like an autumn wind in the trees. Sutherland got to the heart of what he had to say.

"Laddie, I can't see how you raised enough money to pay for this convoy. I estimate we couldn't afford a tenth of what this expedition cost. Tell me what it's all about."

James became taut, his breathing quickening, but he did not hesitate with his answer. "I have come to terms . . . I have made a business arrangement with Cullen and Company."

Sutherland looked as though James had drawn a weapon on him. He stood up, moving to the wall of the tiny cabin and back to the bed, trying to make sense of what he had just heard. He could not.

James forced himself to sit up a little. "I know it's quite unprecedented, Owen, but these are new times. New methods are necessary for success, and if—"

James stopped short as Sutherland swung round and glared down at him. The flickering candlelight on the Scotsman's face warned of a dangerous storm that might break at any moment.

With one hand Sutherland pointed at James, his other clenched in a fist. He said, "You'll withdraw the company from this immediately and let the boatmen represent Cullen's interests to Clark! We'll have no dealings with Bradford Cullen!" James tried to protest, but Sutherland roughly cut him off. "Our share of the goods will be sold to Clark on credit and at no profit, and let Cullen decide what to do with his own! They'll be safe at the Falls until he does so!"

"It's madness!" James cried, loud enough for everyone outside to hear. "After all we've suffered, we're not to make a profit? We're to separate ourselves from Cullen's goods?

You haven't even heard me out! We're to share half the total profits, man! It's a fortune! Surely you're not that mad?"

"No," Sutherland said, suddenly very cool. "I'm not mad."

He went to the doorway and turned, looking calmly at James, who was too furious to lie back, even though he was in agony from his wound.

Sutherland said, "If you think you can become an ally of Cullen's, then it's you who are mad, laddie. He's far more than you can handle, and though times may have changed, he has not! The sooner you learn that, James, the sooner you'll be capable of standing up to him. Until then, you're a—"

"Don't tell me what I am, Sutherland!" James struggled out of his blankets, face flushed, blood staining his shirt and running down to his legs. He was shaking, but he would have his say, and he grabbed at Sutherland's shirt. "I made this expedition! I fought for it, just as you and everyone else fought for it! But I *made* it, and I won't see you sweep it aside and destroy every chance of more wealth than you could imagine, just because of some old stubborn enmity!"

The pain suddenly caused him to gasp, and Sutherland saw he was becoming faint. Telling him to hush, Sutherland eased him back onto the bed. James lay there panting, his face white, eyes wide and unseeing. Sutherland picked up a wet towel from the bedside and wiped James's face. That seemed to bring him around, for he blinked and swallowed, sweat breaking out on his brow. He would not look at Sutherland.

Then Susannah rushed into the room, and Ella followed. The girl cried out James's name and fell onto her knees beside his bed, saying, "Get away from him, Pa! Can't you leave him alone for once? Let him be, please! Oh, James, James!"

Sutherland felt a wrench at his heart. Ella moved to him, putting a hand on his arm. He reached over and touched Susannah's blond hair, stroking it once. Sighing, he turned from the room, leaving his daughter there, to sob over the man she loved with all her young and innocent heart. He

aused a moment as Ella began to draw the curtain closed.
ames had a hand on Susannah's shoulder, and he was
azing at Sutherland while speaking to her: "Don't fret,
usannah . . . he can't stop me. Not now, not even with
ou."

Sutherland did not want to hear that. The others in the
ain cabin tried to look away. After a pause, Sutherland
vent with Ella out to the bow, where they were alone with
he river and the starry night. They stood against each other,
etting the wind and the movement of the boat soothe them.
Meera came out to lie at their feet.

Then Owen spoke quietly. "This whole expedition could
ave cost your lives, and I can't get it out of my mind that
Cullen must have known everything about it . . . that his
gents were aware of your every move, right down to the
noment you would pass the ambush site."

Ella sighed and closed her eyes, not saying what her man
new she was thinking: that James had been taken in by
Cullen.

Ella said softly, "Owen, at least we have our sons back,
nd that's a miracle to me! Now we just have to get home
gain, to Valenya. How I long to see our grandson."

He drew her close, and they looked westward at the stars,
vhile listening to the river rushing past. The boats had been
iven over to the powerful current in a thirty-mile stretch
f water that was free of islands and sandbars. With the oar
et, they could float on safely like this all night and never
ave to steer, as the strong Ohio River carried them on
oward the morning.

Bestsellers you've been hearing about—and want to read